ADMONITION

ADMONITION

Russel T. Shelley

Order this book online at www.trafford.com
or email orders@trafford.com

Most Trafford titles are also available at major online book retailers.

Printed in the United States of America.

ISBN: 978-1-4669-0626-6 (sc)
ISBN: 978-1-4669-0627-3 (e)

Trafford rev. 02/29/2012

www.trafford.com

North America & International
toll-free: 1 888 232 4444 (USA & Canada)
phone: 250 383 6864 • fax: 812 355 4082

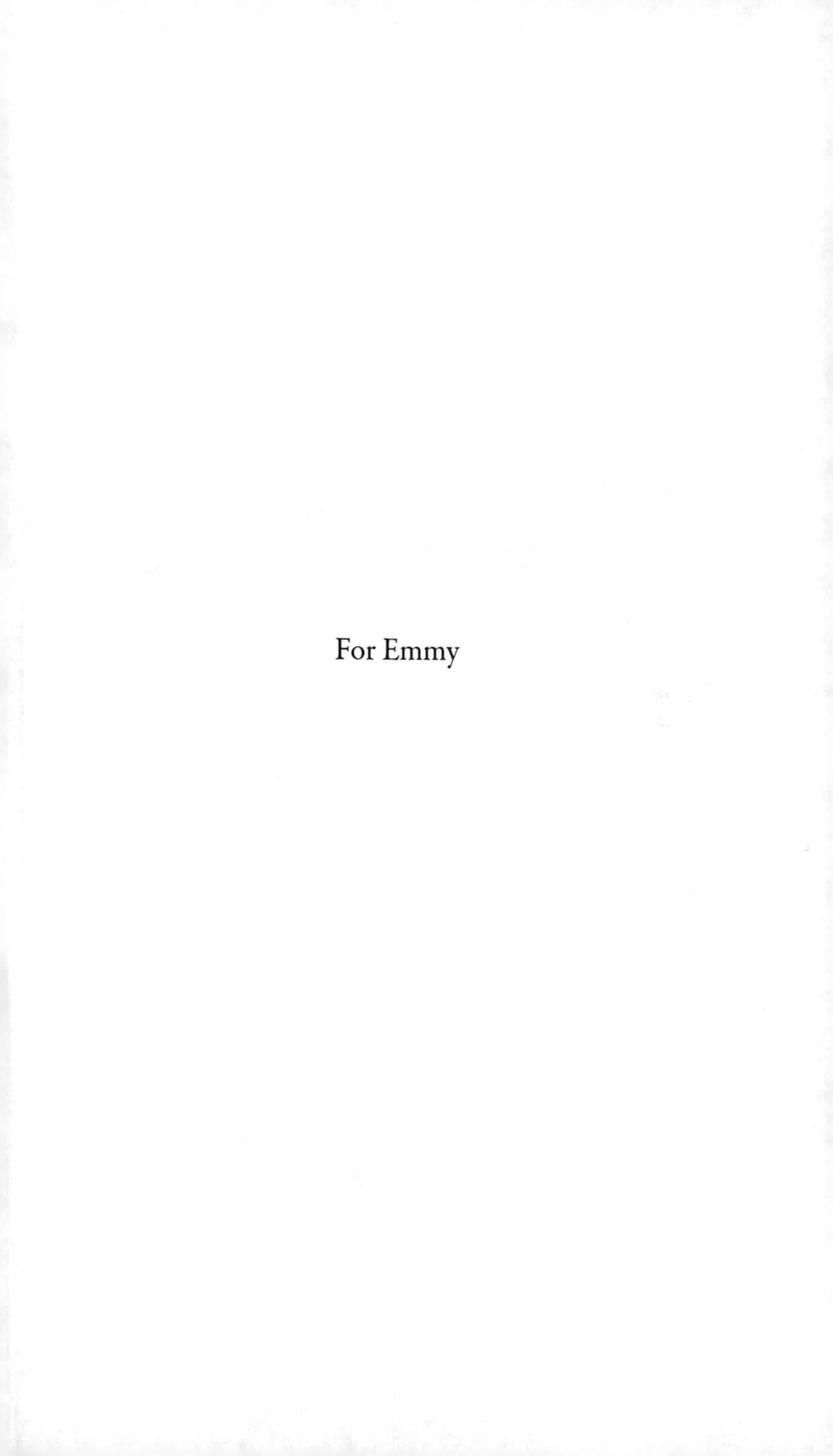

For Emmy

"The oceans of the world are whence we came and to where we must return. If we can."—anon.

admonition: a warning or expression of disapproval

Before he was assassinated, Robert Kennedy admonished us "to tame the savagery of man and make gentle the life of the world."

ONE

February 3rd—approximate position 48° S, 125° W.

The sea was heaving. Under a low lumpy sky the colour of unclean pewter, the Southern Ocean was in a surly mood—grey, massive and chillingly cold. The fact that it was only a couple of weeks past midsummer cut no ice. A steady 25-knot wind had been blowing for hours from the southwest, straight from the Antarctic ice fields, the swells looming up into burly masses of white-topped menace. The water was very deep so there were no vicious steepling breakers, but the swells were large and the tops often fell over themselves, racing down the long slope to the trough at the bottom. It wasn't a gale and it wasn't too dangerous, but it wasn't nice either. This far south you didn't venture upon the ocean unless you had business there, and if you did you gave it some thought.

Ten metres in length, the bright yellow Zodiac semi-inflatable was large, seaworthy and well handled by her skipper, but although thermal-clad and securely harnessed under their life-jackets, the half dozen crew members felt dwarfed by the seas, the whale-catcher and the huge, 11,000 tonne Japanese factory ship, *Kishin Maru*. The Zodiak was a RIB, a rigid inflatable boat, with flexible air-filled sides and a metal hull. It was lightning-fast and could plane even in very rough water. Trouble was, this was very rough water.

The young Sea Shepherd activists were all experienced mariners, most of whom had been involved in many protests, but the violent movement of the Zodiac, a heavy metal clamour from the wind, waves, motor noise and yells from the crew, and the mind-numbing cold, frightened everyone. They were all there on business, but it was the kind that attracted high insurance premiums, if you could find a willing insurer.

They had certainly put themselves in harm's way, the Zodiac skipper, Peter Reichmann, thought as he tried to keep his craft moving fast enough to avoid being rammed by the whale-catcher, which was driving at them, shepherding them away from the carcass of the whale it had freshly killed. Although now unmanned, the vicious-looking weapon on the point of her bow was aimed straight at them, as if the vessel itself was eager to kebab the RIB with the massive harpoon. They'd had a couple of very close looks at that gun, and Reichmann had seen the large flukes, speckled with what looked like rust, on the head of the harpoon sticking obscenely out of its mouth. It was all enough to prevent a close look at the dead whale, but the crew in the Zodiac was sure it was bigger than a minke, the only type supposed to be caught by the Japanese and Norwegian whaling companies operating in the area.

Reichmann increased the throttles of the twin Mercury 250s and swept the Zodiac around the catcher like an Olympic bobsled hurtling sideways around an ice wall, and headed for the whale carcass. But he had come too close to the weathered black, rust-streaked side of the *Kishin Maru.* Suddenly Helen Galanos, who had been trying to film the carcass with a video camera, was caught full on by a powerful jet of ice-cold seawater from a water cannon on the factory ship. She couldn't even scream. Winded, gasping, shocked by the freezing water and unable to see, she lost her grip on the camera. It catapulted into the surging water and disappeared. The crewman on the cannon shouted in triumph, waving excitedly to the officer on the bridge wing. She'd just made his day. These cursed activists could be a real nuisance. They had been waiting to pull the whale up the ramp, but had been commanded by the captain to stop until the protest boat could be neutralized. They all knew the big whale at the stern wasn't a minke, but didn't want to be compelled to let it go. Now they didn't have to.

Within minutes a line had been attached to the tail of the carcass, and it was slowly pulled up the ramp at the stern of the *Kishin Maru*. As it broke free from the surging swells, the onlookers in the Zodiac could only stare in fury and frustration.

"It's a sperm whale!" shouted Peter angrily.

"A large female!" cried Helen.

"Those bastards. They're not just taking minkes. They think they're above the law."

Reichmann beat his hands on the wheel in frustration, knowing they were unable to film the graphic sight. They all carried mobiles as a matter of course, often needing them for some back-up filming if the main camera malfunctioned, but in this case the violent movements of the RIB would have made using a mobile very difficult. The fact that multiple layers of mittens would need to be dragged off stiffened hands, leaving fingers exposed to the numbing wet and wind chill, made it impossible.

In an agony of frustration, they watched the sperm whale being dragged up the ramp, blood pouring down into the sea from the wounds in its head and body. The red run-off streamed into the water at the stern of the mother ship, turning the sea pink. Reichmann was hardened enough to understand the value in publicity of such images, and honest enough to admit to himself that it was worth more than one large sperm whale's life. But not this one. This one died for nothing but the pleasure and profit of Japan. He knew also that within a short time there would be no evidence left of the whale's species identity, for it would very quickly be flensed into pieces of meat and blubber. All remains of the carcass, almost eighty percent of the body, would be dumped back down the ramp and into the sea, and another whale would soon take its place.

Bruised, fuming, helpless and wretchedly cold, sea water sluicing around their legs, the Sea Shepherd protesters turned back toward their mother ship, the *Steve Irwin*, now many miles astern. Bitterly disappointed that they had been unable to capture hard evidence showing the Japanese were clearly and intentionally ignoring the International Whaling Commission requirements, knowing the companies would simply deny the allegations and the world would turn to another channel, they began slowly motoring east. The six young men and women in the RIB ranged in age from twenty-two to thirty-eight, and all were imbued with the fires of conviction and commitment. To a person they embraced marine conservation with the passion required to place themselves between a whale and the killing harpoon, but such an action wasn't often possible. Nor was it totally desirable, although they all would have done it. It was true that some of the older and more experienced members had begun to question their passion and commitment. An unpleasant reality had intruded into their discussions around the big table, a reality that was as old as the culture of protest. Were they being effective? Was what they did making a blind bloody bit of difference? Or were the illegal fishing companies carrying on their business with successful, insulting indifference, impervious to the nuisance value of the protesters' efforts?

They had cleared the stern of the *Kishin Maru* by a few hundred metres when they all felt a heavy thump through the hard sole of the RIB. There was a grinding, clanking noise under the counter of the huge factory ship, and a gout of pink water erupted into the air like the blow from a mortally wounded whale. Only bigger.

"Shit!" screeched the young American marine biologist, Jordan Becker, "look at that!"

Watching intently, not sure yet just what had occurred, the crew in the Zodiac saw the big Japanese whaler begin to slow and turn to port. A large group of officers and seamen gathered at the stern rail, shouting and gesticulating at a great patch of foaming, turbulent, still-pink water.

"I think she's stopping," said Helen, wiping wet strands of black hair from her snub-nosed, elfin face.

"Those little fuckers don't look too pleased. Wonder what happened?"

"Not many floating containers this far south."

But Reichmann had seen that kind of turbulence in the water before. "That wasn't a container, it was an underwater explosion," he said slowly, "but what the hell was it that blew up?"

"Who cares, Peter? The main thing is that the ship seems to be damaged and they will have to cease operations." Helen was excited, her mood swinging rapidly from the flat, angry tears of despair to a grinning pleasure at the possibility that something serious had happened to the Japanese ship. The others in the RIB were by now reflecting Helen's excitement. From down to up in one big red waterspout. Perhaps they would have good news for the campaign controllers on the base ship after all.

'Who cares?' thought Reichmann. 'I bet those Japanese are going to care. Serious damage means a long trip home and costly repairs, as well as lost revenue from the whales they won't be catching. I think we may have just seen the start of a new player in the game. And I don't think the whalers are going to like it.'

TWO

February 16th—approximate position 45° S, 100° E.

Dominic Falduzzi was scared shitless. The Sicilian-born captain of the Belize-registered pirate fishing vessel *Salvona* was sitting in his bridge chair staring darkly at the stern of the ocean-going tug *Stirling,* watching the slow swinging of the long towline connecting the bow of his vessel to the tug. Its lower catenary regularly dipped into the ocean midway between the two vessels, slicing the tops of the swells like a giant cheese cutter. Falduzzi was short, square and aggressive, with deeply lined and weathered features under a thick mat of graying, oily curls, a man of turbulent emotions and unpredictable behaviour. A very experienced seaman and fisherman, he had worked for some years for the Spanish fishing company that owned the *Salvona,* and he loved his vessel more deeply than he had ever loved a woman. He'd had two wives who had given him three fine sons, but no woman he had ever known could breathe such life into a man, could fill his lungs with clean sea air, or excite him as much as winching in a longline full of fish.

But there was no excitement at that thought now. It only caused his bowels to curdle. He tossed off the last of his sambuca with a chunky, very hairy fist and yelled at his steward for a refill, trying again to figure out what had conspired to put him once more in the clutches of the rapacious Australian authorities. Some years before, he had been discovered by an Australian naval vessel well inside the Economic Exclusion Zone of Kerguelen Island, in the deep south of the Indian Ocean, with 190 tonnes of Patagonian toothfish. His vessel had been arrested and an Australian court had fined him and the ship's Spanish owners over a million dollars. They were indifferent to the exclusion zones, having instructed Falduzzi to catch fish wherever he could find them, but they had not been pleased. He would have lost his job, or worse, but he was too good at finding and catching the fish, and they would have had to replace him with someone less experienced. And less profitable.

Gone were the days when just anyone could bring in full tanks of fish each time they went to sea. For many years the cod fishers of the Northern Hemisphere—Americans, Canadians, Scandinavians, British, Dutch, Spanish, Italians—were able to catch the delectable North Sea cod at will. And they did. By the millions of tons. It was piscatorial rape on a global scale, and it couldn't last. In the eighties more than half of the remaining cod population in the North Atlantic and the North Sea was being taken every year. It became clear what had to happen. As the stocks of cod dwindled, and as the European Union reduced quotas, attention naturally swung to the virginal Southern Hemisphere. Falduzzi swung with it. Initially he trawled for prawns, the southern oceans giving up huge quantities of banana, Endeavour and tiger prawns, all big and succulent. But he got word from a cousin working out of Argentina that the new money was to be made catching Patagonian toothfish, and swung again. He developed a technique of fishing sea-mounts that filled his tanks quicker than any other skippers were able, and began to prove very valuable to his Spanish masters. He was feeling on top of the game, indispensable, until his capture at Kerguelen Island. The loss of a million dollars and his vessel was, he knew, a kick in the ass from God for getting cocky. After docking at the Western Australian port of Fremantle, he spent all of the following week in church apologizing, swearing he would remain humble from now on, if God would permit him to continue catching record toothfish numbers. God must have agreed. For the next three years he had kept his head down and harvested thousands of tonnes of the fish without any bother from authorities or activists.

But what had just happened was catastrophic. Four days ago he had been minding his own business, happily reeling in a good catch of toothfish from near Heard Island in the same general area of the Southern Ocean, when his navigator had come to the bridge to tell him that the radio buoys on his number one longline were moving. Cursing the man for a fool, for how could they be moving, he had gone into the navigation room to check. Not only did they appear to be moving, but they were drawing closer together!

The number one longline was a 30-kilometre main line with many branch lines containing 20,000 baited hooks and a heavy mooring cable at each end weighted with anchors. It was all supported by a cluster of floating buoys with radio transmitters constantly broadcasting GPS positions. It was a very expensive piece of gear.

As soon as his number two line had been retrieved, and its catch of toothfish cleaned and packed in the huge freezers, Falduzzi had set a course for the position of the closest end of the main line, increasing the speed of the *Salvona* to full ahead. Although the southern autumn was approaching, the day had been calm and bright, the wind light and the seas moderate and sparkling. It was the kind of day not often enjoyed in the high southern latitudes. Dominic was not enjoying it either. The cluster of brightly coloured buoys had soon been in sight.

"Hook on to the floats and start retrieving," Falduzzi had ordered his mate, a wiry old Spaniard named Carlos. Carlos had spent most of his life at sea in one fishing boat or another and was capable, calm and reliable. He had begun the long wind on the massive winch drum, that would normally take a day to retrieve the full line, but it had stopped almost immediately. The buoys had come in attached only to about 30 metres of cable, and Carlos had attempted to explain to Falduzzi over the deck phone that the end of the cable seemed to have been cut. The captain, short-tempered at the best of times, had turned red and screamed at Carlos to stop being an idiot. He raced out of the wheelhouse and down to the working deck to see for himself.

The end of the cable had been neatly severed as if by a guillotine.

Falduzzi was now white with rage, but there was also uncertainty in his dark brown eyes . . . who or what could have done such a thing?

He had ordered the ship to steam full ahead to the position of the other end, shown by its GPS readings as being 25 kilometres due south. "That's five kilometres short," he muttered.

After an hour's dash the other buoys were sighted and Carlos and his crew went to work. They secured the floats and commenced to winch in the line, but again the drum stopped short. The floats had only 20 metres of cable attached, and that end too had been cut.

Falduzzi's fury was so great that he would have had not a second thought in murdering those responsible for cutting his line, and feeding them to the fish he was trying to catch. But shoving his rage to one side now was the thrill of genuine fear, for he would certainly be held responsible by his masters for the loss of the line, and they were not known for their generous severance payouts. He had told Carlos to steam north to another sea mount and set the number two line, then had walked slowly up to the bridge and collapsed into his chair. The cook, who doubled as a steward, had nervously placed another sambuca by his side and scurried out. Falduzzi enclosed the glass in his large hand, scarred from years of handling lines and hooks, where it peeped out through a forest of black hair, and drank deeply of the fiery liquid. He stared out the window, seeing nothing but approaching darkness.

Suddenly, there had been a loud bang from astern accompanied by a jolting shudder through the vessel, and she lost way, turning slowly to port. Falduzzi had thrown his glass away and again raced down to the stern deck, screaming for Carlos and the crew. Some of the men were staring into the water at the stern, yelling and waving. Falduzzi shoved his way to the stern rail and stared through the encroaching dusk at the large patch of foaming and boiling water in astonishment.

'What the fuck?' he looked at Carlos, eyes wide and uncomprehending.

Carlos shrugged. "Many years ago I used to catch fish in rivers with small plugs of gelignite," he said, nodding his wizened old head and pointing towards the disturbed water with a hand missing one and a half fingers. "The explosions were not large, but the water afterward looked very much like that, only smaller." He gestured at the turbulence in the ocean. "Do you know, I think we too may have just been caught."

"How? Who by?" Falduzzi was beside himself.

Carlos shook his head. "This I don't know, Dominic, but I do think we will need some help."

Neither of the Salvona's twin screws would answer the engine controls, and the rudder had seemed to be jammed about fifteen degrees to port, but there seemed only minimal leaking from the stern tubes around the propeller shafts. Falduzzi had sent a message to the authorities in Western Australia, and a tow had been organized. He had been in such turmoil that he had not thought of jettisoning his catch, so when the Australian naval frigate had arrived, a team of inspectors had boarded the *Salvona* and discovered his catch of toothfish. This time he had over 240 tonnes in the tanks, again well within the territorial exclusion zone around Heard Island. Once again he was placed under arrest, and three armed guards were stationed aboard.

So now, crabbing to port under tow and heading slowly for Fremantle again, where the *Salvona* would almost certainly be confiscated, Falduzzi sat in his wheelhouse, brooding. His thoughts chased themselves around his head like dervishes, all focussing on who or what had attacked him. His first thought, of course, was that it had been a raid by some of those God-damned Sea Shepherd activists, but he had quickly cast the thought aside. There had been no sign of any boating movement anywhere near their positions, and anyway nowadays they all seemed very reluctant to do anything which could be considered illegal.

His emotions built into such a demanding mixture of fury, perplexity and fear that for the first time in over twenty years he felt physically ill on a ship. Under a solid shot of adrenalin, his heart belted his ribs with a wrenching rhythm, and he wondered if he would survive this unbelievable set of catastrophes, let alone keep his job. He began to think seriously of ways to disappear in Fremantle, for there was a large Italian community there, and he knew people.

"What the fuck was it?" he fumed. "What the fuck happened?"

THREE

March 22nd—approximate position 50° S, 11° W.

The weather was foul, and the Norwegian whalers were rolling their guts out. A gale was blowing at forty knots from the south, the swells were huge and the waves were continuously breaking. The sea was more white than grey and the wind was wet and howling. The 9,000-tonne factory ship *Helga Lindberg* had been eased into a turn downwind, beginning to run slowly due north into the South Atlantic Ocean, which was why she was rolling. Her master, Captain Styg Halvorsen, had ordered the two catcher boats to keep station on her stern quarters as they slowly steamed north, waiting for the equinoctial gale to ease. It wasn't that they couldn't operate in rough conditions. It was simply that chasing whales meant steaming in all directions, and if one happened to be straight into the wind and seas, the gunner's aim could be easily thrown off by a wave crashing over him or blinding him with a sheet of nearly-solid spray at just the wrong moment. In wild weather the gunner was harnessed in, of course, but it was neither economic sense nor very pleasant.

Halvorsen cut a striking figure. Tall, strongly built and with a shock of thick fair hair slightly graying, at forty-three he closely resembled the physical makeup of the Norsemen of old. Born of Norwegian parents in Reykjavik, Iceland, he was a modern Scandinavian and technologically current, but there were many hours on the bridge when all he had to do was keep the vessel operating under automatic pilot. Then he would be transformed. He had read *Njal's Saga* many times, and his thoughts easily slipped back a millennium to the time of the Althing, the annual big occasion in ancient Iceland held in the open air at Thingvellir. Halvorsen donned the old traditions as comfortably as he would have worn the skins and armour of the time, reeking with the powerful, familiar smells that provided the environmental reality, and the courage, with which to face another man in a fight for life itself. He had spent many absorbing hours in the museum there, inhaling the brutal menace emanating from the spears, swords and axes of the day, which bespoke of strength, violence and ghastly injuries. But there was a pure truth in such combat. The stronger man, with good luck on his shoulder, was always fated to triumph. "It should still be so," he would growl, "things are too easy nowadays for the young."

Now, however, dressed for working in the extreme cold of the far south, he wore heavy dark blue trousers tucked into sea boots, a thick roll-necked sweater, windcheater and peaked cap. Faint lines of annoyance wrinkled around his pale blue eyes, for the conditions were poor enough to prevent his catcher boats from hunting the minke whales now found in abundance in the Southern Ocean. The Norwegian government had never recognised the International Whaling Commission's treaties, and persisted in conducting whaling operations against minke whales at will. They always avowed that they did not take any other species, but organizations concerned with marine conservation knew differently.

Halvorsen was in the business of whaling and considered his job to be to catch as many whales as he could in the length of the voyage currently under way. The politicians and diplomats could argue oceanic conservation issues in international forums all they wished—it made no difference to him or his company directors. Whale meat was still being exported to Japan for very high prices, and his nation had always been of the sea.

Ducking into the chartroom, Halvorsen stood by the main chart table, where the navigator, Viktor Thyssen, was marking the latest position.

"Hi Viktor," he said, "we going to hit anything soon?"

The young navigation officer smiled. "Not for a while, Styg. We've got over six hundred nautical miles to Gough Island."

"Well, call me when we . . ." Halvorsen began. Suddenly a hollow thump echoed from near the stern of the vessel and the two men felt a mild shock through the deck. Then there was a second bang, louder and more violent, and the large vessel gave a slight lurch forward. They looked at each other in confusion for a few seconds, when the ship's engines slowed to an idle. The captain ran back to the bridge and grabbed the engine-room phone.

"What's up chief?" he barked.

The chief engineer, Welshman Brian Edwards, was immediately on the line.

"Straight after that thump we lost steerage and power to the starboard screw. I shut down both engines as a precaution. What in bloody hell happened, skipper?"

"Don't know yet chief, but you did well. See if we've still got a port screw—increase port engine to slow ahead. And find out if we're leaking."

A few minutes later it became evident that the *Helga* still had a working port screw, but her starboard screw and rudder were either jammed or missing.

The mate, Tomas Bjornson, rushed onto the bridge. "Jesus Styg, did we hit something?"

"Couldn't have, Tomas," Halvorsen said thoughtfully, "or we'd have felt it on the bow first. And there isn't a fishing cable in the sea big enough to damage our propellers or rudder. No, I think something hit *us*."

At that moment the deck phone rang. Halvorsen listened intently, his brow furrowing deeply, said, "OK, thanks Charlie," and turned to Bjornson.

"Come down to the stern rail, Tomas. Apparently there's some kind of disturbance in the water."

Two minutes later the two men, with half a dozen deck crew, were staring over the aft rail at a large patch of churning white water a few hundred metres behind the vessel's stern. It had flattened the swells and wind-driven waves into an unnatural pancake-like smoothness over a hundred metres in diameter. The leading seaman on the working deck was a hard-bitten Scotsman called Charlie Bright; he too was staring at the unnatural shape in the middle of the heavy seas, scratching his head with a puzzled expression on his weathered face. He glanced up at Halvorsen.

"As soon as I heard the noise, I looked at the stern and saw a column of water shoot up above the counter. I've seen plenty of old wartime movies, skipper, and bugger me if it didn't look just like a depth charge going off!"

Halvorsen's mobile shrilled, and Edwards' voice spoke urgently. "Yes skipper, we are leaking! There must be a good-sized hole in the stern somewhere, because there's a fair bit of water coming in. I've had to close the watertight doors to that section, because it was too much for the pumps."

"Good work chief," Halvorsen acknowledged, and walked thoughtfully back to the bridge to begin organising the two catcher boats to provide steering lines to control the direction of the Helga's forward movement. In the heavy conditions it took two hours of rigging, but finally the factory ship began the long journey home under one screw, with steering assistance provided by the catcher boats. Her stern tubes were leaking too, but the pumps were able to cope with the inflow. The directors would probably divert the ship to Singapore for repairs.

The big Norwegian skipper leaned back in his bridge chair, hands clasped tightly behind his head, angry, puzzled, trying to understand what had happened to his ship. He wanted nothing more than to be faced with whoever was responsible for damaging his vessel. His large hands opened and closed unconsciously. He would personally explain to them what they had done wrong, and then he would break some bones. But he kept thinking of the words of his leading seaman.

"Yes, by god, I think we *were* attacked! But what the hell by?"

FOUR

December 17th, some years earlier.

"Jesus, David, you can't be serious!" Arthur Pope's face reflected the incredulity he felt following the words just spoken to him by his CEO and friend, David Roberts. Roberts, Chief Executive Officer and founder of the high-flying Internet company XTRO.com, had just delivered what amounted to a bombshell to his General Manager in his office on the 54th floor of Sydney's MLC Centre. The view of the beautiful harbour city from this level was arresting, as were the artworks and sculptures on the walls and in lighted alcoves in the tastefully furnished room, but Pope could stare only at Roberts.

"'Fraid so, Art. I'm selling all my stock. I should have done it a month ago. All the players in the States are cashing out, and I'm not going to let any more grass grow. Cuban sold Yahoo, did you hear?"

"Yeah, for $90. It's double that now."

Roberts was grinning. 'True, Art, but he still turned $5 billion of paper money into the real thing. And he's always said that no one ever got into trouble by taking a profit. I'm just following his lead."

Pope had commenced his habit of slowly pacing around any room he was in, carefully inspecting each of the paintings and sculptures adorning Roberts' office as though he had never seen them before. Every decorative detail in the room shouted serious money, but the application of good taste had muted the ambience into subtlety. The more serious the matter at hand, the slower was Pope's pacing. This time he actually stopped before completing a full circuit. "Well, $15 is a good price, but it'll be $20 in three months. How many have you accumulated?"

"Taking all my options, close to 70 million I think," said Roberts. "They'll take a while to clear, and the price will drop during the trading, but it'll still be a reasonable severance package. I just have the feeling that some shaky times are coming, and I want to be doing something else when they arrive."

"Shit Robbie, it won't be the same around here now. What will we do without your energy and drive?" Pope was clearly a very disappointed man. His normally enthusiastic, cheerful attitude to the daily requirements of corporate management in a fast-paced, cashed up technocompany had been trashed in an instant. He felt an immediate inner conflict between the thought of losing the driving force behind the company, the awareness of the end of a close working relationship with his good friend, and the exciting realization that he would now be able to make the command decisions needed to take the company to another level. He began to pace again, this time a little quicker.

"Well mate, depending on who picks up my stock, you could be left as the major shareholder. In any event you'll be the new CEO. It'll be your company to take wherever you want to go. But if you want my advice, and I promise this will be all I'll offer, then do what I'm doing and cash out. At least sell a large portion of your stock and diversify the business into other totally unrelated areas like primary producing. I really believe this whole industry is in for a massive shake-up."

"I don't agree, David. I think the company's got a few peaks to climb yet. So I'll probably buy a chunk of your sale package. But what are you going to do with yourself? I know you won't be content to sit and watch TV. You'll have to find some major project to occupy your time or you'll go troppo."

"Oh I'll be occupied for a while stabilizing my assets, and looking for a nice place on the coast somewhere to settle into as my new home base. But you're probably right Art—I'm sure something will turn up to attract my attention."

*

Since leaving the corporate world behind and letting his Paddington town house, Roberts had exchanged his thousand dollar suits for casual clothes and his Lexus sedan for a BMW off-roader, and had moved south. After searching up and down the New South Wales coast he had discovered a home on the oceanfront, just north of Ulladulla. The area of Milton—Ulladulla—Mollymook is a lovely and historic part of the state, well preserved, rural but with a distinctly maritime flavour due to the large fishing fleet which lives in the picturesque harbour in Ulladulla itself. A century ago it was known as Nulladulla, an Australian aboriginal word for 'safe harbour'. The views of the coastal scenery from the large, modern home were sweeping, but the house was set atop a limestone cliff on a large block of sloping bushland, screened from the sight of anyone driving past on the access road. He loved the seclusion and had bought it on the spot.

The product of a private school education at Wesley College in South Perth, Western Australia, Roberts had undergone a staid, nurturing and totally uncomplicated upbringing in a conservative home environment. Geography had played its part, too. The West was a lovely place, and the climate was all the inhabitants said it was, but those who lived on the eastern seaboard of Australia had always considered the West to be behind the East in all ways social, cultural and political, as well as by two or three hours of zone time. One of Australia's longest-serving prime ministers, Sir Robert Menzies, had even once famously made that very point.

His parents, Hal and Becky, were both teachers in government high schools, which was sufficient impetus, even in those days, for them to live frugally enough to provide their only child with a private school upbringing. Quick, intelligent, always neat and clad in the obligatory school uniform, he mostly ignored the standard taunts from the state school kids about 'looking so sweet'. Although bigger than average, sometimes he got into fights with one or two of the more aggressive pugs, when he displayed both a willingness to swing punches, and an aptitude for connecting with eyes and noses. This only occurred a couple of times, after which he was usually left alone.

On the whole Roberts had enjoyed a very innocent childhood. He got together occasionally with some of the local juveniles, a mixture of state school and college kids, and raided the Chinese gardens on the banks of the Swan River, creeping through the tall stands of wild bamboo, stealing vegetables and risking the dire consequences of the owner's saltpeter-charged shotgun. Or at least that was the message spread by all the delinquents of the day. No one could really say they had seen it happen, and no one was game enough to claim they had actually been shot at. When some variety was needed in their schedule they would wander down to the foreshore adjacent to the Mends Street ferry and wait for the old *Duchess* to pull in. She was a bluff-bowed double-ender that steamed across the mile-wide Swan River between Mends Street on the south shore and Barrack Street at the foot of Perth City on the north. The kids took their pleasure from aiming skyrockets, saved from last year's Guy Fawkes night because firecrackers were still legal then, at the big round windows of the pilot's wheelhouse. They never actually hit the windows; wind, trajectory, aim and ballistic instability always came down on the side of the rocket missing its target by wide margins, but the smoke, sound and angry reactions of the ferry operators—and passengers—always satisfied their goals for the day.

Roberts had benefited from his public school education sufficiently to pass out of the secondary education system with high enough grades to be able to progress to the university of his choice and study the major he wanted. At that time in Western Australia the university of anyone's choice was always the University of Western Australia, and the most popular majors were naturally medicine and law. Although architecture and physiotherapy were becoming cool. But Roberts had begun to display signs of a burgeoning individuality. His parents urged him to follow either of the well-beaten tracks to Royal Perth Hospital or to St George's Terrace, where the most prestigious law firms were nestled. But he demurred, politely. He decided he would attend the newly-opened Western Australian Institute of Technology, and study computers. Parental puzzlement and disapproval failed to dissuade him and he enrolled. He loved it. Along the way he took electives in marketing and business administration, passing all with ease and high grades. The fact that he graduated with an associateship rather than a degree bothered him not in the least. Even at his still tender age he understood status and elitism and cared little for either.

So Roberts had matured into a straight-thinking, sharply focused student of the burgeoning technology sector, without undergoing any of the emotional torment, drug addiction, criminal activity or personal tragedy which had tortured the lives of so many of the world's thinkers and creators into wonderful productivity. It was a developmental lack he had always been satisfied was a great advantage in the formation of his character and its backbone of determination and self-belief.

Dark brown hair, straight and spiky, cut short because it was difficult to wear it long in anything resembling neatness, framed a face that was even-featured, good looking enough to be called handsome, sleek and unlined, but a little too fleshy. Now thirty-three years old and jaded, he had decided to hit the refresh button. He was a strapping 188 centimetres in height, but at 105 kilos was overweight and unfit. The clear brown eyes, though, surrounded by whites as yet untouched by any hint of colour or capillaries, were arresting enough to make one reconsider an opinion formed perhaps too hastily, and ratchet it up a little.

"Too many corporate lunches and too much junk food," he had muttered to himself, looking into his shaving mirror one morning and viewing his image with more depth and perception than usual, and had enrolled in the local dojo to take up the martial arts discipline of karate he had begun a decade before. During his school and college days Roberts had, along with most of his male classmates, played Australian Rules football. His size and physical presence had ensured he got a regular game in the college team, and in fact had even managed to play a few dozen games of Reserve-grade football as a ruck-rover/full forward with the Perth Football Club. But it had been a culture of commitment to a particular kind of sporting god he just couldn't get serious about, and he had decided to wean himself away from it. The early training he had begun in karate was something he really had enjoyed, and realized even then that it probably indicated he was more of an individual than a team player. Unless, perhaps, it was his team.

So with the concentrated focus he was always able to apply to any important issue, he sweated, suffered, re-ordered his mind and passed his black belt grading. At the same time he purchased another surf ski and took to the sea in front of his home, reminding himself of how much enjoyment he used to have in the waves of the Indian Ocean at Cottesloe Beach, off the West Australian coast. He paddled for hours in the clear water on the western edge of the Pacific Ocean. Between the dojo and the ocean he regained his fitness, shedding twelve kilos and undergoing a subtle psyche shift. He was astute enough to realise that the pace of his life was slowing, and that he would need to engage in some form of meaningful intellectual activity to retain the charge he got out of life. 'It used to be,' he thought, 'that the biggest charge I got was completing the bloodless takeover of a small mining outfit and turning it into a high performance Internet company. At scandalous cost to them and exorbitant profit to us,' he remembered, surprisingly without much satisfaction.

One morning, a couple of months after his departure, he had gone back to see his friend Art, XTRO's new CEO, who had greeted him with a smile of pleasure.

"Great to see you, David. You're looking very fit. How's life in the sticks?"

"Quiet, peaceful, different," said Roberts over coffee. "How are you doing here?"

"Things are going very well. The stock is $16.50 and climbing, we are into an expansion and diversification program and there could be a merger in the offing. I told you I felt we had new levels to explore."

"You did, Art, and it looks like your strategies are working. But I've still got this feeling of disquiet. I hope you remember what I said to you at the same time."

"Yeah, David, I do. Not being entirely stupid I know full well that positive corporate strategies and basic greed are simply two sides of the same coin. I sold fifteen percent of my holding yesterday."

Roberts grinned. "Well done mate. That will be a nice hedge against any market adversities. You might consider selling some more soon?"

Since that morning, he hadn't seen Pope for six months, during which time the techno-market had turned viciously bearish, dot.com companies had free-fallen and XTRO stock had disintegrated to its current price of 85 cents. He'd had no contact with Pope, and hadn't wanted to phone him in case Pope thought he was calling to do an 'I told you so' on him.

*

Just after moving in, Roberts had advertised in the local community newspaper for a housekeeper/cook, and was delighted with the fourth applicant. Angela Collins was thirty-eight, of medium height and build, with a serenity in her face born of the area in which she lived and the lifestyle that she had created. Her hair was short and naturally curly, tossed into a careless but fetching mass of grey-blond highlights. With a smoothly complexioned face, which captured attention because of a wide mouth and natural smile, and two large and deeply blue eyes, she was a fine looking woman who wore her maturity proudly and comfortably. Her speech was slow and thoughtful, and she impressed as someone who would always be straight, would avoid obsequiousness and who perhaps could transfer some of the calmness of her aura to him.

For he was restless. He kept remembering the caution Art had given him about 'going troppo'—tripping out and relocating into a vastly different mind-set, much as an Australian aborigine goes 'walkabout'. Childless and never married, he nonetheless enjoyed female company and was currently dating Kate Preshaw, the tall, slim and energetic thirty-one year old auburn-haired beauty who anchored the *'Sydney Tonight'* show on Ten. Although 'dating' may not be an entirely accurate description, he mused. They got together only about once a month for a couple of days, either at her unit in Rose Bay or in his home on the coast. They knew they weren't in love, that it wasn't soul-mate stuff, but they reassured each other that it was a mutually satisfactory relationship. Kate was fully occupied with the demands of a busy research and recording schedule for her show, and Roberts kept telling himself that he was thoroughly enjoying the blissful seclusion and healthy lifestyle in his coastal hideaway.

And in the main he was. He had allowed Angie to set the parameters of his new lifestyle, and found he enjoyed her fussing neatness and wonderful meals. She insisted on always using organic fruit and vegetables, occasional free range chicken, and filtered water from their large rainwater tank. She transmitted a gentle non-verbal disapproval of alcohol, against which Roberts just as gently rebelled by opening the occasional bottle of old Penfolds Bin 707, one of his favourites, and offering her a glass. It was as well he didn't smoke—he'd never have withstood the reproach he knew would have been enfolded in quiet sighs and discreet little coughs. He was even beginning to appreciate the subtleties and complexities in the fragrances of the incense she often burned.

He had invested in several small businesses in Ulladulla, and had re-entered the stock market, buying with care and the prescience that never seemed to desert him, but leaving much of the daily operations to a financial manager. He was doing very well, again. It didn't seem to matter what he purchased, apart from one photography shop which went under. He continued to profit. It was all quite satisfying, but he realised there was nothing on his plate that captured his attention for very long. He wasn't stressing about it, but his subconscious knew he was only marking time, waiting for the appearance of his *raison d'etre*.

One day, in late July, the middle of the southern winter, Roberts was having an early morning breakfast in his new home, idly reading the *Australian* newspaper. As he flipped through the broadsheet pages, over poached free-range eggs on wholegrain toast, he became aware that he had passed the business and share price pages without stopping. He knew it wasn't the first time, and wondered whether his persona was undergoing a metamorphosis. An article on the recent Annual Meeting of the International Whaling Commission in London took his eye. He'd always felt drawn to the sea. There was nothing spiritual or unduly significant about it, he assured himself; he just felt good being in it or on it, and took an interest in things of a maritime nature. While he was building his corporate wealth, everything else had been subjugated to his drive to establish XTRO.com as a serious consideration in the world of technology and trading.

Now, however, with time to stop and smell the incense, he found he'd rather read an article about the IWC than the latest business news. As he finished the report Angie came in to clear away the remains of his breakfast, bringing him, with a slight frown, a double espresso from his machine. It had taken him a while to convince her he was serious when he threatened to fire her if she brought him green tea for breakfast. He glanced up, eyes distant, contemplative, a thoughtful expression wrinkling his brow.

"The business of whaling seems to be alive and well. I thought there were only a few whales being taken each year for study, but apparently Japan is allowed over four hundred annually, and Norway doesn't seem to give a shit about international regulations at all."

"It's not only whales either!" Angie's normal equanimity had disappeared. "The illegal and undisclosed catch of tuna, sea bass and whales is raping our seas and reducing the fish population more and more each year. And there's the by-catch too." Her voice had suddenly gained definition and her eyes found a new depth. Roberts gazed at her curiously.

"This is something you really care about, Angie? You seem quite intense. And what's 'by-catch'?"

"There isn't enough caring in the world anymore," Angie said sadly, the depth in her eyes clouding. "It's part of a world-wide indifference to all the things that should matter. The haves of the world, like us, live too easily and don't feel threatened by the possibility of losing anything. Not enough people feel intense about social justice or racial hatred or world poverty or suicide bombers. And 'by-catch' is what they call all the other things that get hooked on the longlines, like dolphins, seals, other fish, sea birds and whales which can tangle in the lines and drown. Oh dear! I'm sorry, David—I'll get off my soapbox now." Angie was acutely embarrassed at what for her was an impassioned outburst.

"No, Angie, don't think that. It's nice to hear someone who is passionate about the world's real ills, rather than tirades from political, religious or corporate zealots who all think they're at the centre of what's important." There was a depth to her thoughts that Roberts hadn't appreciated, and he was surprised at the level of her knowledge. Then he realised he was simply applying a stereotypical prejudice to someone from a semi-rural environment. He went deeper and admitted to himself that Angie's status as a housekeeper had automatically put her into a little box labelled 'to be seen but not bright enough to be heard'. He was ashamed that he had not even considered that she might have had something worth listening to. 'Jesus,' he thought, 'a year ago I wouldn't have bothered to admit that, much less be ashamed of it.'

FIVE

Three days later Roberts was out on the ocean in front of his home, paddling his surf ski over the smooth, gently undulating swells. It was one of those cloudless winter days in Australia which are as bright and clear as the Australian perception of summer in the Swiss Alps, and he had decided to spend the morning paddling up the coast and back.

It was a day that would change his life.

Clad in a half wet-suit, he was revelling in the feeling of the ski cutting through the water, enjoying the sight of terns and gannets diving for fish, their sharp high-pitched cries a musical background to the swishing of his paddle in the clear, brilliantly blue and not-too-polluted ocean. He heard a soft sibilance off to his right like the sound of gentle rain on still water and saw what seemed a cloud of silver sparks moving at sharp angles. A school of baitfish was semi-airborne as it tried to evade some thrashing bonito. The air was sharp and sweet, the marine fragrances evocative. All his senses seemed to be receiving input, closely attuned to the perfection of the environment. It truly was a magnificent day in a very special place. He felt more alive than he had in years.

About two kilometres offshore, thoroughly enjoying the physical effort of driving the ski smoothly north parallel to the rocky shoreline, he became aware of a commotion in the water a couple of kilometres ahead. As he drew nearer, he made out some small boats and jet skis moving slowly around a large submerged object. There appeared to be swimmers in the water as well. Suddenly he saw a large, narrow fin wave in the air, and with a thrill recognised the object as a whale. Its back rose slowly and he saw the familiar shape of a big humpback, but it didn't seem to be swimming.

As he drew closer he realised the whale was entangled in some fishing nets and had suffered some damage trying to free itself. There were swimmers in the water attempting to cut the lines away from its tail fluke and fins. While observing and assessing the situation he had continued to paddle, suddenly finding himself quite close to the whale. It seemed to be calm, not agitated or thrashing around, and one of the swimmers was working on a line around its fin on the side he was approaching.

"Hey mate, can you hold this line while I cut it?" the swimmer called out to him.

Roberts paddled over to the man in the water and grabbed the line, holding it away from the whale's fin. The swimmer began to saw at the line with a knife, and Roberts suddenly realised that the five metre-long fin was moving slowly around in the water, lifting up and down within a metre of his surf ski. The ski now appeared very small and flimsy beside the large fin waving gently above him. The line parted and the swimmer moved down to the tail to cut more lines. Roberts paddled forward away from the fin, in case the whale decided to slap it down into the water and convert him into a pancake. But the humpback continued to maintain a quiet and controlled attitude.

'Jesus,' thought Roberts, 'if he got angry he could turn us all into a big dish of bolognese!'

He glanced down, suddenly aware that his leg was brushing the whale's body, and looked right into its eye. He felt an instant, shocking connection, an indescribable emotion that left him shaking. He couldn't tear his eyes away from the calm, trusting, almost regal look in the creature's eye as it followed his slow forward movement. It was a palm-sized lens offering a glimpse deep into the being of a great, gentle beast. He leaned over and placed his hand on its head, not now thinking it at all incredulous that he would do such a thing. It was enormous, but in no way threatening.

"Glad you don't like bolognese, mate," he murmured to it.

At that moment there was a shout from one of the swimmers near the tail.

"That's the last line—it's free!"

All the swimmers moved away from the whale, and with a gentle flick of its huge flukes it cruised down into the sparkling depths. The people in the water and on the boats were cheering, whistling, some crying, as the massive creature disappeared, and Roberts wasn't at all surprised to find that he was yelling as loudly as anyone.

He began to paddle back down the coast towards his home, high-fiving one of the swimmers as he passed. He had been hugely affected by the events of the morning, and reached his home without remembering anything of the paddle back.

Showered, changed, still on a high, Roberts sat at the dining table staring out over the ocean. But he could see nothing except that eye. Angie placed some sandwiches before him for lunch.

"Are you all right David? You look like you've seen a ghost," she said.

He began to tell her what had happened with the whale up the coast, and to describe how he felt, but the words dried up and he stopped, tears welling in his eyes.

"It's OK David, I know what you're trying to say. Sometimes words just aren't enough." Angie's smile was gentle, compassionate. "It happens to most people who come close to a whale, or even a dolphin which plays with swimmers. There's a connection, an empathy with another creature that's difficult to explain. It's not their size—no one feels the same way about sharks or crocodiles. I think it's the fact that they are mammals like us, and totally non-threatening. But whatever it is, they should never be destroyed under any circumstances!"

"Angie, I touched it, talked to it. It lay there calmly, waiting for us to free it. How in God's name could you kill something like that?"

"Unfortunately, David, the whaling nations think differently. Although so many other nations in the IWC make all kinds of resolutions and even include minke whales in Appendix I, the official list of protected whale species, Japan always takes more than their quota and Norway simply ignores the Commission's rulings. And there isn't a thing anyone can do about it."

Roberts' face set, and his eyes narrowed. "There has to be," he said grimly.

SIX

Two weeks of solid Internet research later, ending in a trip to Sydney to attend a Greenpeace Australia Pacific meeting, Roberts was better informed about illegal fishing and whaling. He had come to learn most of the acronyms involving the organisations which tracked and monitored the activities of the Japanese, Norwegian, Spanish, French, South African, South American and Taiwanese fishing fleets in the Southern and South Pacific Oceans. He had also come to realise that the issue was far more serious than at first apparent, that all manner of fish and whales were being taken from the world's southern regions in alarming numbers. If data provided by Greenpeace were to be accepted, the by-catch was also of astonishing proportions. Tens of thousands of albatross alone were being killed each year.

There was, ostensibly, a full international ban on commercial whaling. There also were quotas established under international treaties supposedly limiting the catch of whales for scientific study. Conservation measures implemented by the Commission for the Conservation of Antarctic Marine Living Resources were clearly ineffective in limiting the huge catches of Patagonian toothfish, or sea bass. Quotas had been established for catches of Southern Bluefin tuna, but Japan had recently announced it was increasing its quota by five hundred tonnes, in the face of opposition from member nations of the Commission for the Conservation of Southern Bluefin Tuna.

"I'm sure all of these commissions are well-meaning, but apart from calling international conferences a couple of times a year for talkfests, and publishing more quotas and restrictions as a result, the whole structure seems to be a paper tiger."

Roberts was talking to three Greenpeace members who had been at the meeting. They had sat together, and Roberts had struck up a conversation with them at its conclusion.

"So outside of the various national exclusion zones, any fishing fleet from any nation can catch whatever they want in whatever quantities they choose, and to hell with any of the treaties decided by the various commissions. Have I got that about right?" queried Roberts.

"Yes," said one of the young activists. "Not only that, but many fishing vessels take catches from inside exclusion zones as well. There are few patrol boats and an awful lot of water to cover."

Roberts frowned. "Is there nothing that can be done to enforce the quotas and restrictions?"

"Apart from blowing the bastards out of the water? No, in the main the only effective action that ever occurs is the Greenpeace protests. We conduct expeditions into the Southern Ocean and hassle the fishing fleets as much as we can. We film their activities and publicise their illegal and over-limit catches in the international forum, and create as much exposure as possible."

"Occasionally," said the young woman, "a naval patrol vessel from New Zealand or Australia or South Africa manages to catch a pirate fishing boat inside an exclusion zone, and brings it into port. The boat is usually impounded and the company heavily fined, but it's a very rare occurrence."

"OK, I think I've got the picture. Thanks for your time. It's been nice talking to you. You all do good work." Roberts got up, prepared to leave.

"Ah, there is maybe one other thing," said the taller of the two men, slightly built, middle aged and unremarkable save for a number of metallic fastenings which appeared to be holding his face together. He seemed hesitant, and glanced at his two younger companions, who had risen and moved away towards another group of young members. "It's not something mentioned often by Greenpeace people, but there is another organization which is more actively involved with campaigns against illegal fishing boats. They have some boats which seek out illegals, and then they, um, get violent. They have rammed some boats, and even blown others up in harbour. Greenpeace considers them too violent, and won't have anything to do with them," said the tall man in a low voice.

"Jesus," Roberts breathed, "that's more like it! Who are these people?"

"They're called 'Sea Shepherd,'" said Roberts' new adviser, "and their leader is one of the men who founded Greenpeace. His name is Paul Watson, a Canadian. Er, I think I'd better go now. Hope you found what you wanted. Who are you?"

"Just a concerned citizen," said Roberts with a faint smile, "and yes thank you, I think I may have."

*

For the past two weeks Roberts had been so busy with his research that he had completely forgotten to call Kate. He had phoned his parents twice in that time, because in spite of his career taking him to the eastern seaboard of the country, and away from the calm and conservative order of their lives, he still loved them deeply and valued their input to his various activities.

But thoughts of Kate hadn't managed to force their way through the busy bubble in which he was currently working. Although it probably went a bit deeper than that, he admitted. He'd been totally immersed in the world of deep sea fishing and whaling, and had come to realise that another direction in his life was crystallising. 'It wasn't quite the traditional, clichéd bolt from the blue', he thought, 'more like the gradual solidifying of an image from one of those old Polaroid cameras.' But the image that had formed in his mind was as real and exciting as any explosive idea which had leapt into his consciousness during the times he had been running his Internet company.

As his thoughts were congealing into just what he wanted to do, so his excitement grew and he felt the urge to share it with someone who would understand it and accept what he was planning as something necessary to which there was clearly no alternative. He almost mentioned it to Angie one night as she was clearing away the dinner dishes, but a natural caution took over. He knew what he was about to become involved in was probably illegal, certainly dangerous and ultimately might cost him very dearly. He resolved to play it securely, allowing details to become known only to those who were involved with him.

He had broached the subject carefully with his parents, who had been enthusiastic about his new interest without really understanding what he was planning. What he hadn't done was ring Kate and talk to her about his scheme. Why? He didn't know. Oh bullshit, yes he did. She wasn't close enough to him to share this kind of excitement. Maybe she wouldn't have thought it exciting. They weren't in tune anymore. He wasn't sure what her reaction would have been, but he simply hadn't thought to include her.

Now he was in Sydney, and finished with the Greenpeace meeting. He rang her on his cell phone.

"Hi Kate, it's me. I've made a quick trip to Sydney, and am wondering where would be a nice place to have dinner. What do you reckon?"

"Hullo David. This is a surprise." The surprise was evident in her voice, but there was also a faint hesitancy too. "Um, I'm actually having dinner with a client tonight, and I may be a bit late. If I'd known you were coming up . . ."

"Yeah, no problem Kate. I'll stay at the Hilton and drive home in the morning. Who's the client?"

"Oh, an American novellist I want to interview on the show. His name's Jay Soderman. He wrote the best seller 'Alms for Allanah', which is currently running out the door. He's a great intellect, sharp-witted and entertaining as hell. Sorry David, it's just not convenient."

"It's OK, Kate, it's my fault for not letting you know what I was doing. Have a nice dinner. I'll call you later."

*

Late afternoon the next day, Roberts arrived at Ulladulla and decided to stop for a beer in the local. 'Whatever happened to a Black Label on ice I wonder?' It was a drink he favoured during his company days, 'and I used to favour it often, too,' he smiled wryly to himself. He didn't think he had become an alcoholic, because he didn't seem to be caught in any cycle of dependency, but he knew he had gone close. They were heady days of wheeling and dealing, of high-powered meetings and negotiations, which involved millions of shares being traded off the floor, and to be candid he missed the excitement and euphoria of a successful deal being completed.

'On the other hand,' he thought, 'there will certainly be some excitement where I'm planning to go in the near future. Be a different kind of thrill, but no less real. In fact, it will probably be more real than all the corporate deals I used to think were so important.'

He walked into the lounge bar of The Federal Hotel in the main street of Ulladulla. The hotel, old by Australian standards, was a classic federation-style construction, two high storeys or floors, commodious verandahs on two sides, the pub bars and lounges below the floor of bedrooms and washrooms or toilets. Roberts ordered a Carlton mid and sat at a table near a large window overlooking the street. His head was filled with thoughts of what he wanted to do, intermixed with disappointment at not being able to see Kate last night, and curiosity about her dinner date. Gradually the noise of conversation at a nearby table intruded on his thoughts, and he glanced at the occupants. One of the men was Raydon Mackie, the sensei of his dojo and master of the style of karate he had just black-belted. Mackie noticed Roberts at the same time and motioned him over.

"Hi David," he said, rising, "come and join the mob. These blokes have all just passed a green grading, and reckon they deserve a beer to celebrate." He introduced the three men to Roberts, who sat down and congratulated them all.

"Very satisfying to pass a grading, isn't it?" he commented. "Doesn't matter whether it's your first belt or your first dan, it's always gratifying to accomplish something that takes so much concentration and thought, not to mention the sweat and punishment. Let me shout." Roberts looked over at the barman and held up five fingers.

"David achieved his black belt a month or so back," said Mackie to the group. "He showed a hell of a lot of focus and determination, and he could go on to a number of dans if he wanted. But I suspect he's gained just what he set out to do. You staying in shape, David?"

"Mostly, Ray. I'm doing a fair bit of paddling out on the water, but haven't done much karate training. Maybe I should come in for some work with you soon?"

"Any time, David. I think these guys would enjoy sparring with you. They're not at your level, but they'd certainly benefit from contact with someone of your ability and style."

"I'll come in tomorrow then. How's business?"

Mackie smiled. "I'm not inundated with clients at the moment. It won't be long before these three achieve their set objectives. Then I might close for a holiday, maybe go back to Japan for some more work, a refresher. We'll see." Mackie was around forty, of medium height, powerfully built, with dark brown, almost auburn coloured hair. He would have been called handsome, even aristocratic, were it not for the nose. He had taken so many hits during his early years of fighting and instruction that it had become very much a blue-collar nose in a white-collar face. He had grown a neatly trimmed moustache, and wore a pair of rimless glasses which added to an almost academic appearance and partially took the eye away from his nose. Roberts liked him immensely. He was intelligent, thoughtful and perceptive, and the pair had developed a mutual liking and respect over the past six months.

Roberts rose. "Nice to meet you guys. Keep training—remember the pleasure you've gained from earning something you can't buy. It just gets better. I'll see you tomorrow, Ray."

*

Later that evening, after dinner, the phone rang. It was Kate in Sydney. Roberts suddenly had a strong feeling this was about to be another significant moment in his life.

"Hi Katie, how was dinner last night?"

"Well, David, that's part of what I want to talk to you about. I know that what you and I have had for a while has been just what we both wanted, and I've been quite satisfied with the relationship. But lately I've been a bit flat, and I think I've just begun to realise why." She was breathless, talking quickly, not letting him in yet. "Last night Jay said that I should be more involved with the life of my relationship partner, and I think he's right."

"Let me guess," Roberts broke in. 'He was an expert on you, me, our relationship and where it wasn't going, and offered his services as a counsellor, confidante, adviser, new lover, or all of the above."

"Please don't be like that." Kate was sharper now, more assured, satisfied she was in control and knew where she was at.

"David," she said slowly, "you're a good and sweet man, and when you were running XTRO you were the most exciting person to be near. I loved the splash, the waves you made all over the techno sector, the deals you brokered which involved such enormous amounts of money. But now you just aren't there any more. You've traded in the Moet for Carlton mid, and the aura has gone. You've disappeared and gone to live in the sticks."

"Well Katie, have you considered that in all those deals, the only things we ever actually made were constructions of paper, large profits for the company, and unhappiness for all the outside punters who lost money due to my cleverness?"

"But David, isn't that what big business is all about?" There was genuine puzzlement in her voice. "Isn't that just what a successful CEO is supposed to do?"

"It wasn't real, Kate. It was a corporation built on deceit and propaganda. Our company spin-doctors were our most important people. The more attractively we could package something the better it sold to the punters."

"Your share and severance package, David. Was that a sham too?"

He paused. "No. No, that was real money, and perhaps that was the worst deceit of all. I made an obscene amount of money out of a house of cards, by selling up at the right time. But maybe I can do something more real with it than where it came from."

"Feed some of Africa's starving millions you mean?" Kate was clearly coming to a close. "David, I'm afraid we've become too far apart in ideals and philosophies. I've become interested in Jay, and I want to explore things with him. You know I've always been honest with you, and so far nothing's happened. But I think I'd like it to, and I hope that doesn't hurt you. I certainly don't want to in any way."

Roberts still felt an emotional jolt at hearing what he had come to realise had happened, even though he knew she was right.

"Yes, Katie, I know you're an honest person, and I believe you. And you're right, we've become estranged in some pretty meaningful directions. I hope you can develop something good with Mr Best Seller. Watch out, though—those guys are very keen travellers."

"Thanks, David. I know what you're saying, and I'm not entirely clueless. But he's a fascinating man and an exciting personality, and interviewing him should also be fun. Take care of yourself, and please keep in touch." Kate's voice ranged through relieved, happy, sad, enthusiastic.

"I will, love. By the way, there's not a lot wrong with helping to feed some of Africa's starving millions, either, provided you can be sure the money is actually going into their mouths. But with that kind of philanthropy there always seems to be a feeling of futility, of pissing against the wind. I think there are many ways one can do something about making this planet a better place for everyone to live, and with a more obvious result. Who knows, Katie, maybe one of these days you'll be chasing me again for a story. You take care too."

"'Bye, David."

Roberts put the phone down with a certain finality. He felt flat, dejected, honest enough to concede that he would miss Kate and her sparklingly insightful commentaries on most current affairs topics. She was warm and very sexy when aroused, and in another concession he knew he would miss that too. But she had certain expectations of what constituted a successful topline mover and shaker, and he quite obviously no longer qualified.

He now had a great many details to sort out, and would begin tomorrow at the dojo. Tonight, however, would be for some solid belts of a very good cognac, a lengthy session with the incomparable voice of Eva Cassidy, and maybe also a little melancholy. Because no matter how calm, reasoned, intellectual and sophisticated you were when you broke up with someone you really cared for, it still created a big empty blob deep down inside, and it still hurt.

SEVEN

The yells, the heavy breathing, the slams of bodies hitting training mats with force, it was the typical noisy, violent ambience of a dojo in full workout mode. Roberts was in the thick of it, battling with two of the novices at once and giving them a going over. With a rapid series of blocks, kicks and throws he put them both down and stood back at ease.

"Nice work David," said Raydon Mackie. He had been coaching the two green belts through a routine, and had put them into a movement with Roberts. Roberts had been working solidly on the heavy bag, and had happily obliged.

"Now try me," Mackie was grinning. "I don't get many chances for a decent workout down here in Ulladulla."

"Shit, Ray, give me a break! I'm out of my league with you."

"Then do what I taught you—concentrate on the things you can do, and stay in that regime. Come on, I'll fight at first dan level."

Mackie removed his glasses and slid them into a pocket in the top of his training shirt. Ordinarily this would not be a good idea, but although he had suffered many blows in his earlier days, now it was nigh-on impossible to lay a hand or foot on him during a workout. For the next ten minutes, the only sounds in the room came from Roberts and Mackie, as they circled, struck, blocked, looked for openings and quickly closed them. The other trainees watched enthralled as the two older men fought in the classical style. Roberts achieved two half strength body strikes and one glancing temple punch, but was put down three times by Mackie, who didn't appear to be breathing hard.

After the last throw, Mackie stepped back to the rest position.

"Good, David," he said, "your technique is rusty but you're not in bad shape. That punch would have felled a lot of fighters. I had to go up a touch to throw you the last time."

"Thank Christ for that," wheezed Roberts, "because I didn't know what else to do. I'm going to have a shower and get changed, and then if you haven't got a lot more on here, I'll buy you lunch."

"What a great idea," smiled Mackie. "If I knock you out next time do I get dinner?"

*

The Cooked Goose Café was like a piece of multi-coloured macramé on a large scale. It had almost every colour of lime-washed paint on the walls, bare floorboards partly covered with throw tiles and timber tables that swayed when elbows leaned on them. There was artwork from three local painters displayed in combinations demonstrating a reckless disregard for artistic sensibilities, multi-hued and -shaped pottery stacked everywhere, and great smells and pleasant chatter. There were bean sprouts, watercress and lentil burgers to please those infatuated with current health food trends, but Roberts liked the place because it was honest and unpretentious and because you could also get real food there.

Over a lunch of warm chicken and salad open sandwiches and cold beer, Roberts regarded Mackie steadily and began to talk.

"Ray," he said, "I've got it in mind to undertake a special kind of project, and I'm going to need a shit-load of help. I won't be able to provide too many details yet, but I'm wondering if you'd be interested in a job? The pay and conditions would be good and there'd probably be a bonus. The downside would be that there'd be a possibility we could be killed or locked up somewhere and forgotten."

"Bloody hell, David," Mackie laughed, "don't hold back. Tell it like it is."

"I'm serious, Ray," smiled Roberts. "I need to put a team together to carry out a lengthy project that should culminate in some affirmative action, and I'm not talking about gender equity. I intend to take a particular kind of fight up to a group of people who appear untouchable. You're the first person I've approached."

"Well just what would you need me to do? I have to admit I'm curious, but I'm not sure I'd be happy about getting into anything illegal. Perhaps you'd better lay it all out and let me work on some concrete facts?"

"Basically, Ray, what I need is a right arm. Someone I can absolutely rely on. Someone to support me in all kinds of situations, and if need be to watch my back. Of necessity I'm going to have to be dealing with some shady types in other countries, and there will be some risk. I won't ever ask you to kill anyone, except in self-defense, nor will I ask you to do anything against your deepest principles. We won't steal anything, but we will be aggressors when we finish preparing. However, I do not in any way intend to cause the death of anyone involved with the, ah, activity, I want to stop. OK so far?"

"It's fascinating so far. How long is this going to take?"

"Probably four or five years to set up, if we work flat out. Maybe another couple to campaign. I'll pay you $250K per year to begin with, plus bonuses."

Mackie blinked. "Jesus, it just got more fascinating! You say you wouldn't ask me to do anything against my principles?"

"Correct. But I think I know you well enough to know that the situation simply won't occur. However, what we end up doing will be against international law."

Mackie looked thoughtful. "You know David, I'd be more concerned about us being immoral than illegal. I guess my business isn't going anywhere special, and there's a young woman I've been training who might want to take it on under a long-term lease. Or even buy it. One year of that salary would be more than I've made since I opened the dojo.

I think I'm in."

"Great, Ray. A handshake is enough of a contract for me, and thanks for taking me on face value. From now on you'll be privy to everything I do, and I'll want your comments and advice on many issues. One thing I don't know—is there a woman in your life? We're going to be moving around the world at pace, and eventually we'll be involved in the campaign."

"Well I'm sure as hell curious about this campaign of yours, David, but no, I'm divorced with no kids and only a casual girlfriend here in Milton. So can you tell me, what in the name of Christ are you planning to do?"

Roberts couldn't help himself... he grinned from ear to ear. "I'm going to buy a submarine, fit it out, gather and train a crew, build a base and go out and stop these bastards who are fishing our seas to extinction. Fun, huh?"

EIGHT

Angie was clearly uncomfortable. Roberts had informed her earlier in the afternoon that he wanted her to join him for dinner that night, and asked her to cook something she really enjoyed also. She had changed for the occasion, putting on her best black knee-length Sandilands, stockings and sandals. The semi-designer clung nicely to her curves, accentuating the fullness of her body and outlining a shape still able to command male attention. She had also done something to her hair Roberts was unable to describe, but it looked neater and shinier. Her eyes were outlined and her lips enhanced by lipstick she normally shunned.

He smiled. "This is wonderful, Angie, and you look gorgeous. But you don't seem to be enjoying it."

"Thank you, David. It's a rabbit casserole with fresh vegetables and herbs, and the meal is fine," she frowned. "It's sitting here with you I'm not enjoying. I shouldn't be here. It's not right." Angie was raised by hard-working parents who, although never becoming aware of Confucius, had instilled in her the simple clarity that everyone had a proper place in the natural scheme of things, that it was unthinkable to consider changing the order. She was paid as Roberts' cook/housekeeper, and so should not be eating with him in a social situation.

"Then let me ease your mind, dear Angie. I wanted to talk to you about something important, and this seemed as pleasant a way of doing it as any. I would like you to become the manager of this house on a long-term basis. I plan to become involved in a special project which will take some time and keep me away from here for long periods. I need someone I can trust to take care of the house for me, and maybe carry out one or two little tasks I may need from time to time. I'll treble your pay and give you access to a well-funded account for whatever you need. You can hire another housekeeper if you wish, as you may become too busy with other matters, but while I'm home I want you to remain the cook. I love your cooking. How are we doing so far?" he grinned.

Angie's soft, attractive face had lost its frown, but was now showing surprise and uncertainty. She looked down at her plate, hesitated, then glanced up at Roberts, her eyes puzzled. She had taken hold of a serviette and had twisted it into a tight roll.

"It would be something I'd very much enjoy doing, David. But I'd be concerned you were trying to make me into someone I'm not."

"I thought you might say something like that, Angie," said Roberts seriously. He knew this was the crucial part. Angie had mature self-belief and was very comfortable with who she was. "But I happen to believe you're wrong if you think your only capabilities lie in cooking and keeping house. I've come to appreciate your capacity to handle anything that could occur around here, and more importantly, I'd trust you with my life. And that's not being overly dramatic, as it happens."

"Thank you, David," she whispered, her eyes moistening, "that means more to me than you know."

"Good, Angie, I'll take that as a yes. And now I'll tell you what I've been planning . . ."

*

"My God, David," Angie gasped, her eyes now wide and sparkling, her face animated, "that's the most incredible thing I've ever heard! And it's so right! Can you really do it?"

"I haven't started yet, but I can't readily think of anything to stop me. My former colleagues at XTRO would tell you that when I get my teeth into something it's not easy to shake me off. And ever since that incident with the whale, my feelings have been stirred up to a point where I'm now completely committed to the idea of stopping the slaughter. I can't think of anything I'd rather do."

"Well I think it's a brilliant idea, and I'm so glad I'm going to be a little part of it." Angie's face was alight with a beautiful smile.

"You realise, Angie, that you won't be able to tell this to anyone at all? It will be illegal, and we will have to maintain very tight security on everything we do. I want you to bring in the necessary tradesmen, all from outside the district, to beef up security both in the grounds and in the house. If ever I'm uncovered, I'm going to be very unpopular with some nasty people, and we'll need to be prepared."

"I understand, David. I'll turn this house into a safe haven for you and your friends. God, I'm so excited at the thought of actually being able to do something real."

"I can see that," smiled Roberts, "you've actually drunk some of this lovely Hill of Grace."

Angie blushed, again very prettily, and quickly put down the glass of aged Henschke cabernet sauvignon Roberts had poured for her. "Oh dear, I didn't mean to do that," she winced. "But it does taste very heady. Perhaps, now I'm a manager . . . ?"

Roberts burst out laughing. "Way to go, Angela. I wonder how many of my best reds will survive my absences now?"

NINE

"Good mornin' gennelmen, what kin ah do for y'all?" The voice was light, well modulated, not at all the kind of voice one would expect to issue from the very large man behind the counter. His heavily jowled face was impassive, although not unfriendly, and his hands, each big enough to cover the top of a good-sized bar stool, rested lightly on the counter top. He was clad in army-type camo shirt and trousers, and the front of a heavy black combat boot peeped around the corner of the counter. A large one.

Roberts and Mackie were standing in a small, well-lit gun shop on SW 25th Avenue, near Beacon Boulevard in an area known as Little Havana, in Miami, Florida, following a long and tiring flight from Sydney earlier in the week. It was late August, but the weather in Miami was still warm and pleasant. According to the locals it was always warm and pleasant.

"We're looking for a Mr Bowater Tallis," Roberts smiled politely up at the man.

"Ah'm Bo," he said evenly, "and you are?"

"My name's Robbie and this is Mack," offered Roberts. "A friend of mine in New York pointed me in your direction, because I'm after some special supplies. He said you may be able to help, or at least to send me to someone who can."

"Maybe you could start bah tellin' me the nature o' these supplahs?" The big man suggested quietly. He hadn't moved or altered his expression.

"We want to buy a fully-equipped and working submarine," said Roberts mildly.

"Well hooley-dooley, now y'all're talkin'!" The impassivity morphed into a smiling, enthusiastically expressive face. "Grab those two stools over there and sit yourselves down. Like a beer?" The massive body finally moved, surprisingly agile; Bo bent down behind the counter, and two Coors appeared, one engulfed in each fist. A third hit the counter top and the caps were flipped off with what had to be an opener inside Tallis' hand. His reserve had dissipated, sloughed away as the natural caution inherent in anyone in a similar occupation was satisfied by the unusual demands of the two foreigners. They just didn't look like trouble, and he knew something about that, anyhow.

"As it happens ah probably kin be of assistance. There's a old German U-boat in dock here raht at the moment, an' ah believe she's still a goin' concern. Maht need some work, 'cause she got stuck on a sand bank in South America recently, an' the owners, the Venezuelan Government, couldn't get her off an' sold her 'as is where is'. A South African salvage company worked her off the bank, patched her leaks an' towed her here. Ah believe ah could arrange a sale for you at a steal—maybe as low as one big one."

"One thousand?" asked Mackie with an innocent expression.

The big man giggled, shaking all over like a truck-sized serve of jello. "Is that British humour?"

"We're Australian," Roberts shook his head, "but we forgive you. We need her to be totally sound, in full working order and completely equipped with all systems and facilities operational."

"Shouldn't be a problem, but y'all'll have to dicker with someone else over the fahnal sale. Leave me y' cell phone number and ah'll be in touch."

"Thanks for the beer, Bo. Hoo roo." Roberts noticed Tallis looking a little puzzled, and put it down to the unusual order he and Mackie had made.

They walked down 25th to their rented Lincoln town car. "A fucking U-boat?" Mackie looked quizzically at Roberts. "Are you dinkum?"

"Well, apparently they worked OK during World War II. Provided it's sound it should do us nicely . . . with a few modifications I have in mind."

"Do you reckon it'll be in good condition?"

Roberts grinned at his friend. "Wouldn't have a clue, mate. That's why we're going to have to find someone who knows all about U-boats, and soon."

*

"Thanks, James, I'll let you know how we go. And there'll be a cheque in the mail tomorrow." Roberts finished the call to his contact in New York. James Redolfo had been a confidante of his for many years, during the heady times of his XTRO days, and Roberts had benefited often when Redolfo had been able to supply him with information of a specific and sensitive nature. So accurate and timely had Redolfo been that Roberts had placed him on a very generous retainer. It had not been insider trading, not exactly, but some of the information had been remarkably confidential and accurate, enabling Roberts to make some impressively prescient and profitable decisions. Of course, these days there was no longer a cheque in the mail; it was a wire transfer to one of Redolfo's accounts, paid by the same anonymous little man in his charcoal-grey suit who had handled all of Roberts' accounting needs during the XTRO days. But Redolfo knew what he meant.

"James still seems to be in business, Ray. His tip on Miami was right on the nose, and he's found the name and address of a man who may be able to help with U-boats. He lives in Seattle, Washington."

That evening the two men took an early American Airlines flight to Sea-Tac airport and checked into the Hilton in downtown Seattle.

"I could get used to this lifestyle," grinned Mackie. "Do you always stay at Hiltons?"

"Not always, but it's a habit I picked up when I was travelling so much between Sydney and the States. They are quality digs, and always have everything I need. I guess I'm known in a lot of them, and that can sometimes be an advantage. They'll have a car and driver ready for us first thing tomorrow morning. C'mon, let's wander down to the Pike Place markets—one of the seafood places there is the best show in town, and we can grab a clam chowder or two. I've never tasted better anywhere in the world."

*

The next morning, Friday September 1st, dawned cool, grey and softly raining.

"Well, it is their fall now, and it usually rains in Seattle," said Roberts with a shrug. "We need to go to N 51st Street please," he told the driver, "number 217."

It was a sloping, tree-lined suburban street with fresh air and distant mountains, lovely in the sunlight which had pushed away the light rain, and the house was a classic double story bungalow. The door was opened to their knock by a tall, spare man with a full head of snow-white hair. His face was in shadow, but his bearing was upright.

"Good morning, we're looking for Gunter Hass," smiled Roberts.

"Well you have found him," said the tall man, stepping out onto the small landing. He had sharp features, a grey-white moustache and large gold-rimmed spectacles. There was a cool look to his eyes that was questioning, as if he knew what was coming.

"Pleased to meet you, Mr Hass. My name is Robbie and this is my friend and colleague, Mack. We would very much like to talk to you about a matter which is important to us, but in no way of concern to you."

"You know who I am?" asked Hass.

"We know who you were, and all we seek is information for a private project. We mean no harm." Roberts spoke calmly, earnestly and with candour in his eyes, telling the old man their full and correct names. "Can we take you to a café or restaurant of your choice? You will be perfectly safe with us."

Hass nodded slightly to himself, as if deciding that the two men indeed were genuine. "I have become very attached to the coffee in this country, and in Seattle in particular. We will go to the Lighthouse, where we can get some Tully's."

*

The place was intimate, funky and satisfyingly noisy, and the wonderful smell of roasting coffee beans had struck them before they were even in the door.

"This is better than Starbuck's." Mackie was becoming used to the idea that coffee came in differing types and tastes. Hass stared at him and Roberts laughed.

"Starbuck's began here in Seattle, but a lot of people think they've been overtaken."

"So, gentlemen, what exactly do you want of me," Hass asked, "if it's not the latest location of stolen Nazi gold in a sunken U-boat off the coast of Argentina?"

Roberts smiled, sympathy obvious on his face. "Have you been hounded much over the years?"

"More than you could imagine," he admitted. "I was very young at the end of the war, only seventeen, although my papers said I was twenty-one. But I was an underofficer on a German U-boat, and was fighting my country's enemies. It was true that there were very few black uniforms in the German Navy, but we still became criminals at the end of the war."

"You're referring to Nazis," said Mackie evenly.

"Yes," nodded Hass, "the average German sailor knew almost nothing of what was occurring in the ghettos and death camps. There were rumours, but no one took any notice and it all seemed very far away. In the confusion at the end I managed to get out of Hamburg and travelled into Norway, where I eventually made a new life training Norwegian naval personnel in some of their captured U-boats. I became an expert, and after many years migrated to the United States, where my expertise as a submariner was recognised. I took back my real name, went through an exhaustive investigatory process, married a dear, lovely woman and have, in the end, had a good life here. I have been retired now for many years, and suddenly here are two young Englishmen who are bringing back so many memories."

Roberts smiled. "We're actually Australian. Tell me, Mr Hass, would you be interested in consulting for us on a special project involving a U-boat? It would mean moving to Florida for a few months, but we would be happy to pay you a generous fee and all relocation expenses. Including your wife?"

"Yes, Mr Roberts, fortunately my wife is still very much alive. But what project? And what could I do?"

"We can't say too much just yet, but we need an expert on U-boats to tell us how to restore one to good working condition. Will you consider our proposal?"

"It sounds most unlikely, and I'm not sure I'd be of much use, but if you're serious, and you appear to be, I will talk to my wife, and see if she would like a holiday in Florida. I'll let you know by this time tomorrow."

TEN

The following Monday Roberts, Mackie, Hass and his plump, charming American wife, Dorothy, flew to Miami. Dorothy had jumped at the chance for a holiday in Miami, and had instantly perceived Roberts and Mackie to be genuine and likeable. Gunter was clearly much more at ease with the situation. They spent the day locating and moving the Hass couple in to a pleasant, furnished apartment in southern Miami, just off South Miami Avenue in Bay Heights, quite near the dock area. During the afternoon a call from Tallis had taken them back to his gun shop to meet a go-between called Julio Mendez, a small, thin, rat-faced little man of indeterminate age and uncertain credentials, painted in tight-fitting black denim, who said he was acting for the Venezuelan Government. He would take care of all necessary paperwork, and the submarine would be available for inspection tomorrow. It was in pristine condition, and well worth the million dollar asking price. He seemed to consider himself of far more importance than that to which his appearance gave any credence.

"So can we arrange settlement now?" he asked in a tone which evoked in Roberts a vision of a mass of bloodworms writhing in some Swan River mud.

"You're kidding, right? You think we should pay you all that money for something we've only heard about and for which we haven't seen a single page of documentation? Get real mate. We'll see you at the dock tomorrow morning."

*

The next morning Roberts was on the phone early to his New York contact, James Redolfo. After a ten minute call he thanked Redolfo and hung up. After collecting Mackie and Hass, the three men drove out to Lummus Island and the Port of Miami. They had been given directions by the obnoxiously oily Julio, and found themselves driving down Australia Way and into Antarctica Way.

Mackie raised an eyebrow at the street signs and looked speculatively at Roberts. "I guess if we needed omens for this project we've got some."

"I've never needed any before," Roberts answered quietly.

"Never turn down a good omen, gentlemen, when you are dealing with affairs of the sea," cautioned the old man. "You can never have too much good luck."

"I always considered I made my own luck in the world of corporate affairs," Roberts said, not in any way arrogantly but with the calm assurance of a person confident in his ability to deal with any situation, familiar or unexpected.

"Maybe so, my young friend," responded Hass, "but when you go to sea you place yourself in the hands of elemental forces over which you have absolutely no influence, and which can either give you the fairest weather, or sink you, with equal indifference. You may need to find some humility, and I urge you to have the utmost respect for the ocean when you venture upon it."

Roberts glanced at the very dignified old man with increased interest. "I hear what you say, Mr Hass. I don't intend to be in any way foolhardy, but I've long believed that I'm the only person in charge of my destiny."

"Please call me Gunter, both of you. Yes, any man who can succeed as you must have, David, will of necessity be a strong character and confident of his own abilities. All I'm trying to say is that out on the deep oceans things sometimes don't go according to plan; sometimes you must fit in with what the fates decree and simply take what comes."

They approached the end of the drive, through some large, open gates, and parked at the side of what looked like a deserted dock in poor repair. The little South American was waiting for them, and Roberts told Hass to wander off and look at whatever he chose.

"I don't want this guy to know who you are," he said, "so just ignore him if he speaks to you."

Roberts and Mackie got out and walked over to Julio.

"Well, where is it?"

The diminutive Cuban actually looked a little sheepish. "Ah, down there," he nodded to the end of the dock.

The three men walked to the end and peered over the rail at something lying low in the stagnant water.

"Jesus Christ!"

"Holy shit!"

Roberts and Mackie stared in disbelief at the rusted, dented and filthy hulk that lay deep in the water below them. With the combination of a low tide and the apparent half-submerged state of the boat, the conning tower, or sail, was actually below the level of the dock. Which was why they hadn't seen it until they moved to its edge. Which was why they were so stunned by its appearance. Aside from looking far smaller than its actual size, it was so covered in rust and grime it looked like a hundred-year-old shipwreck a salvage company had just brought to the surface. They both turned to Mendez and glared at him. He stepped back, startled at the anger radiating from their faces.

"Pristine condition? Fully operational? You're wasting our time, you little prick! A million bucks? I wouldn't give you a hundred for this piece of junk!"

"Senors, I am assured that it is floating, and that it still operates." Mendez was uneasy, subdued, but still selling. "Perhaps you would like to go aboard?"

"Perhaps we would like to drown when it sinks under us, too," said Mackie, his voice heavy with ridicule. Roberts shrugged, still frowning, and beckoned Hass over, motioning him to go aboard.

"Say nothing to anyone—just investigate and observe please, Gunter," he whispered, at the same time digging Mackie gently in the ribs as he passed. "Follow my lead, Ray."

They climbed down a dockside ladder and on to the deck of the old U-boat. It was pitted with rust and only faint remnants of grey paint showed in patches. They clambered up the rust-eaten external ladder on the side of the conning tower, over its side, and down onto the bridge. Julio took out a key and undid a large, crude-looking padlock fixing a welded bracket on the hatch. He grasped the handle, turned it and swung the hatch up, or tried to. It was stuck.

Mackie moved the small man aside, took hold of the handle and exerted pressure. The hatch came up slowly, protestingly, noisily, and he leant back with a snort of disgust.

"Shit, it stinks down there."

Hass moved slowly to the top of the ladder inside the hatch, and then simply disappeared. Roberts followed much more slowly, realizing that Hass was now in very familiar territory. He climbed down into the control room and waited for the others to join him. The smell was bad—musty, dank, metallic, and something else.

Mackie stood beside him. "I've smelled that smell before. Someone died in here somewhere. They've tried to remove the odour with a lot of detergent, but it's difficult to get that smell out of a closed space."

"OK, Julio." Roberts clapped a firm hand on the small man's shoulder. "Show us around. I see you brought some torches. Later you can start the engines and turn on some light." Roberts fixed the uncomfortable go-between with a steely gaze. "*Vamos.*"

An hour later, the three men were back in the tiny control room. Hass came up to Roberts, who frowned a warning at him, shaking his head slightly. Hass was looking very thoughtful. They climbed up into the bridge and down the side of the conning tower on to the pitted deck. Once back on the dock, Roberts turned to Mendez.

"That is nothing but a great big piece of *caja*, Julio. It's rusted almost to death, the engines won't work, most of the instruments have been stripped out of her, we don't even know if it will dive properly, and it stinks. Forget it."

"Senor Robbie, I will bring an engineer back with me this afternoon and get the power plant working, and we will prove it can still move and dive. Please come back here at four PM and we will demonstrate it for you." Mendez was almost imploring in his request to Roberts.

"OK, Julio, we'll be here at four. That will be your last chance to show me the boat is even worth a dollar, let alone the ridiculous amount your people are asking."

The little man ran to his car, jumped in and drove off at speed. Hass turned to Roberts, his face alight and his eyes shining with memories.

"David," he beamed, "isn't she magnificent!"

The two Australians looked incredulously at Hass, as though he had suddenly lost his mind.

"You're having a lend of us, aren't you Gunter?"

While not understanding the Australianism, he read the expressions on top of the body language.

"No, no, she is absolutely beautiful! But I have to tell you, she isn't a U-boat. She is a Russian-built Foxtrot class diesel-electric submarine, based quite closely on the last type of German U-boat built in 1944 and 45. That boat was the Type XXI Electroboat, and had they been able to build them and commission them faster they may have made a difference to the outcome of the war at sea. But this boat is bigger—apart from the massive Japanese I-400 series submersible aircraft carriers she is the largest non-nuclear submarine ever built. She is over ninety metres long and weighs almost 2000 tonnes, and could do sixteen knots. And she is more recent than 1945. She was probably built as late as 1974, and will be in better condition than she looks.

"Well right now it doesn't look like it can even submerge, let alone do sixteen knots," said Mackie.

"Oh, she will dive all right; that is the easy part, if the batteries are still there and the motors will start. She has been stripped of a lot of gear, but there is still much left, and I found a full complement of twenty-two Mk 48 torpedoes. I wonder just what those Venezuelans were doing?"

Roberts' eyes lit up. "She's fully stocked with torpedoes, you say? Will they still work?"

"They are very old, but would probably still run, with some maintenance, maybe some new parts. Incidentally, David, there is a refurbished Foxtrot at Pier 48 in Seattle, where I live, and if my old memory serves me correctly, I believe there is also one at the Maritime Museum in Sydney, where you live." Hass was smiling with excitement and anticipation. "This afternoon will be most interesting."

*

Under the intense gazes of Roberts, Mackie and Hass, Mendez and the marine engineer he had brought worked on the batteries and air start, and after half an hour of attempts, managed to coax one of the old Kolomna diesels into intermittent life. Lights came on and some of the instrumentation left in the control room fired up.

"You see, she moves ahead and astern against the mooring lines," Julio said excitedly. "The ballast tanks are still sound, or she would not be still afloat. We can partially fill and blow some of them, and she will slowly sink and then rise at the dock. But I have to concede that a full sea trial would not be advisable in her current condition. She does need a bit of work." He became apologetic, shrugging his narrow shoulders. "Perhaps we can negotiate a small discount on our asking price," he said with what he probably thought a disarming smile. It in no way disarmed the Australians.

"This boat is in such poor condition it would be a death trap at sea. I doubt we will even want it, let alone pay you for it," said Roberts grimly. "We will see you at Bo's place tomorrow morning at nine to let you know. Make sure you have all the necessary paperwork you claimed you had. There'll be no deal without it," he glared at Julio. "*Comprende, chico*?"

It was clear from the thoughtful look in his dark eyes that the diminutive Cuban did. With a worried frown he walked away to his car, his movements considerably less jaunty. The poor condition of the submarine had caused him to completely forget to swagger. The sale might not be as easy as he first thought. These *extranjeros de mierdas* were proving difficult.

"Well guys, what are we thinking?" Roberts clapped his hands together enthusiastically.

"You're not serious about this piece of shit, David?" Mackie looked askance at his friend. "It's not worth two bob."

"Oh no, Ray, she's probably quite sound, and with some maintenance could be tidied up and made operational," Hass said with concern in his voice. "It would be such a shame to let her lie here and just rot away."

"With the greatest respect, Gunter, you are probably influenced by emotion about this boat." Mackie spoke seriously to the old German sailor. "But we are planning something that will need a sound vessel which can operate for long periods far out to sea. We can't put our trust, not to mention lives, at unnecessary risk with an old death trap."

"It's OK, Ray, I won't be doing anything stupid, but I think Gunter may be right about this boat." Roberts put his hand on Mackie's shoulder. "Yes, it does look like shit, but it's been operating for some years, probably drug running, and I have some plans for its refit. You see, I'm going to strip almost everything out, so I don't mind the missing equipment. I'll use it as a bargaining point, but they've actually saved us some work. Then we'll refit her with the latest in electronics and lightweight furniture, new diesels and batteries, put in a good air-conditioning and filtering system, and buy in some more torpedoes. James told me of a number of refitted diesel subs around, like the two Foxtrots on the west coast and the one in Sydney, as well as a number in Vladivostok and Murmansk, and some US diesel boats like the USS *Blueback* and USS *Barbell*. But for many reasons I want to do the work here in the States, and in as much secrecy as possible. It will cost more here, but I think the work will be of better quality, and all the equipment we will need is more easily available in America than anywhere else." Roberts shrugged, grinned and looked from Mackie to

Hass with an excited expression. He ran his hand through his spiky hair, looked down at the sub. "Don't worry Ray, by the time we're all done here, you won't recognise her. She will look like a million dollars, not the paltry sum I'm going to pay for her. Wonder what her name was?"

*

Next morning on the stroke of nine Roberts and Mackie walked into the gun shop on 25th. Tallis was behind his counter, and Julio was already there, along with a very large, blank-faced man, dark shaggy hair grimly clinging to a massive bullet-shaped head, and swarthy, unhealthily pockmarked skin. He was wearing an expensive dark blue suit that could, at a squeeze, have fit both Roberts and Mackie inside. He was bigger than Tallis, but harder, and decidedly less friendly in appearance.

"Hi Bo," waved Roberts cheerily to the gun shop owner. "Looks like you're doing some business."

"Mornin' Robbie," drawled Tallis, "Julio brought along an advahser. His name's Ricardo." Roberts nodded affably in Ricardo's direction, but drew less of a response than he would have gotten from a street sign.

"I have the papers, senor Robbie," said Julio with more assurance than he had displayed yesterday. "I concede that the boat is not in first class condition, so am prepared to accept a final figure of $900,000."

"My God Julio, I just can't believe your generosity! Only a mere $900,000 for an ex drug-running vessel with all valuable gear stripped out, only one partially working engine, suspect ballast tanks, a death smell almost impossible to remove, and the whole thing hanging together with rust? You're too kind." Roberts' sarcasm was not lost on the little South American, who flushed and glanced at the mountainous Ricardo.

Ricardo moved slowly towards Roberts. "Senor, you will show more respect to Mr Mendez." The voice was as gravelly as would be expected from such a body, especially one cast in the role of an enforcer.

Roberts noticed Mackie quietly remove his glasses and place them carefully in his top pocket. He smiled and turned to the baleful stare emanating from the huge block of muscle standing before him.

"Why?" he asked, the smile still in place, the intentional insolence clear and unambiguous.

At the first movement from Ricardo, Roberts lashed out a foot and connected very solidly with the right knee of the Titanic-sized bodyguard, who groaned and listed to starboard. In the same instant, although it was an extension of the first movement, Roberts lanced out a half strength knuckle strike to the larynx of the unfortunate Ricardo, who gasped and crashed to the floor, shaking some of the display cases. A nod and small smile from Mackie, as he replaced his glasses, was comment enough. Roberts spread his arms wide, palms up, and smiled engagingly at Tallis and Mendez.

"He'll be OK soon, guys. No need to get uptight. We're only here to deal, not to make war on anyone. I don't take kindly to threats, and he made that mistake. So did you, Julio, by bringing him here. As you know, that boat is a pile of shit, but I can use what's left. Unfortunately, it's not worth any more to me than two hundred and fifty thousand. There are quite a few other boats of its kind around, in operating condition, so yours is not an essential item."

Julio looked aghast. "But we can't take anything less than half a million dollars for it," he whined.

"Bugger off," laughed Roberts, "you wouldn't get anywhere near that amount from anyone, and you know it. I'll go to $300,000, but it's now a take it or leave it figure. And that of course also includes the papers. I assume you can make the decision, Julio. Well?"

The little go-between, almost in tears, looked from Ricardo to Tallis. "Don't look at me," said Bo with a shrug, "Ah'm only th' broker."

Ricardo coughed hoarsely, groaned and struggled to sit up, his face very pale and huge chest heaving for air. Mackie walked over to him, leaned down and quietly told him to sit still and he'd feel much better. He reached into the massive man's jacket, drew out a very lethal-looking Glock semi automatic nine millimeter pistol from a shoulder holster, and carefully gave it to Tallis.

Mendez, still shaken and very unhappy, sullenly agreed to the terms set by Roberts. The papers appeared to be in order, but Roberts didn't place much credence in them. The submarine was apparently owned by a company called '*Comanditarios*', which the South American said meant 'silent partners', and leased to the Venezuelan Government, or so the story went. Roberts wrote a cheque made out to the company.

"Ah no, senor, I am sorry but we only deal in cash!" exclaimed the little go-between, again becoming agitated.

"Well, Julio, this time you'll deal in cheques, or not at all. What, do you think we will be able to repair that junk pile and steal it away before you can clear the cheque? We're going to be busy for years," Roberts grinned. He walked over to Tallis. "Thanks for your help, Bo. We appreciate what you've done for us. You can keep the Glock if you like."

"It's been mah pleasure gentlemen. Ah don't believe ah've ever seen Australians operate before, and it's been an education. Come back and see me if y'all need anything else."

"That we will, Bo, because the refit will be comprehensive, and although the vessel is required for research purposes, we want to be able to take care of ourselves in any situation. We'll see you later. So long Julio. You can help your mate up now."

As they were driving back to the hotel, Mackie glanced at Roberts with no small amount of curiosity. With his glasses back in place, he again had the appearance of an elegant, conservative sage who had suffered some unfortunate accident to his nose.

"David, pardon me for being inquisitive, but I think this refit is going to be expensive. As will be our accommodation and living expenses, and Gunter's, and you're paying me a bloody fortune as well."

"Ray, I made a hell of a lot of money when I sold my shares. I haven't re-invested fully yet, partly because I've been too busy, but also because I don't think we've felt the last shock wave to come out of the stock market since 9/11. There's too much uncertainty in my mind. The tech-wreck seems to have levelled out, but I've heard a couple of recent murmurings about something nasty in the wings, and I'm just going to sit on my holdings in two or three banks for a while yet. The interest they are paying on money market loans is making me three or four million dollars a month, anyway. Let's go eat."

*

Dorothy Hass had invited the two men to the apartment for a home-cooked meal, and Roberts accepted with alacrity. He had always enjoyed quality home cooking, and this was no exception.

"Thank you, Dorothy, that was superb," he leaned back in his chair, full, satisfied with the day's work, happy that things appeared to be moving at last.

"Oh David, it was just some southern fried chicken and trimmings," Dorothy chuckled, pleased that it had been appreciated. "I'll get some coffee."

"I'm sorry I haven't had time yet to get in some proper supplies," apologized Gunter. "I've been in this country so long now that I find I prefer bourbon to schnapps, and don't even feel ashamed about it," he said with a rueful smile.

"Coffee'll be fine thanks, Gunter," said Roberts. "Ray, I want you and Gunter to begin organising things with the Miami Port authorities to make everything legal, and to book the nearest dry dock for some extensive work on our new boat. You'll need to find a good marine engineer and full dockside crew—make sure they are all union people. The story is that the vessel is being refitted for extensive cruising in international waters as a research vessel for leasing to the major world wildlife and conservation organisations. Gunter, what we are really going to do is to find as many whalers and illegal fishing boats as we can, and persuade them to stop." Roberts eyed Gunter with a serious expression. "You would have noted my interest when you told me about the torpedoes yesterday? Well, now you know why. If you don't think you can be a party to re-creating a machine of war for such a purpose, it would be a good time to say so." Roberts was on safe ground—he had seen the excitement in Gunter's face and knew the old seaman could not resist the involvement in something that had been such a large part of his life.

"Oh no, David, it's what she was designed for, and I'm very happy to be working on such a project. I'm old, and steeped in diesel submarine knowledge and tradition, but I understand what you require. I won't try to turn her into a museum piece. She can be made as modern as you like, just so she gets to dive again. But I think I have one request to make of you." The old man's eyes were alight with pleasure and excitement. "When she is ready, I want to go too."

Roberts realised now what he had done. "Gunter, what we plan to do will be no picnic, and could be life-threatening. But I promise you this. You will be aboard when she takes her first dive, and if I think you will be OK, you may become a crew member."

Hass was silent for a few seconds, and the look in his old eyes spoke volumes. "Thank you, David," he said quietly. He rose from the table, emotion finally claiming him, and walked slowly from the room.

"Do you think that's wise?" Mackie asked.

"Ray, there are obvious reasons why it would be an advantage to have Gunter's expertise along with us on our campaigning, and he wouldn't eat much, either. But I seem to have changed from a corporate hard-nose who made distasteful decisions easily to someone who now thinks a little less with his head. This project will clearly give Gunter a new lease on life, and perhaps some vindication for the years of international condemnation for the sins of Nazi Germany his generation went through. They weren't all Nazis, and they weren't all bad. And anyhow, I like him."

"Yeah, David, I like him too. Using your heart to make decisions rather than your head probably won't make you any richer, but I guess you're there already."

Roberts smiled. "Well, Ray, I'll let you make the decisions about the crew. Talk to Gunter later and try to get a handle on the type of people we'll need to keep her going, but I want to limit the number to less than thirty if possible. Remember our objective and hire on some special help. You'll have to screen them carefully—I don't want any nutcases, but we'll obviously need some people with fighting experience and knowledge of weaponry. But don't forget to include a capable medico—oh, and a good chef, too."

"He'll be the first picked," laughed Mackie, "and it will be a 'he' too. Most of the best chefs are men and that's the only sexism I have any more. But the crew . . . ?"

"No, I have no sexist objection either. I've seen too much international corporate boardroom in-fighting to believe only the males are the best survivors. You find me the best people you can, and we'll go with what turns up."

"OK, I'll start tomorrow. What have you got planned?"

Roberts looked thoughtful. "I'm going back to Sydney to round up another crew, buy a supply ship and build a base for our submarine."

"Jesus, is that all," Mackie grinned. "Shouldn't cost too much to buy some land on the ocean front and build a port with all necessary facilities, if you can find such a place," he laughed. "Got any idea where to start?"

"Yeah, I do actually," Roberts smiled gently, his eyes twinkling. "But it's not in Australia."

ELEVEN

Thursday and Friday had been blurred. Roberts had set up an operating account for Mackie and had gone to talk to the CEO of the Miami Port Authority. He had explained his requirements for a large and lengthy refitting of his new purchase, that it was for scientific investigation, and that it would mean many jobs and healthy revenue. He gently advised the CEO that if costs were to prove too high he would simply ship the vessel to Taiwan or India or Singapore and do the work there at half the cost. The CEO was warmly receptive to the long-term contract and agreed to a comfortable cost structure, providing the Australians with a working dry dock on the southern side of the island, away from the main port business.

Two Port tugs had moved the old submarine into the dry dock, where she had been carefully positioned by the yard crew over large chocks, and the dock emptied. She had suddenly looked a lot bigger, and a lot worse. "Very bedraggled," thought Roberts, looking at her weedy bottom and filthy, rust-pitted hull, "but not for too long."

Mackie had organized a work team to begin cleaning the outside of the sub, while Hass had been busy drawing up a list of the necessary specialists who would be able to refurbish and refit a vessel of her type. A firm of consultants had been engaged to seek out such people and interview them, and Mackie had then begun searching for another kind of specialist, this kind not so easy to locate.

It had been later one night a week ago that Roberts and Mackie had been walking back to their vehicle after spending some time with the recently installed computer-assisted hydraulics system. They had climbed out of the dry dock and were making their way toward the parking area when four ill-defined shapes appeared out of the shadows caused by the solitary street light on a nearby corner. One of them was twice as big as any of the other three, none of which was small, and limped itself squarely into the path of the now stationary submariners. As it revealed its identity with a rasping "Julio wants to pay his respects, and says you owe him another half million", Mackie removed his glasses and put them in his top pocket, murmuring to Roberts to move sideways so they'd have some room to work.

"Well bugger me, is that you Ricardo?" grinned Roberts, "What's wrong? Weren't you satisfied last time?" At the same time he circled around the menhir-sized Cuban, being careful to stay out of the reach of his massive arms and enormous hands. He heard the sound of quick movement, sharp breathing, rapid blows solidly landing and a series of gasps and moans, all in the space of around four seconds. He didn't even pause in his circling of the behemoth to look at what Mackie was doing, trusting in him to handle the other three without undue exertion.

"OK David, no one's been killed, although a couple are going to need some attention. Sort him out and let's go."

"Well, big guy, do we still have to do this, or would you prefer to cut your losses and piss off?" Roberts said quietly to Ricardo. The massive enforcer hesitated, glanced over a shoulder at his hired muscle spread out on the street, looked thoughtful for a second, then shrugged and growled "He don't pay me enough to keep getting beaten up."

"Smart thinking amigo," Roberts said seriously, stepping close to the huge man and staring intently up at his face, "but do everyone a favour and take a message to the little asshole. Tell him if any of our crew are bothered again, Ray and I will come for him and do some enforcing of our own. *Entiendas, hermano*?"

Ricardo nodded slowly, his eyes, even in the dim light from the lone street lamp, reflecting a certain grudging respect for the two men.

Roberts walked over to where Mackie was looking at the three unconscious forms of Ricardo's companions. "Jesus Ray, is that . . ."

"Yeah David, sorry but this bloke had a knife, so I stuck it in his shoulder to show him what it felt like. His mates can take him to hospital when they all wake up. He's not bleeding too badly."

"OK, Ricardo's still on his feet, so he can look after them." Roberts too looked thoughtful for a moment. "Might be an idea to hire some extra security around the sub for a while, Ray. Just in case."

*

After leaving Mackie with some specific instructions, Roberts flew out of Miami on Friday afternoon for Sydney via Los Angeles. His connections were some hours apart, and it wasn't until after ten PM that he finally departed Los Angeles. First class was improving, and he slept horizontally most of the way across the Pacific, arriving in Sydney early on a Sunday morning.

He picked up his vehicle from the long term car park and drove sedately down the coast to Ulladulla. Turning in to his driveway seemed different, somehow. There was a new two metre-high fence which seemed to go right round the property, and the entrance road had been sealed. It looked as though construction was happening at the fence line. Roberts drove through and parked in the open garage, as Angie came out of the front door with her face lit up in a smile radiant enough to lighten anyone's load.

"Hi, Angie!" Roberts gave her a warm hug. "What on Earth have you been doing?"

"David, it's so good to have you back home again," she said happily, colouring at his embrace. "I've found a bright young electronics man who's had some experience with security systems, and had a new fence erected—he tells me it's a 'smart' fence, whatever that means. The drive has sensors laid under it, I'm having some electronic gates installed, and the garage will be enclosed and automatically operated. There will soon be a complete alarm system installed in and around the house, showing on the control panel inside the house, at the security company and in the local police station. The cameras will be installed around the grounds in a couple more weeks.

And, David, you did leave me an awful lot of money, and the house seemed to be developing into a kind of support system which needed lots of power, so I organized for the installation of a diesel generator as a back-up power plant."

"Wow, Angie, you have been busy, and the generator is a great idea. Let's get some lunch and I'll tell you what I've been up to in Florida."

*

Roberts spent the afternoon paddling and the evening having another very enjoyable home-cooked meal with Angie, something he realized he had been looking forward to with a great deal of pleasure. It was quiet, relaxing quality time for him, something he wasn't enjoying a lot of, but obviously needed. He and Angie talked long into the night, mostly about the project, but Roberts found he was able to unwind and talk about other things with Angie, too. Things he wouldn't have thought he'd be able to, or even want to, with anyone. He deprecated his uninspiring childhood and technological education, telling Angie he sometimes wished he had simply dropped out like many of his contemporaries. There were also times he felt he should have studied arts, for the pure sake of study. All of his tertiary education had been heading in a specific direction, had been aimed at visible and reachable goals. Angie told him about her own youth and development in a small country town, but one not that far from the theatres and concert halls and galleries of Sydney, which she had always considered an advantage. She and her friends could get their measures of culture in small doses, when they wanted them. She had particularly enjoyed 'Phantom of the Opera' on the big stage. The production had captivated her, especially the music. "Do you know, David," she had confided, "I really love some of those superb Andrew Lloyd Webber songs, but I reckon he succeeds only with one or two per play. The rest are pretty ordinary." She had giggled at her lack of appreciation, but Roberts found he was in agreement with her opinion. It was surprising him less and less.

*

The following morning he drove to Sydney and began working on the next phase of the project. Still well connected, he located an ex-Finnish icebreaker of 3,800 tonnes in Taiwan, and a Sydney merchant marine captain who was, he said, temporarily unassigned. Roberts could have secured a capable and experienced master, but he was looking for a man hungry for a job and prepared to do whatever Roberts asked, without argument.

"Captain Christopher Blewett Sanders," he read the name from a flimsy two-paged resume, "dual British and Australian passports." He was sitting in a small conference room in the Sydney Hilton, and had called Sanders in for an interview. "Forgive my bluntness, Captain Sanders, but the name is more impressive than its owner." Sanders was unkempt. His casual, sea-going clothes were rumpled, his eyes bloodshot and his hair as unruly as Roberts' own spiky locks. Slightly less than medium height and wire thin, Sanders was listed as being forty-seven, but he seemed older. His cadaverous face was long and pallid under the messy grey thatch covering the top of it like an office cleaner's mop. 'Jesus,' thought David, 'if they still had chimney sweeps this guy could do it all.'

"Well spotted, Mr Roberts," murmured Sanders, with a trace of English lime in a voice husky with what Roberts was sure was the result of a prolonged workshop involving some detailed comparisons of various kinds of alcoholic beverages. "You picked that up very quickly."

"Forgive me again, Captain, if I observe that someone in significant need of a job, if not a new life, does his chances with the interviewer little good by indulging in sarcasm."

"You're forgiven, Mr Roberts, and your observations are perceptive. Yes, I badly want a ship, and yes, I probably need a new life. But what I won't do is put on a false front to achieve it. I have suffered in the past from the frailty of a rebellious nature, and have always made it very difficult for people to like me. That of course goes for my wife and daughter also, both of whom have recently decided to allow me the courtesy of suffering in solitude. But professionally I am well qualified, experienced and very capable of captaining a ship of the size you mentioned in your fax. My personal situation will have no bearing on the job in question."

"Better, Captain Sanders, but how much bearing on the job in question would alcoholism have?" asked Roberts evenly, tilting his head as he looked Sanders right in one bloodshot eye.

"A very large one, Mr Roberts, if alcoholism were an issue here. But in fact it isn't. I assure you I'm not in denial, and neither am I an alcoholic. True, I've been on a binge for a few days, but that was simply an attempt to get through the recent dissolution of my family unit. I hoped the pain would be dulled, but all that happened was that it was merely postponed." Although cloudy and moist, Sanders' gaze was level and unblinking, his eyes holding a hint of substance deep down in the sorrow.

"Very well, Captain. This folder contains all you need to provide me with a detailed plan of how you would collect a vessel in Kaohsiung Harbour, Taiwan, gather a crew and bring her down here to Sydney for maintenance and providoring. She has been purchased sight unseen. However, she is in survey and has been checked by my agent. I want to see you back here this time tomorrow to convince me I should employ you as her new captain."

"Thank you Mr Roberts, I'll see you then." Sanders offered his hand and walked out of the room without a backward glance, his back a little straighter and his bearing slightly more upright than when he had entered.

*

Roberts stared at the figure waiting for him in the same conference room next morning, and decided to push it a little. "My God, Captain Sanders, is that you?"

"Good morning, Mr Roberts. Thank you for the compliment, backhanded though it may be. I have the information you requested. It should be self explanatory, but I'll be happy to explain it further if there is some of it you don't understand." Sanders was neatly dressed in a captain's uniform, his hair cut and his features clean-shaven. There was no smile though.

Roberts grinned as he took the file, happy to allow Sanders his retaliation. "I'm sure that won't be necessary, Captain. Just tell me, are you confident you can do this job?"

"Yes." A calm, one-word reply—quiet, assured, almost but not quite arrogant.

'That could come later,' thought Roberts, taking a few minutes to leaf through the pages of the file Sanders had provided, 'but I'll take that if he's as capable as I think he is. This stuff is detailed, well prepared and presented—it'll do.'

"OK, Captain Sanders, I'll organize air tickets and an account in Taipei. You need to understand that this is only part of a larger operation. Bring her safely and quickly to Sydney and then we'll talk about what may come next. Contact me from the vessel once you've settled aboard. Her name is *Kontica*. Have a good flight."

Sanders again shook hands with Roberts. "Thank you for the opportunity, Mr Roberts. I'll do my bit, and see you back here in Sydney. Then we can discuss what you require next, and just why you need someone like me to do it."

Roberts grinned again, this time more broadly. "I think you're going to fit in nicely, Captain Sanders."

TWELVE

"We'll be there in about ten minutes, Mr Roberts." The pilot's voice was disembodied but sharp, for the interior of the Embraer Phenom 300 was as quiet as it was luxurious. The air temperature may have been forty below outside, but the people inside the cocoon of comfort could do all the things normally done in a well-appointed office. It was like a flying womb. Roberts had never felt it necessary to revisit his pre-birth time, but somehow he knew it would have been as secure and comfortable as this.

He had chartered the long-range Embraer to take him and three engineers to Macquarie Island, an island in the Southern Ocean about two thousand kilometres south of Australia. It is Australian territory, attached to the state of Tasmania as a reserve, and serves as an observation base for the Australian National Antarctic Research Expeditions (ANARE) research station. It is almost always very cold, very wet and very windy. The average year-round temperature is five degrees Celsius and it rains on an average of three hundred days each year.

Which was the most pressing concern that Roberts had. It was impossible to predict what the weather would be like at the time of arrival, and he certainly couldn't contact the Australian federal department administering the base and ask them. So he had engaged the flight and crossed his fingers. He had instructed the pilot to sweep wide around the island and approach from the south, wanting to concentrate on the southern tip of the island. One of the engineers was doubling as a photographer and would be shooting as much videotape and still shots as possible in the hour of cruising available, before the small jet would have to begin the three hour flight back to Sydney.

Roberts moved up into the cockpit and looked out through the windscreen.

"Raining," he muttered. "shit." The chief pilot, Gordon O'Hara, looked up and grinned.

"Don't worry, Mr Roberts," he said cheerfully, "we'll get some pictures for you. The rain isn't heavy, and we aren't quite there yet. Another few minutes."

"I want to stay around the southern tip, and fly as low and slow as possible," he told O'Hara. "Air Traffic Control regulations are not a primary concern here, as we discussed." He eyed the pilot steadily.

"No problem," said O'Hara, "as long as I don't have to part any wave tops, we'll get right down and dirty. There she is." A high, forbiddingly grey shape materialized out of the low cloud and light rain, and they flew across the tip of the remote piece of Tasmania. "We'll come down lower, and I'll slow her to around a hundred and fifty knots. Go get the cameraman ready."

Roberts returned to the main cabin, where the young marine engineer, Ken Tilley, was already shooting video footage.

"Remember, Ken, I especially want the head of Caroline Cove, and all the southern coastline, as well as Hurd Point."

"No worries, Mr Roberts. I'll describe each location as I film it, and you'll get the best shots possible in the conditions."

"All I can ask, Ken," said Roberts. He moved over to the two other people. Lou James was a very experienced construction engineer, in his late forties and solidly built. He was ruddy and cheerful, with a likeable face topped by short, sandy hair still ungreyed and resisting the male pattern baldness that afflicted so many men of his age. The third member was a wiry, tough looking mining engineer, short, fit, with a wide full-lipped mouth and aquiline nose in a pale round face, framed by closely trimmed dark brown hair. Her name was Kaye Halloran and she was thirty-seven. All three engineers appeared to have purchased their clothes at the same store. The army surplus light brown work shirts with button-down double breast pockets, heavy duck trousers and strong, thick-heeled walking boots almost seemed like uniforms. It must be an engineer thing, thought Roberts. They wore an assortment of jackets, which went part of the way to restoring some individuality, and James would have been smoking if he had been allowed. In spite of the uniform look, though, these people were a far cry from the designer-clad and heeled urban professional presenters who developed and pushed boutique projects in a miasmic cloud of expensiveness. Their affinity was unquestionably with the ruggedness of the Marlborough Man rather than the polished bullshit of Sir Humphrey Appleby. Which of course was exactly what Roberts required. During his selection process he had specifically been looking for people who could think outside the square, work outside their comfort zones, make difficult things happen.

"OK, guys, our voices won't register on the videotape over here, and I've had a chat with Ken already. You each signed confidentiality agreements with me earlier, and this is why. I intend to build and establish a small but very well equipped base somewhere down there," he gestured out the window at the grey, unclear, but obviously wild coastline unrolling past their surprised view. "It will have a partial groyne giving it some shelter from the prevailing weather, and a channel dredged up and into the shoreline, leading into an underground dock big enough to house a vessel of a hundred metres in length, plus accommodation. The ground is steeply sloping almost everywhere around this part of the island, and it should be relatively easy to camouflage the dock from the air. The dock will contain living quarters and repair facilities, and as I'm sure you've now guessed, I want you three experts to build it for me." Roberts flashed his by now well-practised enthusiastic grin, filled with boyish charm, and waited.

"Shit, David, that's a hell of a project." James was not objecting. He was simply stating a clear fact, and Roberts could already see his mind assessing potential problems.

"I see now why you included a mining engineer," mused Halloran thoughtfully, but with unflinching interest in her face. "But isn't this place a reserve? Do you have all the necessary clearances and permits?"

Roberts laughed gently. "That, people, is why I asked you to sign those agreements. Yes, it's a reserve listed on the World Heritage Register, and managed by the Tasmanian Parks and Wildlife Service. But if possible, this base is going to be built in a total secrecy vacuum, completely without the knowledge of any authorities. We won't be building it at Hurd Point, the most southerly tip, because that's one of the world's biggest Royal Penguin rookeries, but we will be dislocating some penguins and seals. No permission would possibly be forthcoming, and of necessity I want to keep my overall operation away from official knowledge and public scrutiny."

"Well, David, would we be liable for prosecution if caught?" asked James with only mild curiosity.

"Probably," admitted Roberts, "but if we can build the base quickly and maintain secrecy, you would ship out and disappear back into anonymity. With your very large pay cheque, of course. But it's a small risk, as is most of life after all."

The two engineers wore very similar expressions—thoughtful, clearly interested, challenged by the idea, and intensely curious. "I'm in," said Halloran almost at once. She was an avidly independent person who had succeeded in a field not generally kind to women, and was used to making quick decisions. She appeared about to burst with curiosity, and Roberts held one hand up to her, palm out and fingers splayed, and glanced enquiringly at James.

"Yes, David, me too. I think you were pretty confident of both of us. What about Ken?"

"I had a chat to him earlier during the flight, as he was going to be busy recording. He accepted quickly, too. Yes, I did my homework on the three of you, and I am aware of your individual circumstances. I particularly wanted field specialists, rather than city or urban professionals, and you can now see why. Adventurers with few roots, used to roughing it and improvising when the expected sometimes doesn't happen," acknowledged Roberts.

"That probably describes all three of us," agreed Halloran, "and the augmentation of a very attractive fee didn't hurt. But it's a fascinating project in a real wilderness area, and the illegality factor was in truth what got me in." Her eyes were sparkling. "I do now, however, have some questions."

"Yes, I can see that Kaye," smiled Roberts, "and I'll bet you're not alone. But why don't we take the opportunity to have as good a look at the island as we can get, and talk more about things on the way back?"

The rain had eased to the point where the occupants of the cruising jet could see the coastline clearly, and each sat in front of a window to soak up the sight. It was not enticing. There was an environmental greyness enshrouding the vista, which filtered out any hint of colour. There was plenty of colour in the cabin, and warmth and comfort, but down there on the edge of the high-rising land it was clearly very cold and comfortless. The surface of the ocean was covered in foam-capped waves, except for extensive areas near the shoreline which appeared to move with an uneasy oiliness. These were patches of giant kelp, fastened securely to the rocks on shore and waving their long, sinuous lengths like a mass of huge soporific eels. The land consisted of a simple combination of stony beaches, rocks and boulders of all sizes, and steeply sloping hillsides covered with tussock grass. There were no bushes or trees. None could win a place in the harshness of this landscape. Only the tussock grass was able to cling, and even grow, in the face of the howling gales that swept the island regularly, even in the height of summer.

But the lonely, uninviting island in the deep south was a home to some. To many, in fact. There were Hookers sea lions, fur and elephant seals aplenty, masses of many different kinds of sea birds, and rookeries of Gentoo, King, Royal and Rockhopper penguins containing millions of members. As well as a base of scientists at the ANARE station on the northern tip of the island.

"And that base at the top of Macquarie contains up to forty scientists and observers in summer, which is why I want to build my base as far away as possible. There are field huts dotted around the coast, the closest to where I'm planning being Hurd Point, and they're connected by a walking trail. So when we come back in our supply vessel, that's going to be your first task, Kaye. I want the trail blown in two places, each several kilometres away from our base, and you'll need to make it look like landslides. It's got to be made impassable. Then we only have to avoid being spotted by the helicopters in November and December that re-supply the field huts." Roberts was filling the engineers in on further details, when O'Hara's voice came over the intercom once again.

"Time to head back, Mr Roberts," he advised. Roberts glanced at Tilley, and the young marine expert flashed a grin.

"OK, boss, I've got loads of video, and about three dozen stills. We're done." Tilley was only thirty-three, but had crammed a large amount of international experience into his relatively short working life to date. A centimetre or two shorter than Roberts, with a very powerful build and craggy good looks, he should have been just closing out a professional football or rugby career, but had been obsessed with marine engineering and conservation since boyhood. It was an odd mix, but Tilley was an unusual man, and totally committed to the ideal of harmonizing marine construction with the conservation of the maritime environment. Halloran patted the seat on the bench next to her with a grin, and he moved over and sat down with a small self-conscious smile.

Roberts confirmed O'Hara's advice and the sleek Embraer turned for home, again sweeping widely out to sea to avoid overflying the ANARE base. He brought out some pre-packaged lunch bags, with bottles of water, juice and beer, and sat down with the three professionals. He smiled again.

"I know you've got plenty of questions, guys, but I really can't tell you much. I've had a preliminary design drawn up, but it will depend on where we decide to site the base. The design will have to undergo field modification, which is another reason I chose people like you. The power generation, living and working quarters will be standard, but we'll need a channel dug into the base, and the base will be dug into a hillside. The whole lot will be camouflaged as best we can, from air and sea. You really don't need to know much more than that." Roberts shrugged his shoulders, an apologetic look on his face. He knew these people wouldn't be satisfied with what he had said, and he didn't blame them. He wouldn't have been, either.

"Are you laying that 'need to know' crap on us, David?" James asked quizzically, as he dug into a brown bag for a sandwich.

"Yeah, he is, Lou. He probably has to." Halloran, twisting the top off a beer with a practiced flick that was a little firmer than usual, was clearly disgruntled. She was also intelligent enough to realise that it was a project fraught with risk, and that they would be able to deny knowledge of whatever it was if it came to court appearances.

"Can you at least tell us what kind of vessel we are building a base for, even if we don't know why?" asked Tilley, quite aware of the firmness of Halloran's thigh pressing into his own.

"I probably shouldn't," Roberts grumbled good naturedly, "but you deserve something. It's a submarine." That got their attention. They glanced at each other in surprise and some puzzlement, but no one commented.

The flight home was quiet, for the three engineers were lost in their own reveries, as they applied their individual expertise to the project requirements, beginning to think of the details and equipment they would need. And then there was the submarine. What the hell was he planning, and why choose this godforsaken part of the globe?

THIRTEEN

On the same day that Roberts and his small team of engineers were checking out Macquarie Island, the CEO of Westral Fisheries, Morgan Hendry, was holding a press conference. Hendry was extraordinarily unremarkable. He conformed almost exactly to the criteria surrounding the average Australian male. Given that such a beast was only statistical, it was unusual in itself to find a man who actually fit the criteria. He was somewhere in his forties, of average height and weight, with brown hair and eyes, and completely without any distinguishing marks. Upon closer inspection, it was possible to decide that his eyes were just a little too near each other and that maybe his chin came more to a point than a manly square. But only just. However, it was when he spoke that he ceased being average. His voice carried a timbre and expression that really was remarkable. You gave it attention purely because of its sound, for it was a voice as compelling as a mixture of Richard Burton's and Kiefer Sutherland's might sound. Then you discovered you were listening to what he was saying, and that what he was saying was worth listening to. He looked like Clark Kent and sounded like Superman.

Hendry's West Australian company was the largest fishing company in Australia, whose major catch was more than two thousand tonnes per annum of Patagonian toothfish. That was another reason why perhaps the guy wasn't that average. To be the CEO of the biggest national company engaged in such a competitive industry should be an indication of a range of abilities and skills enough to ensure anything but ordinary. In fact, he was as hard-headed a businessman as other more incandescent luminaries such as Allan Bond, Donald Trump or Rupert Murdoch. Just not as wealthy. He'd had to stifle a sense of adventure while he established his fishing empire, but at times allowed free reign to a sense of fun.

But not today. Today he was not happy. He had made an announcement in the press the day before outlining his concerns about the overfishing of the Southern Ocean stocks of toothfish by pirate fishing fleets. The pirate vessels were taking as much toothfish as they could catch in any areas they chose, the territorial exclusion zones providing no barriers to their enterprise. There was only one Australian Fisheries vessel and it was not armed, so only the Australian naval frigates, which were occasionally deployed on manoeuvres, were capable of stopping the pirate ships from fishing, and confiscating their catch.

Hendry had bemoaned the lack of enforcement capability that allowed the pirate fishing fleet free reign to take what they could catch. This was something he did often and publicly. It was a problem besetting all the commercial fisheries in the regulated southern countries like Australia, New Zealand and South Africa. But it was the CEO of the biggest operation who had the strongest personality and who had, as a result, gravitated into the position of spokesman. It wasn't that he sought such a role. It was more that the various journalists and newshounds had realised quickly that if you asked him for a quote, you usually got one, and it was nearly always reportable.

On this occasion he had stated that his company was investigating the viability of arming his fishing vessels, and of including trained personnel on board each ship capable of storming the pirate vessels and capturing them for escort back to Australian jurisdiction. The crowd of journos around him had lapped it up. This wasn't just reportable, it was conflagratory. They all knew who would be trying to put out the fire.

The Federal Minister for Fisheries had replied quickly on TV that such an action would not be legal, and he advised Westral not to become involved in unlawful acts which amounted to nothing less than vigilantism and piracy. He may actually have believed this was the proper course of action to take, but it was also the party line that he was committed to espouse.

"We are taking steps to increase our surveillance of the fishing areas, and within three months will have twelve newly-trained inspectors available for such operations. We are looking at the purchase of another Fisheries Department vessel capable of observing and recording any illegal fishing activities in our territorial waters. Mr Hendry and his company should leave the business of illegal fishing activities to the proper authorities."

As he talked, Hendry's scorn for the political dissembling was apparent. "It's all very well for the honourable minister to tell us to stay out of things, but his department is simply not capable of stopping the pirates. The only department that could stop these people would be the Department of the Navy. But we all know there's as much chance of the navy getting into the act as there is of a politician keeping a promise.

The pirates are organized into large and flourishing businesses which use ships from many countries, like Spain, South America and Russia, and crews from Asia and Europe who accept very low wages and poor and unsafe working conditions. Each vessel is taking more than a million dollars worth of toothfish every four months. Clearly they have to be stopped."

One of the reporters asked Hendry about starting a war. "Are you planning to revisit the North Atlantic cod wars which ended up costing lives as well as ships?"

"Of course not. We simply want to stop the illegal fishing activities of the pirate fishing fleets. My company is restricted to a certain catch size, and our livelihood is being threatened by the pirates. We do not intend to harm anyone, just to prevent them from extinguishing the toothfish species. The cod wars were fought between countries—our enemies are pirates. These people fish wherever they like and catch as much as they can. They are completely unconcerned about either taking fish from exclusion zones or denuding fish stocks to the point of extinction. They have been recorded as saying that when all the toothfish have been caught, they will simply catch something else."

The reporter kept on with the same line of questioning, attempting to keep the flames alive. It was developing into a nice piece of controversy and made excellent reading and viewing. "But the bottom line is that you would be breaking the law."

Hendry frowned, his voice becoming even stronger. "On the high seas perhaps, although it would all need to be proved in an international maritime court, but in Australian territorial waters we would simply be making a citizens' arrest. Just who the hell do you think are the bad guys here?"

The news people loved it.

FOURTEEN

The water in the Spanish port of Cadiz was a murky minestrone filled with questionable substances which swirled around the swimming figure in the black wet suit. The man was making his way carefully along the cluttered and filthy bottom of the fishing boat harbour, carrying a net bag within which was a ten-centimetre paint scraper and a large limpet mine. He was doing it slowly, for the mine was packed with high explosive and weighed twenty-seven kilos and he needed to swim in lengthy kangaroo hops, touching down on the bottom every ten or fifteen metres. He was using a torch and wrist compass to make his way unerringly toward a particular fishing vessel which had docked in Cadiz three days ago. It was the whale chaser *El Cazador*, owned by a Spanish company and commanded by a Dutch skipper, Hendrikus van Kuipers, and both skipper and vessel had become famous during the past decade for slaughtering thousands of whales of all species. Nothing was sacrosanct to the pair. When questioned, as he was repeatedly, van Kuipers shrugged and said that if God didn't want him to catch whales, He wouldn't have put so many into the seas.

The swimmer reached the ship, rested beneath its hull for a few minutes, then removed the scraper from the bag, using it to clean an area of the hull about the size of a large dinner plate. He chose a spot near the stern, just under the bilge. With luck the stern tube would be either severed or bent in the explosion. He eased the limpet mine from its net bag and positioned it over the cleaned space, allowing its magnetic clamp to attach to the hull with a light clang. He switched the mine to 'armed', and commenced the swim back to the forty-foot powerboat he and his team had brought into the harbour. His return journey was faster. He boarded the boat without discovery, and it slipped innocently out of the harbour and motored at cruising speed northwest up the coast towards Cape St Vincent and Portugal. The swimmer and his team were all very aware of the *Rainbow Warrior* disaster in New Zealand, when a group of French saboteurs had mined the Greenpeace vessel, sending it to the bottom and in the process killing a photographer who had been aboard. This team was not aiming to replicate the French result, but had there been an unfortunate on board who was injured or killed, they were prepared to accept the casualty, even if the casualty were not.

It was late on a Sunday afternoon, there were few people around and no one working on *El Cazador*, so one hour later when the mine blew with a muffled thump and took a section of the hull with it, the great good fortune was that no crew member was aboard. Within another hour the whaler had settled slowly on the bottom, only the tip of its radio mast showing above the surface. It would be there for some considerable time.

Later the following morning, the Greenpeace Director of European Maritime Operations in Amsterdam, Klaus Hoffman, was becoming irate. "No, my organisation was definitely not involved!" he shouted down the phone to the reporter who was trying to interview him. It was the fourth such phone call that morning. "We do not ever carry out such violent operations. It was probably those maniacs from Sea Shepherd. They are the only people who attack and sink other vessels. They have rammed fishing boats and sunk them at sea, and have offered inducements to anyone who is able to sink whalers! We have absolutely nothing to do with them, and do not ever wish to. Go and talk to them!" He slammed the phone down with some force, muttering to himself about 'ego-tripping megalomaniacs', and stalked out of his well appointed office in the building on Keizersgracht. As he climbed into his BMW, ready for a lunch appointment, he frowned at his Rolex. "Those goddamned terrorists—why can't they just obey the law. Now I am late."

FIFTEEN

"OK, Ray, what I want now is this. Completely strip everything from the port side of the forward torpedo room except the tubes, and seal it off from the starboard side with a strong, watertight bulkhead. Make the starboard side a bit larger, say about 60%. Then I want a two metre hole cut in the top of the pressure hull and the deck plates on the port side, and a bubble of moulded two-centimetre Lexan fitted, so we can stand on a raised platform and visually con the sub, and hopefully aim the torpedoes. An engineer will make sure the bubble is as securely bolted and sealed as possible, and the room has a solid watertight bulkhead and door. He won't like it, and it may reduce our maximum dive depth, but I reckon it'll work well." Roberts was in Florida in mid November with Mackie, standing on the edge of the dry dock on a cool late fall day. "We'll still have the starboard part of the torpedo room with three torpedo tubes, which should be plenty for our purposes. I also want you to have the aft torpedo room completely stripped, tubes as well, ready for new crew quarters."

"Jesus, David—a two-metre hole in the pressure hull? I just bet the engineer won't like it! I'm sure that will go against the grain of everything sacred to a submariner. I'm not sure I like it myself." Mackie looked askance at Roberts, serious doubt in his eyes.

"Don't worry, my friend. Lexan is bulletproof, and there may well be an improved version on the market now which is even better than that. The Lexan will probably be far stronger than the pressure hull itself. It will just need to be securely fastened and sealed, and that's where the engineer comes in."

The exterior of the submarine had been cleaned and de-rusted, with all pits and cracks welded, and the various dents had been expertly panel-beaten. The whole surface was now covered with a rust proof red primer. From above, the huge confines of the dry dock seemed to enclose her like a huge smoked salmon in an outsized can of John West.

"She actually looks pretty good, Ray," Roberts grinned. "Wait until she gets her name and final paint job. Let's have a look inside."

They climbed down and aboard via a series of ladders, into the conning tower and down through the hatch. The interior was a controlled shambles. But it was a clearer and more empty shambles than before, with much furniture, equipment, pipes and cables having been stripped out. A new diesel-driven air conditioning and compressed air system had already been installed, and work was progressing well on the modern hydraulics and new pumps which would replace the old gear. Computer controls would be installed and electronic sensors and equipment would replace much of the engine room controls, so the sub would be able to be driven almost entirely from the control room.

"I think I may have found a driver, David," Mackie said as they climbed back out and up to the top of the dock.

"Great, Ray," Roberts said with a pleased grunt as they reached the top. "Who is he . . . or she?" This last with a grin.

"No David, I doubt that there would be any female diesel sub drivers around. The people with that kind of experience would have gained it in the times when women weren't allowed in navies, let alone on submarines. There are many women in today's navies, and there will be some in our final crew, but they will be of an age that reflects the changing of the times. That is, they'll all be in their twenties and thirties.

The bloke I think will end up being our captain is an ex US naval submarine commander who actually served more time in diesel boats than in nuclear subs, and who is an expert on the American fleet-type vessel. I'm still checking him out, because he will be crucial to our campaign, and we need to be very sure of his capabilities. I also want to examine his psychological profile, not that I'm any expert, but the shrinks who are conducting the tests understand the need for summaries in layman's language." Mackie smiled. "His name is Gus Durrand and he's fifty-two, divorced with two grown children, and looking for work. He seems fit and capable, and so far has impressed with the interviews he's already done."

"Terrific, Ray. Keep pushing ahead as fast as you can. I've got our base vessel, the *Kontica,* in Sydney undergoing a refit and re-supply at the moment, her captain is signing on a crew as we speak, and my engineers in charge of building the base station are also hiring a special team of construction workers. Things are coming together." Roberts appeared satisfied at the progress being made by all the elements of his project team. "But don't take anything for granted. So far no one knows what we're planning, and the story about scientific research will take us a good part of the way. Keep really tight security on things. That shouldn't be hard now . . . . after 9/11 it's become a way of life in America.

Let's go back to Gunter's and Dorothy's for dinner—I remember the last meal we had there with much pleasure. Maybe Gunter has managed to stock in some decent beer by now."

SIXTEEN

Three days out of Sydney, the *Kontica* was heading steadily south into the Southern Ocean. She was now well past Tasmania en route for Macquarie Island, and the seas were building. The wind was strong, urging the seas to build up into hefty swells, deftly slicing off their tops and shredding the leftovers. The motion of the ship was vigorous and powerful. She had been overhauled and stocked in Sydney, and a helipad had been constructed on the stern deck. There was a small long range Bell helicopter securely lashed down on the pad. Her crew list had also been overhauled, with the inclusion of all necessary personnel for a lengthy sojourn in polar regions, including an experienced medical team and facilities. Together with the construction and mining workers, the total ship's complement was now forty six.

Captain Sanders was on the bridge, dressed comfortably in navy blue pullover and trousers, and absolutely in his element. "How are you doing, David?" he asked Roberts with just a hint of satisfaction, as he nuzzled a mug of strong coffee augmented by a shot of rum.

"I must admit I've felt better," Roberts said with a grimace, "but you don't have to be so gleeful about it." Roberts was clad in similar fashion, as were most of the ship's complement. Everyone was now also using thermal underwear.

"It really is quite awesome what a couple of thousand miles of fetch and a steady thirty knot wind can do to this ocean, isn't it?" Sanders mused. "Apart from Macquarie Island, there is nothing between Antarctica and us, so the seas just build and roll. You'll get used to it."

"So, Chris, you clearly don't have any problems with seasickness. How is the rest of you?" Roberts gazed at Sanders with genuine concern, which Sanders understood now was more compassionate than professional. In the past, when confronted with such a query Sanders would draw a shell around himself like an offended armadillo and growl a rebuff. His recent family trauma had pierced his shell and lanced his defensiveness and he was becoming less certain of himself, and more approachable as a result.

"Thank you, David—the rest of me has felt better too. But I think I'm slowly getting there. This position has provided me with time for self-healing, for some introspection, and I feel as though I'm finally able to make changes. I realise now that my wife and I had been growing apart for some time, due mostly to my closed and self-reliant personality. I think I can deal with that, but God I miss my little Sarah. Although at eighteen she's not so little now." Sanders' eyes were sad, wistful, but clear.

"I believe that's the crux of most things these days, Chris. The ability to accept and manage change. It's become a necessary factor in all walks of life—professional, corporate, commercial, personal—sometimes it seems to be promoted by self serving ambitionists just for the sake of it, but mostly it's now a part of modern living. You either accept it and get on with life, or you go down."

Sanders glanced at Roberts over the rim of his coffee mug, seeing the strength and capability of an unusually complete individual. "David, I doubt there's ever been a moment in your life when you haven't known exactly what to do, and been able to do it. But some of us lesser mortals aren't quite so confident."

"Fair enough, Chris. I know mostly what I can do, and so far in my life I haven't made many serious mistakes. But I'm sure I could be an arsehole to live with at times—I never seem to have any self doubt. Anyhow, if you'll allow me a personal comment, you should accept your new circumstances and get on with the business of living. But take your daughter with you as you go. Invest as much time and energy in that relationship as you possibly can. It will nurture her and strengthen you." Roberts got up, wiping his brow. "I'll be glad when I become used to this movement," he groaned softly. "How are the engineers taking it? I want a team meeting soon, when everyone can concentrate."

"I think Lou's doing OK, but the other two have disappeared. Probably in their cabins trying to doze it away," said Sanders.

*

The young marine engineer, Ken Tilley, had a cabin on the port side of the accommodation section, from which soft moans were indeed issuing. But he wasn't seasick. He was on his back in his bunk, hands firmly clasped around the taut, lithe buttocks of his mining engineer colleague, Kaye Halloran. Her naked, well-toned body was sheened in sweat as she pounded and drove over Tilley. Her vigorous movements, plus those of the vessel, combined to cause her fullish breasts to bounce and swing in a circular motion, which almost captured Tilley's attention. But not quite. She had taken him somewhere new, dragging all his senses into a singular focus on the pleasure she was providing. Suddenly, almost simultaneously, he groaned, gasped, cried out 'Oh mother!' and erupted. She smiled, arching her back and allowing her withheld climax to flood, panting and wriggling with her own intense pleasure. She leaned forward, straightening her legs and arms in a feline stretch, sliding over his sweat-slicked body, still fastened at the centre, a soft keening murmur deep in her throat. She was very experienced and always took a great deal of enjoyment from sex. She had applied her expertise to Tilley and had needed to work hard to prevent him from an early explosion. Now, as she lay in the familiar afterglow, tracing the pattern of his face with delicate fingertips while trying to remain in the one very satisfying place, she realised she had enjoyed this screw as much as any in the near past that she could remember. She wondered why. Maybe, she thought, it was because he seemed so naïve and innocent, so damn sweet.

"Hey gorgeous," she murmured, "that was pretty nice. But do you think we could do without the 'oh mother' at the moment of truth?"

Tilley grinned ruefully. "Sorry Kaye," he said, looking like he'd been discovered farting in church. "It wasn't meaningful. It's just an expression. I'll try not to do it again."

"Good," she said, sliding off him and on to the floor, picking up her clothes, "but you'll probably need some more practice. See you later." She dressed and left his cabin. As she was closing the door behind her Lou James staggered past on his way to the bridge.

"How are you and Ken taking this motion, Kaye?"

"Oh, I'm not doing too badly thanks Lou, but I think the poor lad in there is exhausted."

*

"Hi David, Captain," said James as he entered the bridge wing.

"Chris please, Lou. We won't be standing on much ceremony aboard."

"Hi Lou, thanks for coming up. You feeling OK?"

"Yeah, I'm not often troubled by seasickness. But you don't look too healthy David," he said with a slight smile. "I don't suppose I can smoke in here?"

"Certainly not. Why the hell does everyone think seasickness is such a huge joke, unless they suffer from it themselves?" complained Roberts to an entirely unsympathetic audience. "Lou, I want you to take on the responsibilities of Base Commander, when we have a base to command. I think you're the best suited to the task of coordinating the overall construction. Your fee will of course reflect the new requirements. How about it?"

"No problem—be happy to. I've been in charge of some pretty big projects in my time. This one is not a big operation, but it's certainly different, and will need some efficient cooperation between marine workers, miners and construction people. It's a shame I won't be able to put it on my resume."

Roberts smiled out of a pasty face. "Yes, the finished base would make a great case study for many specific areas of construction and research. Too bad." He was by now able to take some coffee, enriched with some of Sanders' special additive, and sipped it slowly, thankful it appeared to be staying down. "One of your machine operators, Lou, is an ex army staff sergeant, Gary Bradley. I'll be needing him for some weapons maintenance and training. I've had a stock of ordnance put aboard, and unless there are any conscientious objectors in the group, all members of the final team will be required to learn the basic operation of automatic pistols and assault rifles."

"Jesus, David!" James exclaimed, eyes widening. "Are we planning to start a war?"

"Far from it Lou," Roberts replied calmly, shaking his head. "I simply want all of our action team to be able to share in defending our project from any threat, even a legitimate one.

It shouldn't be left only to those who are attitudinally aligned. As I said, with the exception of genuine philosophical objectors, everyone will be expected to pull their weight. Is that likely to be a problem for you?"

"No David, I've done my share of fighting when necessary. Most field workers have had to become involved with the defense of themselves or their projects for various reasons. You'll probably find that Kaye is capable of taking care of herself too. It's just that so far I haven't had to resort to military grade weaponry." James was looking thoughtful, but Roberts could see that he was only considering something new, rather than throwing up an automatic barrier.

"Good," he said, sipping more coffee. "And with luck I may be able to get some dinner down tonight."

*

The vessel was running on Eastern Australian Summer Time, and at seven that evening there were more people in the dining area than since the voyage had begun. There was a Captain's Table, at which Sanders and the team leaders would always sit, but Roberts had been working the room, introducing himself to everyone he hadn't met before. He was making it clear that any member of the crew was entitled and encouraged to join the table if there was a space, and to talk about any part of the operation they wished.

"Hi all," he said as he sat down with Sanders, James, Tilley, Halloran and two other men. "David Roberts, Chairman of the Board," he grinned as he shook hands with the two.

"Good evening, David—Lawrence Prescott, Chief Medical Officer," said the taller of the two urbanely. Blonde, tanned and with the face of a media personality, Prescott exuded confidence and charm.

"Hi David—Scott Lambert, GP and I suppose I must be the Deputy Chief Medical Officer." Lambert was shorter than Prescott, but about twice as wide, with a neck the same thickness as his head, and features that appeared to have been moulded in soggy clay and thrown at his face. He smiled, and the irregular became somehow engaging. "Yeah, in answer to your next question, I used to be a front rower for the Warratahs."

"Glad to meet you both, even an ex-Warratah," said Roberts with a slightly puzzled expression, "but I thought we were paying you two guys the same fee? How did we achieve a ranking here?"

"Yes, you are, David," said Prescott smoothly, "but where emergency medical decisions need to be made quickly, it makes sense for the more experienced person to take responsibility for them. I've had extensive experience in general surgery and emergency medicine, as you no doubt know, so I discussed the situation with Scott. He agreed to allow me to take that responsibility. I wasn't being dreadfully serious about the title," he drawled, smiling disarmingly at the table.

"Fine," Roberts appeared satisfied. "Are you both happy with your equipment?"

"We seem to have everything we may need," said Lambert. "There are three very experienced nurses on board and all the gear we have will work really well when it's sitting still," he grinned.

"Once the base is established," Prescott continued, "we will be able to accommodate anything from bandaging a scratch to amputating a limb, with appendix, gall bladder, bowel or heart surgery thrown in. I guess I could even do it here at sea if I had to."

'Very confident, very big ego,' thought Roberts, not missing the easy transition between 'we' and 'I'. 'A superstar in his own mind. OK so long as he can deliver, but I think he may need watching.'

"Glad you're happy gents," Roberts smiled. "I hope we don't ever have to use your many talents. What's for dinner?"

"I recommend the snapper mornay," smiled Sanders, "it's a simple but tasty dish which should stay down OK." Roberts was less certain, but said he'd give it a try.

*

Later, after the two doctors had gone off to locate and meet the nurses, the table was left with the three engineers, Sanders and Roberts.

"David," Sanders looked up from his mornay, "I've been meaning to ask you about our clearances. As the ship's master you handled them all, but I was wondering why you went to Hobart for some time before we sailed, and also just where have we cleared for?"

"Yeah, sorry Chris, I haven't intentionally kept you in the dark. It's just that up to now I haven't felt particularly well. I was waiting until everyone, me included, got over the dreaded lurgy and was able to concentrate on strategy again.

I went to Hobart to visit the headquarters of the Australian Antarctic Division in Kingston, and to attempt to arrange some bona fide permits for research. Shit, you'd think a former corporate high-flyer would be used to interacting with government departments, wouldn't you?" Roberts smiled, but with a solid frown lining his forehead, and shook his head.

James nodded. "Unfortunately, it's not something you can get used to. All private sector professionals are well acquainted with the vagaries of trying to work through the tangles of governmental regulations and requirements. In Australia they come in three sizes, too—commonwealth, state and local. It's the most frustrating, time-consuming and costly part of any project." Tilley and Halloran nodded too, both obviously well aware of what James was talking about.

"Yes, well I certainly got a refresher course in Kingston," Roberts said grimly. "I spent three days working that building. The AAD is a commonwealth government agency under the Department of the Environment, and it is supposed to administer the Australian Antarctic Program. This impressive sounding body has a blanket control over a whole bunch of other organisations engaged in research in the Antarctic. Like, for example, the Bureau of Meteorology, the Australian Geological Survey Organisation, the Ionospheric Prediction Service, the Australian Survey and Land Information Group and parts of the Commonwealth Scientific and Industrial Research Organisation—the CSIRO.

It's a typical bloody government bureaucracy, and there must be several hundred staff in the building. But the heads I wanted to see were all at meetings and couldn't be disturbed. Talk about 'Yes, Minister'. So I went to every department I could find, and took all the papers I'd had prepared for me by a special contact of mine in Sydney. They showed some awesome credentials for a very high-powered body of scientists and documentary makers, all requiring permission to observe, examine and film many aspects of Antarctic and sub-Antarctic life and conditions. I bluffed, bullied and cajoled, and ended up with official permission from five different departments to carry out observations and film wildlife on Macquarie and Heard Islands, and the Australian bases in Antarctica itself. Now all we have to do is make sure no one suspects what we're really doing there."

"It used to be the case that people like me became submerged in masses of red tape," observed James wryly, "but times have changed. There's no more red tape—it's been replaced by email and electronic data transfer over local and wide area networks, not to mention the Internet, which was all supposed to make things easier. But there are now enormous amounts of data being shifted around, so things still take a lot of time. And the electronic indifference of computers seems to be rubbing off on to many staff. Clients have become nuisances—a waste of time. It might be different in the States but Australia has a way to go yet to embrace the culture of service."

"So, Chris, to get off my soapbox and answer your question," said Roberts, "we cleared Australian customs for Cape Town, South Africa. But we can take our own good time to get there, and even alter our destination if we choose. We can spend as much time as we want in the Australian territories in and near Antarctica, on our study and filming excursion. We have now disappeared from official Australian consciousness, and I want to stay that way." Roberts looked at his plate in surprise. "Well, look at that—I've eaten it all! You were right, Chris, it was tasty. Maybe this time I won't have to taste it again, either."

*

At ten o'clock the following morning, Roberts was in the dining area surveying the crowd of people gathered together in little knots of conversation. He had been responsible for hiring every individual, either directly or by his instruction to an agency, and he suddenly realised that he had created a community. There were many discrete parts, kind of like an ant colony, he thought, but the existence of an overall objective would, he intended, coalesce those parts into a working team. Although it wouldn't just happen because he had thrown a group together, he knew—it would be up to him to mould them all into a unit with a common aim. But he was also astute enough to realise that there would be individuals who would simply not fit, and what he could do about them he wasn't yet sure. He'd never much been into social engineering, never studied psychology during his student years. As a result, he had evaded the standard philosophical arguments put condescendingly upon sophomores by jaded professors waiting for yet another sabbatical. In his previous corporate life he'd had no use for group dynamics and emotional politics, but this didn't mean he was ignorant of social structures and their requirements. He just hadn't, before now, felt the need to spend energy on such things.

The seas had eased under a lighter wind, and Roberts was able to climb on a chair without immediately being pitched off. The room quietened. "Hi everyone—please take a seat," he said into a small lapel microphone. "I know this was a compulsory meeting, but thank you all for responding. For those I haven't yet been able to meet, my name is David Roberts, and I guess I'm the head of this new team." For the purpose of gaining the clearances for the expedition Roberts had needed to devise a name for the group almost on the spot in Kingston. "We've renamed the group, and you are now all official employees of the International Foxtrot Corporation. Your contracts will be altered to reflect the new name. Speaking of which," he paused, and went on with a serious expression, "you all signed a specially added secrecy clause. That's because we are going to build a base on the southern end of Macquarie Island, for which we don't have official permission. My lawyers assure me that it won't actually be illegal unless and until the proper authorities officially inform us it is. So I want to maintain secrecy until it is completed, at which time you can all return to Australia with fat fees paid into the accounts of your choice. Whether you inform the local taxation authorities about your large income is up to you; we certainly won't be claiming any of your fees as deductions from our business expenses.

I know you've all agreed to the confidentiality clause, but I want to reinforce that it is very important you don't let slip to anyone back in Australia just what we are doing down here. We won't be able to control or even monitor satellite phones, and it may be that cell phones work also. I'm very serious about security, and I want to stress that I expect loyalty from every team member—you're all being well paid and as soon as we arrive the conditions will improve markedly. The food's pretty good too.

The base is for a special research vessel currently being built in America, to be used almost exclusively in the Southern Ocean, hence the need for a permanent shelter as close to the action as possible. Are there any questions?"

"Morning, Mr Roberts, I'm Bill Babb, surveyor. Did you actually try to get permission to build this base?"

"Hi Bill," Roberts smiled at the lean, grey-haired and stoop-shouldered Babb, "no I didn't. I was quite confident that none would have been forthcoming, because Macquarie Island is part of a world heritage area, and a major reserve within Australian control." He had been anticipating this question would be among the first asked, and was ready for it. "But can I assure you, and anyone else who has any doubts about what we plan to do," he continued earnestly, "that the area we've chosen is not part of any seal or penguin colonies, nor a major nesting area for sea-birds. There will be some fauna we will have to move aside, simply because there is so much there, but once completed, our effect on the ecology of the area will be minimal."

"Mr Roberts, my name is Thea Dunne, one of the registered nurses. I'm happy about not having a significant effect on the indigenous fauna. What I can't understand is the need for another base at the southern end of the island. Why not just use the facilities at the main ANARE station on the northern end?" Tall, spare, angular, early forties, she was a severe looking woman with very short hair showing signs of grey among the dark brown spikes.

"Good morning Thea—thank you, that's another good question. It's complex, but the short answer is that the ANARE base is under government control, with limited accommodation. The Australian Antarctic Division decides who is allowed to spend time there, and just what they should study. There is no permanent shelter for an anchorage there either. My backers want to be independent of any restrictions on what is studied and by whom. Then there is the additional issue of film rights to the series of documentaries planned for the Antarctic and sub-Antarctic region, which my backers will use to recoup part of the costs of establishing the base." Roberts was still comfortable, because this was another obvious question he had expected.

"Excuse me, David," drawled a voice from the rear, "but just what kind of vessel are we building this base for?" It was the tall, blonde figure of Lawrence Prescott, leaning casually against one of the deck supports and looking impossibly handsome. Clearly it was an attitude calculated to impress the rest of the gathering, for there was no doubt that Prescott was very aware of the image he projected.

Roberts became less comfortable. His eyes narrowed imperceptibly and he felt a flash of annoyance. You posing dickhead, he thought, that's one I didn't want. "Another good question, Lawrence," said Roberts evenly, allowing his brow to furrow gently. "You'll perhaps find this difficult to believe, but I'm not sure of all the details. I do know it's about a hundred metres long and will need a ten-metre-deep channel. Apparently it has some special underwater observing facilities not available on standard vessels like this one, but other than that and a few more details like beam and height above water I don't know a lot more." Roberts hoped that would satisfy most of the gathering, but his initial assessment of Prescott as a potential source of trouble was reinforced. "If there's nothing further, I'll see you all at various times here in the dining area. My door's always open to anyone who wants to discuss aspects of the project, and if there's a spot at this table please take it. We should be at the island in a couple of days." He stepped down from the chair and moved over to where James was standing. "Lou, can you get hold of Kaye and Ken and meet me on the bridge in half an hour?"

Thirty minutes later Roberts was standing on the bridge deck, facing Sanders and the three engineers. "That bloody Prescott is becoming a nuisance," he frowned. "Right. You all know what the vessel is, but I don't want it to get out, and now I'm going to tell you why, if you want to know. If not, you can leave the bridge now—even you, Chris, as we're on auto—it won't alter our working arrangements in any way."

Sanders merely raised one eyebrow while the engineers grinned at him and waited expectantly.

"OK, you're all about to become co-conspirators. The submarine is being fitted out with all the latest modern equipment. Except for the torpedoes. They're the old wartime Mk 48s with wire guidance, and they'll be fitted with low explosive heads. I intend to drive her up close and personal to some of these large fishing boats and whalers, and slip a torpedo into their screws and rudders. After a few hits, they all should get the message and depart for more comfortable climes." Roberts eyed them all calmly, a small smile on his lips, one eyebrow raised, the expectant wait now his.

"My god!"

"Well bugger me."

"Bullshit!"

"You're having us on." All of this blended into a simultaneous chorus of surprise and disbelief, although the engineers were wearing broad smiles.

"You're not having us on, are you David," said Halloran slowly, "you really mean to do this. Jesus, what an idea. I love it! When this construction phase is over, I want in on the action. Please?"

"The sub crew will be augmented by some of our team personnel, but that will be a process controlled by my assistant, Ray Mackie. He's the man on the spot in Miami at the moment, organising the submarine's refurbishment, and selecting a skeleton crew for sea trials and then to sail her over here. But it's quite possible, Kaye. What about the rest of you?" Roberts looked at the others with great interest.

"I'm with Kaye," said Tilley quickly. Halloran glanced at him with her eyes only, a small, knowing smile tugging the corners of her generous mouth.

"Count me in too," said James offhandedly. "I don't have much else to do."

"Oh bullshit, Lou," grinned Halloran, "you're busting a gut to join up."

"It might be fun," he smiled.

"I like the idea, David," said Sanders thoughtfully, "but I don't think I'd fit in. Technically it's a crime against international shipping, and they would be within their legal rights to take action against you. Or, in fact, to ask their naval vessels to try to sink you. I'm not being negative here, and I understand they are pirating the whale and fish stocks of the Southern Ocean, I'm just pointing out the practicalities. Also, to be totally candid, I guess I'd still have a significant problem with initiating a violent action against another vessel."

"Well I don't give a fuck about legalities or practicalities," snorted Halloran, "those bastards deserve all they get. My application is the first in, David."

"Duly noted, Kaye," laughed Roberts, "and don't worry, Chris, I understand where you're coming from. You need to consolidate your situation with Sarah, too. I'm glad you three reprobates see things this way—I can't see you missing out on the sub crew.

I'm off to meet the people I haven't caught up with yet. See you all later."

SEVENTEEN

Two days later the *Kontica* arrived at the northern tip of Macquarie Island, and this time Roberts instructed his skipper to take the vessel in quite close to the eastern shore of the peninsula. Cruising slowly down Buckles Bay, in clear view of the ANARE base station, her white hull caught the afternoon light. It had originally been direct sunlight that had found easy passage through the country-sized hole in the ozone layer. But from then on it had needed to work harder as it dove through many layers of varying cloud formations, until it reached the *Kontica* with most of its splendour filtered away. There was enough strength left, however, to pick out the ship's white hull as a stark contrast against the uniform grey seascape.

They moved past some large beds of giant kelp, which flattened the lumpy sea out into an uneasily calm, almost oily surface. Typically, it was blowing raucously from the southwest, the sky was as attractive as freshly-smudged newsprint and it was bitingly cold. But it wasn't raining.

"A lovely summer's day in sub-Antarctica," proclaimed Roberts happily. "Let's pay them our respects.

ANARE base, this is the research vessel *Kontica,* how do you read?"

The reply came instantly over channel sixteen on the VHF radio. "*Kontica,* this is ANARE. We read you five-by-five. Can you identify please?"

Roberts replied with a brief explanation of the study and filming they would be doing at the southern end of the island, adding a couple of the permit authority numbers for weight. "We'll probably be around the southern end for a while, over," he advised, grinning at Sanders.

"Please do not disturb the rookeries at Hurd Point," came sharply back.

"ANARE, be advised we have world-class scientific observers aboard—we are well aware of our responsibilities. Which is why we were granted the permits I just gave you," responded Roberts just as sharply, winking at Sanders. "*Kontica* out."

They steamed down the eastern side of the island, partially sheltered from the weather in the lee of the island. The coast on this side of the 34 km-long, narrow sub-Antarctic island was almost a straight line running south-south west, and as the *Kontica* sailed down its length most of the crew, and all those who smoked, took the chance to go outside and catch their first sight of the place they would call home, at least for a while. It wasn't much of a sight. Everything seemed to be black, white or grey. The wind had muscle and made sure there was always white on top of the ocean. The water under the white was grey on black, the whole a dirty piebald pattern in constant motion. The sky was almost never blue, not even in patches, and the steep rocky cliffs, rising from close to the coastline, were not welcoming. There were no attractive shades of brown, green and purple passing over the contours like the display in a slow-moving kaleidoscope you'd see scrolling over the hills like those in a Scottish landscape. It was really quite dismal.

The scene was almost an affront to the senses. The only spots of brightness and colour to be seen were in the parkas of the crew standing out on the forward deck, huddled against the cold. Ken Tilley was leaning on the rail, clad in all his thermal gear but still feeling the keenness of the wind chill. 'There should be masses of colour in a landscape,' he thought, 'but here it's all been washed out. Or blown out.' He noticed a small patch of drab green on shore, where the ever-present tussock grass clung. "Shit, it's hard to get enthusiastic about this place," he grumbled to himself, "all the adjectives are bad ones. Depressing, uninviting, desolate, forbidding—they're all negative enough, and then you throw in wet, windy and bloody cold as well! These sea birds are obviously in their element though," he mused, "there are thousands of them."

The *Kontica* rounded Hurd Point and steamed west. The seas were heavier here, as the ship moved out of the partial lee of the point. She steamed up past South West Point and then headed slightly east of north to raise the entrance to Caroline Cove. Sanders brought her sharply round and steamed slowly southeast, creeping down as far into the cove as they could safely travel.

"We'll anchor here tonight," said Sanders. "There's too much kelp closer to shore to risk getting tangled in it, and we are in reasonable shelter from the prevailing winds. This'll do." Sanders began the process of getting his main working anchor settled, and dug it in securely by backing the ship down firmly. "Think I'll set two," he decided. "Always been a bit of a belt and braces man."

"Well done, Chris. We'll have a special dinner for all hands tonight, and begin first thing in the morning."

*

"Whaddaya think, Mr Roberts?" the machine operator, Gary Bradley, was eagerly displaying his handiwork. He was the main operator of the small but powerful dredge stowed on the Kontica's stern deck, and he had been working on it, under instruction from Roberts, for three days. He had constructed a light but strong aluminium framework over the main dragline bucket and had hidden it from view with heavy-duty waterproof sheeting. He had also attached a powerful spotlight on an overhead beam, and secured two boxes he had made to look like cameras on each side of the frame.

"Yes, I think that'll do Gary," said Roberts with satisfaction. "Well done. So long as you make sure the bucket isn't working if the ANARE chopper flies over us, it should look just like a floating camera barge. We've actually brought some professional cameras and equipment with us, and on occasions a couple of the crew who are keen amateurs will do some real filming. You can get her launched straight away; put Bill Babb and his gear aboard and use her for the hydrographic survey of the cove. We'll need soundings covering the head of the cove, and then we can sort out just where to make the entrance."

Leaving James aboard to begin organising the work teams for a round-the-clock operation, Roberts took Tilley and Halloran in a small inflatable and went ashore on the short, rocky beach at the head of the cove. It was a spectacular introduction to the environment, for they were surrounded by penguins shooting all around the inflatable like sleek little black and white darts. Although it was blowing the usual twenty knots plus, the shelter was sufficient to make landing through the surge, and a break in the kelp, relatively comfortable.

"What I want you two to do now," he explained as they pulled the dinghy up the beach, "is to explore the walking track on both sides of our cove for a kilometre or so each way. I want you to find suitable spots and blow the trail so that it looks like a landslide. But the damage must be sufficient to prevent any easy repairs. Can you do that?"

"I brought supplies of fracture, plus detonators, as you instructed, so sure, that's no problem at all," Halloran said happily.

"She's as happy as a pig in shit," Tilley laughed. "She can't wait to blow something up."

"OK, off you go. Remember, if the chopper comes over, drop flat and lie still—they'll never spot you in that camouflage gear. When you're ready to return, radio the *Kontica* and someone will come get you. Remember to use our radio code at all times—it will surely be monitored."

Tilley and Halloran moved up the beach and climbed over the rocks and boulders to get on to the walking trail, staring in amazement at the scores of huge elephant seals and thousands of penguins inhabiting the area. The penguins grudgingly moved aside for the two trespassers to pass. The indignantly raucous shrieks and squeals as they did so were deafening.

"I wonder what those funny little penguins are—the ones with the red eyes and attitude," laughed Halloran, as they picked their way through the crowd. "I'll have to look them up in the library when we get back to the ship." The massive elephant seals were sleepily indifferent to the intrusion, making no moves to avoid the humans. The humans made moves to avoid them instead. "God, those mothers are enormous—and don't they stink!" Halloran exclaimed excitedly, wrinkling her nose as they made their way on to the narrow, roughly laid track and started off northwards. They covered about a kilometre on the winding pathway, Halloran studying the lie of the land as they went.

"Kaye," Tilley said slowly, as they walked carefully along the trail, "do you think it might be nice to share a cabin, now we're in a relationship?" He smiled at her, putting one arm around her and giving her a squeeze.

She pulled sharply away from him, surprise on her face and what could have been alarm in her eyes. "Shit no, Ken!"

she exclaimed, "I do not. And who said we're in a bloody relationship?"

His smile faded into a reflection of confusion and uncertainty. "Well, as we're sleeping together, I thought . . ." he tailed off into a very uncomfortable silence under the sudden mask of concern into which her face had stiffened. It was as though her features had melded with the environment. For an instant, they had become frozen, grey and stony, forbidding, totally without encouragement.

Then her eyes lost some of the toughness, softened a little, and her mouth relaxed from its thin line into the normal fullness of her lips. "Ken," she said more gently, "you are a really sweet guy, and I've enjoyed our little romps together enormously. But at this stage of my life I'm just not into relationships. I don't want or need a soul mate, a partner, or whatever passes for a husband these days. I'm fiercely protective of my independence, and totally satisfied with my life as it is. I'm sorry if you got the wrong idea, but in fairness I don't think I encouraged you to think that way. OK?"

Tilley nodded, his face set into an impassive blankness which he desperately hoped would conceal the awful feeling of rejection he was experiencing. He was intelligent enough to understand exactly the picture Kaye was sketching, but it was all very well to be intelligent about it, he thought. It didn't reduce the gut-wrenching nausea that his heart insisted he undergo.

She linked her arm through his and said gaily, only a little of which was forced, "Come on. Help me set up some bang stuff. I reckon we can turn that rise up ahead into a nice, impassable cutaway. Then, if you want, you can ease down my thermal gear and bonk me from behind. I'm feeling horny again."

Tilley looked at her face, now open and impishly cheerful, and simply shook his head in wonder and complete confusion. For the millionth time that week, a man on planet Earth realised he was totally unable to comprehend the workings of the female mind.

*

One week later, as the Foxtrot complement realised that the cold, though unrelenting, wasn't life threatening and the wind wasn't always blowing a gale, the hostile environment had become less hostile. Sanders had shifted the *Kontica* five kilometres around to Hurd Point to anchor there for a few days, the ANARE helicopter had paid the group two visits on days when the weather permitted reasonable visibility, and the work parties had carried on radio conversations relating only to study visits and film shoots. Roberts felt they were now being accepted by the government station people as a necessary nuisance, and would not now be disturbed so much. "However," he thought, "we'll do our serious work in misty or rainy weather and at night, just as a precaution."

Soundings had been done and a working chart was being drawn. Divers had stripped the giant kelp from the area at the head of Caroline Cove, and the positions of the entrance to the base, and the channel to be dredged into it, had been decided. Bradley had begun digging the channel to fifteen metres. He'd had to blast some of the bedrock, and was dumping the dredged material off the point in an arc around to the northeast, the first stages of an underwater breaksea that would provide safe shelter in any weather to vessels inside the cove.

"Lou," Roberts said to James, as they were standing at the rail in fading light, taking the opportunity to enjoy the sight of the fast moving penguins fishing among the diving skuas and petrels, "tomorrow, if it's raining or misty, we'll try to set up our dome." James, gratefully and with intense pleasure, was sucking on a cigarette as though it was his last. The smoke and steam emitting from the slit in his scarf was easily dealt with by the wind. Not always at gale force, true, but down in this part of the world it carried more authority than in the latitudes of comfort. Even with your back to it the wind was in your face. Aggressive, it bullied you into always moving to counter its insistence, constantly demanding attention like a spoiled child. When it wasn't there, you worried. You felt there was something lacking.

"OK, David, it's been ready since yesterday. Ken's done a good job on the sections—I reckon it'll go up without needing a lot of field modification."

Tilley had been supervising the construction, in prefabricated sections, of a large dome that would be assembled at the edge of the water where the channel would meet the shoreline. It would be ten metres high and fifteen wide, and would form the shell under which the excavations for the underground base would begin. It was to be assembled using aluminium frames covered with wire and fibreglass mat, over which many litres of special marine grade epoxy glue would be spread. Beach sand, small rocks and tussock grass would then be applied liberally, creating a strong cover to hide and protect the digging operations as the base was carved out. The dome measured twenty metres at its longest point, where it would meet and merge in with the steeply rising hill behind the shoreline. As soon as possible, a steel roof would be constructed under the dome, and the gap between the roof and the dome cover would have concrete pumped in. The whole would be covered with beach sand, boulders of different sizes, grass and kelp. A large, hydraulically operated reinforced roller door would be built at the entrance, coming down to a metre below the water level in the channel. That too would be camouflaged. From the island, or from a helicopter, it would appear as a large mound of boulders.

The next morning dawned perfectly. Light winds allowed a heavy mist to ooze down over the southern end of the island and reduce visibility to no more than ten metres, and to add to the perfection of the scene rain began to fall, insistently. Roberts, up early to check conditions, rubbed his gloved hands together vigorously to stimulate some circulation—it was two degrees Celsius. There was also a measure of satisfaction in the action. "Just what we need," he muttered contentedly. "A quick coffee and we'll get moving."

With this kind of weather, and the trail having been expertly severed on both sides of Caroline Cove by Halloran and Tilley, Roberts was sure there'd be no interference from the ANARE station members. He sent almost the full ship's complement ashore to experience the conditions and to help wherever they could. Even the medical team went ashore. With a powerful portable generator and compressor, they set up lights and began erecting the dome under Tilley's watchful eye. The legs of the framework were securely cemented in deep holes, and the rest of the dome went up with surprising ease. Heavy-duty wire was run at half-metre intervals over the frame, across which was stretched the fiberglass mats and heavy canvas. The really messy job was mixing the two-pot epoxy marine glue, and spreading it over the mats and canvas. In normal temperatures the glue would 'go off', or begin to harden, within half an hour. This far south, in such cold temperatures, it took much longer, and allowed more time to apply it and cover it with beach detritus. The very burly Scott Lambert accidentally blundered into Thea Dunne, sending her sprawling into a large patch of goo. She screeched, flailing around as she tried to stand, applying great swads of epoxy to herself in the process. Stones, sand and pieces of kelp applied themselves to the epoxy.

"Oh shit, sorry Thea," said Lambert. "You sure are in a fix, by gum. Stick around. I'm of the firm opinion that you should try hard to clean that stuff out of your hair before it sets . . . ."

That was as far as he could go before dissolving into a howl of laughter, eyes shut and hands on knees, whooping.

"You arsehole, Scott! You did that on purpose! My hair . . ." Dunne was nearly in tears herself, not quite knowing what to do next. At that moment Ken Tilley leant into Lambert and gave him a powerful shove, sending him sprawling into Dunne and ending up on his back in the same patch. Tilley stood back, grinning widely while admiring his composition.

"Whatcha up to Scott? Cementing friendships?" Lambert took it well, and the two men helped the nurse up and went off with a can of solvent and some rags.

"OK for you two juveniles, but how will I ever get this gunk out of my hair," she moaned.

Everyone worked in short shifts, regularly taking food and warm drinks. The dredge continued working all the time, under Bradley and another machine operator, cutting the entrance channel, blasting when necessary. The channel that was forming was well defined, and with the installation of directional underwater beacons would act as a guide for the incoming vessel.

At midnight, when the dome had hardened, larger boulders were set on top and at strategic places around it, making it appear more irregular and natural. The channel had by then been cut ten metres inside the dome, and a large set of curtains, appropriately camouflaged with paint, beach sand and hanging kelp, was attached at the entrance. It was only a temporary measure, but Roberts thought it looked fine under the floodlights from any distance away, although he would have a better look at it in the light of day tomorrow. 'Almost like the entrance to a giant igloo,' he thought.

He conferred with James, both men standing on the dredging barge as it took more waste material out to the breakwater site, its bright forward spotlight illuminating the tip of the point.

"Lou, as soon as the entrance area inside the dome is cleared and excavated, and the dock sides are concreted, I want the roof of the dome built as a priority. Coordinate with Kaye and get her drilling team ready to begin tunnelling into the rocky hillside as soon as they can. At last we seem to be getting somewhere." Roberts allowed a hint of excitement to touch his voice, but James didn't appear to share his enthusiasm.

"David, how do we handle it if some of the scientists from the station arrive and want to know what we're doing?" he asked, with a degree of concern.

"I doubt that will happen, Lou. No one can get through on the walking trail, thanks to Kaye and Ken, and the helicopter shouldn't be able to pick up the dome. But if they do, and radio us about it, we'll simply tell them it's a hide for our documentary filming. If in the unlikely event some of them manage to trek to the cove and want to inspect it, they will be told no, in unmistakably definite terms, and be sent on their way. I'd rather have a group of suspicious scientists, than government people who know what we have here."

*

A further week passed, and all of a sudden it was Christmas Eve. The ANARE helicopter had flown over the cove once, during fair weather, without appearing to notice anything unusual. The drilling and tunnelling team was progressing into the hillside, widening out the dock area and cutting deeply into the rock. The excavations for the diesel and fresh water bunkers were taking shape, as were the beginnings of the accommodation areas. The material coming out of the excavations had extended the breakwater a hundred metres to the northeast, and it was now only two or three metres below the surface.

One of the other nurses, Cheryl Wilkes, had pointed out the date to Roberts at breakfast that morning, and he had been surprised to realise that he had simply not been concerned with keeping track of time.

"OK, thanks Cheryl, we'll have to do something about that," he grinned apologetically. "Spread the word that the party will be on tonight in the dining area, and I suppose we should take tomorrow off. Thank you for volunteering to organize the decorations for the party and tomorrow's dinner." A pert little blonde in the tradition of pretty nurses the world over, she grimaced good-naturedly and tossed her head in feigned disgust.

"Serves me right I suppose," she laughed. "I was about to anyway—some of us have just been waiting for a sign that you lot were actually going to celebrate this Christmas."

Roberts laughed with her. "I guess I'd better go see the chef, too," he said.

"I think you'll find Daniel already has things well in hand," she said confidently over her shoulder, as she hurried off.

"Jesus, I must be the only one aboard who hasn't been thinking of Christmas," Roberts admitted to the others at the table. "But it's probably a good time for us to take a break from the hard work done so far. We'll all knock off early this afternoon."

That evening the chef, Daniel Faraday, prepared a buffet for all hands that catered for the palate of the most discerning gourmand. The wet bar had been stocked with plenty of Australian, American and New Zealand beer, with wine and spirits, and with a chef's assistant who doubled as a drink steward. It wasn't long before the combination of the chef's creations and the copious supplies of grog worked their usual wiles over the happily consenting adults. The release of the tensions from the weather and the hard work added to the noise and festivities.

Tables were moved, music began to issue from someone's CD player, and dancing erupted.

Thea Dunne was wandering around the room, moving to the music quite happily by herself. She drifted dreamily into Scott Lambert's field of vision, which wasn't all that easy to do, as he was only a couple of cans short of drunk. Sitting at one of the tables, he raised his eyes above his can with some effort and noticed her more for the navy blue skull cap she was wearing than with any real perception of personal recognition. The Aussies called them beanies and this one was distinctive for the three large white letters on the front, CFC, arranged in a familiar one-on-top-of-the-other pattern. It was faded and ragged around the edges, the way you let a favourite piece of clothing get because it had been with you during a good many of the highs and lows in your life and you couldn't bear to let it go. You'd almost throw away your cat first.

"Bit like the Carlton Football Club itself now, that beanie," observed Lambert, blinking and smiling a little lopsidedly. Lambert had been a talented, and large, rugby player in Sydney, but Australia was a footballing country where it was almost impossible to exist without becoming aware of the footballing clubs, even if only by osmosis. Carlton was one of the earliest clubs in the land, once proud and traditional, but right now not travelling all that well. Fined for salary cap breaches, riven by internal power plays and containing too many unfettered egos, it had been languishing near the bottom of the table, before a new captain and coach had combined to provide its supporters with hope for better things.

"Like it do you, Scottie?" Dunne smiled without a lot of humour, slipping the cap off to reveal a quite bald head only just now showing signs of new hair growth.

"Oh shit, I really am sorry, Thea." Lambert stood up, managing not to stumble, his mind taking a quick sobriety test and coming up a little short. His homely features were twisted into what seemed genuine contrition, and he looked so forlorn she sat at his table.

"Don't worry about it, you big lug," she said, her eyes not totally in focus, "I'm actually getting used to it."

In the cleared space passing for the dance floor Ken Tilley had been dancing, or as near to it as anyone could get in the small clearing, with Kaye Halloran, feeling better about things following a little more romping. He still didn't really know where he stood with her, although he suspected it was on far from solid ground, but he felt it was OK to be optimistic. If he could just keep her happy and not try to get deep and meaningful with her, he reckoned over time he'd be able to convince her he was worth a serious relationship. Jesus, did that mean he was in love?

He had been dragged away by the little blonde nurse, Wilkes, and had been dancing with her for half an hour or so. He begged off, saying he was exhausted, and sat down with a Steinlager. Nobody went outside for fresh air—it was too damn fresh. He couldn't see Halloran, so finished his beer and wandered off to her cabin. He knocked and pushed the door open. "Kaye, are you . . ." he began, before the scene registered.

A naked Halloran was on her knees in front of a figure in a chair, her head moving rhythmically. She stopped at the sound of Tilley's voice, looked up at him with widening eyes, raised her eyebrows and tried to grin apologetically around a mouthful of Lawrence Prescott. Prescott glanced lazily up from his reclining posture in the chair and said in a slightly breathless, but quite unfazed voice, "Hullo young fellow, want to join in?"

Tilley, shocked to the core, enraged, shattered, stared at Halloran for a number of thumping heartbeats. "You shallow little bitch," he groaned thickly, as he took a step into the cabin, pulled her away from the seated Prescott and belted him in the jaw with an angry right cross. Prescott slumped unconscious in the chair, his erection deflating as though someone had undone the end of his balloon.

"Ken!" Halloran shrieked, "Stop it! You don't have any right to attack him! And you don't have any claim on me! I told you I won't be owned by anyone, that I'll do just what I want and not what someone else thinks I should do. If you don't like it, if you're too immature to handle it, don't have anything to do with me. And don't call me shallow! Now fuck off out of here!" she rose furiously, eyes blazing and breasts heaving, completely unaware of her nudity. Tilley backed slowly to the door, turned and walked out in a daze. Halloran slammed it behind him. He flinched, paused, ran both hands through his hair and slumped against the side of the corridor. The slam of the door echoed through his head with a wrenching finality, ending the affair and his hopes for something serious. But then it dawned on him that nothing serious had ever really begun. It was only a construct fabricated in the rose-coloured mist of his own naïveté that had kept his hopes alive. He really should have known better.

*

"Goddamnit Ken, it's Christmas morning and I have to begin the day with our main surgeon having his broken jaw wired, and me having to decide whether to throw my marine engineer in the brig for breaking it! Scott Lambert had to do it under a local anaesthetic so Prescott could advise him." Roberts was annoyed, but didn't seem as angry as he was trying to sound. "I guess at least it'll keep Prescott quiet for a while, though. But are you going to be able to function efficiently with the emotional turmoil you appear to have got yourself into? If not, I'll have to ship you back home."

"Don't worry, David, I've been happier, but it won't stop me from doing the job I came for. I think it's called life experience," he smiled ruefully, sadness showing briefly through the pain in his eyes. "Being so naïve I probably deserved it. After a day or so I'll talk to her and we'll be OK working together again. I'll apologise to Prescott too, and even try to make it sound genuine. I didn't think I hit him that hard. The poor bastard will probably have to suck his Christmas dinner through a straw. I know it's not his fault—he can't help being an arsehole, but I shouldn't have belted him.

Merry Christmas, David."

EIGHTEEN

Lo Nguyen Tay was fat, fifty-two and outrageously wealthy. Commercially based in Jakarta, he owned a small Indonesian island in the Banda Sea called Batuka, on which he had built a fortress-like mansion. "Or is it a mansion-like fortress?" he wondered idly, as his helicopter swept around its northern end and into the light breeze, before planing out and settling gently on the pad. Both, he decided—good defences, plenty of guards and all the comforts of a very expensive home—as his mind switched to the coming meeting he had arranged for the local managers of his varied business interests. Things in general were going smoothly and cash flow was up, and he wanted to expand in certain directions to take advantage of the current prosperity. He well knew that such good times were quite often ephemeral, and that if one were to reap extra benefits during these times one had to act swiftly and without fear. The gods would then smile and grant good fortune.

Lo struggled out of the helicopter and panted up the path to the house, wheezing in the hot, oppressive air. His chief adviser, aide and trusted lieutenant, Chen, had been waiting for his arrival and now escorted him. Lo's fondness for French cuisine was well known by his staff, but he paid for it in the extra kilos he now carried. His doctor had been trying to convince him for months to alter his diet and take less food, but it was a tricky business. How did you give a person like Lo advice he didn't want to hear without earning his displeasure? In the past it had often been the case that the bearer of unwelcome advice had suffered significant health problems of his own in very short order. Lo had never paid any attention to the Western adage about not shooting the messenger.

He gratefully entered the air-conditioned coolness of the big house and went to his rooms, showering and changing into traditional dress for the meeting. Chen had ensured that everything had been ready for his arrival, and now knocked and entered the anteroom.

"Your guests are all here and await you in the conference room. They have been refreshed with tea and sweetmeats."

"Thank you, Chen. We will begin at once. Please arrange for dinner to be served in two hours, followed by the usual after-dinner pleasures according to the individual requirements of our guests." Lo gave his instructions without any hint of arrogance or imperiousness, his unlined half-moon face, topped with thick black hair swept back into a short pony tail, smiling frequently. Like most of those with real power he saw no need to flaunt it, although his general good humour in no way constrained him from instructing Chen, on the spur of any given moment, to arrange an urgent restructuring of his personnel. He walked with measured tread into the large, exquisitely furnished conference room, greeting his twelve managers in turn, with good-humoured ease. He was always calm, smiled often and spoke quietly, although anyone within earshot made very sure they listened carefully to his words. No one in his employ had ever seen him angry; but there were the stories about those who had disappeared, and his presence was always deferred to with the utmost respect. Following his invitation, they all sat, and in the familiar and prearranged order began their reports.

*

Lo had been born in Saigon to parents struggling to keep their family together. It had been only the sale of two of their daughters into Saigon brothels that had kept the family in food and clothing, and as Lo grew older the hardship and desperation became acute. He realised at a very early age that to be able to do anything in his world one needed money and respect. He learned of the value of prostitution from the inside, and during the troubles, when the Americans came, he grew streetwise and gained knowledge and contacts. At sixteen he was running four brothels and employing a staff of forty, most of them older than he. At first, he had done whatever wet work he felt was required to keep his business afloat, and had become quite comfortable with violence and death, as long as he was causing it. Later, he was able to employ a staff of hard men who looked after the persuasive side of his operation. After the war, when the communists took over, he realised he would need to diversify to continue amassing his profits. He turned his hand to arms dealing, for his network had access to a great store of cached weapons, mostly American. And for a time, he also ran drugs. This was a source of great profit for him, but he was always uneasy about the whole scene. There were some heavy players in Asia, and he had no wish to get into any kind of a territorial dispute. After only three years in that business he extracted his organisation from all drug-related operations.

Twenty years later, Lo was a billionaire with a large variety of business interests. His commercial centre was in Jakarta, from where he controlled all of his dealings, many of which were entirely legal. He was still heavily involved in prostitution in

Indonesia, Malaysia, the Philippines, Vietnam and Thailand, and maintained an efficient arms dealership that operated out of Jakarta.

He also owned a fleet of pirate fishing vessels, all of which worked the Southern Ocean zones of exclusion and caught all the Patagonian toothfish they could find.

"Gentlemen," he said in his customarily quiet tones, now turning to address the two men responsible for the fishing operations, "that almost concludes our major business. The final instruction I have is for the fishing managers. Our toothfish operations are lucrative and we will continue to take as much as we can. But the resource is dwindling and finite. What appears to be increasing now is the size of the populations of the whales, and the price of whale meat is high. I want you two to purchase a mother ship and four catcher boats. Get them from the Russians or the Norwegians, and hire their crews also. We will refurbish as necessary, but I want them operating as soon as possible. Engage a good master and instruct him to catch any kind of whale he can. Establish your main market in Japan.

We are now in the whaling business. Thank you all for your attendance. Dinner will be served shortly in the dining room."

NINETEEN

"Nice to meet you at last, David. I've been looking forward to meeting the lunatic who ordered a fucking great hole cut in the pressure hull of this sub." Gus Durrand was smiling as he shook hands with Roberts, but the glint in his dark eyes indicated that he considered the installation of the window bubble in the top of the submarine's forward starboard deck an absolute insanity. Together with Mackie and Hass, they were standing in the conning tower of the submarine in its dry dock, and the bubble was clearly visible poking a good metre above the deck plates.

"Nice to meet you too, Gus," grinned Roberts. "I guess we'll see how it goes when we give her a test drive. But if you think it could be too dangerous, you don't have to accept our offer of the position of commander," he said with guile, innocently raising his eyebrows.

Durrand's square, trim body stiffened, at the same time as his smile thinned. "Don't you worry none about me, David," he said, managing to keep the growl from his voice, "we've built a nice railed platform underneath the goddamned thing, so you can stand right inside it and be the first one out of the sub when it blows."

Roberts burst into laughter. "Thanks Gus," he chuckled, "but that three-quarter inch Lexan is stronger than the seven-eighths inch nickel steel pressure hull itself, and it's been secured by stainless bolts two inches apart, with a layer of special silicone under the flange. Then there's the rubber seal under the deck plates, all of which will simply be forced down flat by the water pressure. I guarantee it won't leak a drop, and I've got a hundred bucks to prove it."

"You're on," said Durrand. Of medium height, he carried himself upright and straight. His hair was a very even coverage of close-cropped metallic grey bristles, and his clothes were blue on blue-navy trousers and light blue denim shirt, both ironed smooth with razor sharp creases, over polished black shoes. His whole appearance shouted navy to those who understood.

"I think I may take a little of that too, David," smiled Gunter Hass, who had been concentrating on the exchange with a small frown on his face. "Although Gus thinks I am just an old fool, an old German fool, I agree with his sentiments about the bubble. It is simply a thing that should not be done to a submarine. It invites trouble."

Durrand's face registered embarrassment, discomfort and something more. With a small shock Roberts realised there was also mistrust in his eyes. "Mr Hass," Durrand said quietly, but with firm resolution, "I already apologised for the remark I made about Krauts last week. I never fought against Germany, and I understand that the German navy during the Second World War was not part of the Nazi machine. I even realise that you are now an American, sir, after so long a time living here. And I never thought you were a fool. But I hope you can understand where I come from too. My upbringing was military all the way, and two of my uncles died under German guns during that war. I will work with you because I'm a pro, but please don't ask me to like you."

Roberts raised a quizzical eyebrow at Mackie, who shrugged slightly and looked unconcerned. "I'll hold you to that, Gus," he said easily into the strained silence that followed Durrand's reaction. "You are both key members of the Foxtrot team and will be expected to work cooperatively, as well as display leadership and provide expert advice. I can't instruct every team member to like each other, but I can insist on cooperation and efficiency. If I don't get it I'll just have to kill you both."

Hass and Durrand stared blankly at him. Mackie developed a strangled cough. "Aussie humour," growled Roberts. "Just watch yourselves."

*

"Oh, this is just great!" Roberts was standing on the platform under the bubble, his head and shoulders above the level of the deck. The bubble was not in fact a neat hemisphere, but rather had been designed with the aerodynamic tear-drop shape of the road racing bicycle riders' helmets in mind, hopefully in order to reduce drag on its surface when the submarine was moving at speed. Controls were positioned on the rail around him, for firing the torpedoes if necessary and for communication with the control room. "What a view it's going to be under water. We'll be able to con the sub right up close to a ship and plant a torpedo just where we want it."

"Yeah, it's a regular *Nautilus* ain't it," grumbled Durrand. "We probably should have a big window in the side somewhere, too, just like old Cap'n Nemo did in the film."

"Now there's an idea, Gus!" Roberts looked around eagerly. The similarity between what he wanted to do and the old Jules Verne classic hadn't escaped him. Both Hass and Durrand made noises of alarm. "Shit David, I was only jokin'," said Durrand quickly.

"It's OK Gus, so was I," laughed Roberts. "You guys probably need to understand that Aussies kid a lot, and are much better at it than Yanks. It's almost a national pastime of ours. We practise on each other, but you don't get many points for kidding Americans. It's too easy." In fact, it went a little deeper than that. One of the very roots of Australian culture is the ability for a 'dinky di' Aussie to be able to 'pull the wool over the eyes' of another. It must be done with a perfectly straight face until the victim becomes aware he has been 'had'. Then both kidder and kiddee alike can enjoy the joke, usually with a beer and a laugh. It is a part of the national psyche, and one of the explanations used by people born outside Australia when describing Australian culture as an oxymoron.

Hass and Durrand still seemed uncertain. "So no hole in the side then, David?" asked Hass hopefully.

Roberts smiled. "No, Gunter. But I do want a larger hatch installed in this 'Bubble Room', like the main entrance hatch in the conning tower. I also want the internal bulkheads and watertight door beefed up, and all electronics well sealed. And I want three more bubbles made, each to the exact specifications of the one installed, and plenty of extra bolts and sealant . . . just in case." He looked at Mackie, who nodded his head in understanding. The other two again were confused, staring at each other as if they weren't sure whether they were still being kidded. Jesus, thought Roberts, if I keep this up I just may drive these two into a friendship of mutual exasperation.

"I want to be able to flood this room quickly, once the watertight door has been closed and locked. Then the hatch and even the torpedo tubes will allow divers to enter or exit, or crew to escape in an emergency. Naturally, we'll need to be able to pump the water out again. It will be in effect a diving chamber. I want lockers installed to contain full thermal wet suits and emergency scuba gear for all crew." This to Mackie also, who nodded again.

"And one more thing, Ray. I want you to get some engineering help and install a hydraulically operated set of shears, like an industrial guillotine, on the forward deck over the bow. It must be in good view from the bubble, and be able to be rotated through ninety degrees. And it should be able to cut through at least six-inch cable. It should be powerful and about six feet long, with a pointed end. Strengthen the bows around it like an icebreaker's and make it operable from the bubble."

Mackie grinned. "Going to be some long lines lost when we get out there," he laughed.

"Speaking of which," said Roberts, "are you able to project when she may be ready for sea trials?"

"I'm hoping inside twelve months, David," said Mackie. "The work is progressing well, and we now have most of the new electronics installed. We've removed the aft torpedo facilities and built new crew quarters with more showers and toilets, the new air system is in and all diesels, electric generators and batteries have been replaced—half the size, twice the power and a lot more efficiency. We've put in a climate-controlled airconditioning system, there's a new hydraulic system aboard, and some special operators have reconditioned all the torpedoes. They've installed new motors and replaced the warheads with those penthrite grenades Bo Tallis got us from Japan . . . the ones they use to kill whales."

Roberts looked grimly satisfied. "Good. I'm going to enjoy giving those bastards some of their own back."

*

It was a jovial group who clustered around the Hass dinner table that night, enjoying the results of Dorothy Hass's expertise at producing five-star food in wholesome quantity. As well as Hass, Roberts and Mackie, the gunshop owner Bo Tallis was there, sitting at one end of the table. He couldn't fit anywhere else, Mackie thought, as he watched him shovel another large portion of oven-roasted strip rump into his mouth, washing it down with a gulp of Victoria Bitter. Mackie had managed to purchase some of the popular Australian beer, simply referred to as 'VB' in that country, and it was proving popular with Tallis too. Dorothy brought another platter of beef strips coated in burgundy sauce to the table, smiling at Roberts as she set it down. Although her round, open face gave the appearance of a happy, ingenuous nature, her eyes were clouded with what Roberts thought may have been worry. Or perhaps sadness. She went back out to the kitchen and Roberts got up and followed her.

"Is everything OK, Dorothy?" he asked concernedly. "You seem a little down."

"Oh I'm just being silly, David. I'm so happy that Gunter has taken to your project with such excitement—he seems like a new man. He's been revitalized and it's like he's got a new reason for living. But he told me the other day that he desperately wants to go off with you all in the submarine, when it's repaired, and I'm worried he might not be able to stand up to it." She looked so forlorn that Roberts hugged her warmly.

"Don't you worry, Dorothy, he'll only be coming if I'm satisfied he's up to it, and if so, I'll look after him. The new lease of life he has must be good for him—he looks more vital and energetic every day."

"Thank you David. But I'll still be worried if he goes."

"There's something else bothering you, isn't there?" Roberts looked closely at her, and she nodded, the sadness he thought he had noticed in the dining room now quite evident.

"Yes, David. I invited Mr Durrand here tonight too, but he said he couldn't make it. Gunter told me what he had said last week, and again today, and I just think it's so unfair that Gunter should have to put up with more racism. He's had so much for so long, you'd think all that would be forgotten by now." She was almost in tears, and for once Roberts didn't quite know what to say. The problem was almost as old as mankind, and would not be solved any time soon. The manifestations of bigotry of all kinds were across every nation on Earth, most dramatically evident in the work of the fundamentalist insanity of 9/11. But it was dreadfully ubiquitous, thought Roberts, as he struggled to find the words to console Dorothy.

"If I thought that Gus was in any way malevolent, he wouldn't still be with us, Dorothy. I'm satisfied that he will behave in a civilised way towards Gunter. He was brought up by his father in a military environment, and lived with the old credo that 'the only good German is a dead one'. He still feels the anger of his father that his uncles were killed by Germans, and probably won't ever change. And he really can't help that. But if at any time I decide his feelings are affecting his judgement in controlling the sub, he will be out." Roberts was serious, and his intensity transmitted itself to Dorothy as she watched his face, her anxiety lessening.

"So please try not to be sad, dear. Gunter still has us to be with, and he won't have to deal with Gus too much. Let's go in and finish off this great meal—your cooking reminds me of someone back home."

They returned to the table, Dorothy looking more at ease, and Mackie glanced up from his plate.

"How are things progressing at the base?"

Roberts nodded, a small grin appearing. "Apart from my chief medico having his jaw busted by a jealous engineer, you mean?" he asked almost rhetorically. "Very well. The tunnelling has finished and the construction of the dock and storage tanks was completed months ago. The accommodation is being fitted out as we speak, and the main generators have been installed. The air heating system is in, as are the main vent pipes. It was necessary to run them through what amounts to a heat exchanger, to cool the exhaust air to the same temperature as the outside air. Otherwise you'd have some almighty big exhausts of steam geysering out of the vents, like great big pointing fingers.

Some of the workers are living in the base, which I've named Igloo, even now. The *Kontica* has been moving around the island, to give the appearance of studying different populations of seals and penguins, and has been back to Sydney twice for more supplies. The next trip will bring the desalination plant, as well as accommodation furniture.

Another six to twelve months should see it completed and ready for the *Flying Fish*."

Mackie and Hass looked up quickly, their interest clear.

"This is the name of our submarine, David?" asked Hass eagerly. "May I ask why you chose that name?"

Roberts' eyes twinkled, partly with a mischievous light. "Well, they are quick, graceful fish which can fly to evade trouble. And did you know their botanical name is *Exocoetus volitans*? How do you reckon the Exocet missile got its name?"

TWENTY

"G'day everyone—welcome to Project Foxtrot, and to the crew of the *Flying Fish*. My name's David Roberts, my funny accent is Australian, and I'm the person responsible for getting us all together. By now you all know Ray and Gus, the two men who have done all the hard work of interviewing and selecting the crew for our special vessel, and I'm very curious to see what kind of people they've chosen." Roberts was speaking to a group of people of all sizes, ages and physical types. He noticed there were also four women present. "Perhaps you're also curious about me, and about what you've signed on for. Our psychological evaluations, and the resulting profiles, have indicated that all of you are the type of people we're looking for, and that you will all be quite at ease with our objectives. However, once I've explained them to you, each one has of course the right to opt out of our project with a bonus and a copy of the secrecy clause you've all signed."

As Roberts was explaining the details of the project, Ray Mackie glanced around the conference room at the Miami Port facility. Some months ago, Gus Durrand had begun to bring Mackie up to speed on the workings of a US diesel fleet boat, a submarine that was bigger and much better equipped than the old wartime German U-boats, and the crew that was needed to operate one. He wanted at least forty members, but after consulting Roberts by satphone Mackie had placed a restriction of twenty-five on Durrand. Durrand had been livid. Goddamn landlubbers! Telling a navy man how to suck eggs!

"Ferchrissakes Mackie, you've never even been to sea, let alone on a goddamn sub! What the fuck would you know about running one!" Chin jutting forward, eyes scornful and flashing with anger, some of the veins in Durrand's neck had appeared about to erupt along with his temper.

"Calm down Gus," Mackie had advised him quietly, not even bothering to remove his glasses. "I'm not treading on your toes, and we're not going to war. David has placed the restriction on the numbers, and although I realise your objections would equally apply to him, he has some good reasons. As you know, many of the operations have been centralized and automated, and there'll be more personnel at the main base. None of them are submariners, but they can be trained as watchkeepers, fire control and engineering assistants. After the sea trials, if you're certain we need extra people to ensure the safety of the boat, we'll get them.

But I guess I don't need to remind you that David's paying the bill, do I?"

At that moment Durrand was sitting in a corner looking glum, and Roberts, finishing his address to the assembled crew, looked over at him. He'd heard about Durrand's reaction to his restriction on crew numbers, but wasn't perturbed in any way. He had asked Mackie for a tough, experienced skipper who would shit on anyone not totally in his corner. From a considerable height. He nodded at him.

"The guy in the corner with the long face is Gus Durrand, your skipper, and he's not convinced there are enough of you to handle the sub. I'm hoping that the advanced electronics plus the centralised systems will allow a smaller crew to take her safely to the main base, where we can augment the numbers with some very keen people there." Roberts paused at the sound of a throat being cleared with a deliberation that carried a clear protest.

"I'm Machinist Mate Carl Wojinski, sir, and I agree with the skipper. I count just twenty-four people here, including the old guy in the corner who surely ain't part of the crew, and I say we'd need twice this number to be fully operational and to stay at sea for some time." The speaker was a large, grizzled, tough looking man in his late forties, with a rasping voice and the air of a veteran campaigner.

"Thanks mate," Roberts acknowledged, "and I'm sure most of the others would agree with you. But why don't we wait for some sea time to see how she handles? I promise you that if after a number of different sea trials all you experienced hands tell me it's unsafe to try to move the submarine with this short crew list, I'll increase it. Just try to keep in mind, though, that the *Flying Fish* is no longer a traditional submarine.

By now the ex-navy submariners here may also have noticed that this crew is not what they would call traditional either. It's a very talented mix of people of all ages, ex-naval and civilian, widely varying backgrounds, both sexes and half a dozen of whom have yet to board their first submarine.

So I hope you'll all understand when I tell you that aboard our submarine there won't be any sirs and salutes, ranks and privileges thereof, or regulations and uniforms, although we do have an issue of high quality thermal trousers and jackets for you, which you may wear or not as you choose. But there will be the expectations—no, demands—of mine and the skipper's, that all crew members will do the job they've been contracted to do to the very best of their ability, without complaint or criticism and totally answerable to Gus and to me. Anyone has a problem, my door will always be open.

If you accept, you'll become part of a special project team in for a long, exciting, at times dangerous ride in a very cold and hostile environment. But we hope it will be rewarding, too, in ways both moral and material.

If anyone has questions, please ask them at any time." Roberts leant back against the wall expectantly, waiting for the first response. It came from a slender, strikingly handsome African American woman of medium height with tight, braided hair.

"Mr Roberts, I'm Cordelia Swan, electronics engineer. Speaking of one of those material rewards, how will we get paid?"

"Hi Cordelia. You'll all be asked to nominate a bank account number, and your contracted amount will be electronically transferred each month by our purser."

"Jesus Christ!" The exclamation came from Wojinski, not loud but clearly exasperated. "We have only half a crew to drive the boat, but we have a goddamned purser?"

"Well sure Carl," Roberts smiled, "who did you think was going to handle all the crew's travel documents and look after your well-being? Besides, Andrew's a multi-talented guy." Roberts waved at someone slouched in a chair at the back of the room. "Stand up and introduce yourself, Andrew."

"Hi, I'm Andy McLeod." The man rose from his chair, unfolding to a height of nearly six and a half feet, with an almost exaggerated muscular development and shoulder width setting off a frame apparently devoid of any excess poundage, even though clearly weighing at least sixteen stone. A face of strong character, pock-marked by childhood measles scars, was underscored by a jaw line to match his shoulders. His teeth, large and white, were all angles and overlaps, seeming to have been arranged with no thought given to regularity or order. One of the front uppers was chipped. This was evident because he was smiling, albeit bashfully, not comfortable with the attention. The top of his head was covered with thinning blond hair, and he appeared to be around forty.

"Purser my ass," someone muttered.

"Oh, he will do those things I mentioned," Roberts chuckled, "but Andy's SEAL background and Special Forces experience also nicely equips him to be responsible for ordnance management and training, and crew hand-to-hand instruction."

"Well big as he is and SEAL or not, he won't be able to show me much I don't already know," Wojinski growled and folded his massive arms emphatically, tattoos peering menacingly from beneath his short-sleeved shirt.

"Ah, I'm afraid he'll have trouble with me too." A small, shabby man sitting at the front of the room spoke apologetically in a mid-western accent. Thin almost to the point of emaciation, very pale with long straight dark hair and huge eyes behind thick glasses, he appeared to be somewhere in his twenties. "My name's Clarence Grimshaw, I'm a computer geek from Silicon Valley existing on onion crisps, diet Coke and cigarettes—well, not cigarettes now—and I don't think I could throw a punch to save my life."

McLeod raised an eyebrow and smiled. "Don't worry Clarence, I can teach you some things, and with practice you'll be surprised at what you can do. And Mr Wojinski, we have a well equipped workout room aboard that I'll be happy to show to you sometime."

"OK folks!" Roberts clapped his hands together and straightened up. "If there isn't anything of more concern, we might leave the housekeeping questions 'til later. I guess it's put up or shut up time. Anyone want out?" He stood calmly, eyebrows slightly raised, radiating openness and unconcern.

No one moved or made a sound. Roberts would have been surprised if they had.

"Thank you all," he said simply. "I guess our psychological workups were accurate and you're all pretty much in tune with what we're about. All right, a little more information then.

As we've noted, this crew is different. I can't demand that you all love each other and get on like one big happy family, but try to remember that each of you is an expert in his or her own field, and pay everyone that respect. If someone shouts at you to do something urgently based on that person's expertise, just do it as fast and as well as you can and, if you need to, discuss it later. For me to use the word 'team' at the moment would be premature and maybe unreasonable, but you have to know that's my ultimate hope.

No one here, not even the navy guys, has had any experience aboard a Foxtrot. No one that is, Carl, except that old guy in the corner, who is very definitely part of the crew. Can I introduce to you all Gunter Hass, a retired U-boat commander and Electroboat and Foxtrot consultant. He will be assisting the skipper in the intensive training schedule ahead of us all, as we learn about our submarine and how she performs at sea.

OK people, that's enough for one day. I'll see you all at 0700 tomorrow for breakfast aboard ship."

*

"Damn fine chow, skipper." The large nametag proclaimed the speaker as Herb Cazaley, Torpedoman, and he was addressing Gus Durrand across the breakfast table in the large, bright and roomy mess. "We be eatin' like this all th' time?" Platters piled with heaps of bacon, fried, poached and scrambled eggs, flapjacks, hash browns, bowls of grits, cereal, muesli, toast, corn bread, juice, fresh fruit salad, yoghurt, tea, coffee, were being rushed out to the tables by two young men whose tags identified them as Gary Duperouzel, Mess Attendant and Peter Cransberg,

Steward. Ray Mackie, sitting at a nearby table, overheard and looked up, swallowing a mouthful of flapjack swimming in maple syrup. "No Herb," he offered quite seriously, "most times we'll be having lunch and dinner."

"Uh, no Mr Mackie, I meant . . ."

"Don't worry about it Herb," Durrand rasped, shaking his head resignedly, "he's an Aussie too. You'll get used to it."

"Listen up everyone." Roberts rose, coffee in hand. "There's no rush, but when you've finished you all may wish to wander around the boat to get a feel for her, then find where you think your station will be. Gus and Gunter will be on hand to assist. Due to the refurbishing with electronics and miniaturization, we have a lot more room and don't have to 'hot bunk' anymore. There are two-person cubicles with one female toilet and shower room and three for men. Pick who you want to bunk with and get settled.

Gunter has been through the boat, and all labels and warnings are now in English. Most stations are working, although either incomplete or not fully configured. Your initial task is to become familiar with your station and advise our Operations Manager, Ray Mackie, what is necessary to bring it to full operational readiness.

I want our first sea trial in five days. See you all at dinner."

*

"Say Skipper, I found my forward torpedo room OK, but it's kinda small and missin' three tubes, and I could only find space to store 'bout ten fish. Then I went to check on 'em an' couldn't find any. Not only that, but there weren't no aft torpedo room at all. Whole lotta small cabins instead. Is this boat fer real?" Cazaley was in the mess with a large mug of coffee in one hand, the other scratching his head in puzzlement as he sat at the table occupied by Durrand and two other men.

"Yeah Herb, it is. We'll probably only need to be shootin' one torpedo at a time, and you may find you'll only need to use one tube. Just be sure to keep all three in perfect working order at all times. The torpedoes, along with all our other special ordnance, are being kept ashore in secure storage until we go through official inspection."

Martin Blake leaned forward with interest as Cazaley was outlining the curious nature of the submarine's main attack weapons system. A tall, very thin man with a prominent hooked nose overhanging a deeply cleft chin, both features put to shame by the magnificence and mobility of a large adam's apple half way down his neck, he too appeared puzzled. "I was a quartermaster, and I've been contracted to navigate and pilot, but I couldn't find a regulation steering station. I found a desk with a lot of computer gear around it which I guess had to be it, because there was a GPS unit there, with some recognizable instruments like a speed readout, depth gauge, gyro compass and such, but there were also other instruments I didn't know."

"That is the steering station Martin; I'll give you a run down on everything there at 1530." Durrand was smiling at last, comforted to some degree by the fact that most of the crew would be as puzzled as these two by the extensive modifications made to the *Flying Fish*, and by their high tech nature.

The other man, purple black and shiny bald, was Theodore Woodville, Ship's Doctor, and about the only person aboard who was reasonably comfortable with his station. "At least the surgery is pretty standard, Captain Durrand, although it's fitted out with the latest and best equipment, so I'm ready and waiting."

"Oh there you are Skipper!" An effervescent little man bounded into the mess, pale blue eyes alive with excitement, all nervous energy and red-haired enthusiasm. "Rick Tomlinson, Radio and Sonar Operator," he fizzed. "I was worried when I came aboard this morning, because I noticed that the sonar arrays had disappeared from the bow bulb and the sail. But I found my cubbyhole and realized we had the latest in high-definition DIDSON sonar, along with some very cool radio and radar gear. And a flat screen with a set of numbered toggles which I turned on, and got some really clear pictures all round the sub. High resolution digital cameras?"

"Yeah Rick . . . nice stuff isn't it," Durrand smiled. "Some of the latest submarines are using this gear and have actually done away with the periscope."

Excusing himself, Durrand made his way to the fitness room, amidships lower deck, where he expected to find McLeod. The outsized purser was sitting on a bench explaining some movement to a subdued Wojinski.

"Why Carl, is that a black eye?" asked Durrand innocently.

"Yeah, he got lucky Skipper," the burly mate growled sheepishly. "He does seem to know a thing or two. He even put Mr Roberts down."

"Only after several minutes and a dirty trick," McLeod deprecated, "but I couldn't get near Ray Mackie. I made a move against him, as he was taking his glasses off, and when I woke up he'd gone off to find the doctor."

"I just wanted to ask you what's happening with our torpedoes and ordnance, Andy?" queried Durrand.

"The Coast Guard and Port Authority inspections will be completed tomorrow Skipper, and tomorrow night Ray and I, with some crew help, will bring it all on board."

TWENTY ONE

It's always sunny in Florida, the locals say. If you grow tired of the greyness and the icy bleakness of unfriendly sidewalks in northern cities, perhaps like Chicago or New York, at this time of the year, they say a little smugly, come to Florida. It does people good to allow some warmth and sunshine back into their souls, as if everyone in the northern world could simply pack up and translocate to Florida, assuming they'd all choose to.

But today wasn't sunny. It was unusually cool under the overcast, and the water was rumpled and unenticing, an unruly breeze sour with the briny tang of a big-city shoreline. A gang of red eyed seagulls stood on the dock, hunched against the wind, their cold scavenging eyes staring at the men in the sail, waiting for a scrap of anything that might suddenly appear near enough to them to cause the usual screeching, flapping brawl. Up in the conning tower Roberts, Durrand, Hass and Mackie paid them no heed, watching four crew members as they took in, coiled expertly and stowed all but two of the new, starkly white dock lines.

Roberts glanced at Mackie and smiled at Hass. "Gunter, you have the look of a major lottery winner just been given the news," he grinned.

"David, it's a beautiful day, I know you and Ray are excited, and Gus is professionally in tune, but it's so hard for me to explain exactly how I feel at this moment. All of that of course, but more . . . I think I feel complete again, after such a very long time." Hass' eyes were now over eighty, but shining with remarkable clarity. "Apart from my dear Dorothy, nothing in my life is as important or fulfilling as what I am doing right now." Even Durrand gave a small nod of understanding, for they were at least both mariners.

"OK Gus, she's all yours," exclaimed Roberts, not trying to conceal his excitement. "Let's go to sea."

*

An hour later, ten miles offshore in plenty of water, the four men climbed down into the main control room and took their stations, Durrand, the last one, closing the bridge hatch behind him. Roberts had a chair in a corner of an alcove containing a large flat screen with a special keyboard and panel, over which Clarence Grimshaw, the computer specialist, was clucking, eyes darting between each indicator in the hope of catching unawares some malfunction, ready to chastise it into submission with a series of keystrokes incomprehensible to ordinary people.

"Attention all hands." Durrand was speaking into a small wireless microphone clipped to his shoulder. "This is the Captain. As you're all well aware by now, this isn't a fleet-type submarine, and it's really no longer a Foxtrot, so we'll have to establish our own Ship's Organisation Book as we go. However, for the ex-navy guys aboard who'll control the dive, we'll use the generic fleet-type procedure already discussed, and see how it goes.

All hands, ready to dive! The diving signal will be two short blasts on the ship's klaxon." He leaned over to a panel near

Grimshaw and pressed a large red button sharply twice. The klaxon sounded throughout the vessel with a familiar urgent stridency, and several things seemed to happen all at the same time.

Hass moved swiftly to the conning tower hatch and closed and dogged it; the diesel engines stopped and the ship was switched to ahead standard battery power; the engine room crew then opened the engine room doors and airlocks; the seaman at the diving station, Clive Chung, was toggling switches rapidly and simultaneously advising Durrand in a low voice of each completed action. "Outboard and inboard engine exhaust valves closed, hull ventilation supply and exhaust valves closed, main induction closed, bow buoyancy vents open, main ballast and safety tank vents open, bow planes rigged out on full dive." His switches were large, sturdy toggles with different but still-familiar shapes, the main induction vent toggle being sensor controlled so it couldn't be opened underwater.

"Take her down to periscope depth," Durrand said sharply.

Andre LeClerc, the Diving Officer, closely checked his panel lights to make sure all hull openings were closed, then bled some air into the ship. "Air pressure constant, watertight integrity, Skipper," he murmured. "Periscope depth, all vents closed, ten knots."

"Very smooth, very quick," observed Durrand. "Having all valves controlled electronically from these two control room stations seems a real improvement.

Well, gentlemen, she works so far!" He turned to Roberts and Mackie as he raised the periscope. Both broke into large smiles.

"Never doubted it for a second Gus—well done! Can we go a bit deeper please?"

"Sure. Just let me check out the scope. Nice optics, good vision . . . couple of ships around, but none near us. What's our heading and what water've we got, nav?"

"095 and a hundred fathoms, Skipper," responded Blake swiftly, "going deeper offshore."

"OK, maintain heading. Clive, flood negative and take us down to 500 feet, twenty degree dive." Durrand's instructions were quick and positive as he snapped up the handles and lowered the periscope. Hass gave a slight cough and looked thoughtful. Roberts took off forward at a fast walk on the sloping deck, grinning at Mackie's questioning glance.

"Want to come and check out the bubble room?" They both moved quickly to the forward torpedo room area now containing the viewing bubble, and Roberts jumped eagerly into the high chair under it. "Too dark to see anything at this depth, but there's no turbulence around the bubble." He flicked a switch on the console and a floodlight on the sail lit up the bows and forward deck with startling clarity, the white-painted cutting tool on the port bow standing out from the royal blue of the hull with an eerie similarity to the harpoon on a whalechaser. The water wasn't clear, but it was clear enough for remarkably good vision, and Mackie discovered that by standing next to the seated Roberts he could see almost as well. Roberts keyed his lapel microphone.

"Hey Gus, you and Gunter owe me a hundred each," he called, with a degree of satisfaction. "Not a drop."

*

Two hours later Durrand, after putting the submarine through a variety of manoevres, including rapid course alterations and speed changes, was standing with the Diving Officer at his console.

"How does she feel Andre?"

"Well, Skipper, she's got more positive buoyancy than I'm used to, maybe because of all the modifications, but the trim is easy and quick to adjust, and she is very smooth. I'm glad you kept the old bubble—it's nice to see a horizontal bubble at a glance, even if the instruments show an up angle on the bow of point three of a degree."

"We'll live with that. Marty, what did all ahead full give us?"

"Not sure I believe it Skipper, but my readout showed 20 knots. I thought these subs could only do 16 submerged?"

"Yeah, but we now have a lot more power and new computer-designed propellers," said Durrand. "I expected an increase in performance, but not quite that much. OK, slow to ahead one-third and bring her up horizontally to periscope depth."

Everyone was back in the control room, all looking pleased with the shakedown.

"Can I have a look through the scope please Gus?"

"Sure David, go for it."

Roberts flipped up the handles as the periscope was raised and glued his face into the moulded viewing socket.

"You're right about the optics Gus," he said as he turned the scope around. "I can see a big container ship bearing 170 at about five miles, coming in to port." Roberts took his face from the viewer and looked quizzically at Durrand, one eyebrow raised.

"Yeah, OK David, I guess that's what we're here for—ahead two thirds, steer 220. Lets go over and take a closer look."

Roberts grinned. "I'll be up in the bubble room Gus. Come at her from behind and just to starboard of her wake. Let me know when we're getting close."

*

"OK David, this new sonar and the high res cameras are very good—we can see schools of fish, five dolphins in front of the bow and the ship about half a mile ahead." Durrand's voice was also clear in the bubble room.

"We're coming up from dead astern at the moment Gus; the water's a little swirly for good vision and the wake's manhandling us a bit. Come right a little." Roberts had already arranged with Durrand to use non-nautical directions when he was conning the *Flying Fish* in to a hostile vessel. The submarine turned a few degrees to starboard and entered clear and stable water. "Good, Gus, straighten up—I can see a disturbance in the water ahead about three hundred yards. Slow down a knot or two."

Durrand issued the command to the pilot just as Roberts said sharply "Gus, I said slow down!"

At the sonar station Tomlinson was jumping up and down in his seat as though trying to relieve a case of hemorrhoids assaulted by a large bowl of night-before chili. He clearly wanted to join the action but knew it wasn't his place.

"All stop!" shouted Durrand.

"Hard right!" yelled Roberts, and the pilot didn't wait for the instruction from Durrand, turning the submarine emphatically to starboard, looking a little apprehensively at his skipper.

"It's OK Martin, you did well. We'll obviously need to work on the procedures during attack manoevering. David, what the hell happened?"

"We just didn't slow down quickly enough, Gus, and were heading straight for the starboard screw; but we missed it by a good thirty yards. Can we come round and try again please?"

"OK," said Durrand, "but this time I want to cut out the middle man. Martin will pilot the boat directly on your instructions, which he did pretty well on that last turn. Goes against the grain, but I guess we're not in the navy any more."

"I was thinking the same thing Gus, but didn't want to step on your toes. Thanks."

*

"All right," breathed Roberts with an excited whistle, "this is better than I hoped for! We're keeping a good steady station just to the right of the ship's course, and the vision is excellent. Gus, can you get the torpedoman up here on the double please."

"Sure David, he's only next door—you've taken half his torpedo room, remember?"

Mackie moved out from under the bubble as Cazaley appeared and stepped up under the large clear dome.

"Jesus, is this cool!" His eyes wide, he stared open-mouthed at the impressive sight of the massive starboard screw of the container ship churning the water into roiling whirls of ice green froth not more than thirty yards ahead off the submarine's port bow. The bubble was about ten yards deeper than the propeller.

"G'day Herb. See how we're paralleling the ship's course? What I want you to tell me is, if we fired a torpedo right now at the ship, would the acoustic head drag it into the screw, or would we have to turn the submarine left on an up angle and aim directly at it as we fired?"

"Aw hell, Mr Roberts, I reckon it'd hit the screw, but you know, we could actually be a bit too close for it to work properly? It might be better to hang back a bit, say four hunnerd yards, and give it time to work fully?"

Roberts smiled at the persistent rising inflections. "Good point Herb. We'll try it, along with several other combinations of distances, angles and techniques. Not just yet though. Hey Skipper," he called to Durrand through the mike, "come up here and check out the bubble. I think it may be about to blow."

Durrand, closely followed by Hass, quickly entered the bubble room, as Roberts and Cazaley moved away from the dome.

"I know you're kidding David, so I... God almighty! I never thought I'd be in a submarine staring out of a fucking window! This just ain't right!"

"Oh my God," breathed Hass. "I have to say this is a sight I never thought to see on a submarine. You're not going to need the wire guidance system on the torpedoes, David. You could fire them point blank just by aiming the submarine, or even use those amazing cameras, and the acoustic heads should take them straight into the noise of the screws."

"Yeah, you're right, Hass," murmured Durrand. "That will save time and simplify the system a lot. The wire guides were only needed to get the torpedoes into the general vicinity of the target vessels.

David, I still don't like it, but I have to concede that it seems to work pretty well. What with the high resolution cameras, the DIDSON sonar and this godawful window, we shouldn't have much trouble putting some of our fish right where they'll hurt the most."

Durrand and Hass, the two submariners, looked thoughtful, Mackie had a quietly satisfied smile spreading across his face and Cazaley's whole body was charged with a predatory tingle. Roberts, in contrast, was standing very still, eyes seemingly glazed and out of focus. But he was looking at something. It was the image in his mind's eye of the first torpedo as it sped out of tube one at the head of a long, luminous, bubbling finger of admonition.

*

"Ray, Gus, Gunter, you've got what I hope will only be about two weeks before I'm back and we can make our departure for Igloo." Roberts was speaking with his lieutenants—managers, leaders, commanders? he thought—just prior to boarding a flight for Sydney to hook up with the imminent departure of the *Kontica* for another supply run to the Macquarie Island base. "I'm really pleased with the shakedown of the *Fish*. She's turned out to be better than I could have wished for in her performance and potential, and after more time and more trials, I'm convinced our procedures and operations will smooth out and become very effective and very safe. I'm also convinced, as I hope you are too Gus, that we can operate her easily and effectively with the reduced crew we currently have. When we get to Igloo Base, we will increase the complement with additions from the base crew. Some of them are busting a gut to get aboard.

I want you to attend to the problems and improvements which showed up during the shakedown, and those which will do so with more sea time, as quickly as possible so we can leave when I get back.

Ray, get hold of Bo and try to stock up as many spare torpedoes as you can, dismantle them and pack them off to Sydney in a seatainer as research equipment.

See you guys in a fortnight."

TWENTY TWO

"Oh yes, this is brilliant!" enthused Roberts to the small group showing him around the Igloo base. "You couldn't see where the entrance was until we were right on it and it opened. You guys have done a terrific job!" He was standing on the dockside of an inner mini-harbour fully 120 metres across, with the three engineers, James, Tilley and Halloran. "This lake of course is so we can turn the *Flying Fish* around once she's in and be able to exit bow first. It's an obvious requirement and why the hell didn't I think of it, but it must have taken a lot of extra work and time." Roberts looked chagrinned, but Halloran just chuckled.

"Go easy on yourself David. Yes it was obvious, but we're the experts and none of us had quite the same loads on our plates as you. We've had to make quite a few decisions on the fly as we came across a number of minor problems, but that's why you hired us after all, isn't it?"

"Yeah, you're right of course Kaye. Let's have a look at the rest of the base."

An hour later they were sitting in a large, very well-appointed mess lounge drinking good quality freshly brewed coffee and munching on anzac biscuits, the 15 centimetre round cookies so enjoyed in Australia. Roberts was close to being speechless.

"I know I've been away for a while, and you guys are going to be spun out by the *Flying Fish*, but this base is unbelievable. You've all done a wonderful job, and there'll certainly be bonuses in it for everyone. The comms room is impressive, as is the sick bay and general habitation area."

"That's very nice David, thank you," Halloran tossed off quickly and completely insincerely, "but the only bonus I want is a spot on board. Don't give a bugger where or what."

Roberts burst out laughing. "Christ Kaye, I don't reckon my life would be worth two bob if I didn't include you in the crew!"

"You're bloody right there mate," muttered James, "and that goes for me and Ken too, as well as a lot of other members of the base team."

"No problem, Lou. In fact, there is room aboard due to the modifications we made, and I want all of the operators to train back-ups for their positions anyway. I think we'll be able to fit another dozen or so aboard before we begin hunting."

"God, I love the sound of that." Halloran was radiating the same kind of body language Roberts had seen on the torpedoman, Cazaley, after he'd experienced the sights through the bubble dome.

Shaking his head, but smiling, Roberts told Halloran that he thought he knew just where she'd fit in. Then his smile faded a little.

"So you two working OK together now Ken?" he looked quizzically at Tilley and Halloran.

"Shit yes, David," responded Halloran with a grin, as Tilley nodded comfortably, "Ken's even got a new girlfriend," she chuckled mischievously. Roberts raised an eyebrow at Tilley.

"I've been seeing a bit of one of the nurses, Cheryl Wilkes, but it's not serious. I'm learning." He glanced at Halloran with a completely expressionless face. She laughed and punched his arm.

"And our Chief Medical Officer's jaw? I presume it's healed by now?" At this, Tilley's impassive expression slipped just a little, and what seemed like a small smile, as mischievous as Halloran's giggle, twitched the corners of his mouth.

"Seems to be fine now David. But Kaye may be able to supply more information about it for you." Halloran's expression faltered slightly too. Roberts raised another eyebrow.

"Well shit, David, the man's gorgeous-looking, urbane, cultured—what can I say?"

"How about arrogant, theatrical, perfumed," muttered James.

"I'm surprised that didn't come from you, Ken," smiled Roberts.

"As I said, David, I'm learning."

*

"So what's the worst problem still unsolved, Lou?" Roberts asked James, as the group moved through the general quarters area.

"One of the heat exchangers in a main vent keeps malfunctioning. When it stops, a jet of water vapour shoots up from the pipe about a hundred metres, for all the world like a bloody great geyser. Lasts a good thirty seconds after we close the vent." James was clearly annoyed, if not alarmed. "I've got all the techs working on the thing, but if they can't fix it we'll need a replacement from Sydney."

"OK Lou, it might be best to keep that vent closed until it's right. The base isn't fully staffed yet or working hard, so it shouldn't be a problem."

"There were those two ANARE people we saw on the cliff path two days ago," Tilley reminded the others. "It seems they've made repairs, and they had glasses on the cove, although Gary and Bill on the dredge were playing filmmakers. They walked off after an hour or so."

"We'll worry about the ANARE crowd only when we have to," said Roberts firmly. "How about the people? Anyone seriously unsettled or causing trouble?"

"No David. Surprising, with a large group of disparate people and talents like we have here, but no real strife that I've been aware of. Gary Bradley had us all outside last week in groups, for some firearms practice with pistols and assault rifles, and there were only a couple of conscientious objectors—one of the machinists and the chef. Gary let them off."

"No one managed to hit any of the local wildlife, I hope?" asked Roberts.

James grinned. "No way. Gary was very careful. He fired some pistol rounds off to get all the birds in the air, at which masses of penguins took off into the water as well. Once the cove was clear, he had us firing only at an elevation out over the water, but he drilled us all very well, and got us to 'collect all our brass', as he kept telling us. It was actually quite fun. That MAC 10's a fearsome thing."

"The wildlife here is pretty awesome. My favourites are the elephant seals in the colony we had in the cove." Halloran was back in good spirits. "The buggers seemed to like sleeping on the beach right where we used to come ashore, and we moved them down the cove a bit by firing pistols in the air a few times. It didn't upset them much, but they grumbled and waddled off a few hundred metres. They complain, shake like dirty blancmange and stink to high heaven—they're gorgeous."

"All right gang," Roberts spoke with satisfaction, even excitement. "Holiday time's over. You seem almost ready to go.

Lou, get all the people who have finished their work here packed and ready to go home. We'll leave for Sydney on the *Kontica* in a day or so, and I'll be back in the States by the end of the week. I don't know how long it'll take us to get here, once the *Fish* departs Florida, but we'll try to do it non-stop. I don't want her to be seen by anyone after we sail.

Then we can start hunting. Funny to be planning to go to war, today of all days," mused Roberts.

The others looked at him blankly.

"November 11th? Armistice Day, you thickheads. No history in your souls?"

TWENTY THREE

Roberts was thinking of the day of the first shakedown trial. It had not been one of Florida's nicer days, but all he could remember was his exhilaration and excitement at how *Flying Fish* had performed. But today was different. The sun was dancing on the water, the air warm and clear, even the breeze seemed to have lost its sourness and carried instead the traces of fresh bread and roasting coffee.

"God, she's beautiful!" He was standing on the dockside, staring at the submarine moored alongside. "How come I never noticed before?" She was painted an overall deep royal blue with white trim, her name on each bow below a stylized flying fish. The same logo was painted in white on each side of the sail. Unintentionally, she had been turned into a real eye catcher. "Shame we have to try to keep her out of the spotlight," he murmured. "Must get some footage of her before we take off. There's bound to be one or two amateur photographers aboard."

Later, in the mess, Roberts was talking to Durrand, Mackie and McLeod. "How're our provisions and clearances going guys? Are we nearly ready to go?" He found it difficult to contain a deep-seated eagerness to begin the campaign which had occupied so much of his waking moments for so long. The others grinned at him knowingly, fully understanding his restlessness and drive. "Yeah, OK you smartarses, before this cruise is done I won't be the only crusader aboard," Roberts growled, albeit sheepishly. "Now when can we leave?"

"Anytime you like David," responded Durrand with an innocent shrug. "We've just been relaxing here waiting for you to get back from holiday."

"I see you're learning too, Gus," Roberts looked mildly disgusted. "We can't have that.

All right then, if the *Fish* and her crew are really ready, we'll leave at first light tomorrow morning."

McLeod and Mackie nodded, smiling, but Durrand's expression froze.

"Sorry David, we can't do that. Tomorrow's Friday."

"Tell me you're kidding again, Gus."

"Never more serious, David. No seaman ever leaves port on a major voyage on a Friday. The only thing worse than that would be to leave on a Black Friday."

At that moment Gunter Hass came in to the mess, his face lighting up with pleasure at seeing his friend again. "Hi David, I heard you'd arrived back. It's good to see you again."

As the two men shook hands, Roberts said to Hass, a touch of exasperation in his voice, "G'day Gunter, you too. But explain to me why we can't set sail tomorrow."

Hass was mildly surprised. "Well of course not David—tomorrow's Friday." He opened his hands palm out, as if no further word would be necessary.

"What is the matter with you two?" Roberts' face had darkened, his voice now hard and uncompromising. "This is bullshit! If I say we sail at ohlighthundred tomorrow morning, that's when we bloody leave!"

Hass took his arm soothingly. "David, my friend, please sit down. I can see you are angry, and it happens too rarely for us to take lightly, but there is something here that you also should think upon. I remember we spoke once before about omens, and you said at the time you had no use for them, that you always made your own luck. But you need to understand that there are no more superstitious people in the world than sailors. All those who venture onto the sea are affected both by fascination and dread in equal measures. Even the hardest of heads and the coolest of minds will pour a libation to Neptune once on a voyage.

If you insist on departing tomorrow, Gus and I will be only two of the regular seamen who won't be aboard." Durrand nodded slightly in agreement.

"Jesus, it's a bloody mutiny," Roberts shook his head resignedly. "OK, can we please leave Saturday?"

*

That evening the whole crew was at dinner in the mess, enjoying a simple but beautifully prepared meal of roasted Australian lamb with wine-dark gravy, mint sauce and baked vegetables. As the slower diners were winding down, Roberts got to his feet.

"Listen up please, everyone. Our departure will be 0600 Saturday, so use tomorrow to do what you need to do before taking off on what may be a long term voyage. I'm sure you've had a lot of rubbernecks down here, and some photos of the *Fish* have been taken and published, but everyone still thinks we're a research vessel heading north. Try to keep it that way please. But if there are any keen photographers on board please feel free to get some record of the *Fish* before we sail.

We will do our best to keep out of sight, but we may need to call in at one of the more isolated ports on the route, although definitely not Cape Town. We are heading for our base in the Southern Ocean, called Igloo. It's cold, wet and windy most of the year, but very comfortable inside—you'll have everything there you want and that's all you need to know about it at present.

Any last minute requirements, see your friendly purser."

*

Saturday afternoon the weather was more Floridan than Chicagoan, and *Flying Fish* was cruising at 15 knots into a light easterly breeze, pushing the small swell and wind waves aside without effort, but sending the resulting spray back over the bridge in lacy curtains of sparkle. It was like a light show for a rock concert, as the dispersing spray picked up the sunlight and diffracted it into continuous rainbows, and the people on the bridge simply enjoyed the sweetness of the experience. They were over a hundred nautical miles offshore and heading due east.

"Bridge, this is sonar. I have a surface vessel tracking us at ten miles astern, and a submarine at twelve miles, both on our heading. The surface vessel is approximately 20,000 tons, and the submarine is an Ohio class." Tomlinson's disembodied voice came clearly through all lapel units.

"Thanks Rick. Stand by," Durrand acknowledged, turning to Roberts, who had exclaimed quietly at the sonar operator's information.

"Are we being shadowed, Gus?" he asked Durrand in some surprise.

"Well hell, David, you didn't think Uncle Sam would let us go without waving goodbye?" Durrand's smile held knowledge gained over a long period of naval experience. "There will also be a couple of planes keeping an eye on us, and we'll surely be tracked by satellite until they lose interest. After all, David, as innocuous as we may be, the *Fish* is still a vessel of war, and the US retains a strong interest in such things, particularly within her own backyard."

"OK, fair enough. Let's keep this heading until we're a thousand nautical miles off Miami, then turn south-east to head for the Cape. While this weather is so good, we can remain on the surface. Could we allow all the crew to spend some time up here, in groups of three or four, to enjoy the moment?"

"Sure, good idea David. I'll get them up."

Roberts turned to Hass, who had been standing quietly on the starboard bridge, wrapped in his own thoughts, an expression of total contentment on his weathered old face. "Don't think you managed to put one over me, you old sea dog. I had a long talk with Dorothy yesterday evening, and that's the reason you're still aboard. I told her I couldn't guarantee your safety, but that I'd care for you like I would my own father, which seemed to satisfy her."

Hass smiled, quite unable to speak for a moment. His eyes glistening, he said very quietly to Roberts, "David, I doubt anyone could understand just what you have done for me with your special project. I too talked to my Dorothy for a long time, and she assured me that she knew what this voyage meant to me, and that she was happy for me to take it. So, my friend, you have my heartfelt gratitude, and my promise that I will earn my keep and not burden you in any way."

Durrand coughed, looked slightly pained, but said nothing. Then, "Once everyone's had some time up here, David, we can submerge and cruise on the snorkel to see how it goes."

Roberts quirked an eyebrow, nodding. "Sounds like a good idea, Gus."

*

"Council of war time, guys." Four days later, Durrand, Hass and Mackie were all squeezed in to Roberts' cabin, as the submarine cruised south-east at twenty feet and fifteen knots under main diesels, the snorkel breathing device bringing fresh air in from the surface.

"Firstly, Gus," said Roberts, "I want you to write up the log to reflect that although you are the captain, I am the owner and master of the *Flying Fish*, and as such will be solely responsible for whatever occurs during the life of our project. Only I will be able to give the order to fire a torpedo. I don't know whether that will provide any worthwhile protection in an international court, but it's the best I can do.

Secondly, exactly what are we going to do in the Southern Ocean?" he asked the group. They all appeared a little surprised by the question.

"Well shit, David, we're going to go looking for any pirate fishing and whaling ships we can find," said Mackie, as though the question didn't need asking.

"OK Ray," smiled Roberts, "we come up on a whaling group, factory ship and catchers, and ask them what they're doing. If they even bother to reply, they will simply say they are engaged in the pursuit of their legal quota of minkes, and tell us to fuck off. And at that stage they actually may be telling the truth. All we'll have done will be to show them who we are. The longliners and tuna boats would do the same—protest their innocence and say they were catching their quota, again only if they bothered to reply. After all, we couldn't identify ourselves, and if we did we wouldn't have any legal authority.

See what I'm getting at?"

"Yeah, I hadn't thought that far ahead," frowned Mackie.

"Well then, David," smiled Hass gently, "what are you planning?"

"We're going to need some good intelligence, which is why I've had a well-equipped communications room established at Igloo Base. I intend to have some quiet talks with certain people in Sea Shepherd, as well as one or two in the Australian fishing industry. That way, we'll be able to target the boats that really are fishing illegally. Of course, any activity we find within or near any of the exclusion zones will be fair game.

You guys are probably not aware of this, but a few years ago in Perth, West Australia, the trial of the crew of a captured pirate toothfishing boat, the *Viarsa*, finished with a predictable 'not guilty' verdict. It took a hot pursuit through the Southern Ocean of a month, millions of taxpayers' dollars and well over two years of legal gymnastics to cause the owners to lose no sleep at all. It was nothing more than a minor inconvenience. The pirates have everything on their side—they simply change the names of their vessels and their countries of registration at will, offload catches at friendly ports, deny everything if caught up with and questioned, and hire expensive silks if ever brought to trial. They even 'fish launder' their catches at sea, by transferring them to other ships." Roberts was speaking calmly, almost mildly, although the others were in no doubt about his convictions.

"Then there're the players in the Southern Bluefin tuna fishing industry—mostly Australia, New Zealand and Japan. It used to be that most tuna found its way into cans. But for more than twenty years the real money's been in sashimi, to the point that eighty percent of the tuna catch is now eaten by Japan. A full-grown adult fish can be over two metres and two hundred kilos, and can fetch more than the price of a luxury car in a Japanese market. So because it's the major consumer, Japan's become the major catcher. Some of its fishing boats aren't really boats any more. They're massive floating factories, setting long lines of a hundred kilometres and tearing the shit out of the tuna population. And of the populations of sharks, other fish species, and albatross. Tens of thousands of birds every year. Greenpeace claims that Japan has illegally caught six billion dollars worth of tuna in the past twenty years." Roberts shook his head slightly, remembering Angie explaining 'by-catch' to him that day back in Ulladulla he began to come alive.

"Is there no one doing anything about this problem?" asked Hass curiously.

"Greenpeace does what it always does. Protests and raises awareness as much as possible. Sea Shepherd does the same, but generally takes more direct action. It confiscates any long lines it comes across without proper identification or if the lines have caught other species or birds. And now, of course, they're throwing stink bombs at the whaling vessels. But officially? The Commission for the Conservation of Southern Bluefin Tuna, the CCSBT, is supposed to be managing the agreement between the three countries. It's held many conventions and meetings and produced mission statements and position papers by the metric ton, as you'd expect from any self-respecting qango. But effective? It's become the self-proliferating biomass that the tuna population used to be and now isn't any more.

But I began this project with one aim in mind—to stop as much whaling as I could. That's why we're going to shoot at any whale catchers or factory ships we find, no matter where they are with their bloody quotas. I could care less about their so-called scientific studies—there haven't been a hell of a lot of scientific papers come out of Japan or Norway during the past decade or so, and those that have appeared aren't worth the paper they came on.

So they're all going to be targets—no matter who they are or how many whales they're still allowed to catch! Fuck 'em!" The calm had vanished along with the mild voice. His face had darkened with a no-compromise expression that clearly came straight from the heart.

The others all wore smiles of varying widths.

"Bring it on!" grinned Durrand.

TWENTY FOUR

Early in the morning of November 27th, within a few hundred metres of the meridian of 30° W longitude, the *Flying Fish* crossed the Equator, but although conditions were flat calm and hot, perfect for a Crossing the Line ceremony, Roberts decided to remain submerged and continue on course. He ignored the grumbles, telling Durrand this was one superstition he was going to stare down, and bugger Neptune if he didn't like it.

"Back in the days of the square riggers, when the only entertainment was what the crew made themselves, the Line crossings were a highlight. But nowadays the crew has access to CDs, DVDs, MP3 devices, Blackberries, Iphones, Ipads, Kindles and satellite TV, apart from the extensive on-board book library. And the workout room. So I don't think maintaining morale is the same problem it used to be." Roberts was laying down some definite ideas in the mess to some of the crew who had raised the subject of the Line crossing.

"What we will stop for in a day or two will be a test firing of our first torpedo. Carl is building a floating contraption from oil drums and planks, and the electronics techs will install a waterproof device in a suspended tank to broadcast the sound of turning propellers.

And Gunter has convinced Gus to drill the crew in rigging for a depth charge attack. Probably not a bad idea—you never know what we may come up against when we start shooting."

*

"Very satisfying," murmured Roberts. He, Durrand, Mackie and McLeod were on the bridge two days later watching as their first torpedo slammed straight into Wojinski's barge and blew it apart with a thump and a waterspout. "Cazaley fired it a little off line, and it homed in nicely on the sound. What did you guys think of the explosion? Not too big? I don't want to blow the sterns off any ships and risk sinking them, but I do want to badly damage propellers and rudders."

The others all agreed the size of the explosion was about right. "But we'll only be able to judge accurately by field testing," grinned the big purser.

Roberts stared through binoculars at the patch of white water half a kilometre off the bow of *Flying Fish*. It had spread out into a large pancake, and it was clearly not something that should have been there. It was an intrusion upon that place and order, and he had the thought that he was about to introduce an unknown factor into the environmental equation of the Southern Ocean—a factor containing the combined energies of about fifty committed people, the *Flying Fish* and a number of carefully aimed torpedoes. During his corporate days with XTRO he had never doubted his decision making, but right at this moment he found himself wondering at the enormity of what he was planning to accomplish. He didn't break out in a sweat, but it was unexpected enough to be a shock to his confidence. He knew with the more familiar pragmatism usually close to the surface of his reasoning that he would continue his quest, but was almost fascinated to observe this apparent chink in his resolve. 'Shit,' he thought, 'a bloody quest? Is that what this is? Are we all knights in a large, submersible suit of royal blue armour, out to do good deeds for God, queen and country?' This thought produced an inaudible nasal snort of self-deprecation, slight enough to be unnoticed by the others, but sufficient to shake himself away from the odd uncertainty that had crept around him like the cold air from an open freezer door. He shivered.

"We're still in the tropics, but there's a cool breeze coming from somewhere," Mackie noted.

*

Steering 135°, *Flying Fish* drove steadily on through November and into December at an average cruising speed of twelve knots. She passed Cape Town over 350 nautical miles offshore, moving comfortably from the South Atlantic Ocean into the cold, windswept reaches of the Southern Ocean, running at depth when storm fronts came through. Although summer, this was a part of the world that could be monumentally indifferent to influence from the seasons. Sometimes a ferocious squall would hurtle down on the surface-cruising submarine, and diving to a hundred feet until it passed was the most comfortable and efficient action to take. Gradually, she came around to a course of 095°, passing south of Prince Edward Island and aiming to head between Kerguelen and Heard Islands. They saw no signs of any whalers, and Roberts realised he would have to rely on intelligence from his sources to come to grips with his targets.

Xmas Day, and a huge meal of turkey and trimmings saved for the occasion by chef Richard Flanagan, was spent somewhere near 50°S, 100°E in the quiet and comfort of fifteen fathoms of water. Many of the crew had bonded into friendships, some had remained aloof and alone, and self-proclaimed geek Clarence Grimshaw had indeed learned some moves from McLeod that put a bounce in his step.

"Better watch yourself, Clarrie, or you'll be turning into a terminator." The strong tones, heavily coated with a Scottish overlay, were amused. Janice Mackenzie was the hydraulic and pneumatic engineer, a short stocky woman in a blue boiler suit with cut off sleeves. It could have been a working uniform, but looked more like something from a designer boutique for activists. Mackenzie could have been 35 or she could have been 45. She kept her fair hair very short and wore no visible makeup, which all added up to a quite nondescript appearance; however, a careful observer would have noticed a fine balance to her features and a sparkling intelligence in her hooded blue eyes.

"Oh you're just smitten with my body," laughed Grimshaw.

"Not unless you're about to undergo a sex-change operation darling," snorted Mackenzie. "At the moment you're just not my type."

Grimshaw stopped laughing, then chuckled to cover his embarrassment.

"Oh. Er, sorry," he stammered.

"God Clarrie, this is the 21st century. Haven't you met a real live dyke before? You and I are very much the same, you know—we both like pretty girls." Mackenzie was grinning at Grimshaw, openly enjoying his discomfort, and she chuckled throatily as he turned and walked swiftly back into the workout room.

In the mess, many of the crew were relaxing, enjoying the drill-free day and the advanced electronics which allowed the vessel to remain on course, speed and depth automatically, albeit with some crew members on stand-by watch. The marine diesel engineer, Agostino Cabrillo, a short dark and furry little Italian-American, asked the favorite question of the day. "When do we get there skipper?"

"Well Aggie, if we maintain our average cruising speed and don't hit any icebergs, we should be at Igloo base by January second," Durrand said with a thoughtful expression.

"Icebergs!" Cabrillo was startled. "How do we know where they are? Can we see them on radar?"

"Relax Aggie," Durrand laughed, "I'm only kidding. It's summertime, and there aren't any bergs this far north. We're quite safe. David was right, it's easy to kid Americans."

"I'm Italian," scowled Cabrillo.

"Couple generations ago, maybe," grinned Durrand. "Now you're as Italian as I am."

TWENTY FIVE

The unpleasant patch of water between Tasmania and New Zealand was nobody's favourite sea. As ill-tempered as the early Dutch navigator who also gave his name to Tasmania, the Tasman Sea was usually grey and annoyingly lumpy. Today, however, the sun was shining and things were easy. The *Kronos* had been driving south into a surprisingly placid Tasman for the past nine hours, ahead of a wake that could have been ruled by a celestial navigator with a heavenly parallel, so straight was it. A white, gently widening slash across the deep blue of the strangely quiet water, it was being carved by the powerful jet motor of the thirty-metre aluminium and fiberglass craft named not for a music group, or a science fiction hero, or even an ancient mythological god, but for one of Australia's prehistoric marine megafauna called Kronosaurus. It was a boat with a difference, for the main central hull was flanked on opposite sides by large outriggers containing living quarters for the crew of eleven. It had a top speed of forty-two knots, and was currently cruising at thirty-five, due to the benign state of the sea. It was painted a startling, all-over bright red.

'Even the Tasman can enjoy summer at times', thought Callie Fraser, as she swept her eyes over the slave instruments on the dashboard of her elevated steering station—compass heading, speed, engine revs and fuel situation.

"How soon before we raise the whalers, Neville?" she asked the navigator, Neville Ray. He was an old sea dog, grey, grizzled and fifty-seven, but he had been with Callie as her navigator on the last eight Sydney-Hobart yacht races, and was happiest with his head down and nose buried in his instrument array in the nav. station. He was never seasick.

"At this rate, Callie, we should raise the two chasers in thirty-two minutes, give or take. The mother ship is a further thirty miles south." Callie, fit, strong, capable and one hundred and eighty centimetres tall, was the master of this unusual vessel, due to her experience as a lifelong mariner and her history in the previous thirteen Sydney-Hobarts, in all of which she had competed and in two of which she had been on the winning yacht. But it wasn't only her blue-water credentials which had landed her the command of the *Kronos.* For many years now Callie had been a lecturer in marine biology at the University of New South Wales, and had become well-known for her stance on the need for marine conservation, with a particular focus on the whaling industry that was no longer supposed to exist. Although a blue-water sailor, she eagerly accepted the offer of command of the power boat *Kronos* because it was a vessel capable of joining the campaign against the Japanese whalers being fought by Sea Shepherd on the *Steve Irwin*.

"All hands ready, Joe?" she queried the vessel's bosun, Joe Karpas.

"They will be by the time we reach the whalers", he grinned, showing a mounting excitement. "They're just giving all the cameras a final check, along with the stink bombs." Stink bombs were about the only type of ordnance the protesters were able to hit the whalers with. They were fashioned professionally by combining a solution of silicone infused with hydrogen sulphide gas and mixed with some thinners, then sealed into large, emptied floodlight bulbs. They would break when thrown at almost any surface and splatter it with the sticky concoction that smelled bad enough to cause vomiting.

"OK. Make sure that everyone on deck is securely harnessed to the safety lines before we close with the whalers. You know how crazy it can get out here when we're shepherding." Callie was referring to the actions of the *Kronos* when she was darting around the whalers at high speed, harrying them away from the whales they were attempting to harpoon.

The war against the whalers had been running for some years, and it was fair to say that the whaling companies were no longer indifferent to the conservationists. They ensured that all their whaling vessels had the word "RESEARCH" painted in large white letters on both sides, and drove their boats aggressively near the protesters, firing powerful water cannons at them when in range. It was also fair to say, however, that they still took as many whales each season as they chose, and if some of them were species other than minkes, then that was simply an unfortunate case of mistaken identity. The protest campaign had begun with Greenpeace trying to raise public awareness about the illegal whaling that was occurring, but the whaling companies had their own publicity machines that countered all the arguments from protest groups and political pronouncements and even the multitude of motions resulting from each succeeding IWC meeting. Basically, the whalers kept repeating their mantra of "We only catch minkes, we only take our quotas and the whales are all for research purposes".

It was also true to observe that where once the protest campaign had been exciting, morally uplifting and great fun, especially when chasing the chasers in small runabouts and capturing graphic photos of harpooned whales bleeding into the sea and being dragged up the ramp of a mother ship to be butchered, latterly it had become something darker. There was more of a grim determination about the protesters these days, an obsession to do everything they could to stop the whalers from taking any whales at all, let alone their quotas. The *Steve Irwin* had hit some of the chasers, shunting them off course without causing terminal damage, and volunteers had been encouraged to board some of the whalers at sea and make token arrests. Things were getting more serious. There was more danger present now.

"We're all set now Callie", said one of the deck hands, Robert Fenwick, poking his head into the wheelhouse. "How soon will we raise the whalers?"

"They should be coming into view about now, Bob, and we should be up with them in a few minutes. Stand by." A shout from on deck caused Fenwick to hurry out, and he called to Callie that they could now clearly see two whalers off the port bow. She altered course to port a fraction, and eased the *Kronos* back to twenty knots, steering for a point of interception with the leading chaser. Within minutes the trailing whaler turned hard to port and ran straight at *Kronos*, but Callie, smoothly caressing the steering joystick and throttle lever, swept her vessel around to starboard and cut behind the chaser, skipping easily through her wake and arcing around to port to run down the leading whaler, which they now saw was chasing a whale. Pushing the throttle open, Callie tore down the starboard side of the chaser, close enough for two of the deck hands to throw stink bombs on to her deck, and pulled over to port just ahead of the chaser's bow. She cut back her speed and maintained station some twenty metres ahead of the chaser, and began to slow. She was confident the chaser wouldn't ram her stern, as there were three more crew members taking videos of the action. The whale pulled ahead of the *Kronos* and dived, hopefully to sound and stay away from the whalers.

The high, sharp bow of the chaser advanced on the stern of the *Kronos,* not slowing appreciably, until the gun platform was almost over her stern rail. Two deckies were clipped to the rail, taking videos of the chaser, their cameras pointing steeply upwards as the bow arched over them. The little Japanese gunner behind the harpoon was either grinning or snarling at them, aiming his menacing weapon right at them. Callie, watching closely, yelled at them to hang on, and shoved the throttle sharply forward. The *Kronos* responded with a surge of power, digging her stern in to the water and accelerating away from the threatening bows of the whaler. 'God', she thought, 'I think she really would have rammed us!'

"Hey Callie", Joe said as he came into the wheelhouse, "that was a bit too close! It looked to me as though they were actually trying to hit us." He seemed to be more curious than worried, due probably to the superior speed and manoeuvreability of the *Kronos.*

Callie conned the vessel around in a wide starboard arc, easing down on the throttle to an idle. The other crew members came into the large midships wheelhouse, chattering excitedly about the successful shepherd, and the proximity of the whaler.

"They wouldn't actually have hit us, would they Callie?" asked one of the professional photographers, Suzanne Olsen, along for the opportunity of making a film for the promotion of marine environmental awareness.

"No, Sue, I don't think so", said Callie, quite sure in her own mind that that was exactly what the whaler intended. "We have the legs of anything out here at the moment anyway," she assured the young woman.

As if to underscore the old adage that you can never take anything on the ocean for granted, the large diesel powering the water jet suddenly coughed throatily and died, leaving a silence accentuated by the hiss of the water down the hulls and the distant rumble of the whale chasers as they circled.

The engineer, Jake Lowe, thrust his head up from the engine room hatch. “Callie, sorry but I just shut her down for a while. I noticed some water in the main fuel filter glass, and I need to bleed the lines before it gets into the injectors and burns them out. Buggered if I know how we suddenly got water in the tank. It'll only take me about ten minutes. OK?”

For some reason Callie felt a small sense of disquiet, but kept it to herself. “Sure Jake, get it done as quick as you can, eh? The chasers may be on to other whales soon.”

Lowe disappeared down the hatch, and some of the crew went on deck to watch the whalers. Callie, Joe and Stuart Symes, an experienced diver and underwater cameraman, poured themselves cups of coffee from the espresso machine attached to the forward bulkhead.

“Joe, I'm not sure what it is, but something feels different out here today,” Callie said thoughtfully.

“Yeah, I'm getting it too, Callie. How the hell did we get water in our fuel?”

“Don't know, but it couldn't have got there by accident,” she slowly shook her head, causing the mass of dark auburn curls framing her pretty, oval face to flutter as if in a breeze.

Sue Olsen poked her head in the wheelhouse doorway. “Callie, those two chasers are heading our way. They're about a kilometre off at the moment.” She looked worried.

“Thanks Sue. I'll keep an eye on them.” Callie appeared calm and in control, but she was now filled with a real sense of something very wrong occurring. “What's Neil doing on the bow?” Neil Jancey, one of the older mechanics, had slipped his snap shackle from the safety line and was climbing on to the bow rail.

"Neil, get down!" she yelled through the partly-opened wheelhouse windscreen. "Jesus, he's gone in! What the hell?"

"He didn't fall in Callie—he jumped!" Joe shouted. He raced out and up to the bow, where the mechanic could be seen swimming away from the *Kronos* as fast as his orange life vest and yellow wet weather gear would allow.

"Joe! The chasers!" Sue Olsen was clearly frightened now, for both whalers were maintaining their heading straight for the *Kronos*, which was still dead in the water. Their high bow waves showed an increase in their speed, and they were now only a matter of three hundred metres off and closing fast.

"Jake!" Callie yelled down the engine room hatch, "get the motor going! Now!"

"Another minute, Callie!" he shouted.

"Too late," she said quite calmly. "Neville, get a mayday out! Fast as you can!"

"Nooo!"

"You murdering bastards!"

"Mayday, mayday, mayday, this is the *Kronos* in the northern Tasman. We are about to be rammed by Japanese whalers. Our position is 41° 20'S, 163 °11'E and we are . . ."

The two whalers, only twenty metres apart, were thundering down on the stricken vessel, engines roaring, bow waves crashing, but no gunners in sight. The tiny figure of the swimming Neil Jancey was ploughed under by the starboard whaler, just before both boats rammed at full speed into the *Kronos*. With a dreadful sound of rending metal and tearing fiberglass, they drove straight through the sections of what had seconds before been a beautiful red vessel, their screws chewing up the debris into small pieces, most of which sank immediately. The chasers eased their speed down, turning in a wide circle to inspect what was left. There were no signs of any survivors, and only shattered remains of bulkheads, a wooden first aid box and two unbroken stink bombs. There was the beginning of a large diesel slick flattening the sea surface around the bits of wreckage, and what looked like some bloodstains in the water. Nothing else.

The *Kronos* and all her crew had vanished as though a celestial delete key had been pressed. The physical remnants of their existence were also disappearing, and the only witnesses to the violence of their ending were the Japanese whalers that had caused it.

TWENTY SIX

The inhabitants of Igloo had been alerted that the submarine was about to arrive, and every one of them had gathered on the landing dock to watch for her.

"Hope they won't have any trouble finding their way inside." Bill Babb was speaking quietly to Gary Bradley, both men standing on the dock inside the main doors to the Igloo base.

"I just hope they can find the base—it's a grey old day outside, and fair pissing down," said Bradley.

"Don't worry," Babb assured him, "they have the GPS coordinates of the entry passage to within a metre, and the high res cameras all round the bows should let them con the sub in visually. Mark told me a while back they were less than half an hour out, so they should nearly be here." The base radio operator, Anthony 'Mark' Coney, had been keeping a listening watch for the *Flying Fish* for the last three days, and had been advising the twenty people left in Igloo of updated arrival times. Coney's nickname was always going to be unavoidable, but in truth he would have accepted almost anything that effectively replaced Tony Coney—sometimes parents just didn't get it. All twenty, plus most of the complement of the *Kontica*, were now gathered on the dock waiting expectantly for the submarine to appear. The Igloo's main door had been raised to its full height, but even though it was mid-morning, visibility was no more than twenty metres outside.

Suddenly, a long dark cigar-shaped shadow appeared inside the main door and glided easily into the floodlit water of the base harbour, accompanied by a muted growling noise which echoed resonantly around the dock area. The surface of the water broke into a swirling, heaving mass of turbulence as the glistening blue submarine stopped its forward motion and rose into view near the dock. As the sail emerged, water cascading down and around it, the large white flying fish logo emblazoned on its side seemed almost to flash with internal lighting. The watchers on the dock were stunned into silence at the dramatic sight.

"Now that's what I call an entrance," murmured Lawrence Prescott.

Two sailors clambered out of the hatch and down on to the decks. Lines were thrown and she was hauled hard alongside; a minute later whistles and yells reverberated around the dock as Roberts poked his head out through the hatch and waved down from the bridge.

"Give us an hour to get squared away, then we'll all meet in the mess for lunch and a briefing," he called to Lou James, a huge grin on his face.

*

During lunch each person, including Chris Sanders and the crew of the *Kontica*, had stood and introduced themselves, and the full group then went off to tour the base. Roberts realised the intense interest the base people had in checking out the submarine, so he asked Durrand to take them all aboard when the sub crew had finished inspecting the base facilities. He then called the command group into the conference room.

"Gus will be here shortly, and you guys can all tour the *Fish* later, after she's been turned around and squared away. Right now I want to make sure we're preparing properly for our first hunting trip. Lou, I want you to ensure that every base member chooses a submarine station to train on as back-up for the first crew." He grinned at Kaye Halloran. "I think I know who wants to become the world's first torpedowoman." Halloran smiled sweetly back, but with a fierce glint in her eyes.

"Yeah, she's been pestering me a lot lately about getting aboard," James laughed. "Some of the people will slot nicely into the same role as they have on the base, like the chef, mess steward, medical people, radio man, and I guess Gary Bradley will join that outsized purser as an assistant ordnance trainer."

"Try to organize two complete shifts, because I want one shift to remain at the base during each trip, as a precaution," Roberts said thoughtfully.

"As a precaution against what, David?" asked Ken Tilley curiously.

"I'm afraid that sooner or later we are going to become public, and the base may even be discovered. We may need to defend ourselves from whoever it is that appears first, depending on their identities and objectives. They may be semi-friendly, or they may be very hostile. We have to be ready for whatever comes. Everyone engaged on the campaign needs to be aware of the possibility they may become involved in violent action at some time in the near future." Roberts spoke slowly and earnestly, and the group was quiet for a few moments, each beginning to realise that exciting adventure could so easily change into danger and death.

"I think we need a lot more weapons training, David," Halloran mused quietly. Her smile had disappeared, but not the glint in her eyes.

"That will be a large part of what our training routine will become, Kaye," said Roberts. "Lets go and have a look at our new boat."

*

A few days later, Roberts was taking his leave from the group, as the *Kontica* made ready to return to Sydney. Both base and boat crews were becoming familiar with each others' domains, and McLeod and Bradley were arranging regular training sessions with all the available ordnance.

"While I'm away, Lou, I want you and Gus to coordinate practice runs out in the *Fish* with the regular crew and both shifts of back-ups. Go out every day, but if a whaler blunders into your path, under no circumstances are you to move against it. Follow it and film it, but keep your distance."

"What are you going to be doing, David?"

"I plan to meet some people who might be able to help us find our targets more easily," he replied. "See you all in a couple of weeks."

*

Not long after his return to Sydney, Roberts was in earnest conference in a suite in the Sydney Hilton with a half dozen fascinated listeners, one of whom was the outspoken Morgan Hendry, CEO of Westral Fisheries. Some of the others were representatives of Greenpeace and a large South Australian tuna fishing company. The last member was a man who may have been connected to the Sea Shepherd group, although not admitting as much.

"So gentlemen, as you can imagine, I'm not able to disclose very much in the way of concrete information, but I can say that my special projects group is now in a position to take positive affirmative action against any whaling or pirate fishing vessels we come across in the Southern Ocean. We will, therefore, be grateful for assistance in locating said vessels, which is the reason for this meeting. All we require is information, as current as possible, on the coordinates of any vessels engaged in whaling operations, or any pirate fishing boats setting longlines in restricted areas, or any tuna boats you suspect are catching more than their quotas. Be genuine and accurate about this, gentlemen, for I can assure you that any vessels you point us at will be admonished with significant prejudice."

"Boy," said Hendry, eyes gleaming, voice as compelling as always, "I'd love to know what you're on about. But whatever it is, count me and my company right in!"

There were murmurs of agreement from the others around the table, especially the man who may have been from Sea Shepherd, and the talk then revolved around the logistics of transferring the information to the radio base at Igloo.

"Just what and where the hell is this Igloo, David?" asked Hendry curiously.

"Arnold, if I told you that I'd have to kill you, as they say," smiled Roberts. "Just trust me that it's a viable proposition, and that you'll see very quick results."

TWENTY SEVEN

Once again, all hands were gathered in the base mess over dinner, and Roberts was addressing them, every part of his body language, expression and voice conveying a suppressed excitement.

"I've had word from the Australian contacts that a Japanese whaling group is right now heading into the Southern Ocean to begin operations. There's a large factory ship and two or three chasers. It will take us about five days cruising to get to where they should be, so we'll be leaving early tomorrow morning. Make sure the *Fish* is fully provisioned for a lengthy voyage. We could be out for a while, depending on the information we receive.

Time to see if all the training you've been doing has been effective."

'Time to find out if it's all actually going to work,' he thought.

*

One week later, after a two thousand nautical mile fast cruise WNW, the submarine had surfaced and picked up the whaling group on radar.

"Looks like a small boat messing about in the middle of things too, skipper," an animated Rick Tomlinson called to Durrand.

"Thanks Rick. Marty, give us a course to the largest ship in the group—it has to be the factory ship, then come up on it like we've practised, from astern and to starboard."

About twenty minutes later the *Flying Fish* was moving slowly on station astern of the Japanese factory ship *Kishin Maru*. Roberts, inside the bubble, called to Durrand.

"Gus, it looks like a Zodiac is right in the thick of things—no, hang on, they seem to be moving away to the east. Marty, come left a touch. Herb, ready tube one?"

"Tube one ready," came Cazaley's tense but quick reply.

"Fire one!" shouted Roberts, and as soon as he saw the silver spear shoot from the bows, shouted again "hard right, Martin!"

Only a few seconds later there was a muffled thump both heard and felt through the submarine as a minor tremor.

"Gus, come round and get pictures of the damage."

As the *Fish* came back on a parallel course to the stricken whaling ship, Roberts and Mackie had a clear view of the large rudder, blown over to port and tangled up with the twisted wreckage of the starboard propeller.

"Perfect!" breathed Roberts. "The strength of those grenades in the heads is spot on. The rudder's not moving, and neither is that propeller. With luck the shaft snapped as well. She isn't going to process any whales for a while. They'll all have to piss off to wherever they came from for repairs, and if they come back, we'll hit them again.

All hands, that was a direct hit. The ship is seriously disabled and will have to be towed somewhere for repairs—somewhere a long ways off, and the chasers will have to go with her. Well done all!"

Shouts and whistles echoed around the submarine, and there were some exuberant high-fives slapped, for it was the first engagement and their first 'kill'.

OK Gus, set a course for Heard Island at good cruising speed and issue a grog ration to all hands."

*

A week later found the *Flying Fish* cruising slowly in a wide circle around 55°S, 80°E. Roberts had just received an update via Rick Tomlinson in the radio room and was conferring with Durrand, Blake and Hass.

"The intel suggests that the pirate vessel won't be here for another couple of days, and the weather up top is unusually fine and clear at present, so if you agree Gus, we'll grab some surface time and air out the boat."

"OK David. What have you got planned for this pirate?"

"Yes, I too am curious about our next move, David," said Gunter Hass. "The action against the Japanese vessel was so successful I'm looking forward to seeing what else we can manage."

"If it is indeed a longliner after toothfish, as our information has it, he probably knows his spots and will set his number one line in about 140 fathoms over a sea mount and move off to set another some miles away. While he's gone, we'll test our bow shears on the anchor lines. If they work as they should, the net will sink to the bottom and the buoys will start drifting. He will at some point notice from the changing GPS coordinates that his buoys are moving, and come racing back to investigate. At that time he'll get surprise number two," Roberts said grimly.

"A torpedo up the backside," chuckled Blake.

"Oh dear, how quickly we become bloodthirsty," Roberts opined, shaking his head in resignation.

"Now I know you're kidding me, Mr Roberts," smiled Blake.

"Well done Martin. The next step is to put one over on Ray Mackie. You manage that and you'll have arrived."

*

Early morning on the 12th dawned brilliantly, with a light breeze and small swell topping the wonderful blue of really deep water with what was almost a dainty covering of ruffles. Visibility was as clear as grandmother's old cut lead crystal vases, and the air, incisively cold and tangy, was fresher than anyone really had a right to enjoy, thought Roberts, as he lounged on the bridge of the submarine. Suddenly, Tomlinson spoke urgently into his lapel mike, and Roberts began sliding down through the hatch as he listened to Tomlinson's message.

"I'm detecting radar emissions from a vessel about 40 miles away; I'm sure it's him. Our profile has to be lower than his, and I'm sure our radar is of better quality, as it's about the best you can get, so he won't know we're here yet." The words tumbled out in a rush from the wired Tomlinson, and in spite of himself Roberts grinned, infected with the radio man's excitement.

"I'm sure you're right, Rick," he said. "Gus, would you please take her down and stand by until we see where he's going to set his line?"

By noon the fishing boat was about five miles to port and had commenced laying its longline in a northerly direction. Durrand risked a periscope shot and was able to read her name—the *Salvona*. After an hour she was hull down, still setting the line. When she had disappeared completely over the horizon, Roberts moved into the bubble and began to con the submarine slowly towards the near set of buoys holding one end of the longline. He opened the shears on the bow to their maximum width of nearly three metres and brought the *Fish* slowly towards the cable stretching from the buoys on the surface down to the deep-set line and its anchors. It disappeared into the deep blue at an angle of about 40°, and Roberts rotated the shears until they were perpendicular to it.

"Come right a bit Marty," he murmured into his microphone, "and keep her at dead slow. More right, now." This sharply and a bit louder. "Shit," he swore, "we've missed it. Stop and reverse for a moment. The line is bent around the starboard bow plane." The submarine moved slowly backwards, and Roberts conned it forward once more.

"Ah, that's better. All stop, Marty. The line is in the shears. Here goes." Roberts toggled the switch controlling the jaw movement and the shears severed the 50mm cable as if it wasn't there, the end snaking away into the gloom.

"Great," called Roberts. "The cutter went through the cable like a hot knife through a block of Watsonia butter. Let's move up to the other set of buoys, chop them off and wait for the reaction."

*

An hour later, the *Flying Fish* was moving slowly away from the now-floating buoys that had recently been attached to the other end of the longline, 30 km to the north. The cable had been cut just as easily, this time on the first pass, and the crew was waiting for the reaction from the *Salvona*.

"Mr Roberts, why are we bothering with the longline? Why not just hit the fishing boat?" The pilot, Martin Blake, was asking Roberts the same question other crew members had been pondering.

"We could have gone straight for the *Salvona*, Martin, but I want the word to get around that none of their gear is now safe. The 30km longline is very valuable financially, but that's not the main point. It's their primary piece of equipment, not easily replaced, and I want them and others to know we can take it from them whenever we decide to. My belief is that it's a psychological strike as well as a material one, and should cause at least as much concern as a direct attack on their vessel.

Gus, can we please move south to the first set of buoys? After the *Salvona* retrieves the northern set, she'll probably steam south hoping the line is still attached to the southern set of buoys. We'll hit her there."

The submarine cruised south for an hour and a half and Durrand put her into a stationary position at periscope depth, a few hundred metres from the drifting buoys. She lurked, waiting.

Not long after, Tomlinson advised the approach of a fast-moving vessel on a direct bearing for the buoys, and within a few more minutes the *Salvona* appeared, a large white bow wave showing her haste to get to the buoys and winch them in. Had they been on the surface, they'd have heard Falduzzi's screams of rage at the discovery he had lost his line. A minute or two later, the fishing boat turned north again and moved off at about ten knots. The *Flying Fish* followed, matching course and speed.

"Gus, the weather is so good I think we'll try for a longer shot," mused Roberts, "maybe from half a kilometre back. How far away are we at present?"

"About seven hundred metres, Mr Roberts," came the quick response from Blake.

"OK, take her in to five hundred metres. I can't see the *Salvona* from here. Are you picking her up on the DIDSON sonar, Clarrie?"

"Yeah, Mr Roberts, clear as day. This stuff works a treat. I can even see something on the high res cameras—our bow is pointing straight at her."

"Good. Tube one ready, Herb?"

"Tube one ready," Cazaley replied instantly.

"Fire one," Roberts said firmly, and again watched enthralled as the long shaft of creamy white turbulence speared out from the bows, the stark whiteness of the shears seeming to point the way to the target. This time the wait was longer, the crew listening tensely, and after about a minute the expected thump came; not loud, and felt as much as heard, but everyone started breathing again.

"Stay on course Martin, and let's have a look," said Roberts with satisfaction.

Two minutes later, the *Fish* came slowly up on the stalled pirate vessel.

"Wow!" exclaimed Roberts, "we blew off her starboard screw completely, and her rudder is twisted right over to port. She's going to be out of action for a while, too."

Roberts and Mackie walked back to the control room, where Durrand, Hass and some of the crew were reviewing the action and its result with an air of excitement and satisfaction.

"Two hits, two 'kills', David—good shooting, although 'kills' is probably not the word to use," said Hass.

"It is if it means disablement and out of action, Gunter. I'll be very happy if our attacks result only in this type of 'kill'. I don't want to injure or kill anyone, as I've said all along, because these people are only doing what they consider is their job and are not trying to harm us in any way. But I intend to stop them doing their job, and so far, so good.

The long range shot worked fine too, Gus, but I think I prefer getting up close. Let's wait around for an hour or so to make sure they're not going to sink, and while we're waiting I'll put a call through to my contacts back in Oz, to see if they've got any more action for us."

An hour later found the *Flying Fish* steaming due west at around ten knots, for word had come via Roberts' Australian contacts that the *Steve Irwin*, the Sea Sherpherd's main working vessel, was tracking a Norwegian whaling group consisting of a large factory ship and two chaser boats. They were heading into the South Atlantic, clearly intending to begin operations as soon as they came upon any minke and humpback whales.

TWENTY EIGHT

It had been another long haul for the *Flying Fish* and her crew, and had tested the resources they all used for relaxing and entertaining themselves, and each other. For living aboard a working submarine needed application and commitment. It was easy to rile someone, and it got easier the longer they remained at sea without the diversion of an attack. Many of the crew had already changed cabins, and one or two fights had occurred. Andy McLeod had quickly stepped in to defuse these outbreaks, usually getting both parties into the workout room for a controlled contest, but the naturally aggressive Wojinski had applied what McLeod had shown him to a couple of the crew who took exception to his abrasive manner. They had both needed treatment from the doctor, and Durrand had to speak to the burly mate.

The submarine nurse, Helen Quartermaine, a homely, ginger-freckled American, didn't invite much male attention, but the base nurse, Cheryl Wilkes, did. Although Australian, she looked sweet as American apple pie. Her cute, curly blond hair hanging lazily over a snub nose set slightly off-centre between smoky green eyes, which always seemed to be smiling, drew appreciative glances the way wild figs draw fruit bats in Darwin.

She had been hit on in turn by the ERA, Bob Jesaulenko, Andre LeClerc and Janice McKenzie, and Ken Tilley, also aboard as part of the back-up operations group, was getting tired of warning them all off. He was actually getting tired of Cheryl, too, and her constant attention-seeking, but wasn't prepared to say anything just yet.

"The two guys didn't want to make anything of it," he was telling Roberts quietly in his cabin, "but I can't very well threaten to deck Janice. She just told me to fuck off and mind my own business and she'd sort it out with Cheryl. Hard to argue with really," he sighed, with a small chuckle.

"No, I can see why the two guys wouldn't go on with anything," smiled Roberts as he glanced at Tilley's large and powerful body, "but McKenzie is her own woman and isn't afraid of being classified, stereotyped or told that lesbians should be confined to their own world and shouldn't bother 'normal' people. You'll have to let Cheryl work it out with her. If she doesn't want McKenzie's attention and McKenzie doesn't take the hint, then I'll have to sort it out."

Suddenly Tomlinson's voice came over the intercom, excited and staccato-like as ever.

"Mr Roberts, I have a message from the *Steve Irwin* to say they have to return to base for repairs and re-provisioning, but they sent the coordinates of the Norwegian whaling group, which coincide with a reading I just got on my long-range radar. We could be on them in a couple of hours."

"Thanks Rick, be right there," replied Roberts as he rose from his chair, clapping Tilley on the shoulder as he moved past. "I don't see it as a serious problem, Ken, and I reckon things will improve markedly in the ship now we're into it again. But if you really have trouble, let me know quickly and I'll attend to it."

Roberts reached the control room. "What've we got Gus?" he asked expectantly, "and why are we moving so much?"

Durrand grinned. "We're moving around a little because I brought her up to periscope depth, and there's a nasty gale blowing on top. What we've got is a group of three ships—a very big mother ship and two chasers. The factory ship looks at least 10,000 tonnes. They're steaming slowly north, probably because it's too rough to catch whales at present. We're twenty feet down and feeling the waves and swells, so you can imagine what it's like up there."

"OK, let's catch them up and come in on our standard approach. This time I want to get in close."

After half an hour and some minor course corrections, Roberts was in the bubble and calling out sharply.

"Marty, come right a touch, we're getting into her wake and it's hard to see clearly."

"OK David," a different voice responded quickly, "how's that?"

"Is that you Lou? Good, keep her steady there."

"Will do. Yes, Martin felt I was ready to take the controls this time, and Gus agreed."

"Right, that's a good track. I can just see the prop turbulence. God, she's a big one! Her stern is enormous. Slow it down a little more, Lou, we're getting close. Tube one ready Herb?"

"Tube one's been ready for hours, David," came an excited female voice.

"Jesus, Kaye, you too!" Roberts laughed. "OK, stand by . . . stand by . . . . fire one!" Roberts called sharply.

"Fire one—yeehaa!" shouted Halloran, and once more the silver trail sped away from the bows.

"Hard right," called Roberts. Nothing happened.

"Hard right Lou, fast!" shouted Roberts, but the submarine remained on course. There came a violent thump and a force seemed to push her to starboard, followed by a loud clang and a jarring, jolting crash. The vessel stopped its forward movement.

"Hard astern!" shouted Roberts, and as the *Flying Fish* powered backwards, Roberts raced into the control room.

"Jesus Gus, what happened? Why didn't we come right after the tube fired?"

"Don't know yet David, but Clarrie and Cordelia are checking the electronics as we speak. I've got a damage control party checking the bow section as well. We'll come around and film the damage as usual—the controls seem to be functioning all right now."

"OK, I'll get back in the bubble. I want to see what the result is. Let me know if we're sinking," he grinned, but it was a grin more of excitement and tension than of humour. A few minutes later the *Fish* was back on the same track and idling up to the factory ship.

"God, I hope the cameras are getting all this! We did some damage this time—the starboard screw is missing! The shaft must have snapped near the stern tube, and the prop has come loose and fallen right out! The rudder looks like it's been jammed too. And there's a large hole in the stern," said Roberts in an awed voice, "about the size of our bow shears. We must have rammed her, and with the movement of the big ship as we pulled out astern, we enlarged it considerably. Are we leaking too Gus?"

"Yeah David, damage control reports that there's a strained weld around the reinforcement we put in at the base of the shears, which is leaking, but it's manageable. We'll repair it on the way back to Base, when the weather improves and we can get some surface time in."

Roberts moved back into the control room. "It looks like we were very close to the explosion, then we continued on and rammed the ship with the shears. It says a lot for the construction of the refitting, and for the reinforcement around the shears. I think we'll call it the ram from now on . . . it seems to be quite effective."

"Wow, that was the coolest thing I've ever done!" Halloran bounded into the control room. "We gave that big boy a lover's kiss," she bubbled, laughing, "with a bit of tongue as well. When can we do it again?"

Roberts shook his head. "Incorrigible, Kaye, even salacious. You put the rest of these macho submariners to shame."

"But it was a good shot, eh David?" she twinkled, her adrenaline still pumping.

"Yeah. Have the electronics guys figured out what went wrong yet?"

"We think so Mr Roberts," said Swan. "It seems it was nothing more than a faulty connection in one of the buses in Clarrie's computer. We'll beef it up and go over all the other control connections so it can't happen again."

"Good, thanks Cordelia. Clarrie, how did you get it working again so rapidly?"

Grimshaw looked a little sheepish and actually blushed. "Ah, I slapped it" he said. "Sometimes a good talking-to isn't enough."

"Jesus," groaned Roberts. "Gus, can you take us home please?"

TWENTY NINE

It was April and once more all hands were gathered in the base mess for a big dinner and conference. Roberts got up, slowly, for it had been a huge meal of Californian rib eye steaks with all the trimmings, and turned on his lapel microphone.

"Hi everyone," he began, "hope you all enjoyed the meal as much as I did. It was a joint effort from Daniel and Richard—thank you both. I know it's been a long campaign so far, but it's also been very successful. We've accomplished exactly what I hoped we'd be able to do with the *Flying Fish*. Now I need to go back to Australia to see just what's happening in the world of pirate fishing and illegal whaling.

You've all done everything I asked of you, and I'm going to arrange a hefty bonus for each of you. Should anyone wish to leave the project at this point, I'll release you from your contract and pay you out in full. The *Kontica* will be leaving for Sydney in a couple of days, so you can return at that time.

In fact, I intend to arrange R&R in Sydney for all hands in two shifts, the first to leave in two days. Remember the secrecy clause, especially now we've been active. There will be people looking for answers by now. Volunteers first, then Lou will decide. While he's away, Ken's in charge of the base."

*

"While I'm away, Gus, make sure the repairs we made to the *Fish* are going to hold, and get her ready for another trip. I want to find out whether we've made any noise yet, and try to get a line on possible repercussions."

"Are you expecting any, David?" asked Gunter.

"Oh yes, there's no doubt in my mind that we have begun to upset some powerful and ruthless people. I believe it's just a matter of time before the smarter ones put two and two together. Our trail isn't that difficult to pick up, but whether they'll find Igloo is another matter. I hope not, or we could be in for a rough time.

Give each group about five days in Sydney, Lou. Put them all up in the Hilton and charge it to me. See you back here in a fortnight."

*

"Morgan, Brock, Trevor, good to see you all again." Roberts was in conference with his contact people in the Esplanade Hotel in Fremantle. He had called the meeting over in West Australia so he could visit his parents, and Hendry's Westral head office was also based there. The hotel was the best in Fremantle, set on Marine Terrace a couple of stones' throws from the fishing boat harbours, across a grassy, pine tree-dotted park. The waterfront had been developed into a sprawl of boatyards, restaurants, seafood eateries and a boutique brewery called Little Creatures. It was a popular place for Sunday outings, but the whole area was alive with people every day. Fremantle itself had once been quite a sleepy hollow, but then in 1983 *Australia II* won the America's Cup and the 1987 defense had been held off Fremantle. The once-sleepy city awoke with a rush.

"You seem to have been busy, David, if the scattered reports we've been able to locate are correct," he enthused. "We've picked up stories of two different whaling operations whose factory ships were apparently disabled by underwater collisions or explosions—one Japanese, one Norwegian. The parent companies have both said their ships were engaged in lawful whaling for scientific purposes, and neither was reported to have made their quotas. They have no idea what it was that caused the damage, but said their factory ships would be laid up for weeks being repaired. The *Helga Lindberg* would be out of action for at least two months, as they needed a new propeller shaft fitted."

"Good," Roberts said with satisfaction. "It's been fascinating. So far it's all working out well, thanks to the accurate and up-to-the-minute information I'm getting from you blokes. So far, it doesn't sound as though anyone's connected the dots yet."

"David," said Trevor Lane slowly, "my friends at Sea Shepherd would dearly love to know exactly what you're doing. Whatever it is makes all the efforts of the crew on the *Steve Irwin* seem like custard pies at twenty paces. Are you able to tell us anything about your operations?"

"They're not the only ones," rejoined Hendry emphatically, "I'd give a million dollars to be in on whatever you're up to mate," he smiled.

"Some of us in Greenpeace were talking the other day, and came up with what we think is actually happening," said Brock Hewitt. "I'm surprised the people at Sea Shepherd haven't come to the same conclusion, given that they already operate a mini-submarine."

"Well, actually, we did give some thought to that possibility," admitted Lane, "but it would need to be a much larger one than ours, I mean theirs, and fitted out with very special equipment."

"Jesus, a bloody submarine! Of course it is! I should have thought of it myself," Hendry admonished himself. "My God, David, I remember now seeing some footage of a large blue submarine leaving a dock in Florida some time back. A special research vessel, they said, bound for northern waters. Just about the right time frame, too," he grinned ruefully. "I guess it turned right instead of left after clearing port, wouldn't you say, David?"

"Could be, Morgan, could be," said Roberts, with an expressionless face.

"And if it really is a sub, then that damage can only have been caused by torpedoes," said Lane. "That's something Sea Shepherd hasn't got, and couldn't use if they did."

"Oh, this is too good to be true," Hendry laughed delightedly. "If that's really what it is, I'd give five million dollars to be part of it, not one."

"OK, guys, I'm still not saying a word, but you're all experienced men of the ocean, and smart. If you've put something feasible together, other like-minded people can do the same. It reinforces the need for total secrecy, as we're all working toward much the same goals.

The special submersible research vessel *Flying Fish* is a matter of public record in Miami, Florida, where she was refurbished and fitted out. There were even some photos and that short video taken of her before she sailed. But hopefully that's where the well of detailed information will dry up. And I urge you gentlemen to encourage the drought by not repeating your conclusions outside this room, in fact by actively disagreeing with any similar conclusions you hear, to the point of ridicule."

"David, you may not have heard about this yet," Lane broke in, "but a special power boat called the *Kronos*, which had been harassing whaling groups and allowing whales being chased to evade harpooning, was recently reported lost at sea. A partial mayday broadcast was heard by two vessels and the Hobart Sea Rescue, that the *Kronos* was about to be rammed by Japanese whalers, but nothing more than that was reported. A helicopter was sent to search the area around the position she gave, but nothing was seen other than a few pieces of wreckage in a fading patch of oil. The Japanese whalers in the area were radioed and asked if they had seen the *Kronos*, but they denied seeing or having any contact with her.

It seems quite certain that the whalers sank her. There were eleven crew members aboard." There was sadness and sorrow in his face, and a glint of steel in his eyes.

The group fell silent, shocked to the core that such an action could be deliberate.

"God damn," groaned Hendry, "I knew some of her crew. I'd like to see you sink that whole bloody group, David! Oh shit, no I wouldn't. I know it isn't the basic working man at fault here, but we have to be able to do something," he gritted, blinking back tears of sorrow and frustration.

"It's dreadful to hear about that, Trevor, but we won't be altering our basic strategy. Speaking of which, there is maybe one other incident you seem not have come across yet," Roberts continued. "We did find that pirate fishing boat near Heard Island; we sent his number one longline to the bottom, and disabled him in the same way as the whalers. She was the *Salvona*." "I hadn't heard about that one," said Hendry. "They must have kept it quiet for some reason. Perhaps the government is still smarting over the *Viarsa* farce and doesn't want to create another media circus too soon."

"Maybe," conceded Roberts. "I don't really care what happens to these pirates legally. To me it's more important that the owners realise what happened out on the water, and what will keep on happening if they keep on fishing," he growled. "I think we have a lot more work to do before there are serious unofficial moratoriums called by any of the fishing companies. So I want you all to remain focused on the project, and keep the accurate and current intelligence flowing through."

"We may have figured out how tonight, David, but I doubt anyone here has a clue about where," said Hendry.

"Good," replied Roberts, "that means no one else will either. Not yet, anyway."

*

At that same moment, not more than a few kilometres away, members of the Fremantle Water Police were puzzling over the identity of a body which had been discovered floating in Cockburn Sound, some ten kilometres south-west of the Fremantle Harbour mouth.

"No papers, prints not on file and the fish haven't left much of his face. Difficult to establish an identity easily," mused the sergeant on duty. "About 170 cms and 90 kgs—short, squat and heavy, could be Italian or Greek. Someone's shoved a knife into his back and twisted it. Lot of damage. We'll have to send his prints and general description, along with the photos, to Interpol to try to get a line on him," he said. "Look at the scars on his hands. I reckon he was a fisherman. Hairy bugger too."

THIRTY

Lo Nguyen Tay, the Vietnamese billionaire, had been drawing the quarterly meeting to a close in his mansion on Batuka, the mood relaxed and the members anticipating the usual fine dinner and entertainment to follow.

"And the report from our fishing managers?" he enquired in his quiet, cultured voice.

The same two men were there as before, but this time they seemed tense, even nervous. They glanced at each other, which was enough for Lo to lean forward slightly and fasten his complete attention on the pair. One of them spoke.

"Mr Lo," he began, clearing his throat, "we regret we do not bring good news." Lo said nothing, his silent stillness encouraging the speaker to enlarge.

"The large Norwegian whaler we purchased recently, the *Helga Lindberg*, was whaling in the South Atlantic five days ago, when she suffered significant damage and had to be escorted to Singapore for repairs. These repairs will take, we are informed, over three months. A propeller was lost, the rudder was jammed and a hole approximately half a metre across was punched in the stern, below the waterline. It is not as yet known just how this damage was inflicted."

Lo stared at the two men dispassionately, his gaze calm and without a trace of malevolence, but the men knew their very lives were being weighed. They simply sat there, sweating, unable to breathe, waiting for judgement.

"Inflicted?" Lo murmured. "Are you saying the ship was somehow attacked?"

"We believe that is the only possible explanation, Mr Lo. The damage is consistent with some kind of explosion."

"Very well gentlemen," the fat man wheezed gently after another pause, "I want you to determine exactly what happened, and who was responsible. I want you to do this within two weeks. Further failure will not see me in such a benevolent mood. Do you understand?"

It was clear to all at the table that they understood perfectly.

*

Two days later, the two fishing managers were in a conference room in a high-rise office building in the Jakarta central business district, earnestly discussing their pressing problem. The men looked so alike they could have been mistaken for twins, although one was a centimetre taller. It was he who spoke.

"I just received word from a contact in Manila that our vessel may not have been the only one to suffer similar damage recently. It seems there was a Japanese whaling ship in the Southern Ocean which was in the process of drawing a whale on board when it was struck by something, and received the same kind of propeller and rudder damage, although without being holed."

"This is becoming interesting," said the other thoughtfully. "I have this morning heard from one of my informants in Europe that a fishing vessel engaged in longlining for toothfish, also in the Southern Ocean, was damaged in exactly the same manner over a month ago. The vessel was towed to the West Australian port of Fremantle, where the skipper has since disappeared. Apparently the Spanish owners were unhappy with the situation and had hired another fish finder before the vessel was even brought into Fremantle."

"It is beginning to appear as though there is a force at work intent upon preventing our lawful fishing ventures. It would be as well for us to discover quickly who is behind this force, and to take steps to eliminate him. Otherwise we will inevitably share the fate of this poor skipper," he said grimly. His companion nodded, needing no outline of the situation to encourage him to apply his full concentration to the task. Fear was always a greater inducement than reward, as he well knew.

*

There is a popular newspaper in Sydney called the *Sydney Morning Herald*, and on its staff is an investigative journalist by the name of Les Patterson. Although not yet able to boast a Pulitzer, the thirty-three year old ex professional tennis player is in fact a very good journo. One who has a wide circle of contacts in all walks of life, and who uses them all mercilessly. He is, however, such a charmer, with a very well-developed sense of humour, that his contacts invariably end up thanking him for giving him their assistance. He is tall and rapier-thin, with features to match, is always dressed casually, even sloppily at times, as though he cared nothing for fashion, but is never dirty or unkempt. He both drinks and smokes a lot now, after finishing a reasonably lucrative career playing the European tennis circuit for eight years, but yet somehow manages to retain an appearance of fitness and good health.

In Australia, and even to a degree in England and America, his name is particularly well-known, but not because of him. Dame Edna Everage is Barry Humphries' better-known alter-ego, but Sir Les Patterson, his other and somewhat less refined persona, has become Australia's unofficial cultural attaché to the world. In fact, Patterson the reporter had become so tired of having to say to everyone on meeting them for the first time, "no, I'm the other one" that he had at one time seriously considered changing his name by deed poll to something like Courtney Silverside. Now, resignedly, he has given up and just answers to the nickname of 'sir'.

On a morning at much the same time as Roberts was returning to Sydney after his meeting in Fremantle, Patterson was trolling through one of his favourite blog sites when something pinged on his antenna. It was a report of some damage sustained by a Japanese whaling ship operating in the Southern Ocean not long ago. The blogger was exulting that it had to be towed back to its base for repairs, which would save a number of whales that otherwise would have been killed.

"I'm sure I saw another . . ." he muttered to himself, quickly running through a number of URLs. "Yeah, here it is." He read the report now on screen and sat still for a minute, thinking. "Shit, there could be something in this," he said softly. He tagged it and sent it to a special box which would keep it on his daily desktop. "You just never know," he said to himself, again softly. He hadn't become a capable and experienced journo either by ignoring his instincts, or by talking too loudly.

*

Coincidentally, at about the time Patterson was having his curiosity aroused, a group of businessmen in Kagoshima, on

Japan's southern island of Kyushu, was meeting to discuss the same topic. They were on the 45th floor of an office tower with a spectacular view of the active volcano, Sakurajima, across the bay. Kagoshima is a port city with ready access to the East China Sea and the western Pacific. In another coincidence, it is also a sister city to Perth, in West Australia.

"Gentlemen, has a full analysis been prepared?" asked Sato Takamori, chairman of the corporation controlling the whaling operations of several fleets of catchers in the Southern Ocean. He was referring to the damage sustained by the *Kishin Maru*. Takamori was an extremely wealthy and powerful man, and wore his influence as only one who has been born to the cloth can do. His family had been one of Japan's most influential for a great many years, and he had the ear of all those who mattered in his country. It was rumoured, but not loudly, that a certain proportion of his family's wealth and power was supported, even enhanced, by very close ties with one of Japan's most powerful Yakuza gangs.

"As much as we can ascertain at present, Mr Chairman," said a staffer. "You all have copies in front of you. The ship was struck heavily and suffered serious damage to its stern and drive units. The damage appeared to be the result of an explosion. Its cause is at present not known."

"It hasn't cost us much in overall revenue terms," said the chairman, "but if it was some sort of strike against us, and our other vessels are now targets, then we obviously need to draw up a strategy to combat whoever it is. The primary objective, of course, is to find out who is responsible, and what they are doing. Once we know that, we can deal with them," he said dismissively. "Make it happen."

*

Roberts had decided to take a few days off and spend some time at Ulladulla, bringing Angie up to speed. He drove his BMW SUV down from Sydney, where he kept it in the Hilton underground storage, and aimed his new remote, left for him at the hotel, at the impressive set of steel gates in front of the double doors to the garage. Both the gates and the doors opened silently and he drove in. They closed just as silently, and very quickly, he noted. He opened the vehicle door and eased out, stretching as he did so, and found a craggy-faced man in combat fatigues standing in the doorway to the house, watching him closely.

"Mr Roberts?" the man queried sharply, his hands behind his back.

"That's right," David answered slowly. "Who might you be?"

"Forgive me sir, but could I please see some ID?"

"Oh Allen, it's OK! That's David," Angie's voice came through the doorway in a rush, followed by her person. "Sorry David, I should have been ready for you, but I was doing something away from the screens. This is Allen Bell, a security man I hired last month as a live-in guard. He's ex British SAS, and came highly recommended by James Redolpho."

"Hi Allen, nice to meet you. Angie, lovely to see you again," giving her a huge hug and enjoying her colourful discomfort. "Bloody good idea Angie, and nice to see he was waiting for me and ready for trouble. What kind of weapon do you have behind your back Allen?" he grinned.

"Hi Mr Roberts," Bell smiled, "it's a Sig Saur 9mm, my preferred pistol," he said as he brought it out and holstered it at his shoulder.

"OK, the two of you come into the house and give me a few minutes to freshen up. I guess it's nearly dinner time Angie. I don't suppose . . . ?"

"Of course, David, I have a nice meal waiting in the oven. Why don't you get acquainted with Allen while I get it ready, and you can tell us what's been happening while we eat."

Roberts smiled happily to himself, pleased at the way Angie was managing the house and with her easy confidence in making decisions.

"Have I got any decent reds left Angie?" he asked innocently.

"Of course David, I've only been drinking the Penfolds ones called 'Grange' something," she smiled sweetly, chuckling at his sharp and slightly pained look. "They go really nicely with barbecued chops and sausages."

Some time later, after Roberts had outlined what had occurred in the Southern Ocean and Bell had gotten used to saying 'David', Angie, eyes shining like the blue headlights on a new Alpha, said "David, can I please go on the next trip? It's just the most wonderful thing you're doing—exactly what you said you hoped to do all those years ago."

"Sorry Angie, but I don't want to expose you to the dangers I believe are in store for us. It could also be dangerous here, and I need to go over some things with you both about that. But once the big boys cotton on to us, they'll be trying to remove us permanently from the scene, and I don't want you anywhere near that sort of action.

Allen, I want you to make yourself known to the lads at the local karate dojo, and hire any who agree as supernumeraries. Then I want you to come to Sydney with me when I'm leaving again for Igloo and pick up some special ordnance from the *Kontica*. Bring it back here and deploy it ready for anything that may occur. I don't know how much time we have, but I expect some sort of reaction within a month.

Angie, thank you for that lovely meal. It's one of the things that keep me going, knowing I can come home to a meal like that in this beautiful place."

Bell excused himself, and Roberts and Angie took coffees out on to the terrace overlooking the ocean.

"Red wine, coffee, god Angie, you'll be smoking next," Roberts chuckled, very comfortable with Angie's presence. "I think you're realizing now how much there is to Angela Collins," he said quietly. "I know I am. You're making all the right decisions and you seem to be able to produce a new capability whenever it's needed. I'd have no hesitation in recommending you for a general manager's position in a large firm or corporation right now, and I'm sure you're still expanding your talents."

"David, thank you for your support. I know now you were right about me being able to do a little more than keep house, although I think you're flattering me somewhat, but whatever I've managed to do, or become, has been because you encouraged and advised me. You're a wonderful man and I won't be able to say that again—blame the wine."

"You're one of this planet's lovely people, Angie," smiled Roberts as they leant on the terrace rail, staring at the luminous path made by the full moon down the ocean's surface to their spot on the rail. He put an arm around her and gave her a kiss on the cheek. Or he meant to. Angie turned her head at the same time, and the kiss found her lips, moist, full and moaningly eager, and the one arm became two and a passionate embrace that time ignored.

Finally they came up for air, still tightly embracing. "Oh David, I'm so sorry," murmured Angie.

"Angela, don't you dare apologise!" said Roberts sternly. "That felt about as right to me as anything I've ever done," he assured her. "I can only hope you felt it too."

"I think I've been waiting my whole life for something like that, David," she said softly, her eyes now shining on high beam. "What happens now?"

"Well, my gorgeous woman, if you haven't anything better to do, I'd love to take you to bed."

Angie's grin was tinged with mischief. "What about the dishes?"

Roberts' grin was tinged with an expletive.

*

Later, quite some time later, Roberts murmured "Angie, just for once I'm stuck for words."

"Out of breath, David?"

"There is that, my love," he smiled into the darkness, "but the experience I've just had was quite new to me, and I don't mean I was a virgin."

"That I could tell. But I have to say I found myself somewhere I hadn't been before, too, if that's what you mean."

"Yes," breathed Roberts, "yes, that's exactly what I mean. I thoroughly enjoyed the sex and exploring your very tasty body, but at the same time I was running through a lot of different feelings and emotions, almost like a reactor in meltdown. The explosion came at the right time, too," he smiled.

"Me too David," she whispered. "At various times during the last hour I found myself quietly weeping for a number of reasons, like I'm doing now. But this one is for pure joy."

"Well beautiful, I don't quite know what the outcome of all this will be, but please don't make any plans to change your employment for the foreseeable future."

Angie paused, serious. "That sounds a little like a commitment, David. I love the sound of it, but are you sure?"

"Well, Angie, this has hit me like Alien versus Predator, and my whole life has changed during the course of the last hour or so, but yes, I've never been surer of anything quite as much before. I want you in my life, Angela."

"Then that's where I'll be. Could we try the sex bit again, just to be sure?"

THIRTY ONE

The southern winter was approaching, the weather perfectly in tune with the season. Almost every day was bitterly cold, frequently raining or sleeting, and blowing either a half gale or a full gale. Inside Igloo, deep within the rock base of Macquarie Island, it was quiet and calm, warm and snug, but the Foxtrot members were preparing for another sortie into the raging Southern Ocean. The *Flying Fish*, her bow pointing west toward the entrance, was gently tugging against her mooring lines, as if she had an urgent appointment to keep.

"We have more good intel advising us of three whaling groups, three pirate fishing boats and a fleet of Japanese tuna boats, so make sure we are fully provisioned and our total store of ten torpedoes is aboard." Roberts was in council with his command group prior to departing. "We know the best ways of dealing with the boats we come up with now, so I want this trip to be fast and full-on. We're going for volume this time, and I don't want to return to base with a single torpedo. Bo Tallis has organised a replacement set of twenty four, and they're on the way to Sydney right now."

"Did you find any knowledge of our doings anywhere, David?" asked Lou James.

"'Doings'. I like that word, Lou," smiled Roberts. "No, my informants group had managed to come up with a submarine as our modus operandi, and Hendry connected it to the *Flying Fish* in Florida, but this is a group with special knowledge. None of them could hazard a guess as to where our base was, so I'm confident that we'll be safe from any retaliation for at least a month. But we can't afford to relax in any way.

Let's go hunting."

*

It was more than two weeks into the latest excursion and the whalers had been hit again. The Japanese and Norwegian ships had been operating quite close to each other, and had been disabled on consecutive days. Next to be chastised was a Russian group whaling in the southern Indian Ocean, catching humpbacks. The word about the submarine may have been spreading, because the three catcher boats were all driving at full revs around the stern of the stricken factory ship, evidently trying to ram the submarine in the event it wasn't deep enough.

"Good," Roberts said with satisfaction, "maybe they'll start to take notice and give some thought to an extended holiday. Gus, let's head for the Bight. That's where those tuna boats have been reported working. It's almost in our backyard."

*

After a couple of days heading ENE at cruising speed, the *Flying Fish* was crossing the 120° E longitude meridian at approximately the latitude of the middle of Bass Straight. She was heading roughly for the Great Australian Bight, that enormous chunk of missing continent across the southern part of Australia, where a good part of the Southern Bluefin tuna fishing occurred. The day was fine, sunny and fresh, with good swells and some breaking waves. There were many gannets diving on the detritus from the long lines, pieces of bait and scraps caught in the line, and they were always an indicator of where a line may have been set. Unfortunately, there were also albatross wheeling around and diving on the baits, especially on the lines not equipped with an anti-bird device. The coordinates supplied for the operating area of the tuna boats were as accurate as always, and they had already located and sunk three long lines before coming upon the first tuna vessel.

"Geez skipper, these things are as big as the whaling factory ships!" Grimshaw was getting a very clear picture of the massive boat with sonar and then the cameras. "She's almost still in the water. Must be winding in one of her long lines."

"We'll move behind her and slip a fish into her gear, then bear away and try to cut the line as it comes in." The submarine curved around to starboard and straightened, firing a torpedo as she bore on the tuna boat. The now-familiar explosion did its work and the large vessel stopped. The winching in of the long line stopped at the same time, understandably. "While they figure out what happened, let's have a go at the line," said Durrand. The submarine curved around in a tight circle, slowing to just over a knot, and Roberts conned it in towards the line.

"Easy now," he called to Blake, "nearly there." He opened the jaws of the cutter, rotating them so they were at an angle of ninety degrees to the sloping line, and the *Fish* slowly moved forward, the line slipping between the jaws. As it did so, Roberts closed them, neatly severing the line. "Good. We'll have to follow it back to the other end and cut that too, Gus," he said. "There are plenty of tuna on the line, but I'd rather see them go to the bottom and feed the food chain here in the ocean than end up feeding wealthy patrons in high-priced Japanese restaurants.

Oh, shit! Shit! There's a guy floating in the water! He doesn't seem to be moving. He has a vest on, but he's still going to drown if they don't get to him quickly. He must've been near the emergency brake on the winch and been knocked overboard, or slipped and hit his head before falling in.

Andy! Emergency! Bubble room, fast! Ray, let's get out of here!" Roberts and Mackie raced out of the bubble room as McLeod ran past, slamming the watertight door behind him. Back in the control room, Roberts told Durrand he wanted to try to save the fisherman's life, in case his crew couldn't get to him or didn't realise he was in the water.

"Andy, once you're suited up, get out as fast as you can. Try to get him breathing as you take him to their ship. Once they've got him, get the hell away as quick as you can. Don't give them a chance to shoot you or capture you. We'll keep the *Fish* right here and keep you on visual with the cameras."

The bubble room was quickly flooded and McLeod gave the OK. The hatch that had been installed as an extra was opened from the control room and the big purser shot out in a large cloud of big bubbles, swimming powerfully past their nonchalant ascent for the surface thirty feet above him. He could be seen clearly on the control screen, his image captured by the forward cameras, as he swam quickly to the unmoving fisherman. He was shouting at the ship fifty metres from him, although no sound could be heard in the submarine. Reaching the man in the water McLeod expertly flipped him upright and commenced mouth-to-mouth resuscitation, interspersed with blows to his chest. He continued this process while swimming toward the huge tuna boat, taking the man right up to the side of the vessel. The crew had become aware of the drama and had lowered one of the cradles used to lift the tuna from the water. It was a perfect fit for the injured man, who was now showing signs of movement. As soon as the cradle began to rise, with the fisherman securely inside it, McLeod dived straight down, still swimming strongly, heading for the submarine which had crept closer to the tuna boat as it followed the big man's progress. He entered the still-open hatch and Grimshaw closed it behind him, activating the control to pump out the water from the room.

Once clear, the watertight door was opened and Roberts, Durrand and then Mackie fell in to the bubble room, wide-eyed and breathless, as McLeod was stowing his underwater gear.

"You beauty Andy!" Roberts shook his hand. "Was that guy moving when you left him?"

"Yeah David, he was coughing and spewing. I reckon he'll be OK."

"Good job, mate. Everything seemed to work very well. Go and grab a coffee or something stronger and get some rest.

Then we can cut the other end of this line, and find some more tuna boats."

*

Some four weeks later, in the dead of a freezing night filled with the sounds of crashing waves, screaming wind and surf booming over the breakwater, the *Flying Fish* scraped her way down the channel, her 2,000 tonnes being shoved from side to side by the turbulence of the water as though she were a model boat being operated on a pond in a London park. She moved gratefully into the harbour under the main door and was moored alongside the dock, to be turned around later. Her crew were all glad, in varying degrees, to step on to the dock, three of them having decided to call it quits.

"Debriefing in an hour, guys, after we clear her away."

*

"These trips are certainly long and arduous," Roberts was saying to the command group, "but we were very successful in hitting our targets. We disabled all three of the whaling factory ships, three pirate fishing boats and those four Japanese tuna boats. Not to mention all the long lines we've sunk. So, ten fish, ten hits. I think the message is now very visible, and must be having an effect."

"Will we be continuing operations then, David?" asked Lou James.

"We certainly will, Lou. That was my original intention, and I see no reason to stop now. I want all these fishing companies to realise that if they come down here to take fish, it will cost them more than their profit in lost time and major repairs.

Make sure the *Fish* is re-provisioned and ready to go, and we'll all take some R&R back in Sydney. There should be another two dozen torpedoes waiting for us there. I've heard that there has also been some publicity, which I want to check out.

What's our crew status? We've now lost seven members. Do we still have a good balance, or should we recruit more when we're in Sydney?"

"I think we're still OK, David. I have to concede that you were right about being able to operate the sub with a reduced crew. We've still got at least two people able to handle each station. We even have three doctors and three nurses in total—maybe we could let one or two of them go?" replied Durrand.

"No, Gus, so far it's been plain sailing, but at some time we'll meet some retaliation, and unfortunately I think we'll need all the medical help we have. But what I am going to do is to bring back half-a-dozen special hands, well-trained and experienced guys who are no strangers to violence, to take charge of our Base security.

Let's have dinner and sort out the roster for Sydney."

THIRTY TWO

On a cool winter's morning a few days later, Roberts and Angie were having coffee on the terrace of their home in Ulladulla.

"David, do you remember a few years ago reading the account of the whaling catches here, and becoming interested in the issue at that time?"

"Very clearly, Angie. It wasn't long after that I had that epiphanous encounter with the trapped whale up the coast. Boy, was that ever a life-changing experience."

"Well, here's another interesting newspaper article I kept for you—see what you think."

Roberts took the paper Angie handed him, opened to an article by Les Patterson that had appeared about two weeks ago in the *Sydney Morning Herald,* and read:

"A Protector for the Whales?

Strange happenings in the Southern Ocean there are. An unknown and powerful Force disrupting fishing and whaling vessels in the furious fifties there appears to be. While it may not have anything to do

with Luke Skywalker, nonetheless it seems to have been effective in causing a number of whaling groups, as well as pirate fishing boats and tuna boats, to take some time off for R&R. In this case, R&R could well stand for reflection and rethinking.

For, according to reports coming in from unrelated but reliable sources, as many as ten vessels of different sizes and types have suffered damage during the past couple of months. Damage serious enough to cause them to need towing back to their various bases for repairs and re-fitting. The best information to filter through from these reports is that the damage has been almost exclusively to the sterns of the vessels, that is to their propellers and rudders, and that it has been both extensive and expensive.

But what is the manifestation of this Force, I hear you asking. To date no one has seen anything, or if they have they aren't saying. But the fact that all the damage has been to the sterns of the vessels would appear to rule out collisions with floating objects. So, if it's not accidental, dear readers, ergo, it must be deliberate. And if it's deliberate, a number of questions tumble over themselves on their way out: What is it? How does it happen? From where does it come? Why these vessels? And the biggest question of all, who is behind it?

Sea Shepherd, a group which has been called the military arm of Greenpeace, although the two organisations really don't see eye-to-eye, is known to have committed violence against pirate fishing boats and whalers in the past. It is also believed to own a submarine, albeit a little yellow one. Are the

two connected by the Force? Or has the *Nautilus* been reincarnated? Is the Evil Empire—those corporations raping the fish populations and killing the whales—finally getting its comeuppance?

So far no one has been killed or injured and no vessels have been sunk, so the Force clearly is benign, on the side of truth, justice and the way of the whale. One might even opine that it's doing the job that should have been done by the governments of the world long ago. Therefore, all that remains to be said is . . . . may the Force be with you."

"Yes," smiled Roberts, "I've read stuff by sir Les before. I quite like him. He's got his finger on the pulse all right, and I'm pleased he's put that Sea Shepherd bit in. It might keep attention off us for a while yet. But I don't intend to go to sleep either. We have to make sure we're ready for anything that might come our way unexpectedly."

*

"No gents and ladies, I'm sorry but I don't know any more than you've all read in the papers so far. I enjoyed Mr Patterson's piece in the *Herald* the other day, and I reckon he's pretty well spot-on." Morgan Hendry had been asked for his views on the apparent happenings in the Southern Ocean by a group of journalists, as he was Australia's largest player in the area. Also because he always agreed to comment and his comments were nearly always printably pithy.

"Do you agree that those boats were attacked by something, Mr Hendry?" asked one of the reporters.

"It's too early to tell yet. We need to wait until more figures come in," Hendry said with a perfectly straight face. Two or three of the more astute groaned. "Come on Mr Hendry, give us a break—it's not election night. What do you really think is happening down there?"

"OK, what I think is that there is something down south which is taking action against whalers and illegal fishers, and I'm afraid I can only applaud whoever is responsible. I'm almost sorry it isn't me," he grinned.

"Even so Mr Hendry, the whalers say they are all under their legal quotas, as do the tuna boats, and the longliners say they weren't catching fish in restricted areas."

"I think all the arguments about whaling have been made, both pro and con, and I come down squarely on the side of the whales. Those chasers that say they haven't caught their so-called 'quotas' yet know full well that no one could ever prove otherwise unless they were on the actual boats, as the carcasses just get dumped back down the ramps and into the sea. And they simply deny catching any other types of whales—even though they've been observed doing so.

The tuna boats have become huge factory ships in themselves, able to take enormous amounts of tuna on a single long line. There've even been official estimates from government sources that the Japanese boats have been understating their catches by as much as 50%, and could have been doing so for twenty years.

And don't get me started on the toothfish pirates. They use every trick in the book to confuse the authorities—changing the names and even the shapes of boats, altering company records, offloading catches to other vessels at sea, and denying everything of which they're accused.

So, people, you can see where I stand. And it isn't because I want a clear run at the fish without competition. My vessels strictly adhere to the quotas—they have to, as they are regularly and carefully inspected on reaching port, something which doesn't happen to the Japanese boats."

"But Mr Hendry, whatever is attacking the boats out there doesn't seem interested in your vessels. Isn't that a bit odd?"

"I don't think so, Martine. Our vessels are very recognizable, as are all Australian ships well-known to be observing the quotas. I think whoever or whatever is out there knows that too. As for the whaling ships, it seems that any whaling at all is a no-no, regardless of nationality."

"Are you saying that no Australian boat ever catches more than its quota, Mr Hendry?" One of the reporters was a very short and wiry little man with very bright brown eyes, in which intelligent curiosity outshone journalistic malevolence.

"No, Brad," Hendry replied slowly, "I won't say that. Unfortunately, I know otherwise. But if you'll allow me, I also know two other things. One is that the companies overfishing their quotas have done so rarely, and who they are is no secret. The second thing is that none of my boats has ever done so. Any skipper of mine who intentionally catches more than his quota is risking instant dismissal. And they are all very aware of that." His riveting voice carried the resonance of truth and conviction.

"But surely attacking a vessel is tantamount to declaring war? How can you justify that kind of action?" A sharp-faced woman of approaching middle age, dressed in a trouser suit of power grey, got back to the main topic. The one more likely to hold viewers' attention.

"Yes, it is war, Martine, but there really is a good side and a bad side in this one. Do any of you honestly believe it's a good thing to plunder toothfish and tuna to extinction? To kill more and more whales because their numbers have risen?"

"I doubt it, Mr Hendry," said the woman, "but I have a problem with the method of protest in this case, if indeed there is some sort of vessel attacking the fishing boats. For a start, it's clearly against international law, and it will inevitably lead to injury or death."

"That's a fair point, Martine, and hard to argue with. I guess whoever it is has got to the stage where they don't see lawful protests having any effect, and want to do something positive to prevent species extinction. And I'd have to agree that injury or death may indeed be likely as a result of these protests. But inevitability? Only God and the Prime Minister can claim to know that."

*

Not long after the Q&A session with Morgan Hendry, in another part of the country parliament had risen and the Minister for Agriculture, Fisheries and Forestry was trying to make a quick and unnoticed exit. He failed. A media throng waylaid him, knowing where he would likely be coming out of Parliament House, and he realised he was going to have to give them some time. He quietened them down, saying "Only time for a few quick ones I'm afraid."

"Mr Minister," the loudest and most insistent voice, belonging to 'A Current Affair', imposed itself on the group. "Can you comment on the government's response to the situation in the Southern Ocean?"

Too experienced either to stonewall or obfuscate, the Minister replied. "Clearly we can't make any decisions about something that may not even have happened. All we have are some unsubstantiated reports and an article in the *Herald* trying to pull them all together. We are simply going to have to wait until these attacks, if that's what they are, have been confirmed."

"But it seems likely, Mr Minister, that the reports are genuine. Is the government not going to do anything about them?"

"We have plans to dispatch a patrol boat into the general area of our exclusion zone around Heard Island, and will have two Orion search planes make a number of flights through the areas mentioned in the reports."

"One patrol boat and two planes? That'll hardly frighten them off, Mr Minister."

"Could I remind you all that as yet nothing has been confirmed? If and when it has, we'll take all necessary steps to ensure all vessels engaged in lawful fishing activities will be protected."

"But Mr Minister, what will your department actually do? It was only a few years ago that the government spent a million dollars in a hot pursuit of a pirate longliner, the *Viarsa*, brought him back for trial, and let a QC earn a fortune for getting him off all charges. It seems that whatever is crippling these fishing vessels is doing your job for you."

Stung, the Minister replied sharply, "I'm sure I don't need to remind you that episode occurred under the previous government! Our policies will need time to demonstrate their effectiveness. But what you all seem to be admiring is nothing short of piracy itself! It's against all maritime international law, and whoever is responsible should be facing arrest and imprisonment. There's never been any room in a civilised society for vigilantes.

I'm sorry, that's all I have time for at the moment."

THIRTY THREE

"Tube one ready?" Roberts asked quietly, some three weeks later. The *Flying Fish* really was flying, in hot pursuit of one of the whale chasers that was part of the Norwegian whaling group they had sent north for repairs nearly nine months earlier. The chaser was pursuing a whale at around fifteen knots and the *Fish* was closing on the chaser at twenty. She was half a kilometre ahead, the sonar array painting her in bright green detail, when Cazaley's voice replied instantly, "Tube one ready Mr Roberts."

"Fire one," came from Roberts, this a little louder and more forceful. "Maintain course, reduce speed to three knots, let's check the damage."

Within a few minutes the submarine was cruising slowly under the now-stationary chaser, photographing the familiar damage to the screws and rudder.

"Excellent," breathed Roberts with satisfaction, "a twisted and mangled mess. We'll leave the other chasers for towing. But I want that factory ship again. Where is she?"

Two hours later the *Kishin Maru* was in the sights of the stalking submarine, about eight miles away. Durrand ordered the *Fish* to be submerged to a depth of twenty fathoms, as he and Roberts had decided to shoot at each target from a distance.

"Not so much fun," Roberts had said, "but a lot safer. We can aim the *Fish* right at the targets with the sonar, and the new acoustic heads on the torpedoes are taking them right into the propellers.

"Tube two ready?" queried Roberts after a twenty minute run to the large factory ship.

"Two ready," came from Cazaley.

"Fire two," called Roberts. "Maintain course and depth, slow to three knots."

The familiar thumping jolt told the crew they had scored another hit, and the submarine approached the Japanese vessel, also now stationary ahead of them.

Suddenly a loud pinging noise reverberated around the submarine, a noise few of the crew had heard before.

"What the hell is that?" A puzzled Mackie turned to Roberts, both still in the bubble after the torpedo had been fired. They jumped down and hurried to the control room. Durrand was peering at the sonar display.

"All stop!" he called to Blake sharply.

"What is it Gus?" asked Roberts with some urgency. He could sense the tension in the room.

"We're being tracked by active sonar," grated Durrand. "It must be the factory ship. These guys aren't stupid—if your contacts could work out what was happening then so could others. They may have installed some anti-sub equipment during their repair and re-fit."

With a deafening boom an explosion close to the submarine's port stern quarter shook it the way a terrier shakes a rabbit, throwing everyone off their feet and causing a number of alarms to begin hooting and wailing.

"Damage control!" shouted Durrand. "Hard a'starboard! Full ahead! Find out if we're leaking—quickly now!"

"Skipper, we've got serious water coming in at stern tube 3!" came a shout over the intercom from Jesaulenko. "Can you reduce pressure?"

"Clive, up angle 30°—get us up quickly!"

"No Gus, no!" came a strangled shout from Gunter Hass. "Clive, belay that order!"

Chung hesitated, as Durrand snarled "The fuck you doing, Hass? I'm in charge of this boat!"

"Gus, there's a problem with Foxtrots that I thought you would have known about. Clive, take her up quickly, but not at more than 20°!"

Chung looked at Durrand, who nodded curtly, and began bringing the *Fish* up to periscope depth at 20° bow angle.

"OK, Hass, talk!" barked Durrand. "What was that shit all about?"

"Gus, there is an inherent problem with the Foxtrot design that is common knowledge among the fraternity of users. I assumed you were aware of it when you dived her at 20° during our sea trials. If a Foxtrot is dived or surfaced at 30° or more she can lose control, and if that happens I'm sure you know the rest." Hass stared at Durrand grimly. Durrand's face had turned the colour of wet chalk. "Jesus," he whispered. Blake and Chung looked at each other, their wide eyes reflecting the horror they both understood could have been theirs.

"Christ, Gunter, what on earth are you talking about?" asked Roberts, his face showing puzzlement and surprise, but not mirroring the shock clearly displayed by the submariners around him.

"David, I may have nearly killed us all," Durrand said slowly, painfully. "I didn't know about that Foxtrot problem. If Hass is right, and I don't doubt it for a minute, we may have lost control on the way up at that steep angle. That means she could have turned turtle, and we then would have lost buoyancy."

"Jesus, Gus, are you saying . . . ?"

"Yeah, David, straight to the bottom, which here is around twenty thousand feet down. By the time we got there we'd have long been crushed flatter'n a jam tin under a steamroller."

"God almighty! That was a bit too close, Gus."

"Yeah. Let me sort out the situation, then you can decide what to do about me. Damage control, report! Any injuries, report! Clive, hold at periscope depth—I want a look at the big ship."

"Water inflow easing, skipper," Jesaulenko sounded calmer, "but we'll need some serious repairs to shaft 3, and probably propeller 3 too."

"Three casualties, captain. A concussion, a broken nose and a fractured forearm," the nurse, Helen Quartermaine, responded. "They're all in sick bay being treated by the doctor."

"I can see that son-of-a-bitch clearly, about a half mile off, and dead still. He's almost certainly got the same damage as last time. And I can see what looks very much like a depth-charge launcher on his stern counter. It looks like an old wartime model, but it can probably fire charges a few kilometres. His firing control system may not be as coordinated as a naval ship's, but we need to get out of here fast all the same. We won't worry about photos this time—Marty, set a course for Igloo. Clive, when we're out of sight of the whalers, we'll run home on the surface. If you get word from Rick of any vessels approaching, submerge to periscope depth until we're past, then surface again. The less water pressure on that stern tube, the better.

OK, my cabin please, David. You too, Mr Hass, if you will."

A few minutes later, Durrand was speaking to Roberts and Hass in the privacy of his cabin, his voice quiet and his manner subdued, almost sorrowful.

"I fucked up big time, David, and if it hadn't been for Mr Hass' knowledge and quick action, we'd probably all now be dead. I offer my resignation as captain effective immediately in favour of Mr Hass. I will of course act in any position you require until we reach base, then I'll ship out.

Mr Hass, I apologise to you for my attitude since we met. You are a true seaman and you clearly know your job better than I do mine."

"Right, Gus, that's enough." Roberts had been listening to Durrand with something approaching a smile, but replaced it quickly with a stern look and a cool voice. "Yes, you fucked up royally, but we didn't sink and we may not have anyway. Apart from that one error, you handled the attack on us capably and calmly. You're a bloody good captain with the trust and confidence of the whole crew. I doubt Gunter wants to become captain, and I don't want him to either.

So cut the crap and get back to doing what we're paying you for. On balance, you're doing it very well." Roberts finally allowed the small smile he had covered to show, and Durrand nodded his thanks.

"David is quite correct, Gus. I most certainly don't want to be captain. Those days are long behind me, and I'm sure the crew would agree," Gunter assured Durrand. "I believe David is also correct in his assessment of your capabilities. You have proved to be a strong and reliable skipper who has gained the respect and confidence of all the crew—including me—and it would be counter-productive to try to replace you now."

Durrand stared at Hass for a time. "Thank you Gunter," he said quietly.

"You're welcome, my friend," said Hass with a smile.

*

A week later the *Flying* Fish was back in the Igloo harbour and being prepared for repairs she needed to her hull and stern tube 3. Propeller 3 also needed to be replaced.

"Ironic, David," Hass was saying with a small smile, "that we now need repairs to the same damage we have been causing the fishing vessels. At least the depth charges can only travel downwards, and explode at a pre-set depth. They must shoot and hope, whereas we can shoot and our torpedoes will only explode if they actually hit. That depth charge which damaged us must have been at least ten metres away from our hull, and although they are very powerful, the further they are away from the hull the less damage they can cause.

This time, we were fortunate."

"Yes, I know Gunter. They took us by surprise, and I should have thought of it. Next time we'll shoot from further away, and stay away. Our sonar and cameras give us a good look at the targets—we don't need to get as close as we used to.

Lou, get her ready for sea again as soon as you can. I'm going back to Sydney in the *Kontica*. I'm a little worried about Ulladulla now that the Evil Empire seems to be getting closer."

THIRTY FOUR

Roberts had been back home in Ulladulla for four days, reviewing security and relaxing with Angie. That night, some time after midnight, a muffled explosion sounded back up behind the house, followed quickly by a scream and some loud moans. The moans were not audible in the house, but the explosion and scream had attracted an almost instant reaction.

"David, Angie, up quickly!" came an urgent command over the house interphone system in their bedroom. Roberts was awake fast and dressing, urging Angie to do the same. Bell, who had called to Roberts, was activating alarms and tooling up, ready to go outside to investigate.

"Angie, stay by the tunnel door. If I give you the word, get into it and go down to the beach. Get the dinghy ready and wait for us. Allen and I will see just who's trying to hit us." Roberts ran out to find Bell near the back door, confident his precautions would be effective. Some time ago he'd had a tunnel dug under the house from an entrance inside; it descended to a small beach at the foot of the cliff on which the house had been built, and Roberts had concealed an inflatable dinghy with a 30hp outboard motor under a hide.

"Allen, let's wait for the boys to arrive, then see who and how many there are. Can you get them on camera?"

"Yeah, we should be able to see them," muttered Bell. "Yes, there are two beside that tree, and two more back up the hill a ways. I reckon one of our APMs took out a couple of them. They look like they're ready to assault, but there's only four of them now." Against government regulations outlawing mantraps, Roberts had set Bell the task of deploying some reduced-power anti-personnel mines, similar to defence-issue Claymores, but with only half of the charge.

"OK Allen, we'll wait a bit and see what they do. The boys should be here soon anyway."

The four shadowy figures in the back of the house joined and moved down to the back entrance.

"I think they're going to try to blow the door," said Roberts quietly. "We can't have that." He glanced at Bell, raising his eyebrows questioningly. Bell nodded grimly. He touched the keypad of a device he had strapped to his left forearm and two sharp blasts in quick succession were heard, this time close outside the steel-reinforced back door. Another keystroke and powerful lights instantly removed all shadows, turning the back area into a stage with now only two moving players. Bell spoke into a small microphone on the device.

"Drop your weapons and raise your hands! Do it now!"

The two remaining figures looked at each other, startled and confused at the strange turn of events which now saw them reduced to two, spotlit mercilessly and very much on the defensive.

"Be a bloody good idea to do what he says, guys," called another voice from the edge of the lighted area, a part of the yard that still had concealing shadows. That did it, and the two attackers dropped their assault rifles and slowly raised their arms.

Five trim figures emerged from the shadows and stepped cautiously into the lighted area. They all carried weapons, either pistols or assault rifles, and surrounded the two black-clad invaders still standing. At the same time, Roberts and Bell came out of the back door.

"Nice work people. Quick response," Roberts said to the leader of the group from the dojo.

"No problem, Mr Roberts. Any time. We'll send you our bill, shall we?" chuckled Sarah Sanders.

"Have you spoken to your father yet, young lady?" asked Roberts sternly. "Does he know what you're getting up to?"

"I love my father very much Mr Roberts, and since he began working for you he's become so much more approachable. But he's still very conservative and I know he wouldn't approve of me getting involved with the project. He continues to think of me as his little girl, and doesn't realise I can take care of myself quite well now," said Sanders with quiet confidence.

"That's all well and good, Sarah, but if you want to remain working with the project you'll talk to him about it, and soon. I know you're an adult capable of making your own decisions, and of being responsible for them, but your father is special to our project, and just incidentally a friend of mine. So that gives me the right to interfere," Roberts said, with a raised eyebrow and a narrow-eyed glare. But there was also a smile in there somewhere that he kept to himself.

"Now, if you want to be paid, sort out who and how many there were, and find out their status. I want to know how they found us, and I want it all cleaned up before I go back to bed."

*

Bell, Sanders, Roberts and Angie were in the living room discussing the attack over coffees and brandy. Sarah was outlining the situation as it now appeared.

"There were six of them initially, a mixture of Vietnamese nationals and mercenaries hired specifically for this job," she was saying.

"Which was what, exactly?" queried Roberts.

"To kill you and anyone else who happened to be in the house at the time," replied Sarah flatly. "The two still alive were shaken up badly by our response. They thought they'd be able to get in easily and take care of you without any problems. When we told them we would feed them to the sharks they told us everything we wanted to know. They were sent by the 'Twins', two fishing managers working for someone called Mr Lo out of Jakarta. He owns the Norwegian whaling group using the *Helga Lindberg*, as well as a number of toothfishing longliners. You're starting to cost him serious money."

"Good," said Roberts with satisfaction. "That's exactly what I want. What happened after the attackers got over our fence?"

"Two were taken out with the APM, one killed and the other badly injured. He's since died. The two who were trying to set the charge on the back door were both killed by the automatic shotguns set above the door. All four bodies have been taken out to sea in the dinghy by two of our guys. They'll weight them properly and sink them a few kilometres out to sea.

What do you want us to do with the two we captured?"

"These guys are murderers who would have killed us all without a second thought," Roberts said slowly, with ice in his voice, "but that doesn't make it right for us to do the same. I'm comfortable with killing anyone who attacks us, as they did tonight, and especially as they would have killed Angie also, but I won't kill in cold blood. So these two will be spared. In fact, it will be to our benefit for them to return to tell the story of what happened to their comrades. Tell them the four who died are feeding the sharks right now, and there are plenty more sharks out there waiting for anyone else who comes back here. I doubt they'll try again."

*

The next morning Roberts and Angie were having a late breakfast, musing over the events of the early hours and what they had done. Angie was pale and withdrawn, clearly shocked at what had resulted.

"God, David, I must admit I never thought it would come to this," she said with real sorrow in her voice and tears in her eyes. "I know they were bad people who were trying to do us harm, but four of their lives have ended because of us. That's a huge burden to carry."

"Yes it is a burden, Angie, but you should try to lighten it somewhat with some rational thoughts. It's not our intention to kill or even harm anyone. All we are doing is costing them money. It was their decision to send a killing team after us. And I'd suggest strongly to you that their lives didn't end because of us, but rather because of their actions in attacking us. If they hadn't invaded our home, they'd still all be alive."

"I know what you're saying, David, and I understand your argument. I guess the loss of life, human or animal, will always affect me in some way. I'm sorry but I doubt that will ever change."

"Oh my dear Angie, I don't ever want it to. That's one of the key elements of what makes you so special, and why I love you so much," smiled Roberts.

"Damn it, now you've got me crying again." But as well as tears, there were brilliant eyes and a shining smile.

"What I do want now, though, Angie, is for you to pack a large suitcase or two and get ready to travel. As I said last night, I don't think they'll come back here again, but there are probably other interested parties after us by now, and it's not worth taking any more risks. I want you to come with me to Igloo. I can protect you better there than here."

"Oh David, I'd love to. I've wanted to see both the base and the submarine for ages! I don't care how long we have to stay there. I'll enjoy being with you and feeling as though I'm really part of the campaign."

THIRTY FIVE

Back at Igloo, Roberts had received word from his contacts that the Japanese group, with the *Kishin Maru* factory ship back in action, was again hunting whales in the southern Pacific Ocean. While in Sydney Roberts had seen some video footage of interviews with the chairman of the group involved in hunting whales, Sato Takamori, who had been scathing of whoever was attacking his ships in their lawful pursuit of the legal whale quota.

"We take only minke whales, and only catch up to our quota each year. No one can show any evidence to the contrary. These pirates must be found and stopped. They are a scourge on the ocean. They are trying to stop our vessels from carrying out legal commercial fishing operations, and I have asked our government for protection. If they continue to attack us, we will be forced to defend ourselves."

"Fascinating," he had said to himself. "I wonder just what his government will do to protect him."

Roberts had taken a few hours off, to show a very excited Angie over the base, and then over the submarine.

"David, it's incredible what you've managed to build here. It truly is an awesome feat. I only hope one day that you'll be able to legitimise it and show it to the world."

Now, just prior to sailing for the southern Pacific, Roberts was instructing the communications man, 'Mark' Coney, to keep a careful listening watch for word from the *Fish*, and for any information concerning vessel movement in the area they were heading for.

"I don't know exactly what to expect, but whatever happens I'm sure it will be trouble of some kind."

They set a course of 080° to pass south of New Zealand's Campbell Island, heading for the last set of coordinates they had received from Australia. These would be updated by Coney as they travelled, so they would be able to head almost directly for the whalers. The Sea Shepherd's *Steve Irwin* was also in the area, harassing the whalers and trying to film evidence of them overcatching their quota or taking other whale species, always a hit-or-miss undertaking, and this was another aid in locating the group.

Four days later, after a fast run mostly at snorkelling depth due to the heavy winter conditions, the *Fish* was approaching the area being worked by the whalers. It was late afternoon and through the periscope sighting was difficult due to the gloom, wind-driven spray and heavy rain.

"Lovely weather for a party," muttered Durrand.

"Our sonar's picked them up skipper," called Tomlinson, as a familiar loud pinging once again echoed through the submarine, "and theirs has picked us up."

"Maintain course and speed Marty," said Durrand, "while I get a look at them."

Tomlinson was riveted to his console. "Skipper!" he called urgently, "I'm showing four images—two large and two small. The two small I can identify as the chasers, and the largest image is the right size for the *Kishin Maru*. But the other blip is about half the size of the factory ship. If I didn't know better, I'd have to say it looks like a naval vessel, about the size and shape of a frigate. Can't be!" Tomlinson shook his head.

Durrand was glued to the periscope. "Haven't lost your touch Rick," he said slowly. "It's a naval ship right enough, and keeping close station on the *Kishin Maru*. It's too dark now to see the flag, but I'll bet it's got a rising sun on it. It certainly looks like a frigate, but I don't think Japan has much of an active navy these days.

Whaddaya reckon, David?"

"Well, she knows we're here, but I don't think she'll risk any kind of international incident by firing on us first," Roberts said thoughtfully. "I'm very tempted . . . if we made a fast run at the *Kishin Maru*, what do you think the frigate would do Gus?"

"Not sure David. She's trying to keep between the *Maru* and us—we'd have to go under her to get close to the whaler. Whether or not she'd drop a charge on us I don't know, but I'm game if you are. We'll sure as hell only get one pass though."

"Gus, what's the draft of both ships?" asked Roberts curiously.

"The whaler's would be about thirty feet, the frigate's probably twenty," replied Durrand quickly. "Yes, I see where you're heading—I think we could get away with it," he grinned.

"OK, Gus, let's do it. Make a run at the whaler at sixty feet to pass under the frigate, then plant a torpedo in the Maru's ass. Keep going until we're right under the *Maru*, then all stop. The frigate obviously won't be able to throw depth charges at us while we stay under the whaler, which is about five times our size. There'll be plenty of room under her, and we can keep station easily with the sonar and cameras controlling our thrusters. They won't be moving for a while anyway.

When you're ready."

The submarine dived to sixty feet and came around on a direct heading for the factory ship, moving in at ten knots. The frigate was alive with crewmen moving in all directions as she came to action stations. A depth charge was thrown into the path of the submarine to warn her away, the explosion throwing up a mountain of white water that was shredded into tatters by the gale force winds, but it was set at thirty feet and blew well ahead of the *Fish*. The crew had been warned to rig for depth charges, and were braced and ready. The result was less violent than before, and the submarine passed smoothly under the frigate, heading straight for the whaler. As she passed the frigate, she fired tube one and for the third time that year ruined the Kishin Maru's stern gear. She passed under the hull of the large whaler and reversed her screws to come to a dead stop under the now-crippled vessel.

"Great work everyone," called Durrand. "Clive, keep her at depth. Clarrie, keep monitoring the whaler with the cameras. Light her up if you need to—they certainly know where we are. Advise Martin if we need to adjust position. Rick, what's the frigate doing?"

"Seems to be circling round the *Maru*, skipper. What happens next?"

"We can stay here almost indefinitely," mused Durrand, "but at some point we'll need to leave the scene. In this weather it'll take them a long time to organise a tow for the *Maru* and get her moving north again. What do you want to do David?"

"Let's stay here tonight and have a look at things tomorrow morning. I didn't think Japan had a navy these days either. I'd like a look at that ship in daylight."

*

As a weak and watery dawn began to make sense of the hidden shapes in the cold, moving darkness, the crew of the *Flying Fish* all returned to action stations again. They were all fed and rested, the only people who had needed to be on watch those necessary to keep the submarine on station, and their back-ups.

"Morning Clarrie. That frigate still there?" asked Roberts cheerily, leaning in to Grimshaw's screen while finishing off a piece of vegemite toast.

"Yes, Mr Roberts, she's still circling slowly around us both. She's about half a kilometre off and seems to take about half an hour to get around. She's doing less than ten knots." Grimshaw politely turned his face away from Roberts so his wrinkled nose wouldn't be seen. Many people considered that vegemite was an Australian attack on international culinary culture. Grimshaw was one of them.

"I'm sure she could get up to speed quickly enough if we made a break, even at serious depth, and I reckon she could outrun us comfortably. So we'll need to consider other options," Roberts said slowly, thoughtfully, swallowing the last piece of the unconsciously offending toast. A small grin appeared.

"Clarrie, given the speed of the frigate, and that our bows are pointing in the same direction as those of the *Kishin Maru*, could you calculate the exact second her stern would be passing the line of our bows?"

"Easily," smiled Grimshaw, his nose unwrinkled again. "Would you also want the number of seconds prior to that we'd need to fire our torpedo so the two would end up in the same place at the same time?" he asked innocently.

"Now there's an idea, Clarrie," said Roberts. "Why not?"

Twenty minutes later Roberts was giving quiet instructions. "This time, Herb, I want you to fire on Clarrie's countdown. Martin, keep her steady. As soon as the torpedo's away, ease her out from under the *Maru*. I want a look at that frigate after the strike."

"Tube one ready?" asked Clarrie with a huge grin. "God, I've wanted to say that for months."

"Tube one ready," came the breathless voice of Kaye Halloran.

"Coming up . . . coming up . . . 3 . . . 2 . . . 1 . . . fire one!" called Clarrie.

"Fire one!" instantly responded Halloran.

As they all waited expectantly for the sound and thump of the strike, Durrand shook his head slightly. "Jesus, that's the first time I've ever fired on a warship of another country," he said almost wonderingly.

The sound of the hit pulsed through the vessel, signalling that they had crossed another barrier, and the campaign may have escalated to a different level.

"OK, Gus, let's have a look at her," said Roberts soberly. The submarine moved slowly out from under the *Kishin Maru* and rose to periscope depth. Durrand took a long look at the frigate as they moved slowly towards her.

"TV 3509," he read slowly. "That's a Japanese training vessel—I can't see her name, but I think it's the *Kushima*."

"She may be a training vessel, but she's armed at least with depth charges, and probably more. I think we should keep our distance," said Roberts.

"Yeah, she'll certainly have live ammo for her surface guns, but she's stopped in the water at the moment. They're probably assessing the damage. I reckon one screw's gone, and maybe her rudder's been damaged as well. I doubt she's crippled, but she'll probably have to make for port and lay up for repairs.

Scratch three more, guys. We're starting to take a bit of a toll. Wonder whether the word's getting out."

"Well done people," Roberts told the crew. "We could have turned away when we sighted the frigate, but we're here for a purpose. Once we were committed and contained, we had no alternative as I saw it to getting safely away.

We're still aiming solely at damaging the shipping we target, and doing all we can to ensure no one is hurt or killed. But that frigate, training vessel or no, would have sunk us and been satisfied if we had all perished, so I'm not feeling too bad about the damage we're doing.

Gus, can we head back to the Bight? There are reports of a fleet of tuna boats taking large catches of Southern bluefin again."

*

A week later the *Flying Fish* and crew were back in Igloo Base, after disabling three more large tuna boats—all Japanese long liners—and sinking their lines. While the submarine was being turned around and squared away ready for re-provisioning, Roberts and his managers were discussing the operations to date.

"So far we have fifteen hits. We must be making a serious dent in the operations of both the whalers and tuna boats. They are costly vessels to set up and must be even more so to repair after we've been at them. The Norwegians aren't back yet, so we'll take some more R&R back in Sydney while I get a handle on the publicity which seems to be generating. Sort out the shifts, Lou, and we'll move out in a day or so."

THIRTY SIX

The contact group was meeting in a quiet corner of one of the Sydney Hilton's lounge bars. There was enough soft music and muted noise to cover their conversation with a blanket of privacy, as they sipped at drinks and nibbled antipasto and pork crackle.

"The hornets' nest is starting to stir," Morgan Hendry was saying, with evident satisfaction. "There've been many newspaper articles and television current affairs programs speculating on just what is going on down south. But no one so far has been able to present any hard facts. According to a source I have in the federal parliament, the government has received a request through the Japanese consul asking for information on any Australian submarines operating in the Southern Ocean. The stories of the damaged fishing and whaling vessels have been picked up by overseas news services, and every one I've seen has the same spin—how good it is that these illegal fishing boats are being forced to interrupt or even in some cases halt their activities. Even though, as you'd expect, the whalers are all maintaining an air of injured innocence, claiming that they are being forced by pirates to stop their legal whaling operations, the majority of reports are hailing the interruptions as a win for the whales." Hendry and the others were clearly pleased with the results of Roberts' campaign so far.

"That's good to hear, guys," said Roberts, "but have any of you seen any mention of my name or my home in Ulladulla?"

"No, David," replied Trevor Lane, "all the reports so far have only recounted the damage to the vessels, especially to the Japanese training ship. That one has caused a real stir. The Japs are furious that someone has apparently fired on one of their naval vessels, and they want blood. But at the moment they don't know whose."

"Well, for your information only, I can tell you that last month we had a covert team of intruders attack my home at Ulladulla, and they weren't there for R&R. They'd been sent by a Mr Lo, a Vietnamese billionaire from Indonesia, who controls a fleet of toothfishing boats and a whaling group. His managers had put two and two together much as you blokes did, came up with a submarine and somehow discovered that I was connected with it. I suspect we have a slimy little South American in Florida to thank for that."

"Jesus, David!" exclaimed Brock Hewitt, "obviously they didn't succeed in what they were trying to do, but was there anyone hurt?"

"Four of them were killed and we sent the other two home with a warning," said Roberts soberly. "Fortunately none of us were injured. Angie had hired a very reliable security man, and he had enlisted the aid of a team of young karate enthusiasts from Ray's old dojo. They are all keen as mustard and have been trained by the security man, Allen Bell, who had installed a few strategic devices around the place which worked very well. The dojo team cleaned up the resulting mess."

"God almighty," breathed Hewitt, "that's awful! Did the local police get into the act?" He was clearly shaken by Roberts' story, and the general mood of the group had darkened as they realised the picnic, if there had ever been one, was definitely over.

"No, Brock," Roberts shook his head, "the foreign bodies were buried at sea and the remaining two were able to walk away, which they did very quickly. There's no evidence left of what happened and those two won't be talking. If they survive their return, that is.

Thing is, if Lo found us, there's no reason why others can't do the same, and I expect them to. Like the Japanese, for example. That's why I moved Angie to Igloo base, so there isn't anyone left at Ulladulla to attack. Except Allen Bell and his gadgets, which wouldn't be the smartest thing to do."

"OK David," mused Hendry quietly, in a group that had grown serious and thoughtful, "currently you personally aren't in the public domain, and neither is the *Flying Fish*. But that state of affairs probably won't last much longer. Have you got any plans about how to handle things from here?"

"Yes, Morgan, I have. I want to become proactive with regard to the publicity. I don't under any circumstances want to step into the limelight, but if it's inevitable, then I want to control it as much as possible. Can you arrange an interview with Les Patterson?"

"No problem," smiled Hendry, "he's already contacted me and asked if I have any idea of what's really happening to the fishing and whaling boats. He will absolutely leap at it."

*

The next morning Roberts, Hendry and a clearly expectant Les Patterson were sitting at the large and beautifully polished red wood jarrah table in one of the hotel's smaller conference rooms in its business centre. Hendry had just introduced

Patterson to Roberts, who was advising the journalist of some ground rules.

"Les, I've read some of your pieces and I like their flavour. I know Morgan has told you almost nothing, under instruction, and I wish I could keep it that way. But things are hotting up, and I see no alternative to getting some information out to the public on our terms. But you'll agree to print only what I authorize or this will be our first and last interview, and you won't like that one bit. Trust me on this."

"Mr Roberts, all I know at present is that you are somehow connected with what's happening to the whaling and fishing boats in the Southern Ocean, and to the damage to that Japanese frigate. But I will not knowingly print lies or bullshit, and I won't be censored. I will, however, agree to print only what you approve. I can smell a pretty big story here, and as you say, I don't want to miss out on it. Are you planning to give information to other reporters as well?" Patterson was plainly anxious about having sole rights to a story which could turn out to be one of the biggest of the year.

"Call me David," said Roberts, "and I'll call you sir. No, I'm happy for you to break it to the world, as long as you break only what I tell you."

Patterson cringed slightly at the 'sir', but manfully shrugged it off as a form of payment for what he hoped he was about to receive. His face was frank, open and looked almost ingenuous, but Roberts wasn't deceived.

"Tell me what you've gleaned so far, sir," he suggested to Patterson with a faint smile.

"Clearly, what's doing the damage is a submarine, and I imagine it's yours. It has to be firing torpedoes at the vessels that have suffered damage so far, and it must have fired on that Japanese cruiser as well. I don't know anything about the sub yet, although I've got something that just came in on a research vessel in the USA which may be a submarine. But I haven't the foggiest where your base of operations is." Patterson looked at Roberts, returning the small smile and raising him an eyebrow.

"Yes, not bad, sir," Roberts replied. "It is a submarine, a Foxtrot class that we refurbished, about a hundred metres long and called the *Flying Fish*. I'll let you see some video of her soon, as well as film of some of the damage done to the ships we've—ah—seen. She's registered in New Caledonia but has a mostly American/Australian crew. When we get to fly a flag, it will be the Boxing Kangaroo. Your assessment about the torpedoes could be correct, but I admit nothing.

We operate out of a special base, but its location will be kept strictly confidential. Attempts have already been made on our lives and I don't want to encourage any others. I'll talk to you more about that in a minute. How are we doing so far?"

"Great!" enthused Patterson as he checked his small, voice-actuated tape recorder. "I think I've got a handle on the 'why', but can you confirm it?"

"Sure. We are very much into conservation of all marine species, especially whales, and if no more whalers or pirate fishing boats ever came into the Southern Ocean we'd be overjoyed. I guess we'd have to take a trip north," Roberts grinned. Then more seriously, "but we are in no way threatening the lives or health of any persons, pirates or no. All we hope for is that the vessels sustain damage that renders them incapable of continuing to fish to extinction species such as toothfish, Southern bluefin tuna and all whales."

"Got no problems with all that, David, it's the 'how' that I think some of my readers may be less enthusiastic about. Were you to be actually firing torpedoes at these vessels, you would in fact be committing piracy on the high seas, would you not?" The eyes were now quite piercing, the expression less open.

"I understand, Les, that an experienced journalist such as yourself has to play devil's advocate in every interview, regardless of your own personal views, and in this case your question is fair. If in fact torpedoes were being fired, then yes, it would be piracy in the case of the whaling and fishing boats, and an act of war in the case of the Japanese training vessel. Although I guess that a physical declaration of war would theoretically be made by the first aggressive act, which may have come from the frigate via a depth charge.

In any event, as far as I and my crew are concerned, not one of the governments of the countries espousing a commitment to marine conservation has managed to accomplish one damned thing of any practical use in preventing illegal fishing and over-quota whaling. The lives of the diplomats and foreign affairs junketers have become too comfortable—their talkfests move at the speed of a Galapagos tortoise taking the sun. We insist it's way past time for affirmative action.

The general public will have to make up its collective mind about the rights and wrongs of whatever is happening down south. I just hope they'll be presented with balanced arguments devoid of rhetoric and emotive viewpoints. Mind you, it's bloody difficult to ignore your emotions when you're within touching distance of a humpback whale."

"Beautiful stuff," exhaled Patterson. "OK, if you won't confirm the torpedoes, can you tell me something about the crew?"

"Sorry Les, absolutely not. The only name you will hear is mine, and you're not authorized to print that yet. The reasons should be obvious."

"Yes, David, they are, but a good reporter will always try it on. It's surprising how often something pops out," smiled Patterson.

"Right sir, the base. All I will say is that it isn't in Australia, but nobody who isn't part of the Foxtrot Corporation knows where it is. Not yet anyway," said Roberts.

"Don't look at me, sir," shrugged Hendry, "I haven't a clue where it is either, but I'd give an awfully large percentage of this year's profits to see it."

"And that, Les, is what I really want to talk to you about . . . ."

*

That night, following the interview and a lengthy discussion between Roberts and Patterson, the reporter leaned back in his chair as he finished his latest piece for the *Sydney Morning Herald.* He reviewed it, made some amendments, rewrote a sentence here and there, and finally was satisfied. He was also satisfied with the deal he made with Roberts. Although not admitting it, his sympathies lay solidly with Roberts' cause, and extracting a promise from Roberts to show him over the base and the submarine, when possible, in return for the construct of a base in red herring country, had been strawberries on the banana cream sponge.

Sir Galahad or Henry Morgan?

Yesterday I had an interview with a man who, whether he likes it or not, is going to become quite well-known in the near future. He's put together a team of people from America, Australia and Britain and encased them in a rather special 'research vessel'. It's a submarine, and apart from the beautiful royal blue colour and a large white flying fish on the sail, it looks like an old wartime model. But this

model, folks, comes equipped with some interesting high-tech modifications.

You know all those whaling and fishing boats that have been mysteriously damaged in the Southern Ocean while carrying out their 'strictly lawful' enterprises? This submarine, which I understand is called the *Flying Fish,* has coincidentally happened to be quite close to each vessel when it suffered the damage, and has used its high-tech scanning and recording equipment to capture images of the damage to each vessel. Which, folks, I'm here to tell you doesn't look an awful lot. Some broken propellers, a few bent rudders and a hole in a hull or two. Enough, though, to send these ships back home for repairs.

The man-in-charge (I wanted to call him Captain Nemo, but was helped to resist by the flashing eye and scowling mein) claimed his vessel was merely standing by each of the stricken boats to render assistance should it be needed. In fact, he mentioned in passing that his crew had already been able to assist one fisherman who had fallen overboard. He said it looked to him and his crew as though the disabled ships had been struck by floating containers. The people carrying out the repairs on the vessels have said the damage looks to them as though the ships had been struck by running torpedoes. While this mysterious masked man has admitted nothing and there is no evidence of torpedoes, or whence their 'running' may have originated, I guess it takes neither the imagination of Stephen Spielberg nor the intelligence of Albert Einstein to arrive at four here, folks.

And then there's the little matter of the Japanese naval training vessel *Kushima,* which claims it, too, was struck by one of these torpedoes while escorting a whaling group. The masked man said the container that did the damage may have been blown upwards into the vessel by the depth charge the *Kushima* dropped on it, but the Japanese deny carrying any arms or weapons aboard their ship. They are outraged and claim that an act of war has been committed against them. But by whom, you might ask? They did too, but their consul in Canberra was told emphatically by our minister that Australia had no submarines operating in the Southern Ocean, and that if we did they would have carefully refrained from firing any torpedoes at the *Kushima*. Anyway, you'd have to hope that if one of our submarines fired a torpedo at the *Kushima* there wouldn't have been anything left to complain about, or our Department of Defense isn't getting enough bang for its bucks.

Finally (for now, but watch this space folks), there's one other interesting aspect of this story that emerges as a real puzzle: Where the hell are these affirmative activists located? Nowhere in Australia, that's for sure. But they must have a significant base of operations somewhere—significant enough to maintain and provision both a submarine and the crew to run it. And you'd think, again without input from Spielberg or Einstein, that it would need to be somewhere in or near to the Southern Ocean. Well naturally this intrepid reporter asked the man the same question (albeit without the 'where the hell'—his flashing eye was quite intimidating), and using his guarded, carefully-worded explanation, plus one or two hints he had dropped earlier, came up with what could be an accurate result.

Folks, the base has to be in Tierra del Fuego—the Land of Fire! And here's some geography for you: The most southerly city in the world is its capital, Ushuaia, and south of that is the Wollaston Islands group, only a few kilometres north of Cape Horn itself. Somewhere in there, I believe, is the base of this band of brothers and sisters. It is a very remote location, almost inaccessible, has extreme weather but is sheltered from the violence of the South Atlantic and Southern Oceans. It provides excellent access to the Southern Ocean through any number of waterways and neither the Chilean nor the Argentinian governments bother about the area apart from some infrequent patrols.

So, folks, there you have it—friend or foe? Knight in shining armour or bloodthirsty, black-hearted pirate? Maybe the truth, as it does so often, lies somewhere in-between. Certainly no blood seems to have been spilled, and those who are suffering are doing so only in the hip pocket. Those who *were* suffering—the whales et al—are getting some time out.

On balance, and after only a little soul-searching, I found I came down pretty quickly on the side of these cetacean crusaders.

Get on to our blog site and post your side.

THIRTY SEVEN

The mansion on the Indonesian island of Batuka, with Lo in attendance, was hosting its quarterly general meeting. There was a palpable tenseness around the table, for it was not lost on any of those present that only one of the twins—the taller one—was sitting in his accustomed place. Chillingly, there was now not even another place set. There was nothing outwardly different about the speech or actions of any of the members. That would have been unthinkable. Nonetheless, there was an air of uneasiness permeating the room, the discomfort seeming to increase when Chen glided across the carpet to speak quietly to Lo for a minute. He finished, moving away as silently as he had entered, and Lo turned his attention to the group at the table.

"Gentlemen," he began in his customary soft tone, "I want to begin this meeting with a report from our fishing manager. His colleague, unfortunately, will not be able to join us. He has decided that his future lies in diving rather than fishing, and has left to gain practical experience." By now everyone around the large table was fully aware that it had been Chen who had arranged this practical experience, and that it had included free diving in very deep water with plenty of weights.

The remaining twin, face completely impassive, voice matching, all emotion and expression laundered from his presentation, said, "Mr Lo, gentlemen, I advise that our maritime operations have been forced to halt pending the satisfactory removal of the cause of the interruption. That cause has been determined to be a certain Australian businessman called David Roberts and a submarine he has outfitted. It has a trained crew and is attacking any whaling vessels it sees in the Southern Ocean, together with toothfishing boats and tuna catchers. We mounted an operation against his home base in a place called Ulladulla, in New South Wales, but he had organised a small army of highly trained soldiers who were able to prevent our operatives from completing their task. There were only two survivors, neither of whom are able to be located, but one of them contacted an agent of mine, who advised me of the details.

His base of operations has been reported in the newspapers as being somewhere in Tierra Del Fuego, and we have dispatched some small patrol boats to attempt to locate it. So far we have been unable to do so." He glanced at Lo impassively, for he had long ago become resigned to his probable fate. He felt sure it would not be long before he followed his former colleague into a similar career change.

"Recommendations?" murmured Lo on a rising inflection.

"Roberts' home now appears deserted, Mr Lo, and we have so far been unable to determine where he is operating from. I believe we need some significant assistance, perhaps in the form of the Japanese, whose operations are also being affected. Should you agree, I recommend a personal approach to the CEO of the group controlling the Japanese whaling interests, a Mr Takamori. He is a very wealthy and powerful man in his country and I believe he has the ear of his government. I am confident he would be prepared to join forces with us in resolving this problem."

Lo considered this advice for a short period, then nodded once. "Our fishing operation is one of our more lucrative enterprises. I do not wish to roll over and tuck my tail between my legs because some little crusading flea is biting my rear end." On their lives no one dared make a sound or show the slightest expression at the image Lo had painted. "I will contact Mr Takamori and enlist his aid in squashing this flea. I hope very sincerely that your confidence is not found to have been misplaced."

The remaining fishing manager did also, with a fervour that quite surprised him. Neither his fervour nor surprise, however, was remotely revealed in the submissive lowering of his eyes and nod of his head.

*

Only a day or two later a similar meeting was occurring once again in Kagoshima, Japan. This one, however, was of a distinctly different flavour. It was presided over, as usual, by the head of the Japanese whaling group, Sato Takamori, and on this occasion he was less than imperturbable.

"Did I not give instructions last meeting concerning this *gaijin* and his submarine? Did I not make myself clear?" he growled to the others in attendance. "He is now causing us unacceptable losses, and I want him eliminated!"

"Excuse me, Takamori-san, but all we know at present is his name, David Roberts, and that he has a submarine based somewhere in the Southern Ocean. Just where is still unknown. The western press have picked him up, although his name is not yet public, and are lionizing him and his exploits. We need more information before we can organise a counter-offensive."

"Very well." The harsh, staccato tones shot from Takamori like an old gatling gun on full crank. "I have been approached by the head of certain maritime operations, including whaling, based in Indonesia. This Mr Lo is in a similar position to our group, and has suggested we combine our resources and find this madman's hideout. Then we can send in teams to remove it."

"As the head of our legal department, Takamori-san, I would advise caution. It would depend very much on just where their base is situated. We would not want to cause an international incident," said one of the older members of the group.

"*Manko!*" snarled Takamori, "those devils have already fired on a Japanese naval ship! I don't give a damn about causing an incident. I want them stopped and I don't care how! Liaise with these Viets in Jakarta and find them. When we know where they are we can plan accordingly.

Get it done!"

*

It was clearly the time of meetings, for in Sydney Roberts was conferring again with his contact group. Also present at this time was Les Patterson.

Brock Hewitt sounded almost reverent. "David, do you realise what's happening out there? You're becoming bigger than Ben Hur. Les' article has caused worldwide fascination with your exploits, and public opinion is running over ninety percent in your favour."

"Yeah, David, after my latest piece our blog site recorded more hits than at any other time, and they're still coming in. I've had requests from over fifty other journos from all round Australia, and many more from overseas, for some inside information. Especially for the name of this hero. Kate Preshaw from *'Sydney Tonight'* is very keen to get an interview." Patterson shook his head slightly. "It's easily the most interest I've ever had in any of my stuff before," he smiled, a little ruefully.

"Kate Preshaw eh?" Roberts said with a grin. "Well, we'd better give her what she wants. Set it up sir, but don't tell her who it is yet. I want you there too. I guess we can't keep a lid on it for much longer anyway. At least your 'disclosure' of the location of our base may have sent a few of the nasties on a long chase to nowhere."

"I believe so, David," Patterson said with a certain satisfaction. "I've had a couple of reports in from some South American colleagues in Chile who have heard via contacts in their government that several large power boats have been seen cruising near Puerto Williams and Ushuaia, presumably investigating the Wollaston Islands. Most of them have apparently called in at Punta Arenas for supplies and fuel, and their crews have visited the bars and the brothels. Word has filtered out from both sources that they are searching for the elusive submarine base."

"Good." Roberts nodded, although with a small frown. "I wonder if we'll be able to maintain secrecy at Igloo."

"So, David, that's what the base is called? Is it on a map somewhere?" Patterson eagerly fired the questions at Roberts.

"No sir," laughed Roberts," at least not on any map south of Alaska. Call Kate and tell her you'll introduce the leader of the conservation group to her and to her viewers on air during the next show."

THIRTY EIGHT

"Why are you so late! The show has been on now for twenty three minutes, and Kate and the crew have been in a huge flap! Quickly, come with me and get some fast make-up on." Patterson and Roberts had deliberately arrived at the television studios late, but the young production assistant was all experience and efficiency, propelling them both into the make-up room. "Mr Patterson, Kate wants you to go on first for a couple of minutes, to set it up for your friend. What's his name?"

"Sorry miss, that'll be for the live telecast," said Patterson, while Roberts looked around with interest at Kate's world of lights, strange equipment and fast-moving people.

"OK," the PA spoke quietly into a headphone mike, then addressed the two men. "You're on in four minutes, Mr Patterson, and your friend will walk on to the set when Kate's ready. Please follow me to the sound stage."

They walked quickly behind the young woman, who led them through a maze of passages and doors, before the last and largest one of which she turned to them and whispered, "Quietly now, this is the backstage area. Just come in and sit down on one of the chairs. Try not to make any noise."

Preshaw was wrapping up an interview with a local formula one driver who had won his last start in Germany, and was moving into world ranking calculations. A couple of minutes later a burst of applause from the studio audience sounded as the young driver came around the side of the set with a stylishly dressed female assistant. She took hold of Patterson's arm and waited, poised for a cue. She obviously heard something which went past the two men, for she urged Patterson around the same side of the set from where the young driver had appeared. Applause rang out again, as Patterson walked up to the lounge chairs and small table where Preshaw was waiting.

"Hi sir, thanks for coming on," Preshaw said in a low voice, laughing as Patterson grimaced. "People, a warm welcome for Les Patterson, the reporter who has broken the story of the mysterious stranger and his amazing machine, the *Flying Fish*, a submarine that seems to be causing havoc among the whaling and fishing industry in the Southern Ocean." She grinned as Patterson sank onto the chair Preshaw indicated. "Les and I are friends from way back, so I get to call him 'sir'. Most of you in the audience will know his pieces in the *Sydney Morning Herald* and I doubt there's a person in the country who hasn't read his latest report on this fascinating crusade which seems to be occurring on our doorstep.

But what you people in the audience don't know is that you're in for a real treat tonight! Thanks to Les, we've managed to secure an interview with the man himself, the one who's put this team together and is pointing his submarine at what he considers are 'maritime undesirables'. He's waiting backstage right now, and I can tell you I haven't even met him myself yet. So, people, please give a very special welcome to the mysterious stranger who is so much in the news at the moment."

The audience burst into a loud and excited applause, more vigorous than the cues called for, some whistling and shouting, as the assistant led Roberts around the side of the stage and on to the set. Patterson and Preshaw had risen, and at the sight of Roberts Preshaw's jaw fell audibly and she gave a small shriek. Her years of experience deserted her for an instant as she recognized Roberts, and she stood still, quite stunned at the sight of the man she had once known so well. Her face was a picture, first white, then red, as a number of expressions chased themselves over it, all beautifully caught by the camera. After a few seconds of immobility, which the audience in the studio and all those watching at home were very interested to observe, her *sang froid* returned and the professional took over.

"My God . . . David! Is it really you? My God!" She smiled hugely as she hugged him and motioned him to a seat around the low table. "People, as you've all no doubt realised by now, this man and I are old friends too. I'm very pleased to be able to introduce to you, live on our show, Mr David Roberts, the man who appears to be responsible for the rash of broken whaling and fishing boats currently operating in the southern hemisphere. Or trying to." Once again the audience erupted into a loud and prolonged applause, and by now the production team had picked up the unusual reaction, as had Kate.

"The audience is clearly in favour of what's happening, David, even if we don't actually know what that is. I'm just dying to hear all about it, and I'll bet a good percentage of the country's population is too. Please, can you tell us?" Preshaw had regained her presence, and used it to good effect, her gaze at Roberts a study in wide-eyed, imploring expectation.

"Boy, Kate, you've certainly become what I think they call the 'consummate professional'," said Roberts with an admiring and very disarming smile. "and still as lovely as ever." Preshaw's colour rose slightly again as her presence faltered, before resuming her camera face. "Yes, I'm happy to tell you about our beautiful *Flying Fish*, and how we seem to stumble across so many ships and fishing boats in need of assistance." A number of people in the high-spirited studio audience were chuckling, one man laughing loudly while stuffing a handkerchief into his mouth.

"Our vessel is an old Foxtrot submarine which we've modified to take advantage of current technology, and our crew consists of about equal numbers of Americans and Australians, with the odd Brit thrown in. We range across the Southern Ocean and often come upon other ships and boats fishing or whaling. They all seem to suffer damage to their stern sections, or backsides, and we stand by to offer assistance in the event of any sinkings. It appears to have happened about twenty times to date, and we've noted a decrease in the amount and frequency of fishing and whaling operations over the past year or so."

"David," Kate said, no longer smiling, "you seem to have skirted around the core of the matter, one that I think would be of major interest to everyone watching. Just how is this mysterious damage being inflicted? The reports coming from the shipyards where the vessels are being repaired suggest that it is torpedo damage—that it can't be anything else. Is that what you're doing?"

"Kate, in the best interests of legal tradition, or political doublespeak, I can neither confirm nor deny that we are using torpedoes. But it may be worth noting that so far no vessel has been sunk and no person has been injured or killed on them. It appears they are simply being encouraged to cease operating in the Southern Ocean, regardless of whether they are 'legal' or not.

"And I guess you can't confirm or deny you fired a torpedo at a Japanese naval vessel either, David," Kate asked seriously.

"Correct Kate, I can't. But we were in the vicinity of that incident with the *Kushima*, and what I can confirm is that she dropped what could only be a depth charge in the water near us. Any damage she sustained came after that."

"But as I understand it, the *Kushima* was only trying to protect her country's whaling ship that was operating in the same area."

"You mean the one only catching her legal quota of minke whales for scientific purposes, Kate?" asked Roberts with raised eyebrows. He wasn't smiling now either.

"Well, that is what they claim, David," replied Preshaw. "It's the same claim made by the tuna-fishing boats, and the toothfishing longliners all maintain they don't fish anywhere near the exclusion zones."

"And I swear I saw Elvis alive and well yesterday, shopping in Centrepoint," nodded Roberts equably. More chuckles from the audience. "Do you remember the pirate fishing boat caught red-handed in the Heard Island exclusion zone about four years ago? She was the *Viarsa*, and after a long chase she was captured and brought back to Perth for her crew to stand trial. What happened?" asked Roberts rhetorically. "Nothing. The 'not guilty' verdict simply ensured a return to illegal toothfishing for the crew and that several highly-paid lawyers became even richer.

"Kate," said Roberts earnestly, turning to the audience, "and all of you watching this program tonight, be sure of one thing. Our seas *are* being ravished. Some species *are* being fished to extinction. Whales other than minkes *are* being hunted and killed—there may be only a few hundred blue whales left alive on our planet, and they are the largest creatures ever to have existed! And it's all just for one simple reason: profit. The directors of these marine factories are as indifferent to species extinction as they are to swatting a fly. They would be equally indifferent to eliminating me and my team." Roberts spoke quietly but earnestly, and completely won the audience. They were enthralled by what he was saying. "The Japanese, Norwegians, Spaniards and others, they are all either overcatching their so-called 'quotas', or simply ignoring them. Regardless of what they all say about the lack of evidence to prove such a claim, believe me, it's happening."

It was clear the audience did.

"David, for the benefit of the audience and viewers can I point out that some years ago you were a real high-flier in the business world and made a fortune on the stock market before apparently opting out. Was it this crusade of yours that persuaded you to change the course of your life?" Kate asked the question for the camera, but her genuine curiosity was plain to see.

"No Kate, I decided to 'opt out' as you put it because I grew disenchanted with doing big deals that made me and my company a lot of money, but actually produced nothing of benefit to society. My 'crusade'—again as you put it; you do have a way with words—began the day I went paddling up the coast and came across a humpback whale trapped in fishing nets. Some swimmers and jet-skiers were trying to cut it free, and it was lying calmly in the water, waiting. I got close to it and helped one of the swimmers cut some net from one of its fins, and realised suddenly that I was within touching distance of it. So I did. And stared right into its eye." Roberts paused, his feelings clear even though he was speaking almost dispassionately. "I doubt there'd be a single person who's been close to a whale who didn't feel something of what I experienced that morning," he said quietly. "It was unforgettable."

Preshaw waited a few seconds, milking the moment, delighted at the way the audience was responding to Roberts, before continuing.

"David," she said in a serious tone, candour painted across her face, "I haven't had time to mention this, but we've had the Fisheries Minister standing by in our Canberra studios since you came on. He's been listening to what you've had to say."

Roberts burst out laughing. "Haven't had time, Kate? Just slipped your mind? Or maybe your timing is perfect to the second," he grinned, obviously comfortable with the situation. Preshaw didn't look nearly as comfortable at being so easily caught out and again her composure slid momentarily. But only for a moment. She smiled and raised her voice slightly, turning to a large monitor hooked up to the Canberra studio equipment.

"Good evening Mr Minister. Thank you so much for your patience. I'm sorry you had to wait so long. Can I introduce you to Mr Les Patterson of the *Sydney Morning Herald*, and Mr David Roberts, I guess of the *Flying Fish*?"

"Good evening Kate. Not at all. I'm pleased to be asked onto your show, and have been fascinated to listen to Mr Roberts and his tales of derring-do. Good evening to you both, gentlemen." The minister's very expensive hair treatment ensured that the lock of dark, lightly silvered hair dropped exactly over his left eye, so he could casually wave his hand at it and brush it back. Preshaw, very experienced in TV presentation, smiled to herself at his styled and schooled appearance.

"I'm glad you're in such good spirits, Minister," grinned Kate, enjoying the ease with which she was able to segue. "It wasn't too long ago you seemed less pleased with what it was reported was occurring in the Southern Ocean. In fact, if I remember correctly (she remembered perfectly, as she had researched the topic that morning and included the notes on her clipboard), you said in an interview that the people responsible for the damage to the fishing vessels were pirates, and should be prosecuted for what they were doing. Do you still feel that way?"

Preshaw wasn't the only experienced TV performer in the interview. The Minister smiled a little sadly as though at an errant schoolchild, saying "Oh Kate, I never called anyone a pirate. I said what was occurring was akin to piracy, at a time when we all knew little of what actually was happening." He had been observing the audience reaction to Roberts closely too, and was as capable of reading the play as were the TV people. One aspect of the experience gained by politicians who have been in office for any length of time is the ability to judge the mood of a group of people to a very fine tolerance. Another is the skill to make minor amendments to something said previously so it now sounded like its complete opposite. "Now we've all heard the 'Clayton's admission' from Mr Roberts—the admission you make when you're not making an admission—we are in a better position to analyse the situation and decide on an appropriate response."

"Nice to hear you say so Mr Minister. Do you still claim that there's never been any place in a civilised society for vigilantes?"

Now the Minister's composure exfoliated, his shining smile decreasing to half its size. "I don't believe I made that exact claim, Kate," he said, not quite so happily. "I may have been alluding to the dangers of untrained people trying to take the law into their own hands, which is clearly inadvisable. But again I point out to you and our viewers that this was before anyone knew exactly what was happening, who was involved, and why they were doing it."

"It was actually an exact quote Mr Minister, but we won't labor the point. Can you tell us how you feel about what is happening now that you are more informed?"

"I can tell you and the viewers, Kate, that my government is relieved to know that the vessel inflicting the damage on these whaling and fishing boats is not one registered in this country. We are pleased also to learn that no injury has befallen anyone, but sincerely regret the damage sustained by these vessels. My government is vehemently opposed to whaling of any kind, and to any vessels taking catches exceeding their quotas, and loses no opportunity to present this point of view at all IWC meetings. However, we can not condone violent action of any kind against any vessel. It just simply is not acceptable." The Minister was back in stride, speaking confidently and comfortably.

"But Minister, this is nothing we haven't heard a number of times already. What are you going to do about the situation now?" asked Kate with just the right amount of exasperation. "If anything," she added, with an apologetic shrug. This drew a small carefully controlled frown from the Minister, who didn't, however, allow it to encroach upon his voice.

"Kate, viewers, I can assure you all that we as a government are doing everything possible to manage the situation. We have all our patrol boats and planes on active duty at present, with trained inspectors on all vessels. As you would all be able to understand, it is a huge area we have to cover, so inevitably there will be some places we can't investigate. But all those engaged in illegal fishing enterprises know very well that the full weight of Australian authority will be upon them should they transgress."

"Like what happened to the *Viarsa* you mean?" Kate asked evenly.

"Well, Kate, in all fairness her captain and crew were tried in a court of law and found not guilty. What else could have been done?" The Minister smiled ruefully, shrugging as he tried to imply he would have liked to see them imprisoned for life. It didn't work very well, and the audience sensed it. They began to murmur.

"The government could have ordered them sunk the moment they began to flee from the exclusion zone, Minister," said Roberts mildly.

The Minister brushed his lock back. "If that's a serious suggestion, Mr Roberts, it perhaps underscores the difference between your philosophy and the government's. That incident occurred, of course, during the time of the previous government, but I'm not sure we would have done things differently had we been in power at that time. We are not barbarians who take the opportunity to destroy boats and risk killing their crews because they are illegally fishing. We must operate within the law at all times." He managed not to appear patronizing, but couldn't prevent some condescension flavouring his tone.

"Then maybe you should be changing the laws. You've certainly had enough time to begin doing so," said Roberts flatly. "Any boat that tries to flee after being caught fishing in an exclusion zone, and after having a warning shot fired across her bows, deserves to be sunk."

"Er, Mr Minister, could I ask a question?" Les Patterson spoke diffidently, although his eyes held a gleam not apparent to the Minister in the Canberra studio. He continued without pause, his words coming a fraction of a second before the Minister could reply. "Have you considered asking any of the private companies for help in locating the illegal fishing boats? I think I know one company which would be pleased to assist the government in apprehending these people."

"Good evening Mr Patterson. I enjoy your work. Yes, you probably do." The Minister was back in control now, on familiar territory. He hadn't enjoyed Roberts' direct and pointed comments, especially as they had been pointed directly at him. "But I'm afraid we'd be concerned that involving private vessels in conflict situations could lead to unwanted, perhaps even unwarranted, confrontations, which might escalate into violence. It could be seen that the private vessels had a stake in the apprehension of foreign fishing boats, that the Australian government was unfairly protecting its own boats."

"Fair enough Minister, but what about allowing them to provide you with information on the locations of the vessels taking fish in the exclusion zones?"

The Minister casually brushed the lock back again while appearing to give the suggestion some thought. "That would seem to be a good idea Mr Patterson. I'll take it up with my staff in the near future," he nodded approvingly, his thoughts in fact only concentrated on his appearance and how he was faring in the interview. "Well, Kate, it's been a pleasure, but if there's nothing more I really must . . ."

"There is one more thing I'd like to ask, Minister, if you don't mind?" Roberts was mild, non-aggressive, almost affable.

"Certainly, Mr Roberts." This time the Minister got his reply in before being upstaged. He smiled.

"I'd like to know if you have a naval presence in the Southern Ocean, and if not, are you going to?"

"That really is the province of the Minister for Defense, Mr Roberts, and I'm certainly not in the position of second-guessing what he will decide. To the best of my knowledge we don't at the moment have any naval vessels in the Southern Ocean. That isn't to say, of course, that we won't undertake training manoevres there at some time in the future, but as I said, that's for the Minister for Defense to decide. But I don't believe there are any plans to send a naval vessel into the area, due to the possibility of causing the situation to become more inflamed.

Now I'm sorry but I must be off, Kate. I'm late for another appointment." One final time the Minister waved his lock back, as he rose to leave.

"Oh dear, I'm very sorry to have held you up Minister. Thank you so much for coming on our show and giving us some of your valuable time. It was most illuminating," Kate said to a retreating back, clad suavely in one of the latest Stratton three-piecers.

"And thank you both very much, too. Les, I'm very grateful you persuaded David to out himself, so to speak. David, I still can't quite believe it's you behind this fascinating campaign, even if you won't admit it." Turning to the audience, Preshaw said "Would you all thank the two men for being here tonight with us?"

The applause was long and deafening.

*

Fifteen minutes later, Kate joined the two at one of the tables in a small cafeteria, where they were relaxing over a coffee. She was pumped.

"It probably doesn't mean a lot to you guys, but we just rated through the roof!" Shining eyes, high colour and a beaming smile told the two men that the figures she had just received were as good as they got.

"Congratulations Kate," Roberts smiled in genuine pleasure. "You certainly have become a leading light in the world of Australian TV entertainment. Watching you operate tonight, it was obvious that you were always in control. I'm glad we were able to help with the success of tonight's show."

"Thank you. But without Les' help and you coming on the show, we would only have rated our average, which hasn't been all that flash lately. You have been more help than you know.

It's nosey I know, David, but is there a woman in your life these days?" she continued.

"There sure is, Kate. Some years ago I hired a housekeeper to look after me in Ulladulla. I didn't realise until recently just what a treasure she was. To my great good fortune, I do now. Her name's Angie.

How about you, Kate? What have you been up to in the intervening years since we were attached to each other?"

"Oh, I married that author I was telling you about, Jay Soderman, and for a time we had a wonderful relationship. But he stopped writing, started drinking and kept travelling, as I remember you said he might. I discovered he was usually accompanied by friends when he travelled, said friends being young, female and attractive. We've been separated for eight months now, and I've been too busy to deal with it properly, or to search for a replacement." The euphoria of the ratings result had been replaced by a certain wistfulness, and Roberts couldn't help feeling sad for her.

"I'm sorry Kate. But don't worry, it'll happen. I hope it doesn't take as long for you as it did for me. We'd better go, Les. I don't want to keep my friends waiting."

"David, could we please stay in touch? I don't want to let this go, and I have the feeling there's more to come." Kate was still the professional, still thinking and working.

"Sure Kate. My number in Ulladulla is the same as before, and I'll give you my mobile number too. But I'm away a fair bit, so don't worry if you can't reach me. You can get a message to me through Les, who knows how to contact me. See you later." Roberts and Paterson both gave her a hug and kiss on the cheek, and left the studios. They made their way through the large car park towards Roberts' SUV. He was fishing in his pocket for the keys, when a voice spoke sharply from behind them.

"Please stop there, Mr Roberts! Lift your hands and turn around, slowly. Your friend, too."

Roberts' face displayed no surprise as he did so, lifting his hands half way. There were four black-clothed figures in a half circle around him and Patterson, all in ski masks.

"Yes," he said to nobody in particular, "I thought my TV appearance may result in some close encounters. But this is a private car park. How did you get in?"

"We persuaded the guards to let us enter. Don't be concerned for them, Mr Roberts. They are still alive. You, however, may not be so fortunate. You are proving too much of a nuisance with your stupid submarine." The leader of the four spoke with a pronounced Asian accent, and all four drew knives as they moved closer.

"Will you allow my friend here to go? He doesn't have anything to do with what's happening. And he's a well-known reporter, who hasn't seen any of your faces." Roberts was quite calm and spoke quietly and reasonably.

"We know very well who he is, Mr Roberts. But he has allied himself to your cause, and so he must stay and face what is to come. If you accept the punishment we must provide, you may live. We know of your fighting prowess, Mr Roberts, but I have to advise you that we are all above first dan, so you are at a distinct disadvantage."

"Oh I wouldn't say that exactly, son," came Ray Mackie's voice from behind the assailants. "Just be cool and put the knives down, slowly."

The speaker had frozen at Mackie's first words. Now, in a very fast movement, he spun round with his arm raised, about to throw his knife at Mackie. Faster still, however, were the two low coughs from the silenced Sig Saur in the hands of Allen Bell. The man staggered, the knife fell and he dropped on top of it.

"You ninjas were told to be cool," said Bell, as three members of the dojo team also moved into view. In all, there were now five figures surrounding the assailants, who all slowly put their knives on the bitumen of the car park. Bell walked up to the man on the ground, knelt and examined him. Looking up at Mackie he shook his head slightly.

"Guess these guys never heard the old one about not bringing knives to a gun fight," he said.

Patterson, visibly shaken, slumped back against Roberts' SUV. "Jesus Christ, David," he muttered, "you might have warned me. I think I wet myself. I suppose these are the friends you didn't want to keep waiting."

"Yeah, sorry Les, but I didn't want to alarm you in case nobody showed up. If it's any consolation, you were never in any real danger. My guys were close by all the time, and as you've seen, they're pretty capable." Roberts spoke now to the three men, standing quietly under guard.

"You people will have to learn that you're not welcome here. Tell your master that he should consider redeveloping his operations. Whaling is out. So is toothfishing. If he sends anyone else against us, they will be dealt with more severely. Now pick up your man and get out of here. We will be calling the police in five minutes."

Two of the remaining three picked up their dead comrade and carried him to a black Suburban parked off to one side. They were gone inside two minutes.

"OK guys, well done. Let's check on the guards, then shoot through. I'll take you home, Les. Are you going to be all right?"

"Sure David. This sort of thing happens to me all the time."

Roberts grinned as he climbed into his vehicle. "Yeah, I think you'll be OK. It hit me pretty much the same way the first time I saw violent death, too. But I believe that if you've got anything inside you at all, you can handle it. Especially when you come to accept that these people are trying to kill us to ensure their profits remain high. They are dying because of that, not because we're seeking them out."

"When are you going to call the police?" asked Patterson, thinking he knew the answer already.

"I'm not," said Roberts flatly. "Let's go."

*

It was an exclusive walled residence on the western side of Sydney's Rose Bay with a small funicular railway leading up the steep slope to the front entrance. In this area exclusive meant unimaginably expensive, affordable only to those with the kind of money they really didn't need to count. The tradesman's gate in a front corner provided only steps, quite a lot of them. High above, inside the house, was the owner, a very wealthy merchant and investment banker, and three other men, all in their thirties, all successful in one field or another. Although 'successful' may not have been the most apposite adjective for the doctor in the group. Currently, he was leaning back in an expensive, empire green leather-covered orthopaedic recliner, eyes closed, quietly sniffling. He had just done a very high quality line, and was absorbed in himself, his handsome face set in a slight frown as he dwelt upon his enhanced sense of injustice. Tears formed freely as he once again considered his ill luck in listening to the stock market tip his banker friend had assured him was inside knowledge. It had cost him over three hundred large as well as his latest bonus. The fact that he had received four tips prior to this one, all of which had netted him a profit of $278,000, made this loss seem all the worse.

"Gerry, you really are an arsehole," he whimpered to the banker, who was sitting comfortably with the other two, all nursing cocktails. None of them had indulged in the hits available on the glass dining table. Several lines were carefully constructed, all precisely parallel and framed by four exquisite Lladro figurines. "You told me that information was rock-solid. You've cost me a packet." He dabbed at his eyes, the tears now almost entirely due to the blow.

"Oh Lawrence, don't be so precious. Even I get it wrong now and again. It's only money, but your account is seriously in the red, so I had to sell it to James. You owe him now." The banker was speaking languidly, appearing unconcerned at the situation, but as he glanced at the others, his eyes held a subtle gleam.

"Jesus Gerry, you didn't! You couldn't have! Not James." Prescott groaned softly. James was the English name of a Korean money-lender known to the crowd in which these people moved. His reputation as a hard man was deserved. He was also known to be impatient, and recalcitrant debtors were not treated kindly. One default meant hospital; two meant a disappearance.

"What the hell am I going to do?" Prescott was almost in shock. "I don't have that much, and my next bonus isn't due for a month." He was stunned, not quite in focus.

"Well Lawrence, if you concentrate on what I'm saying, I may have a suggestion," said his friend, with another knowing look at the other two men. "You haven't told us much about what you're doing, but you have indicated on some earlier breaks that it's something to do with what's been going on in the Southern Ocean. If you have some hard information about that, it could be worth money to you. Even as much as your debt to James." He was now watching Prescott keenly, gauging whether the man was understanding what he was saying.

"I've been sworn to secrecy about that, Gerry, as I've told you before." Prescott was clearly not disoriented and was now gazing at the banker with reproach in his eyes. "I'm not a half-wit, Gerry, nor am I too high too appreciate what you're trying to do."

"Good, old man. That means you're capable of imagining what James is likely to do if you can't make the payment next week. Especially as you're a doctor and all," murmured Gerry.

"Christ, I thought you were a friend." Prescott was clearly disgusted with himself and the situation he had gotten into. But he knew he couldn't get out of it by running, or borrowing from any other party. "It's going to cost you my debt plus a hundred thousand, Gerry. Otherwise I will take my chances with James." He was bluffing, due to the fact that he couldn't tolerate the thought of damage being done to him, and the pain with which it would undoubtedly be accompanied, but was sufficiently smooth to carry it off.

"OK, Lawrence. I'll arrange it. Be back here tomorrow at the same time. I'll give you your banking details, and you can give us the information we need. By the way old son, is that a slight lisp you seem to have developed?"

"That's what a jaw broken in two places and a couple of missing teeth will do for you, Gerry—compliments of a Neanderthal engineering team member who objected to something I was doing with his girlfriend some time ago."

His good friend rose, a wide smile on his face containing neither warmth nor sympathy and going nowhere near his eyes. He held out a hand to Prescott. "Then I'll see you out old chum, shall I?"

THIRTY NINE

Several government ministers were in the cabinet room in Parliament House, Canberra, in a special session. The extraordinary meeting had been called by the Prime Minister an hour ago and the members were all coffee'd, tea'd and watered up and waiting expectantly.

"Ladies and gentlemen," began the PM, "thank you for getting here promptly. I won't take much of your time, as I'm well aware how much of it you don't have to spare. It concerns the matter of the, er, happenings in the Southern Ocean. I take it you've all seen the *Sydney Tonight* show? Monty of course was on it. What did the rest of you think of it?"

"I thought Monty was his usual assured self and handled things very well," offered the Minister for Foreign Affairs.

"I thought so too," a senior advisor agreed.

"I meant what did you think of this man Roberts?" the PM said pointedly, with a hint of emphasis.

"PM," said the Minister for Defense slowly, "I have to say I like what he's doing, but I also think he has the capacity to become a large headache. Most probably for me."

The Minister for Fisheries chimed in. "He is clearly a very capable person with significant resources, and knows exactly what he wants to achieve. He put me on the spot tonight, and I'm not sure I got out of it all that well. There's no doubt of one thing though. He certainly has public support now, and it's growing fast in Australia and America."

"We should be seen to be assisting him while being able to retain deniability, PM. It will hurt us if we do nothing," came from the advisor.

"PM, I'm having some new rules of engagement drafted at the moment, which will allow our vessels to shoot at illegal fishing boats caught in the act, and who refuse to stop. We'll also be supplying the boarding forces with tear gas, capsicum spray and abrasive acoustic devices," the Defence Minister said thoughtfully. "But what else we can do in any proactive sense I'm not sure. What does concern me, however, is the capacity for these situations to escalate into confrontations which would see violence occur, and lives put at risk."

The Prime Minister made a quick decision. "I like what he's doing too, people, but we can't afford to be seen to encourage him. He is after all breaking international law. However, I also don't like the Japanese badgering us with insinuations about involvement, and I especially don't like them dropping depth charges in our backyard from a training vessel.

What I want you to do is this. I want you to dispatch a small fleet of naval ships, nothing too, ah, ostentatious, and send it on manoevres in the Southern Ocean around our exclusion zones. Make sure it operates near any whaling groups—they clearly attract Mr Roberts' attention. I want a presence there if anything untoward were to occur. Liaise with the Secretary of State in Washington. They may want to send a unit or two as well. Get it done soonest please.

Thank you all for your time."

*

"Good morning Angie, David. Nice to have you aboard again. Are we planning to move out soon?" Chris Sanders was speaking with Roberts and Angie after their arrival on the *Kontica* at the Sydney docks.

"Hi Chris," smiled Angie. "G'day Chris," nodded Roberts. "Yes, I want to sail at your earliest convenience please. I've done the publicity bit and drawn the expected flak, and I've also had word of more whaling movements due very soon in the southern Atlantic. I'm keen to get moving into the area and see what's happening."

"Very well, David. We can sail first thing tomorrow. We're nearly done providoring and all our tanks are full. We've loaded the extra stores you sent to the boat, and all those on shore leave are back on board. We have an extra complement of a security man and something called a 'dojo team'—all in all seven more bodies, one of which appears to belong to my daughter Sarah." Sanders looked at Roberts quizzically, an eyebrow raised. "Perhaps you could enlighten me?" he asked.

"Shit," growled Roberts, "hasn't she had a word with you about what she's doing yet? I told her to do so quick smart, the little bugger. Can you get her up here to the bridge?"

A few minutes later, after Angie had left to stow their gear in the master's cabin, Sarah arrived on the bridge, a little flushed and breathless. She knew why she had been summoned, and entered hesitantly.

"Mr Roberts, I was going to talk to dad as soon as he had some spare time, but he's been very busy," she said in a rush, "and I didn't want to disturb him."

"Hello darling. Talk to me about what?" Sanders asked her curiously. "I saw you come aboard and found your name on the manifest. Why are you here?"

"Well, dad, I'm actually part of the 'dojo team,'" she said, glancing at Roberts, who scowled at her.

"Which is what exactly?" asked Sanders, beginning to feel stirrings of alarm.

"Chris, it's a response team I've had training with our security man, Allen Bell, to handle any problems which might arise. So far they've been able to intercept two groups of would-be assailants who've been sent against me. Sarah is one of the leaders in the group, and can handle herself particularly well. But I told her to speak with you some weeks ago." He frowned again at Sarah, who had the grace to look abashed and chastened all at once. But there was a gleam in her downcast eyes and the hint of a smile in one corner of her mouth.

"God Sarah, do you mean you fight? No, please tell me that's not it. I couldn't bear it if something happened to you. Not on top of everything else." Sanders was quite distraught, then anger overcame him.

"David! Did you . . ."

"No Chris, I didn't know anything about her until she had been in the dojo for months, and had proved herself so capable. I then told her I wanted her to talk to you before committing to the job. She said she would, and I assumed she had." He scowled again.

"Dad, I'm sorry but I knew you'd be upset, and I just couldn't bring myself to tell you. I'm sorry Mr Roberts. Does this mean I can't keep the job?" She was pretty sure of herself, but there was some trepidation in her voice as she spoke to Roberts.

"Your father will decide that, young lady. Whichever way it goes, it should be some sort of a lesson for you," he smiled grimly. "You're an integral part of the team, but no one is irreplaceable. Chris, let me know the outcome before we sail."

*

Two days later the *Kontica* was driving into a smart southerly chop, seemingly enjoying the fresh conditions as she rose to each wave, parting it neatly and disdainfully casting aside the resulting spray. Sarah had spoken earnestly to her father for almost an hour after Roberts had left them to it. She had been mature and intelligent enough not to play on his emotions, preferring to argue her case logically and calmly. It nearly wasn't enough. Sanders couldn't see her through any eyes other than a father's, but in the end he came to realise that she was completely committed to the project and wanted nothing else. He had resigned himself to capitulation, hoping desperately that she was as capable as Roberts had said. She had gained some maturity in a hurry, and was happy and excited as she left the bridge.

At the moment though, she would have traded places with any nine-to-fiver she could have talked into agreeing. She had never felt worse in her life. She was clinging to the high rail in the waist of the ship hurling the remains of last night's dinner into the boisterous seas of the Southern Ocean. There wasn't much left. She had been doing so for the best part of an hour, and her stomach muscles were becoming strained. She had passed the stage where she was afraid she would die. Now, she had reached the point where she was afraid she wouldn't. Sanders had checked on her half an hour before, clipping a line around her waist, then left her to the misery of one of the worst feelings it is possible to experience. Forget sea bands, pills, patches and what-have-you, the only gilt-edged remedy for the scourge of seafarers everywhere is to sit under a shady tree. So she endured . . .

Inside, in the mess, Roberts, Angie, Sanders and Bell were snacking on a light lunch, discussing the information Roberts had just received from Hendry's group. At that moment Lawrence Prescott came into the mess, saw them at the table, checked, gave a slight wave of acknowledgement and walked back out.

"Odd," said a slightly perplexed Roberts, "he must be feeling off colour too. Glad I seem to have gained my sea legs.

This message I got from Morgan is interesting. It seems there is some unusual activity surrounding the whaling groups. Russian, Norwegian, US, Japanese naval ships, even some of our own, are moving into the South Atlantic as we speak. There are reported to be at least two, possibly three whaling groups either working there now, or about to begin soon. Looks like we've stirred things up a bit. Could get crowded down there. I'll need to talk this over with Gus and Gunter, but I'm still very keen to get amongst them."

*

Two more days at an easy fifteen knots saw the *Kontica* approaching the entrance to Caroline Cove. Bradley and his team had piled several very large boulders at the end of the undersea breakwater, big enough to withstand the force of the winter seas that so often swept into the cove. They, or rather the spray and white water always surrounding them, served as an effective starboard marker to those who knew about it, and the *Kontica* rounded it now as she crept into the now more sheltered waters of the inner cove. Roberts and Angie were on the bridge as Sanders conned the vessel to its anchorage. The door flew open and Sarah rushed in, flushed from the cold wind.

"Mr Roberts, there's a group of people on the trail above the top of the cove. They've got binoculars, and are watching us right now. And there's been a helicopter circling us for about three minutes. Where's Igloo? How do we get in?" She stopped, breathless, as Roberts held both his hands up, waving her down.

"Thanks Sarah. Glad you're still with us. You look like you're over your seasickness," he smiled sympathetically, remembering his own troubles. They seemed to have happened a century ago. "The main entrance is that large hill of boulders, which we can't use while those people are watching. And I'm not going in through the personnel door either, for the same reason. Let's go ashore Chris. I want to see who they are and what they want. It must be a party from the ANARE base, finally waking up."

An hour later the helicopter had disappeared. Roberts and several members of the dojo team, plus Allen Bell, took one of the Kontica's small semi-inflatable launches ashore, landing in the surging swells on a part of the stony beach well away from the Igloo entrance. After dragging the dory up the beach, clear of the restless water surging after them, Roberts, Sarah and Bell clambered up the rocks to where the group of people was standing. Everyone was clothed in cold-weather gear, bulky trousers and parkas, boots, mittens and hoods with scarves. Although all wore clear glass goggles to prevent eye damage from the biting wind and occasional sleet, identification was impossible. Clad in what amounted to a standard Antarctic outdoor uniform, a mother wouldn't have recognized a son.

One of the group stepped close to Bell and shouted what was probably an introduction. Some of his words were inaudible, the howling wind having little trouble whisking them off into nowhere. It was like a sound system with some faulty wiring.

". . . Dr Bond," he yelled, ". . . scientific colleagues . . . ANARE . . . the hell . . . doing?"

Bell glanced at Roberts, who shook his head and motioned for them all to follow him back down he slope to the dory. ". . . protected," he called over his shoulder.

Down on the beach the wind was less strident and conversation was at least possible, if not comfortable. The group stopped about thirty metres away from the dory with the dojo team sitting huddled in its lee, watching them.

"As I said, we are from the ANARE base and have been waiting for word of the Kontica's arrival. Our helicopter has been observing and filming your ship and apparent lack of any signs of your so-called 'scientific study'. You seem to have spent a large amount of time around the southern end of the island, and we are becoming very concerned at the effect you must be having on the wildlife populations here.

Just what the hell is going on here!" Bond was irate, his complexion visibly reddening through the clear goggles.

Roberts spoke, muffled through the scarf and parka, mildly, but with his eyes unflinchingly set on Bond. "We've been through this with your people before, Dr Bond. We have a lengthy program of sub-Antarctic wildlife study we are working through, and we'll be staying around this part of the island until we finish."

"Yes, well we've come to the conclusion that that's a load of bullshit, sir! The *Kontica* has spent far more time around Hurd Point and Caroline Cove than we consider necessary for mere films of penguins and seals. I repeat, what the hell are you up to?

And just who would I be speaking to?" He glared at Roberts, the part of his face visible through the goggles now thunderous.

Roberts paused, shrugged slightly and said, calmly, "My name's David Roberts."

The shortest member of the group moved sharply, and what sounded very much like "Hai!" sounded through his scarf. Bond stepped back a pace, said "Ah, the pirate. We've heard of you. What are you doing here?"

Roberts stepped toward the short man, peering intently through his goggles, now seeing eyes with a pronounced epicanthic fold framed by thick glasses. "And who might you be?" he asked curiously.

"That's Dr Hidekari, a visiting Japanese marine biologist, if it's any of your concern," growled Bond. "He arrived a few days ago, and asked to accompany us to Hurd Point."

"Just happened to be visiting, eh?" said Roberts, smiling at the man without a lot of humour. "Well well, what a coincidence. I'll bet you even know something about marine biology too," he said sardonically. "Dr Bond, we have nothing further to discuss. Please take your colleagues and go back to your base. We have some more filming to do, and you're holding us up."

"Who the devil do you think you are, ordering us around on our island! I want you and your crew to come back to the ANARE base with us for a formal investigation!" The crusty old scientist was outraged, quivering with a fury directly contrasting the stillness of Roberts.

"Firstly, Dr Bond, it isn't your island. It belongs to Tasmania. Secondly, what you want is not the major concern here." Roberts was speaking as quietly as the still-boisterous wind would allow, but his words carried utter conviction. "If you are having trouble deciding what to do, my security advisor will help you make up your mind." Bell had been rummaging through the pockets of his bulky parka, and suddenly withdrew his Sig Saur, examining it keenly for any salt spray or lint from his jacket. He began to clean it, made no threatening move towards the scientists, didn't even look at them, but the message was as sharp and cold as the screeching wind. The scientists, except for Bond and Hidekari, stepped further back, and turned to leave. Bond stared at Roberts with contempt. Hidekari stared at him with venom. Both then turned and walked off after their colleagues, back up the slope to the track.

With a nod to Bell and a wave at one of the concealed external cameras, Roberts motioned to his companions to follow him back to the dory. The crew dragged it back into the water and they jumped in quickly, wetly, and headed back to the *Kontica.* Half an hour later, after the scientists had disappeared north towards the ANARE base, the dory motored back to the entrance and shot into Igloo through the partially-raised main door. Sarah and the dojo people were rubbernecking all the way in, astounded at what they were seeing.

"God, Mr Roberts, this is just incredible," gasped Sarah. They were standing on the dock, the royal blue of the submarine shining in the cavern lighting. The sail with its white flying fish towered above them. "Dad described it to me after we'd settled things back aboard the ship, but I didn't get the size of it, or the sophistication of the technology. It's so cool. I can't wait to have a look aboard the *Flying Fish*. It's all just awesome!" She was as excited as the child she used to be on Xmas morning, sitting under the tree opening all her carefully wrapped presents, both parents sitting there with her opening their gifts to each other. A fleeting sadness passed across her face for an instant, as remembrance brought the images of long ago suddenly to life and she knew those times were gone for good. But she was too positive in her make-up to stay down for long, and within moments was eagerly walking, trotting really, across the gang-plank and on to the deck of the submarine, followed by the equally excited dojo team. It was something they had all been anticipating with great excitement since, following the attack at the TV studio, Roberts had asked them whether they wanted to transfer to the base to reinforce its defence. They had all leaped at the chance.

*

Some time later Roberts was conferring with his core group in the mess, Allen Bell now part of the planning process. Kaye Halloran was sharing some of her concerns.

"We were watching the proceedings through the cameras, David, and after Allen began cleaning his pistol, they took off quickly. But why did you let them go? Wouldn't it have been a better idea to shoot them all? OK, just kidding, but shouldn't we have detained them here so they couldn't spread the word?" She was frowning at the missed opportunity.

"Don't worry Kaye, I gave it some thought as we were talking. But if we had kept them here, or even just that poisonous little Hidekari, the alarm would still have been raised when they failed to return. I think you'll find Hidekari's employer is a man called Takamori, who will be alerted by either his failure to return, or by him directly when he does. So I decided it wasn't worth the hassle of keeping prisoners. It will take them some time to organise whatever they're planning, and it won't be easy for them to get here. And if and when they do, they may find a surprise or two waiting.

What I'm more curious about is just how did Takamori know to send a scout to Macquarie Island? Especially as he had been looking so recently in the Wollaston Islands. I'm afraid it means that we have a leak somewhere." Roberts was, as always, quiet and confident. He never gave an impression that things were too much for him. His unflappable demeanour was so laid-back one could be forgiven for thinking he was about to start yawning. None of those present had met his like before, as none had traversed the world of big and bitter business.

So none of them had any inkling of the turmoil of thoughts chasing themselves through his racing mind as he analysed the situation and tried to stay two steps ahead of anything that might now occur. His boardroom experience had schooled him in becoming unreadable while thinking and planning furiously. It was now an unconscious process that had the effect of transmitting a calmness to the others. It was as reassuring as it was contagious.

"Well it's done now. We need to get moving quickly. It'll take us nearly a week to reach the South Atlantic location we've been given, by which time it will be pretty crowded down there. So we need to try to figure just what all those players are going to do." Roberts looked at them all in turn, encouraging thought and comment from each. He had reached his own conclusions by now, but wanted them all to share their ideas. And their worries.

Halloran was the first to speak, soberly, her words measured as she arranged her thoughts. "We're going to come under attack, David, aren't we?" she said with something like wonder. "Some of those navy ships are actually going to try to sink us." Her normal ebullience was now subdued. "This time it's really serious." She too looked at them all in turn, before her face shed the look of mild disbelief and assumed first a determined set, then an eye-crinkling smile. "I don't give a shit, I'm in anyway." She leaned back, picked up her coffee mug with finality, her contribution done. Roberts smiled, said nothing.

Lou James took it up next. "Don't know much about naval warfare, guys, but I have a feeling Kaye's right. You will be attacked if you enter their space, wherever or whatever that is. But by what, or how, or with what I wouldn't have a clue. My obvious concerns are for your safety. If you can't guarantee it, I'd have to suggest taking an extended break and waiting for things to cool down." Again Roberts said nothing, just glanced at Gus Durrand.

"OK guys, I guess I'm the resident 'expert' in naval warfare, even though I've never been under fire. Done a lot of training though, which may help some. As David said, we have to try to second-guess them all. Will they shoot at us? Yeah, I reckon they will, especially if we fire a torpedo at one of the whalers. They'll all have sonar, so they will know where we are, and plenty of depth charge rocket launchers too. Their torpedoes'll only worry us if we're on the surface or shallow. We need to make some decisions before we go, if we go at all. Any battle plan will depend on the deployment of whatever vessels are in the vicinity." He looked questioningly at Roberts, who now responded.

"Firstly, I have to say I agree with your assessments. I'm sure if we dare to mix it with the big boys they'll try to send us to the bottom. But you know Lou, I'm just not able to take a break. I got this crazy idea and I can't stop and hope it works itself out. I'm not made that way. I have to stay with it until something gives, and I hope to have a few of the crew with me. I guess Kaye will be one," he smiled at her gratefully, "and I'm counting on a few others. But it's now going to have to be strictly voluntary. And you people here on the base will almost certainly be hit at some point, depending on how long it takes those two syndicate heads to organise their vessel and teams. Allen, you'll have to see to the defenses." Bell nodded calmly.

"Gus?" Roberts raised his eyebrows. Durrand said nothing, just grinned. "Thanks mate." Roberts looked at him for a few seconds with real warmth, then he nodded too. "Lou, would you call everyone into the mess for a general meeting please? Say in one hour. I have to lay it all out for everyone, and send those who want to opt out back on the *Kontica*."

Exactly one hour and ten minutes later the meeting was over. Every person present, save four, had decided quickly to remain with the project. The American electronics technician, Natalie Mentelle, the two conscientious objectors from the base, the machinist and the chef, Daniel Faraday, and, surprisingly to Roberts, Lawrence Prescott, had been the ones to request to go back to Sydney. Roberts had thanked them all sincerely and told them they'd receive their guaranteed bonuses plus a generous payout sum. He would miss Daniel's cooking, but then remembered that Angie was now on the base and smiled.

"Wonder why Prescott's going?" he murmured to himself. "Not that I'm complaining. He may be vain and insufferably egotistical, but he never struck me as the nervous type. I wonder . . ." Roberts walked over to Bell, taking him aside for a quiet word.

"Allen, I want you to wait until the dory is about to leave for the *Kontica*, and make some last-minute excuse to get Prescott out of it. Tell him he has an emergency of some kind, I don't care. But make sure the dory and the *Kontica* leave without him. OK?"

"No problem David." Allen seemed to find nothing in any way unusual about Roberts' order, which Roberts realised was simply a result of the man's professionalism.

"Good. But my main concern is the attack I'm sure is coming. Will you be ready?" Roberts didn't appear anxious, but Bell read him. "Don't worry David, I'll be taking special care of her. She'll be well out of harm's way. And yes, we'll be ready. Gary Bradley is a good man, and it'd help if you left Andy McLeod and Ray Mackie here too. The dojo team is a good group and they're training up well. We'll be arranging some of that special ordnance outside, and even if they know where the personnel door is, as you suspect, they'll pay on the way in," Bell said grimly.

"OK Allen. I was planning to leave Andy behind this time. He'll be more useful here when the fun starts. But Ray said he wanted to be on the *Fish* for what could be potentially climactic action, and he deserves his spot. Also, he's been with me since the beginning, and I feel more comfortable having him close by." Roberts seemed satisfied. "When you deploy the people, make sure that Prescott has an automatic rifle and is in the first line. But keep an eye on him. I have a feeling he may no longer be completely trustworthy. Kaye told me he spoke to her quite intensely a short while ago, trying to convince her to go back to Sydney with him. Could be he's simply in love with her, or it could be something else. Kaye being Kaye, she just told him to fuck off, but she felt there was something a little off about the way he spoke, and told me."

"Yeah, I'll look after him too, David," smiled Bell.

FORTY

Five days later the *Flying Fish* was heading steadily westwards. She had passed Heard Island to the south the day before, and was now angling up towards the United Kingdom's Gough Island, a lonely little piece of rock on the southern edge of the South Atlantic. It was nearing October in the Southern Ocean, but the environment here was the antithesis of springtime in the Rockies. The vicinity of this cold, windswept chunk of Great Britain was where the whaling fleets had been reported to be working, and the submarine would be there in a little over twenty four hours. Roberts, Durrand, Hass and Mackie were conferring over hot coffee in the mess. The past few years had seen Mackie and Roberts travelling many thousands of miles, mostly at a height of around ten kilometres and a speed not too far removed from that of sound waves. Mackie never tired of the feeling of wonder he always had sitting in a comfortably stable seat, being plied with quality wining and dining, knowing that just a few centimetres away it was minus fifty degrees and blowing a thousand kilometres an hour. He had the same feeling now, contentedly cradling a steaming hot espresso, warm, dry and comfortable, travelling easily at fifteen knots thirty metres below a moody, near freezing ocean rapidly losing its temper. He knew, though, that it wasn't going to last, that pleasure and pain are rarely far apart, so he took care to enjoy every sip of the freshly ground, dark Columbian roast they were currently using in the Italian coffee machine he had insisted on purchasing for the mess. He was becoming something of a coffee snob, he thought, but he now really could tell the difference between good quality fresh ground espresso and a packet of Nescafe 3-in-1 MyCup.

"Full speed ahead, David?" Durrand was asking with a quiet smile.

"Yes Gus," Roberts nodded, not returning the smile. "It seems as though all we've done so far has been a kind of preamble, a lead-up to something definitive. We can't stop now. Whatever we find when we get there, if there are whalers operating I want to stop the bastards. Just how we go about it will depend on your assessment of the positions of whatever shipping we find.

But I'd like to offer something for when the shit hits the fan. I don't in any way intend to try to teach you to suck eggs, Gus, but what did you think of our tactic of sitting under the *Kishin Maru* the way we did?"

"It was a goddamned hoot, David! It worked well on a couple levels. No one could touch us, it was easy to keep station with our computerized diving controls and deck-mounted bow and stern thrusters, and we could move out at our choosing. You think we should mebbe try it again?"

"Well, you're the skipper, Gus, but I can't see much wrong with it. And there's something else to consider. If there really are those ships from different countries in the area, it could very well get chaotic up there. Especially given that at least vessels from the Australian and U.S. navies will be friendly. Or should be. Even if they're not, I doubt they'd actually fire on us. It might turn into a classic clusterfuck, which could only be to our advantage." Now Roberts was smiling, but the smile was closer to the focused expression on the face of a hunting wolf than that of a quiet, pleasant-natured tactician discussing the rules of play in a college football game.

*

Late morning the following day found the submarine four hundred nautical miles south-east of Gough Island. Tomlinson called out excitedly, “Got a sonar contact skipper! A long way off yet, but there’s more than one ship. Bearing is 345° true.”

“Ah! They’re here. Thanks Rick,” replied Durrand with some satisfaction. “Stations everyone. We’ll go up for a quick look. Periscope depth please, Clive. Ease her up.” Some ten minutes later Durrand raised the periscope with a soft hiss from the hydraulics.

“Whoo hoo, it’s grey and rough out there,” Durrand said, as the submarine began pitching and rolling in the disturbed water twenty feet below the surface. “But I can see some shipping. At least one whaling mother and some chasers, as well as some frigates and what looks like a destroyer. Geez, I think she’s Russian. Can you sort them all out Rick?”

“Yes skipper, Clarrie’s getting an overall plot on screen now. It will be the best way to plan the doings.” His enthusiasm was infectious. All their adrenal glands were on speed dial. The idea this could be some kind of concluding statement to their original objective had spread through the submarine over the past few days, and all were eager to get started.

Durrand and Roberts were studying the large screen at Grimshaw’s station as though it were about to give birth. Clarrie had programmed the display to show the submarine as a small purple flying fish icon, and different shapes and colours for other vessels. The whalers looked like little yellow whales.

“As soon as you can identify the ships for me, skipper, I’ll assign them their correct colours. The Aussie and US ships will be green, all others red. Once identified, the plot will automatically keep track. You can see we've got two whaling groups, a factory ship and three chasers in each group. Have to be our old friends the Norwegians and the Japanese again. Boy are they ever going to be pissed!"

"Gus, let's circle the area slowly while we build up our plot. They know we're here by now, so we don't have to worry about being coy. Let's see what they're going to do about us." Durrand nodded and gave the order to Blake.

An hour later Durand had identified naval vessels from Australia, the US and Norway, all now showing on Grimshaw's screen. The Japanese training ship *Kushima* was hovering around the edge of what Roberts had dubbed 'the pitch', an area of ocean about twenty miles square where the whalers were working. The factory ships were diagonally opposite each other, nearly thirty miles apart. The destroyer was indeed Russian, a Udaloy II class ship of about 7,000 tonnes, probably from the Russian Pacific fleet. "Someone's got some serious pull," said Durrand. "That destroyer is a hunter-killer carrying anti-submarine rockets and missiles. She can launch rockets at us from a couple of miles, and missiles from torpedo tubes in the waist. We have some defence-capable ECMs (electronic counter-measures) courtesy of David's contact and Bo Tallis, but I don't want to have to rely on them. If she gets close enough to us, and she can do at least thirty-five knots, she'll probably sink us."

"OK Gus, here's where you earn that fabulous salary of yours," Roberts grinned. "Tactics, that's what we want now. We've gotta have some tactics. Take a minute or two. See what you can come up with." Even Hass was chuckling at Roberts and his routine, not realizing it was carefully structured to reduce tensions and create an air of easy confidence. Many times during his business career Roberts had presided over boardroom fights with millions of dollars riding on their outcomes. Some of them had degenerated into vicious corporate brawls resulting in huge financial gains and losses, and on two occasions lives had been given away by those who were unable to deal with the failure their losses had engendered. Roberts had entered the corporate world armed with his wits, determination and an unquenchable thirst for competition. He loved the complexities involved in the deals he structured and the tensions inherent in the fire and ice of the boardroom struggles. He was at his best during those times, and became totally confident in the particular set of skills he had developed. After his thirst finally reached the quenchable stage and he changed the course of his life, he didn't shed his experience and special capabilities like a snake renewing its skin. They were merely shuffled into a less active part of his brain and put on hold for a time.

This time.

Durrand leaned back from the screen decisively, nodding to himself slightly. "Yes. We'll hit the big Norwegian mother first. It's closest to us, and the Russian is too far away from it to stop us. Probably doesn't care too much about it anyway. The Norwegian frigate is close enough, but they'd have to bomb us as we passed, and that would be the first hostility. They won't risk starting anything, so we've really got a free pass for the first go. Bad luck for the *Helga*. After we hit her, we'll head straight for the *Maru*. Martin, when we move, I want all we have.

David, Gunter, any comments or suggestions?" Both shook their heads silently, both smiling to themselves. Roberts had stilled down to a Zen-like calm. Hass was gazing at nothing obvious to the others, but an inner completeness had engulfed him with a feeling of near joy. His heart was full. He was as happy as he could ever remember. His breathing quickened, his sight dimmed and his ears heard only the whistling roar of his blood racing itself through his body. For the smallest instant he felt a flashing white pain fill his chest, and then he died where he sat, slumping sideways in his seat.

"Gunter?" called Durrand sharply. "David!" he yelled. Roberts came out of his trance and quickly knelt in front of Hass, loosening his collar and feeling for a pulse in his neck. "Call the doctor, quickly!" he said to Durrand in a voice suddenly strangled, very scared. He lifted Hass with ease and carried him at a shambling run to the sick bay. Dr Woodville met him at the door, motioned him to one of he tables, and went to work.

"God, Theo, please don't let him go." Roberts was distraught. Woodville looked up, calmly, sadly, said only "I'm sorry David, he's already gone." Roberts sank to the floor, head in hands, silent tears making their way through the cracks between his fingers. His whole being shook. He couldn't move. He'd brought a lovely old man out of comfortable retirement and taken him to his death. And Dorothy—what could he possibly say to her? He was almost in shock, and Woodville moved away from Hass to tend to Roberts. Mackie came into the room, silent, anguished, tears in his eyes.

Back in the control room, Durrand was alerting the crew. "I came to like and respect that old man, and I'm very sad at his passing. But we've a job to do now, and I want to get it done with no other casualties. At least, none on our side.

Full ahead, Martin. Steer for the *Helga*. Rick, let me know when we're half a kilometre away. Tube one ready?" The commands came quickly, firmly, drawing an equally rapid reply from Cazaley. "Tube one ready!"

The *Flying Fish* accelerated to twenty knots and headed straight for the big Norwegian factory ship. All surface ships were now at full power and converging on the southern part of 'the pitch', but only the Norwegian frigate was close. The submarine powered past her at a depth of fifteen metres, a hundred or so metres off her port side. There was a flurry of activity both on deck and on the bridge, but as Durrand had reasoned, the Norwegians didn't want to fire the first shot, so no depth charge hurtled out of the frigate. The submarine was five hundred metres behind the *Helga* when she fired her first torpedo, immediately altering course to the north-east on a bearing to intercept the *Kishin Maru*. A few minutes later the water behind the *Helga* erupted in the now-familiar spout and for the fourth time her stern gear was reduced to a twisted mess. Her captain was on deck, screaming his rage at the nearby frigate. "You stupid, useless cretins!" he howled, "what's the use in having a navy if it won't protect its citizens! Why the fuck didn't you shoot him as he passed, you bloody morons!" Halvorsen was beside himself. "You deliberately made us the sacrificial lamb, you bastards!" No one aboard the frigate could hear him, of course, but all on the bridge could see him, as they drew near to check on the damage.

"Get a damage report from him when he calms down," the captain ordered. "At the moment he seems a bit worked up. I doubt he's sinking. Where's that goddamned submarine?" On hearing his sonar operator confirm the *Flying Fish* was bearing down on the *Kishin Maru* at full speed, the captain shrugged. "Our duty is to stay with the *Helga*. We can't be worried about the Japanese ship. It looks like the Russians are heading for him at speed. Maybe they can stop him," he observed. There was a smile in his words which didn't quite reach his face. The helmsman glanced at him curiously, before quickly turning his eyes back to the bows, the *Helga* and the compass. "As much as Captain Halvorsen wishes to rant, the submarine is no longer of concern to us. Our instruction from the Secretary was under no circumstances to initiate hostilities of any kind. If he returns to threaten the *Helga* again we will sink him. But it seems he is no longer interested in us, so we will simply watch the action from here." The helmsman thought to himself that the captain seemed almost pleased with what had happened, as though he were looking forward to seeing what the submarine would do next. 'Strange,' he thought, 'it's almost as if he's on their side. Why would that be?'

*

The atmosphere in the control room of the submarine was different now. Only a matter of half an hour before, the general mood had been buoyant, with the expectations of an exciting and successful conclusion to the project. They had felt almost bulletproof, such was their confidence in the *Flying Fish* and in their own capabilities. The death of Gunter Hass had hit them all hard, none more so than Roberts. He was still in the sick bay, quiet under a mild sedative given him by the doctor. He could not yet get past the awful weight of his guilt in taking Hass away from Dorothy. It was crushing, the mass compounded by the sorrow of his own loss of a good friend. The total of it all was enough to bury him in a miasma that, while not evil, was nonetheless enough to enshroud him to the point of physical and psychological immobility. He had finally come face to face with what he knew to be a ghastly failure and had been powerless to prevent it and could not undo it. His mind began to slide away from ugliness into a conjured focus on his most treasured image. Angie was sitting at breakfast on the terrace of their Ulladulla home on a clear morning with the sun already risen over an ocean more blue and sparkling than in reality it could ever be. He grasped the picture with a desperation only familiar to someone with a terminal illness given a new drug, and just could not release it. At that low point he wasn't even aware of Mackie's hand resting on his shoulder, his friend simply sitting with him for as long as it took.

Durrand had set the submarine on a direct heading for the Japanese whaler. The Russian destroyer, now approaching fast from the north-west but still four to five miles away, clearly had not been placed under the same restriction as had the Norwegian ship, for she had readied her rocket launcher and now fired charges in rapid succession. The launcher was an RBU-6000 Smerch-2, a powerful unit that fired unguided depth charges some miles, like outsized RPGs. The *Flying Fish*, however, was still outside the effective range of the charges, which exploded with great force but accomplished little other than tossing the *Fish* around in some turbulence. Once the submarine was away from the influence of the Russian charges, she closed on the *Kishin Maru* and fired tube two from a kilometre astern of the whaler. Due to the advanced sonar and camera facilities aboard, it was almost impossible to miss a target, and yet again the *Maru* felt the wrath of admonishment served by a torpedo up the ass. The submarine turned to starboard and came to a bearing of 100°, preparing to ease her speed down to fifteen knots, and go deep. The Russian cruiser, meanwhile, had swept around in a tight turn at her flank speed, and was heading on an intercept course toward the *Fish*.

Fascinated observers to what had unfolded over the past hour or so had been two of the Australian ships, a corvette and a frigate. They were of similar size, and were also now moving fast on a course to overtake the submarine, aboard which Durrand had been rivetted to the operations screen. He could not outrun the destroyer and knew they were in for a torrid time from which they might not emerge. But the positions of the Australian vessels were intriguing. They were coming up fast from the submarine's port quarter, and Durrand was unsure quite what they were planning.

"David, are you good to come to the control room, please?" he called into his comms mike. He sorely missed the incisiveness of Roberts and his strategic advice, but his call was unanswered. In barely five minutes the two ships had come up to the submarine, which was still at a depth of fifteen metres, and had moved into a parallel flanking pattern on either side of the *Fish*, each vessel on station a hundred metres away They matched her speed exactly, and the strange convoy travelled south-westwards at fifteen knots, Durrand holding his order to dive deeper. He had a feeling they may be safer exactly where they were.

The Russian destroyer now closed rapidly on the group from astern, her course suggesting to the Australians that she was going to charge straight through the middle of the group, a course that would take her directly over the submarine. A flurry of messages swirled around the depressingly grey, bitingly cold and sleet-shot atmosphere. "Russian Udaloy-class destroyer approaching us from astern, this is the frigate HMAS *Parmelia*. You are standing in to an unsafe position. Please adjust your course to pass us either to port or starboard. Do not attempt to steam between us." The commander of the frigate was terse, his message blunt and unequivocal. "Under no circumstances are you to fire rockets or missiles while in our vicinity. That would clearly imperil our vessels and we would have no alternative but to consider it an unwarranted act of aggression. We would be compelled to respond with force. Please bear away!"

The Russian captain was equally short. "This is Captain Sergei Malenkov of the Russian destroyer *Krasny Ognevoy*. We are in international waters and will sail where we choose. You may not be aware of it, but there is a dangerous pirate submarine near both your vessels. She has already fired upon a ship friendly to my country so you are in danger also. I suggest you alter your courses away from each other and allow my ship to dispatch the submarine before it tries to sink you both."

The Australian skippers, in scrambled contact with each other at all times, grinned at the Russian captain's ploy, but neither altered course by as much as a degree. The destroyer steamed at over thirty knots right between the two Australian ships, the two hundred metre gap suddenly seeming to be plugged by a large grey warship smashing the big quartering swells into huge sheets of spray. The Russian vessel's name meant 'red fire', but its appearance now was almost chimerical, colourless and barely visible behind the enormous billows of spray in the deepening gloom. Malenkov had instructed his first officer to have some ratings roll six charges over the side manually as they passed over the submarine, but his sonar operator called urgently over the comms system.

"Captain, the submarine has vanished! It is no longer on screen."

"Hold the depth charges!" Malenkov spoke quickly to the first officer. "Sonar, where the hell did it go, and why didn't you see it?" he demanded fiercely.

"Sir, I apologise. I left the screen for no more than twenty seconds to make an adjustment to the incoming signal and it disappeared. It must have changed course and passed under one of the ships. It is not showing on screen yet, but if we move ahead of the ships, it will be visible either to the north or south." The sonar operator was respectful but not remorseful. He knew he had done nothing wrong. The submarine simply had changed strategy during a recalibration, and he would acquire its signal again shortly.

Fifteen minutes later the *Krasny Ognevoy* was five miles ahead of the two Australian warships and searching for the submarine. Its sonar operator was now not so confident. "I'm sorry, captain, I can't pick it up. The only answer is that it has moved under one of the ships and is still there. I cannot identify which one. Both signals are of equal size and strength, but it must be there."

"Yes, it must be," mused Malenkov thoughtfully. "It could not have moved far enough away in a quarter hour. Good tactic," he nodded, impressed. "We can't get at it without sinking both the Australian ships, and that might be a bit of overkill. As long as they stay together we can't touch her." He came to a rapid decision. "Helm, steer 060°. We've done all we can here. I'm not in the loop, but I understand we were only here as a favour to some well-connected Japanese businessman anyway. Let's go back to the Pacific fleet."

*

Aboard the *Flying Fish* Durrand was sweating. He had correctly decided that the Australian warships offered them no danger, were in fact giving them cover, and had kept station with them until Tomlinson called urgently with news of the Russian destroyer's movements. Once it had become clear she was going to chase them down, Durrand had waited until the last moment and jinked to starboard under the corvette. Although the warship was pitching and tossing in the heavy seas they had little trouble keeping under her at a steady fifteen knots sou'-west. They had observed the departure of the destroyer with relief.

"Good to see the last of her," Durrand said thankfully as he wiped his brow. "The US boats have gone too. But what happened to the *Kushima,* Rick? Did you see her move off ?"

"Yeah skipper, she disappeared to the east about a half hour ago. She's off the screen now."

"She's probably gone home too. Marty, lay a course for Igloo. We'll do the same." He glanced around the control room with a tired smile. "Good job everyone. I think we're just about done. I'm going to check on David."

In the sick bay Roberts was awake but still, almost unnaturally so. Not catatonic, not even comatose, just still.

Mackie, sitting beside his cot, was just as still. Durrand glanced at Dr Woodville, questioningly.

"Sorry captain, but he's been unresponsive since Mr Hass died. I sedated him to give him some quiet time, hoping he'd relax and come back naturally. Do you want me to try to rouse him now?"

"Yeah, doc, if you please. I need him up and about. Sorry, Ray, but we have some things to do and I want his input."

Mackie nodded. Woodville injected a stimulant into Roberts and massaged his arm. Roberts stirred, moaned softly and his wide open eyes suddenly looked about him with recognition. "Ray, Gus," he said softly, his voice hoarse and unsteady, hesitating as conscious thought gradually returned. "What happened?"

"Hi David, good to see you at last," Durrand smiled with genuine affection, and not a little relief. Mackie just looked relieved—his affection was hard-wired. "We knocked over those two whalers again and got chased by a Russian destroyer. We might not have survived but for the two Aussie boats flanking us like a protective shield. The Russian drove straight through the middle of them, but I saw what he was planning and moved the *Fish* under the corvette. He kept going and when he couldn't find us outside the shield he decided enough was enough and pissed off."

Roberts swung himself off the cot, groaning with the effort it required to move again, although the effort was entirely psychological. "God," he said, dragging his hands down his face, "sorry Gus. I totally wimped out. Gunter . . ." he paused, looking at Mackie, his face sad beyond sorrow. But the stimulant was effective. He shook his head with a small decisive toss. "OK guys, let's go back to work. Gus, it sounds like you made all the right moves. Well done mate." They moved back to the control room, where the crew all greeted Roberts with lighthearted insults, all obviously pleased to see him back in the land of the responsive. "Hey all," Roberts dredged up a wan smile, "sorry to be such a pussy. Seems like you all managed to stay afloat without a lot of trouble. Gus, can we come up to periscope depth please? I want to send a message to those Aussie ships."

A little later, Roberts was on the radio, broadcasting in clear. "To the Australian corvette and frigate currently operating around 50°S, 15°E, this is David Roberts aboard the submarine *Flying Fish*. I acknowledge your flanking manoeuvre was clearly intended to shepherd us away from the commercial vessels. When the Russian destroyer drove between you we were concerned for our safety and had to move under your corvette to get out of his way. Although unintended, your actions inadvertently assisted us to avoid the destroyer and may have saved our lives. We are grateful. *Flying Fish* out." Roberts grinned at Durrand. "That'll give them an out if questions are asked back home, although I'd like to think they were acting under unofficial instructions anyway." His grin faded. "Now we have to bury Gunter."

*

"Are you sure, David?" Durrand was looking sceptically at Roberts, seriously unconvinced about what Roberts had just outlined. "I'm not sure it'd be the right thing to do."

"Don't worry, Gus, I am. I came to know Gunter very closely, and I'm as sure about this as anything before in my life. He was a true submariner to his core and would want nothing more than to finish this way. Ask Theo to prepare him please. Assemble all hands when he's ready." Roberts spoke firmly, his conviction enough to satisfy Durrand. Mackie gave a small nod of confirmation.

Later, most of the crew was crammed into the torpedo room, the overflow outside in the passageways. Hass' weighted body was tightly bound to a small metal frame, the whole covered with both a German and an American flag. Roberts stood alongside it, looking at the flags but seeing only his friend, wise, gentle, unassuming, yet knowing exactly when to make a hard decision. As Roberts had to do now.

"Gunter Hass was a product of his time and of both his countries. He was a wonderful man who will be missed and remembered," he said simply. "God speed, my friend." He and Mackie eased Hass's body into the torpedo tube and Cazaley closed and dogged the door. "Tube one ready?"

"Tube one ready," Cazaley replied quietly.

"Fire one," whispered Roberts.

*

Roberts, Mackie and Durrand were quietly toasting Hass in the mess a short time after, recalling much of the involvement in their lives he had happily created, knowing they were enhanced because of it. It was a scene that had been played countless times before upon the death of someone much loved and respected. The location, however, was a first.

"Gunter showed me something about myself I hadn't been aware of," Durrand said thoughtfully. "Simply by being who he was spotlighted my prejudice and proved how unreasonable it was. 'The only good German is a dead one.' That was hammered into me a long time ago and I came to accept it as an axiom. How wrong can a guy be? Right at this moment I'm mourning a dead German very much. Were they really so different from the rest of the world? I doubt it. And I guess the same goes for the Japanese too."

"God, the Japanese!" Roberts sat up, startled. "Gus, what did you tell me about the *Kushima*?" he said with some urgency.

"What? Why, only that she disappeared from the scene some time during our 'doings', David. What's up?"

"I've been disgracefully out of it, guys. I should have thought of it much earlier than this. I've been expecting some kind of action against Igloo, but any invaders will have to get there first. The *Kushima* . . ."

"Jesus, yes David, you could be right." Mackie was now looking worried. "Gus, do you think . . ."

Durrand leaped up. "You got it guys," he threw over his shoulder as he ran towards the control room. In less than a minute the submarine was at full speed, heading for Igloo at maximum revs. Roberts entered the control room just behind Durrand.

"Rick, please stay in constant touch with Mark at Igloo. Tell him to keep a very sharp watch for any strange vessels, or even helicopters. I want to know the minute anything appears that shouldn't be there." Roberts didn't give the impression he was concerned, but by now the others could read the subtle signs he emitted and knew that he was anxious to get back. In fact, he was desperate, terrified they would arrive to find the base destroyed and a number of his people dead. He couldn't get Angie out of his mind. He had failed Gunter, and had been shattered. If Angie was injured or killed, he knew he would simply stop. There could be no continuance, not of his project, not of his life. He went to his cabin, collapsed on to his cot in a formless pile and was instantly asleep. The drugs administered by Dr Woodville had taken their toll and it had been a big day.

FORTY ONE

The day just happened to be one of the very few around Macquarie Island during which neither rail fell nor wind blew. Well, not a lot of wind—there would always be some movement in the air down here—but when it turned into night, there was about it a clarity you just didn't see in more comfortable latitudes. The stars, many more than viewed from anywhere near habitation, burned fiercely like the raging fires they all were, and the steady disk of Jupiter outshone them all. There was even half a moon. It was all enough to substitute an unreal luminosity for the normally drenched, howling blackness of ninety nine percent of the nights in this area.

Which was not at all what the thirty heavily armed, black-clad figures in the two semi-rigid inflatables wanted. Both boats were heading in from the delivery ship on a course for Caroline Cove at a steady and quiet ten knots, trailing streams of phosphorescence in their wakes. The clear night, relatively calm conditions and sparkling tails of green light would have appeared beautiful to anyone with an eye for it, but no eye on either boat beheld any beauty that night. Most were cursing, quietly, the unusual visibility which was actually throwing shadows. It was a little after two AM.

*

Snug inside the climate-controlled comfort of Igloo Base, most of the complement was fast asleep. Most, but not all. Since the departure of the *Flying Fish*, Allen Bell and Andy McLeod had been busy planning a welcome for any uninvited visitors. Part of the preparations had been the setting up of a network of highly sensitive microphones, extra cameras and some powerful hydrophones in the cove, together with a 24-7 listening coverage. Lou James was on shift in the small hours that night, watching a muted DVD replay of an Australian Rules football match from a few seasons back. Fremantle and St Kilda had been playing in Tasmania, and in the last frantic seconds of the game Fremantle were leading by one point. The siren sounded to end the game, but the umpires couldn't hear it over the crowd noise and allowed play to continue long enough for St Kilda to kick a point and draw level. Clearly Fremantle had been robbed of a win. Although James was actually a St Kilda fan, he was relieved that the Australian Football League had taken the almost unprecedented step of reversing the result and declaring Fremantle the winners. James was absorbed in the final scenes of pandemonium, when he gradually became aware of a low-pitched, soft buzzing sound coming from the outer cove hydrophone. It was a sound he didn't recognise and he knew it wasn't the equipment. Under strict instructions, he called Bell and McLeod, both of whom trotted into the communications room within thirty seconds. Still dressing, they glanced at each other and McLeod said tersely, "One or two powerful outboards at low revs. They should be on the beach in about ten minutes." Bell nodded and sounded the general alarm.

Such was the drilling the base personnel had been put through that by the time the two boats filled with blackly indistinct shapes had reached the small stony beach, they were all up, dressed, armed and waiting in their allotted positions. Lawrence Prescott had been armed with an Uzi submachine gun and placed behind a crate just inside the personnel door. When putting him there, Bell had muttered in his ear and Prescott had gone very pasty. McLeod had glanced enquiringly at Bell.

"I told him if he moved I'd shoot him myself," he grinned.

*

On the beach, Force One leader murmured to Force Two.

"The personnel door should be up the beach, behind and to the south of the large rock outcrop which conceals the main entrance. We'll go through the door with an RPG, or two if necessary, and mop up everything inside. I just wish it wasn't so goddamned clear."

"Doesn't matter," whispered Force Two. "They're only a bunch of whale huggers. I know we were told they had some expert help and were practicing, but come on! We've got thirty experienced guys who know what it's like to return fire. This job is a milk run."

At that same instant, two modified claymores, buried under a foot of beach stones, exploded with an ear-bursting and mind-numbing force. For seven of the intruders who were caught in the hail of metal and stone shrapnel, it was also heart-stopping. The Force Two leader was one of the seven, his head turned into a red splash by a baseball-sized rock flung by the claymore at many times the speed of a good fastball. Both inflatables instantly deflated as they were shredded and tossed in the air, and powerful floodlights turned the night even brighter.

"Get those lights!" yelled Force One, "and move up to the door. On the double!"

His men didn't need instructions. They were shooting out the lights as they scrambled up the rocky beach and headed for the personnel door. The detonations of three more mines didn't take them by surprise this time, but it did cost them five more of their number. There was neither time nor medics to tend wounded, so the rest of the soldiers hustled up to the entrance to the personnel door and spread out around it. One of them let fly with an RPG which exploded right on the camouflage over the large steel door, leaving it twisted on its hinges. Another man fired a second grenade, which blew the door inwards in a cloud of smoke. Light from inside immediately diffused out through the smoke in a quite appealingly golden glow. It didn't appeal much to the Force One leader, however. He knew now that he and his men were in a fight to the finish—his boats were gone and forty percent of his men had been neutralized before the targets had needed to fire an angry shot. He also assumed that the first few men inside the door would be met by a deadly crossfire, and ordered a blanket of grenades with an immediate follow-up incursion. His men knew the score. They had signed on for this kind of action at very high rates of pay, but in most cases they simply enjoyed the rush of lethal action as much as the serious salaries.

*

A little earlier, Bell, McLeod, James and Coney had been in the communications room watching the boats being dragged up the beach by the intruders. The conditions were so sharp and bright they could see the men and their weapons quite clearly.

"They obviously know exactly where they're going," Bell had mused. "Does anyone think these jokers are here to have a beer and a chat with us?" He had glanced around at the others, all of whom shook their heads grimly. "OK Mark, which are the mines closest to the boats?" Coney had pointed to two switches and Bell had closed them firmly. "Lights now, Mark," he said, and Coney toggled three more in rapid succession. Bell, McLeod and James had then left the comms room at a run, heading for the dock area.

Now, following the two blasts on the personnel door, the second of which had blown the door clean off and hurtled it into the water, the base people were in place and waiting for the first shots to come from McLeod or Bell. Suddenly the area around and inside the missing door erupted in flames, shrapnel and smoke. The two men waited a second to avoid flying debris, then raised their heads and began firing their Mac 10s into the smoke around the entrance. At the same moment half a dozen invaders ran through the opening firing as they came, but for a second or two they had no targets. The defenders did though, and four of the runners went down, the other two scrambling for cover. One of them dived behind the same crate concealing Prescott, and Bell waited for the sound of firing to come from him. Nothing happened.

"Shit, that bloody Prescott," grunted Bell. "He must have given up straight away. I'll sort him out later. Although come to think of it, these guys probably won't be taking any prisoners." He mentally shrugged and kept firing at the two who had taken cover and were shooting back. McLeod was positioned about thirty metres away from Bell, with James and some of the others towards the rear of the dock behind machinery and in doorways. McLeod sent an RPG of his own through the now open doorway, the explosion outside causing more havoc among the attackers. Under covering fire from the two already inside, however, five more had managed to enter the cavern and take cover, pouring fire into the dock area. They began to advance on the defenders, their military experience and superior fighting skills becoming a telling factor. The base staff were trying gamely to ignore the incredible noise of the weaponry and the ferocious whine of passing bullets, but for all bar Bell and McLeod it was their first time under fire. The attacking force had been reduced to eleven, but they were eleven hardened and capable soldiers who knew exactly what to do.

Coinciding with a lull in the shooting came the gentle rumble of the main entrance doorway rising. The Force One leader glanced at it quickly through the smoke, saw the entrance was all water with no way for flankers to outmanoevre his men, and gave his concentration back to the advance. Suddenly the gentle rumble switched to a powerful roar as a three metre wave smashed awesomely in through the big main entrance. It topped the dock platform by a good metre, its force more than sufficient to upend the attackers on that part of the dock and sweep them into the walls. Many of them lost their weapons in the mini-tsunami. The roar had deepened and increased, as a large, round, blue missile with what looked like a thick white spear on the front swept out of the smoky darkness and into the harbour. The *Flying Fish* had arrived, its propellers thrashing in emergency reverse to bring it to a rapid stop.

There were people on the bridge in the conning tower, one of whom was cradling an M60 machine gun under his arm. Three others had Mac 10s, all of which were pointing at the invaders still standing, shocked into immobility. The engines came to 'all stop' and the deafening roar became a gentle rumble again. Carl Wojinski, the man with the M60, grinned nastily at the black-clothed intruders.

"Any of youse mothers still keen to tango?" he growled, as the water that had flooded the dock ran back into the harbour with a sound as innocent as the tinkle of a fresh mountain stream.

The Force One leader had managed to hang on to his AK 47. He slowly rose from where he had been knocked aside by the wave, staring intently at the top of the conning tower. All he could see were four pairs of cold, angry eyes behind the sights of four large bore rifle barrels. It was enough to make a quick decision for him, for he was a professional rather than a patriot and saw no point in throwing his life away. He glanced at his men, shook his head, shrugged and laid his weapon on the wet cement floor of the dock. They took their cue from him and those who still had their rifles laid them down as well.

One of the four in the tower was Roberts, and he had observed the leader signalling to his men. He called to the man to take his hood off. The leader did so, slowly, revealing a round, red-cheeked face under a thick mane of flaming red hair, underscored with a full red beard. His eyes were ice-blue. Had his hair and beard been white, and his belly three sizes larger, he could have done duty as a Rent-a Santa, for his face lent itself to cheerful expression. Right now, however, his expression was grim, defeated; his eyes were calculating, unafraid, as he proceeded to strip himself of his ordnance. A rifle barrel speared sharply into his left kidney, sending him writhing to the floor.

"It's OK, pal, we'll do that for ya," said McLeod. "Any more of your guys still outside?"

"Dunno," gasped the leader from the floor. "There were eleven of us left who got in. You do the math."

"American, huh? Thought you'd all be Japanese," drawled the towering McLeod, as Mackie and some of the ex-navies from the submarine began checking outside and rounding up those still standing inside. "Guess you're a mercenary group hired in Europe. Probably most of you have done stints in Africa and the Middle East. But we know you were put together by Lo and Takamori."

"Then you know more than I do, and I was the leader of the strike team. You're probably ex-SEAL or Special Forces, so you should know that a team like this is put together by a middle man. We're all totally deniable. You gonna do us all?" The eyes now were simply curious, for the decision had been made to surrender and he was no longer in control of the situation. He thought ruefully that maybe he never was—these guys were too well-prepared, too well led.

McLeod glanced up, and the leader rose painfully to see Roberts standing next to him, eyes drilling through the ice-blue and into his being. He saw death there.

"Your job, which you happily signed on for, you piece of shit, was to infiltrate this base, murder everyone you found and sink the *Fish*. You would even have killed my Angie. If you moved against me now, I'd willingly kill you with my bare hands, but my handicap is that I can't do it in cold blood."

The leader stared at Roberts, hearing the suppressed fury in his voice, and although a hardened campaigner with many kills, he remained quite motionless, knowing with complete certainty that he was one small move away from becoming dead. He slowly put his hands out to be cuffed.

"Behind the back, china," growled Bell.

"You knew where we were and just how to get in," said Roberts flatly. "How?"

"Yes, we had good intel," admitted the leader quietly. "One of your guys got caught in a coke ring in Sydney and bought his way out with information. I don't know his name, but I think he was a doctor."

"Shit!" exclaimed Bell, glancing at Roberts. "I forgot about Larry!" He raced over to the crate he had installed Prescott behind, and bent down out of sight. "I need help over here!" he shouted. Roberts and two crew members ran over and saw Bell trying to stem some serious blood loss from Prescott's chest. "I think he caught some shrapnel when they blew the door off," he grated. "I shouldn't have put him so close. He's nearly gone."

"Don't beat yourself about it, Allen," said Roberts. "I'm sure he was the Judas. He's just got some ironic payback. Get him into the sickbay and see if the doctors can do something for him."

At that moment Mackie walked up to the group, trying to put his glasses back on over a nose that now wasn't so much dilapidated as condemned and ready for demolition. It was more twisted than usual and now also swollen and bleeding. Mackie was holding a handkerchief over it to soak up the blood.

"Jesus, Ray," groaned Roberts, "not again! What happened?"

"We were outside rounding up three of the grunts when one of them cold-cocked me with his rifle. I just didn't see it coming. I must be getting old," he tried to smile, but clearly was disturbed about it. His voice was nasaly and muffled through the blood-soaked cloth.

"Don't be too worried, Ray. There still isn't anyone I know who can clean your pipes."

"Ah no, it isn't that, David. I reacted too strongly and hit him too hard. I broke his neck. It's actually the first time I've ever killed anyone." Through his damaged nose and the handkerchief over it, Mackie was pensive, thoughtful, even sad. "I'm not distraught and I don't need counselling thanks David," he smiled a little. "I realise very well that these guys were trying to kill us all and that any injuries or deaths were part of the deal. It's just that all my training and the skills I've developed have been aimed at avoiding the kill. I'm afraid I let a little of my pain and anger through, and it cost a man his life. That's why I said I'm getting old. It's my first failure."

"Failure?" Roberts yelped. He clasped his friend by both shoulders, staring intently into his eyes. "You haven't failed, mate. Apart from Angie, the best decision I ever made was to ask you to join me. You've done everything I could ever ask for and I owe you more than I can ever pay. Do you think I wasn't aware of you when I collapsed in the submarine?" Roberts was silent for some seconds, his eyes filling.

"I believe Theo Woodville has done quite a bit of plastic surgery in the States. When the heavy stuff is over we'll get him to have a go at your nose."

"Thanks David. For everything." Mackie's eyes were now filling too.

*

Scott Lambert was bending over the figure lying very still on the hospital bed in one of the small recovery rooms. Lambert was inspecting the large, angry wound on the right side of the man's chest for any sign of infection or weeping. It was extensive, for the shrapnel had taken some tissue and mashed parts of three ribs, and had been closed with a mixture of clips and sutures. The brown stain of the Betadine solution liberally coating his chest contrasted sharply with the white of Prescott's skin, the whole area rising and falling slightly and slowly, the monitor displaying a ragged but continuing heart beat. Roberts came in to the room, noticing the small frown on Lambert's face which quickly disappeared. He didn't have to ask.

"He came out of surgery OK, and is reasonably stable. We had to take part of his right lung, Theo needed to do some fancy by-pass work and about five centimetres of rib had been pulverized. The piece of shrapnel, or bullet, or whatever did the damage, passed through him and left a sizeable inspection port in his back, too, so he's now got quite a bit of patchwork in him. Is he going to live? Probably. He isn't out of the woods, but he wouldn't have had better treatment in Sydney. Theo's very good."

"Thank Christ for that," whispered Prescott, startling them both.

"Jesus, Lawrence, you shouldn't be awake yet," said Lambert in surprise.

"Sounds as though I'm lucky to be awake at all," came another slow, laboured whisper. Prescott moved his head slightly, and focused on Roberts.

"Sorry David, couldn't see any other way out. Hope no one else was hurt." He sank into unconsciousness. Roberts looked disgusted, glanced at Lambert and turned to leave.

"Thanks, Scott. You blokes did well, although I'm not sure he deserved it. Keep me informed of his progress will you?"

*

This time it was a small conference room rather than the mess. Roberts glanced around him with feeling at the assembled group: Halloran, James, Tilley, Durrand, McLeod, Bell, Angie, Sarah Sanders and Ray Mackie, face swathed in bandages and sporting a couple of very black eyes.

"Getting to be quite a crowd," he smiled. "You look really nice, Ray."

"Thanks David. Doc Woodville said I'd be quite surprised at the results, when all the swelling and bruising fades."

"Good. Well, people, we've done about everything I set out to do, and I doubt we'll have any more trouble from the nasties. The *Kontica* will be here in a few days, and we'll all go back in her for a break in Sydney. Andy and Ray, could you see me later? I want to arrange the bonuses. We'll all have a week in the Hilton, then I'll pay everyone off.

Has the damage been repaired? The bodies taken out to sea and buried? The personnel door replaced? I'd like to leave the base in good condition."

"Yeah, David, we've taken care of the raiders and things are nearly as good as new here," said James. "Are we all being let go now?"

"Well, I guess it's the end of all the contracts," said Roberts slowly. "There's not a lot left to do."

"I think Lou means he doesn't want to leave, David," said Kaye Halloran, serious for once. "Neither do I. I'm going to feel kind of empty after this. Going back to the mundanity of suburbia, or what passes for it with us engineers, will be very tame after what we've been doing."

"'Mundanity'?" smiled Roberts. "'Us engineers'? Maybe you could teach English somewhere instead, Kaye," he chuckled.

"OK smartarse, you know what I mean. Sorry, Angie, I meant Mr. smartarse," grumbled Halloran. "But I remember way back before we started belting whalers that you said you hoped to form a team. Well, I think you were more successful than you realise. Most of us risked death for this project . . . hell, not for the project, for the people in it . . . and we're now all part of a very strong team. I know of many lifelong friendships that've been formed. We can't just break all that up now and go back to square one!

And what are you going to do with our beautiful *Fish*?"

Roberts grew thoughtful. "Haven't really considered that yet, Kaye, to be honest. Maybe that means I don't want to leave either. And I hear what you're saying about the group. They really are special people. I've got a lot more friends now than before I started, and wouldn't want to lose contact with any of them. You've given me something to think about, Kaye.

What do you think we should do with the *Fish*, Angie?"

She smiled sweetly. "Honeymoon cruises perhaps, David?" The others roared with laughter at his discomfort. "I think if you can resist all the purchase offers that should pour in, and keep the federal government away from her, something fitting will turn up in good time."

"As usual, you're right, Angie. When the story breaks there'll certainly be some interest generated in her." He looked around him, seeing more than the four walls of the conference room. "And in this wonderful place you people built, too. I may own the *Fish*, but the ownership of Igloo is less clear cut."

*

The farewell dinner had been huge, presided over by Richard Flanagan with Angie assisting, and all had been happily surprised to hear their bonuses were to be doubled. Roberts had shrugged off their thanks. "Danger money," he laughed. They placed all systems on standby and shut and coded the doors, ferrying all personnel and gear, including the ten prisoners, out to the anchored *Kontica*. Chris Sanders was both nervous and excited, wanting to hear everything about the final actions at sea, and on the base. He'd had an inkling of what was likely to occur, and was in an agony of worry and suspense knowing he had allowed his daughter to be a part of it all. "Let's get under way, Chris, and Sarah and I will fill you in on all details. There's a lot to tell." A subdued Roberts was on the bridge talking to Sanders. Angie was there also, looking at him with a slight frown.

"Is there something worrying you now David?" she asked.

"Yes, love," he said quietly. "As soon as the *Kontica* docks, I'm going to get the first flight I can to Miami. I have to go and see Dorothy Hass."

"Oh David," Angie said softly, "of course. I'm coming with you."

As the *Kontica* pulled out of Caroline Cove, Kaye Halloran wasn't the only one with tears in her eyes.

*

A few days later, Dorothy Hass opened her door to a knock. She saw David Roberts standing there with an attractive fair-haired woman she didn't know. Her face lit up with pleasure as she stepped out to him. Then she saw his face clearly and stopped, and the light died. She folded her arms around him and buried her face in his chest, and let her tears flow.

"Dorothy . . ." The word was wrenched from his soul as his eyes closed and anguish wracked his being.

"Shh, David, don't say anything. I'm so sorry for what you must have gone through." Dorothy's face, still streaming tears, looked up at him with a sad smile. "It was his heart, wasn't it." It wasn't a question.

"God, Dorothy, I've taken your husband from you and you're sorry for what I've gone through?"

She took his hand, saying "Come inside and I'll fix something to drink. You must be the Angie David's talked so much about. Please come in, darling."

They sat around her small table, each nursing a large brandy. "It's actually a good cognac. Gunter paid a fortune for it last year and I brought it from Seattle, as he loved a small nip occasionally." She smiled sadly. "He thought I didn't know, but he had discovered a problem with one of his heart valves, and like most men kept it to himself and slowly began to eat better and exercise more. I just couldn't bring myself to talk to him about it, and then you came into our lives and he was so happy. I should have warned you, David, and that's why I'm sorry for putting you through such grief."

"Dorothy, he was so good on the boat. He actually saved all our lives at one time. Gus Durrand came to like and respect him, and the crew loved him. He was a very special man. And I was devastated when he died because I knew I had failed. I couldn't bring him back to you."

"Dear David, what you did was to help make the last years of my Gunter's life as happy as he had ever been. I'll miss him every hour of whatever life I have left, but you should be easy knowing you enriched us both by what you did. And by who you are.

Angie, enjoy your life with this man as much and for as long as you can. You are a very fortunate person."

"Thank you Dorothy. The last few years of my life have been enriched too," Angie said softly but with total conviction. "What we want now, though, is for you to gather whatever you can't live without and come home to Sydney with us. We want you to stay with us for a day, or a week, or a year or a lifetime, whichever you want."

Emotions like surprise, grief and pleasure are mutually exclusive, but they chased themselves across Dorothy's face in quick succession. She gulped.

"Thank you, both of you. I would like to do that very much."

FORTY TWO

It had been five days since Roberts, Angie and Dorothy Hass had arrived in Sydney, five days that had passed like a carousel in overdrive. Roberts had met his 'special interest group', giving them a detailed account of what had occurred in the murk of the southern Atlantic Ocean that day. They had all listened in complete silence, scarcely taking time to breathe let alone gulp from water bottles or tumblers of scotch.

"Kerr-rist, David!" Morgan Hendry was the first to give voice to his feelings when Roberts finished. His grin split his face open. "God, I wish I'd been there! Do you think the story will reach the media?"

"Of course it will, Morgan," Roberts laughed. "If none of you lot break it, someone from one or more of those boats in the action will. That is, if we don't do it ourselves. Mightn't be a bad idea to give Sir Les another interview."

"And Kate Preshaw's been on my wheel every week for news of you. I'm sure she'd love you to do another appearance on her show."

"David," said the Greenpeace man, Brock Hewitt, "I'm rapt in what you've done, even though it doesn't fall strictly within the basic ideals of my organisation. But it seems to me that you've accomplished what you originally wanted to do. Are you going to stop now?"

"Yeah, David," came rapidly from Trevor Lane, before Roberts could answer. "I think what you've done is fantastic too, but unlike Brock, it does fall smack in the centre of the ideals of my organisation. I reckon Sea Shepherd would be very interested in purchasing the *Flying Fish* if you don't have any further use for her."

"Thanks guys," smiled Roberts. "I think I'm going to hear those two questions in particular repeated many times in the next few days. Are we going to stop now? Certainly we're going to pause, but I don't know whether all the other members of the Foxtrot Corporation will allow us to stop. Is she for sale, Trevor? Would you sell your mother?

But one thing I can guarantee . . ." Roberts' face was trying not to burst out laughing, but his eyes were flashing with merriment. "If any of you would be interested, when we've finished our business in Sydney, I think I can organise a trip to Igloo before they try to confiscate it, and a ride in the *Fish* . . ." He got no further, drowned out by the gleeful yells of the others in the room.

"Holy shit, David, I bet you could sell those rides for about fifty large a head!" cried Hendry, face lit and eyes luminous. "I reckon even the PM would want to go!"

*

"I'd like a tour of the base and the submarine, Mr Roberts, if the logistics could be arranged." Following a further article from Les Patterson and another appearance on *Sydney Tonight*, the Prime Minister of Australia, together with three ministers and an adviser, was meeting with Roberts, Durrand and Mackie. Mackie's face had lost its black eyes and his nose, following some serious work by the submarine's surgeon, was now a thing of ordinariness, which compared to its predecessor, made it a thing of beauty in the eyes of all who remembered the original. "The base, Igloo I believe you've called it, is of course on Australian territory, and as you gained no approval to build it, its construction was illegal. It must therefore be confiscated and placed under the control of the Australian Government."

"You might get an argument from the Tasmanian Premier, Prime Minister," suggested Roberts innocently.

"Yes, well, er, I'm sure the Attorney-General will be able to sort all that out," the PM dismissed the suggestion with a small hand wave. "I also doubt we'll need to canvass the area of prosecution or any form of legal action against you for trespass or unlawful construction on government land without permission," the PM said with a wry smile. "You and your group seem to have become almost as popular as the Beatles."

"Yes, well perhaps not quite." Roberts kept his face straight and unsmiling with a bit of an effort. "But confiscation? That base cost me an arm and a leg! If you are going to take it all over, I suppose we'll have to go there and remove all our equipment. It would, of course, then be inoperable. And there's the small matter of where we would then be able to berth the *Flying Fish* without a base."

"I can see how you became so successful in business, Mr Roberts," the Prime Minister said, wincing slightly. "Why don't we leave it for the present that you may use it to wind up your 'operations', then we'll sit down and dicker."

"Fair enough, PM. I want to give a tour to a party of people who have given us support first, then we'll organise a visit for you and your staff."

"Thank you, Mr Roberts. I want you to know two things. Firstly, I want to thank you for your message to the two ships' captains after they had interceded in your, er, contretemps, shall we say, with that Russian destroyer. It helped to ease what could have been a difficult diplomatic situation.

Secondly, and I intend that this stays right here in this room, I want to tell you that I actually approve of what you and your group did. Unofficially, of course. And I'd have to add that I hope it is 'did' and not 'are doing.'" The PM smiled at Roberts and the other two, shaking hands firmly with all three. "You've clearly had a significant effect, as I hear that the Southern Ocean whaling operations of those two large companies have both been halted indefinitely. I doubt we'll see many toothfishing boats in our exclusion zones for a while either."

"Thanks for the support, PM, even if it is clandestine. But I believe all we did was to give the whalers some food for thought. Yes, they've stopped for the moment, but I very much doubt they've given up. I'm sure you're very well aware of the farce that the IWC's become," Roberts said grimly, looking at the suddenly-uncomfortable Minister of Fisheries. "Do you really think you and the Kiwis and others are going to achieve anything by boycotting the IWC meetings?

The Japanese continually claim their whalers are catching whales solely for scientific study, their JARPA II program, but no one denies the whale meat ends up in restaurants. Japan has gathered enough of the supporting nations together to win an IWC vote to 'normalise' whaling. As you know, that is simply their code word for a return to commercial whaling. And it's about to happen. For all their moralising and stated good intentions, the Japanese are nothing more than high-tech fishermen, capable of plunging their greedy little hands into the world's oceans and dragging whole species into their cooking pots.

I know, I'm soapboxing again, and I'm sorry, people, but all I can see in the official and politically correct future is the death of much of the oceans' marine life. Sea Shepherd is virtually ineffective these days. Paul Watson has threatened to give the whalers a 'steel enema' by ramming their sterns with his ships and attempting to seriously damage their ramps. You know they say that a collision at sea can ruin your entire day, and such an action would have the potential to sink both vessels and cause injury or death to crews, and I hear his frustration with bureaucracy very keenly. But then you have politicians from places like New Zealand phoning him to express concern at his suggestion! The New Zealand government has promised him they will do everything they can to stop the Japanese from killing whales, especially the highly endangered Humpback. Well, hooray! What exactly would that be I wonder?

See, PM, you've just advised me to cease what we've been doing, and the Kiwis have asked Sea Shepherd not to ram any of the whalers. I mean absolutely no disrespect here, but just what do you federal governments want? You are publicly critical of people or organisations that try to take action against practices which are clearly, demonstrably, bad for our planet. Yet at the federal level, nothing's happening! If anything, things are going backwards, for we will surely see commercial whaling back on the seas this year." Roberts stopped, knowing he was getting close to saying something that would be a little inappropriate. He realised he was in a forum not available to many, and didn't want to diminish the effect his words clearly were having.

"Mr Roberts, I'm not going to waste our time with platitudes like 'I hear what you're saying' or 'we're doing everything in our power'. I well know that people get sick of hearing politicians dissemble. But you have to understand that publicly, and that's your word, we simply are not able to condone any overt act by a non-government force that could be construed as terrorism or piracy. We are constrained to having to operate via governmental channels of diplomacy. And dammit, that means legally!" The Prime Minister allowed a little personal feeling to surface, knowing the ministers and staff would keep the faith, and putting trust in this man Roberts. The PM could read honour and principle in others very well, for it was not something much in evidence in political circles and stood out like the Opera House on a sunny day when it appeared.

The adviser coughed discreetly and glanced at his watch. The PM nodded, sad to end an enjoyable meeting. "I'm sorry, gentlemen, but we are about half an hour over time, which may indicate to you how important I felt this meeting was. Good luck for the future, Mr Roberts, and to you too, Captain Durrand, Mr Mackie."

"Thank you PM. All the best to you in the next election."

FORTY THREE

One of the smaller dining rooms in the Hilton had been reserved for the Foxtrot group, who were all present and enjoying a real sea-food feast. It was one of the quality times that could be appreciated by the members of a special team of people who had been living lives moulded by the circumstances of their cause. It had meant that for almost three years they had been constrained by the requirements of the fight they had taken to the whalers and illegal fishing boats, and they were now beginning to understand the stress and pressure under which they had all been working. It was leaching from them all in great dollops of relief and they were really enjoying the food, the atmosphere and most of all the company.

Roberts got to his feet at the end of one of the large tables, holding a glass of Australian Para liqueur port. It had been produced by Seppelts in 1947.

"I'd like to propose a toast," he said mildly, as the room quietened. "To Gunter," he said simply.

Gus Durrand was sitting in the middle of another table, and quickly rose, turning to face Dorothy Hass, sitting next to Roberts and Angie.

"I'd very much like to second that, David," he said earnestly. "Ma'am, I want to apologise to you for my earlier attitude. I say to you, in front of this group of special people, that I was wrong. I came to respect and admire your husband, for he truly was a very fine man, and I deeply regret that he's no longer with us." He raised his glass to Dorothy, and said, "To Gunter."

Tears ran down Dorothy's face as she stood, but her voice was steady and strong.

"You really are special people. Thank you Captain Durrand, I accept and appreciate your sentiments. And thank you all too for allowing my Gunter to fulfill his life in the best possible way he could have done." She sat down slowly, head bowed, as Angie curled an arm around her and laid her head against Dorothy's.

Roberts, still on his feet, took a moment and continued speaking, contemplatively, still quietly.

"You know, people, when you think about it, there's a hell of a lot of expertise and capability in this room. Be a pity to let it all go to waste." He paused, looking at the men and women gathered around the tables in the tastefully-appointed dining room. "Yesterday, when we were talking with the PM, I came to the realization that these bastards aren't going to go away. We may have forced them to take a break, but sometime soon Japan is going to win a legal return to commercial whaling. They won't need the spurious cover of JARPA II any more—they'll be able to go at it full-on. It won't matter that they'll be restricted to minkes and a small number of humpbacks and fins. They'll continue to take any whale unlucky enough to swim into their sights. It will then be only a few years before some of those species will be lost forever. The blue whale will be one of them.

So what am I rabbiting on about, guys? Kaye Halloran was speaking from the heart when she said she didn't want to see this group wound up. My point of view may be more rational, but it comes to the same thing. I don't want to cease operations either. I think there's going to be a lot more work for us to do in the near future." Roberts stopped, as a chorus of shrieks, yells and laughter broke out all over the room. "You've all been paid up and signed off, and I was going to ask if any of you would be interested in another contract? Looks like a few of you might be," he smiled.

"David, I'd be surprised if anyone here wasn't," laughed Halloran. "Except maybe for dear Lawrence. What did you do with him?"

"Oh, I told him all his medicals would be covered, but that when he was able to get out of bed he should do so with some haste, and disappear. If I ever saw him again he'd find himself back in hospital quicker than he left it."

"And those ten 'guests' we had, David?" asked Gary Bradley.

Roberts' smile turned grim, his eyes now the grey of a steel whetstone. "I asked some of the guys to give me a hand with them," he replied quietly. "Ray, Allen, Andy and Carl helped me escort them on board the *Kushima*, which had docked in Sydney a short time ago. They were all cuffed and hobbled, and we did it at about two the other morning. There were only three sentries at that hour, and we persuaded them to allow us aboard." The group hanging on every word all grinned at the use of the word 'persuaded'. "We left them all in the care of the Japanese. I told the captain, after he'd been roused, that we were simply returning his property to him. He tried to protest, but I'm afraid I didn't give him any alternatives. I told him I would be alerting the immigration authorities to be on the lookout for ten suspected terrorists last seen near the *Kushima*. I think he got the message. He seemed a little shocked, and asked if there were no more than ten."

"You're not going to inform the immigration people, are you David," Bradley was commenting rather than asking a question.

"Of course not. But I have the feeling that those guys are on shaky ground anyway. The Vietnamese, Tay, will probably cut his losses, but I suspect with Takamori it's more personal. His culture won't permit him to accept such a loss without attempting to save face. Part of that could be to deal harshly with those mercs, another part could be to come after us and try to close us down permanently.

So we'll all need to be constantly on the alert until we're back at Igloo. I'm going to ask the PM to take formal possession of it and lease it back to us for a peppercorn rent for the next five years. I think they'll agree, if they can keep the Tasmanian Premier at bay. Of course, that means we'll also need to keep the dear old *Kontica* running too."

Sitting towards the rear of the dining room, Chris Sanders smiled contentedly to himself. He was getting used to the idea of his sweet little daughter Sarah being a part of such a tough bunch of people, and loving it so much. 'And being as tough as any of them,' he thought, shaking his head in wonder.

"Don't look so pleased with yourself, daddy," chuckled Sarah, sitting next to him. "The dojo boys and I will be right there with you."

"You being a member of this unusual group is the only cloud on my horizon," he smiled, "and I'm trying hard to come to terms with that."

"I know you are daddy. You just have to realise that I'm as well trained, or better, than any of them, and very determined to be the best I can. What I can't get over is how well you're looking. You've put on a little weight and are looking better than I can remember. I think this job is agreeing with you."

Sanders nodded slowly, but he knew it wasn't just the job. He had stopped beating himself up over his marriage dissolution, realising that any breakdown of a relationship always involved both people, that his wife had cared little for reviving her disinterest. It had been a fair base on which to build a new life, and David Roberts had come along with his proposal at exactly the right time. Then he had re-discovered Sarah. He had been horrified to learn what she had gotten into, but had the good sense to appreciate very quickly that trying to force her out of it would have simply driven her away. He was personally growing, too.

"So guys, all those of you who would like to come back for more, stay and enjoy Sydney and the Hilton for a few more days while we can set up the contracts. Then you can visit your friendly purser again. See you around." Roberts smiled, waved and sat down with Angie to pay some closer attention to the lovely liqueur port.

*

The following morning Roberts, Angie and Ray Mackie were making their way down to the permanent car-parking bay in the second underground level below the Hilton, on which Roberts paid rental. It enabled him to bring his SUV from Ulladulla, and to use it while they were in Sydney. Which was not, in today's world of all-encompassing electronic communication, a difficult thing to discover. So it should not have come as much of a surprise to Roberts to see a man standing by his BMW. A tall, wide and very angry-looking man, who straightened and moved towards the group as they approached the vehicle. Mackie removed his glasses, angling away from Roberts and taking Angie with him.

"Are you David Roberts?" the big man growled in what sounded like a Swedish accent, glaring at him with quite unconcealed fury.

Roberts stopped, allowing Mackie and Angie to move away. "Yes, I am," he replied mildly. "Who's asking?"

"I am Captain Styg Halvorsen of the whaling factory ship *Helga Lindberg*, and you and I have some business to conduct," he grated. "You have attacked my vessel four times, causing great damage and much lost time and revenue. It is time for you to pay." He swung a large, red and raw-boned fist at Roberts' head that very nearly connected. It would have ended the business before it really began being conducted, had it landed. It was a fist that was scarred and dimpled and not very hairy. Clearly it had been in a number of such business discussions in the past.

"Careful, David," came softly from Mackie, "he's not as big as Ricardo, but much faster and more dangerous. Be respectful. Do you want me to . . . ?"

"No thanks, Ray, his fight is with me." Roberts slowly circled the big Norseman, watchful, concentrating. The moves came and were blocked or evaded, Roberts counter-striking without trying to cripple the big man. After six or seven minutes, both had taken punishment, but Roberts was holding back whereas Halvorsen was intent on annihilation. Eventually the training Roberts had received, together with his general fitness level, began to tell. He slipped inside one of the large Scandinavian's strikes and hit him hard below the heart, instantly following with a chop to the underside of the jaw. Halvorsen collapsed, groaning softly, struggling to rise. Roberts bent down to him, panting.

"Enough, mate. You've nearly done me, and I don't want to put you in hospital." The whaler's eyes had lost their fury. He had been beaten in a good fight and accepted that his opponent had won the day.

"Very entertaining. Heartwarming stuff." The voice, fluently English with a pronounced Asian accent, came sibilantly from the darkness. Roberts and Mackie started, flashing looks around them, as three slight figures glided from the shadows among the cars in the deserted car park. They too were dressed completely in tight-fitting black, including hoods and masks. Each man was pointing a pistol, and Roberts saw that they were pointing at him, Mackie and Angie. His bowels tightened, fear invading him in a cold inrush of horror. Angie! He glanced at Mackie, shaking his head slightly.

"Yes, Mr Roberts, you'd do well to be still. No knives this time. Those Vietnamese were women. We are the personal samurai of Takamori-san, and it is our duty to avenge the wrongs you have done to him. Your time is over, Mr Roberts.

Captain Halvorsen, we were hoping you would be able to deal with him, but unfortunately you were not strong enough. We will finish your business for you. You may go." The Japanese dismissed the Swede, who had struggled to his feet. "Shigata-san, if you please?" The shorter of the other two men, the one holding a pistol on Angie, slipped a hand into his jacket and brought out a slim metal cylinder. He pressed a button on its side and a slender blade shot out. He drove it into Angie, who gasped, cried out in agony, and slumped to the floor. Her assailant sank down with her, withdrawing the blade, watching dispassionately as blood began pouring out of Angie's side. "Well, perhaps one knife," he murmured, with a slight smile.

Roberts watched in complete terror. His world turned red and dim, and he was only vaguely aware of the other two Japanese leveling their pistols at him and Mackie. But there was still something buried deep in his core that resisted the urge to accept his fate, now that Angie was dying. He smouldered, raising his eyes to meet those of the man about to kill him. The man checked, momentarily taken aback by the totally feral look on the face of the man in front of him.

At that instant there was the sound of a solid blow and a choked gasp came from the attacker who had stabbed Angie. He collapsed on the cement floor of the car park, driven there by the same large fist that had attempted to send Roberts into the harbour. The four other members of the tableau had been snap-frozen into motionlessness by the completely unexpected event, but it was Roberts and Mackie who unfroze first. It may have been that they were quicker than the ninjas, or that they were being powered by extra adrenaline due to the attack on Angie. In any event, they were both more than the Japanese could handle. They fell on the two smaller men with a speed and ferocity both implacable and merciless and this time there was no holding back.

The two Japanese died quickly.

Roberts fell to his knees alongside the now-unconscious Angie.

"Ray, ambulance, quickly!" he gasped, as Mackie pulled his phone out and frantically began dialing 000. "She's still alive. I'll try to stop the bleeding." He wadded up his handkerchief and pressed it over the wound in her side. He held it there, closing his eyes. He couldn't pray because he didn't believe. He just felt, with every atom of the being he was, and his world shrank down to his hands, as he pushed the blood-drenched handkerchief hard into the wound, and to the woman lying on the cold grey floor. Nothing else registered. Nothing else intruded. Not even the squeal of the tyres on the ambulance as it stopped nearby, or the noise of the paramedics as they clattered the stretcher on to the floor. But he was ready to kill the ambulance officer who tried to pull him away from his woman.

"David! It's OK! These guys are here for her now. Let them do their job." Mackie spoke insistently to Roberts, his words getting through and registering enough for Roberts to come back. Mackie squeezed Roberts' shoulder as they stood up and moved back, allowing the paramedics to stabilise the bleeding, put Angie on a drip and tie her in to the stretcher.

"Where are you taking her?" demanded Roberts, as they lifted her and eased the stretcher into the back of the vehicle.

"The closest is Sydney Hospital in Macquarie Street," said one of them, as he turned to get into the driver's seat.

"I'm coming with you," said Roberts, and jumped into the still-open rear door. The other officer followed him in and pulled the door shut.

As the ambulance screamed its way up and out of the car park with full lights and siren, Mackie mentally shook himself and turned to Halvorsen, who had been standing quietly, observing the terrible anguish and frantic actions of Roberts with an unreadable expression.

"Well, captain, that was one timely blow back there. If you hadn't joined in the way you did, all three of us would probably be dead. I think we owe you big time."

"I hate you people for what you've done to me, and I wanted to kill Roberts when we were fighting. But he beat me the way one man should beat another, and I don't make war on women. To me, those little black men seemed evil, and stabbing the woman like that, smiling about it, just was not right. I was not thinking about debts, or about what your group has been doing. I just reacted the way, I think, I always would."

"Needless to say, captain, we are very grateful that you did. I'm sure this has all been caught on security cameras, so I'm going to have to ring the police now. But I doubt there will be any comeback. We were after all only defending ourselves from attackers with guns. The one you hit is stirring. Hang on while I have a word with him."

Mackie stepped over to the Japanese who had stabbed Angie.

"Hey, sunshine, are you awake properly?" The man stared up at Mackie with hate emanating from every pore. But there was also fear behind the glare. His eyes glanced sideways at his two comrades lying motionless, their necks forming unnatural angles with their shoulders. "Yeah, I'm afraid they were the ones who paid, mate. You should be happy that you're still alive, and that it's me talking to you and not David. I have a message for you to take back to your master. Tell him that now, because of what you did to the woman, his life is no longer safe. And neither is his family.

And the best of luck with your own life. I doubt it's going to be a long one." His hand blurred as he chopped the man on the side of his neck. "No need to tie him now; he'll be out for another hour or so, and the police will be here soon.

Captain Halvorsen, my name's Ray Mackie, and I very much hope you'll allow me to take you up to the bar and buy you a drink."

*

"The police have flooded level two of the car park and we've just finished giving statements, David." Two hours had passed and Mackie was on the phone to Roberts. "I waited to call you in the hope that Angie may have been treated. I guess I was also scared to ring," he said in a very subdued voice.

"It's OK, Ray, I know how you feel about her. In fact she's been in surgery for over an hour, and it's going to be some more time yet. The surgeon came out a few minutes ago to tell me she would be all right, but there was significant internal laceration, although no artery was severed. The repair work'll take some time and her convalescence will be lengthy, but she should be well again in a month or two. That shit-eating little bastard . . ." he choked and stopped.

"Yeah, he was the only one still breathing, and the cops have taken over here now. So he's been taken over too. But I gave him a message to take back to Takamori, because he'll probably be bailed and flee the country. His duty will compel him to give it to his master, and I have little doubt that his master will then be compelled to deal with him. If he's lucky he'll be permitted to commit seppuku. The police have gone and Styg and I have been sitting in the bar getting mellow."

"Styg?" As well as the question, Mackie could hear a number of undertones in the sharp reply.

"Yes, funny thing that, David. You may have missed it in the furore of what happened, but it was Halvorsen who belted the man who stabbed Angie, and allowed us to sort out the other two. He and I've been talking about it for a while. To be honest, David, I've concluded that he's a good bloke. I like him."

"OK, Ray, I trust your judgement totally. Ask him to stay with you until I can get there. I want to wait until Angie's in recovery."

*

"Captain Halvorsen, I owe you more than I can probably pay." Roberts, back at the hotel after seeing Angie into recovery, had been briefed by Mackie while he downed a large single malt. It hadn't taken long. "Clearly what you did was the distraction that allowed us to deal with the two ninjas with the guns. And just as clearly it saved our lives. More importantly, it saved Angie's. That alone means I wouldn't be able to repay such a debt. I didn't and don't dislike you . . . after what you did I never could. I understand perfectly that you feel hatred for me. But I believe in always being up front. I have to tell you that you are immersed in an occupation I'm trying to end, and I'll continue to do so. If we catch you at the business of whaling in the Southern Ocean again, we'll do our best to blow your stern gear off again. I really wish you could be persuaded to seek other employment, but knowing your heritage I'm sure you wouldn't consider such a thing for a second.

Having said all that, captain, I also want you to know this: if at any time in the future while I'm still alive you find yourself in trouble and need help, whether it be on your behalf or that of family or friend, you need only to let me know. You'll have whatever I can give. You know my resources are not inconsiderable.

And I'd also like to shake your hand and say thank you." Roberts put his empty glass down and held out his hand. Halvorsen gazed at him steadily for some seconds, then seemed to give a slight shrug. He clasped Roberts' offered hand and squeezed ferociously, but a faint smile played across his features. Roberts nodded, put strength into his own grip, smiled himself and said "Thank you captain. You're a very strong and honourable man."

"Unfortunately, Mr Roberts, not as strong an adversary as you."

"Oh, that's more training than strength, captain. I've got Ray to thank for that."

"What I saw you do needs, I think, more than just training. You must also have the inside power. I realize now that you could have hurt me badly if you had wanted to, and that you didn't showed strength, not weakness. You would have made a good Norseman. You do not give up easily."

"You've probably told Ray, captain, but can you tell me why you helped us?"

"Mr Roberts, it wasn't a case of helping you. I wanted to kill you. But I saw what that little man did to the woman, and I saw him enjoy it. My ancestors could be called evil men too, for they raped and killed. But they didn't fight women and they didn't kill for pleasure. They enjoyed the fighting, and they loved to win. But they also had a certain kind of honour and would respect an opponent who showed courage, especially if he beat some of them. Those Japanese men showed no honour in attacking the woman, and my action was quite reflexive. And I would do it again.

But that does not mean all of a sudden I will change my way of life. I am a whaler and will continue to hunt whales. I can't speak for other whalers, Mr Roberts, but none of my gunners will ever shoot at blues or sperms, in spite of your assertions. We are not all ignorant of conservation issues. But we do believe there are now a great many minkes and fins and humpbacks, and that the numbers we kill make absolutely no difference to the populations. My people have a long maritime tradition and see no reason to give it up. If you come after us again we will do our best to sink you. And if we both survive I will be happy to buy you a drink next time." He turned to leave.

"Captain, I meant what I said about owing you," Roberts said.

"Thank you, Mr Roberts. I know you did."

FORTY FOUR

It had been a lengthy period in hospital, Roberts guarding Angie day and night, and another three weeks at their home in Ulladulla. The security had been boosted, and Bell and at least two members of the dojo team had stayed at the house at all times. There had been no incidents.

Now, they were all once again on the *Kontica* heading for Igloo Base.

"Geez, it's great to be back, David. I can't wait to see the *Fish* again." Kaye Halloran was sitting at table one in the mess with the regulars. Roberts grinned at her enthusiasm. She was always positive, irrepressible, and he valued her very highly as a key member of the group.

"Yeah, I agree, Kaye. I must admit I've missed that beautiful boat. She's going to need some TLC when we get there. I want her to be completely fit for active duty before we take off again."

"David, we've all heard the story of what happened at the hotel, and I think I can even understand why the Norwegian did what he did. But is that going to change the thinking on our basic strategy?" Lou James asked the question.

"I've been wondering about that too, David," said Gus Durrand. "It sure sounds like he saved all your asses, and you must feel very grateful to him. I know I would be. He really sounds like my kinda guy."

"Yeah, Gus, Ray was right about him. I like him too, even apart from what he did for us. But Lou, he's still engaged in the very thing we're trying our best to eliminate. As much as I admire him, and owe him everything I have, the one thing I can't give him is immunity from interference. I just can't do it.

So if we have to fire on the *Helga Lindberg* again, we will. He said he'd be trying to sink us if we do, so there won't be any surprises. I just hope to God no one gets hurt."

"Where are we heading first, David?" asked Ken Tilley.

"First, we have to tend to the *Fish*. Then we must arrange the tour of Igloo and the submarine for the people who have helped us so much. I'm going to tell the Prime Minister and that bunch of ministers and advisers they can come along with the others, so we get it all over in the one visit. Kate Preshaw will enjoy that, and I guess the PM never says no to extra publicity.

Then, people, I think we'll need to look at moving north. I believe the usual suspects are taking an extended break from the Southern Ocean, so if we want to take the fight to the whalers, we have to go where they are. And currently that's now in the northern oceans. Going to be a big job. Going to take a while."

No one at the table looked in any way disappointed at the prospect.